"Targets. Bearing Five-two-zero meters. Break contact. Engage left." Karstil switched to internal. "Take her down! Smoke!" Karstil felt the Liberator drop away as it dived for the doubtful security of one of the narrow valleys. A 150mm round cracked overhead, just where the turret would have been if the tank had continued. Smoke from the launcher bloomed behind him, and then the tank was below the level of the ridges, hurtling along between the spines.

The sheer sides of the cliffs flashed past in a blur, their sharp protrusions lost in the blinding speed. Ahead, the valley took a sharp turn to the left; too sharp for the Liberator to make at its current speed. The far wall approached inexorably; it would be a final resting place for the plunging tank.

Other FASA Novels

Renegade Legion:
by William H. Keith, Jr.
Renegade's Honor

BattleTech:
by William H. Keith, Jr.
Decision at Thunder Rift
Mercenary's Star
The Price of Glory

by Michael A. Stackpole
Warrior: En Garde
Warrior: Riposte
Warrior: Coupe
Lethal Heritage

by Robert Charrette
Wolves on the Border
Heir to the Dragon

DAMNED IF WE DO...

◆

BY
PETER L. RICE

FASA CORPORATION

◆

1990

FASA Corporation
P.O. Box 6930
Chicago, IL 60680

Cover Art: Steve Venters
Cover Design: Dana Knutson

DAMNED
IF WE DO...

CARALIS

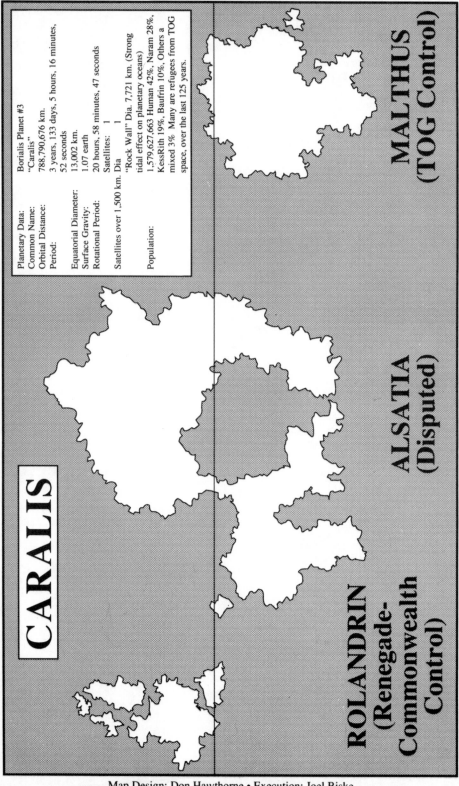

Planetary Data:	
Common Name:	Borialis Planet #3
	"Caralis"
Orbital Distance:	788,790,676 km.
Period:	3 years, 133 days, 5 hours, 16 minutes, 52 seconds
Equatorial Diameter:	13,002 km.
Surface Gravity:	1.07 earth
Rotational Period:	20 hours, 58 minutes, 47 seconds
Satellites:	1
Satellites over 1,500 km. Dia	1
	"Rock Wall" Dia. 7,721 km. (Strong tidal effect on planetary oceans)
Population:	1,579,627,663 Human 42%, Naram 28%, KessRith 19%, Baufrin 10%, Others a mixed 3% Many are refugees from TOG space, over the last 125 years.

MALTHUS
(TOG Control)

ALSATIA
(Disputed)

ROLANDRIN
(Renegade-
Commonwealth
Control)

Map Design: Don Hawthorne • Execution: Joel Biske

PROLOGUE

In the nearly five thousand years since Humans first left Terra and took to the stars in 2056, the history of the race has risen to peaks of glory and descended almost to the point of extinction.

Now, in the year 6831, it is Humans who dominate the Galaxy under the sway of the Terran Overlord Government, or TOG. Ruled by Caesars out of New Rome, this government holds that the Humans of Terra are superior to all other races, and enforces its absolute power through any means necessary—be it propaganda, terror, brute force, or enslavement. Faced with TOG's eight million Legions and its iron-fisted Caesars, who dares oppose the mightiest army the Galaxy has ever known?

The answer lies across the Galaxy, some 70,000 light years from Terra at the far end of the Orion Arm. These thousands of stars encompass the government known as the Human-Baufrin Commonwealth, the seat of armed resistance to TOG since the Terran Overlord Government first came to power in 6681.

In that year, a number Imperial legions fled the tyranny of the new TOG government, finding refuge among the people of the distant Commonwealth. They and their descendants are now known as the Renegade Legions, fighting side by side with their Commonwealth allies against TOG.

BOOK I
POWER
DOWN

1

In Orbit Over Caralis
Shannedam County, The Commonwealth
5 January 6829

Centurion Umbros Canaxthantin warily settled himself into the padded command seat of his Eradicator antiaircraft grav vehicle and thumbed on the Satellite Communications and Data Transfer (SCDT) circuit. Carefully studying the information glowing across the Data Display Panel dominating the commander's station, he saw the blue squares that marked the other vehicles of his unit, their identification numbers showing beneath. Preparing for launch from the transport vessel, the vehicles were firing up their grav generators. As status indicators began to scroll across the screen, each unit reported up and ready to move.

Centurion Canaxthantin and the other air defense vehicles in his command were part of a convoy of reinforcements on their way to the planet Caralis, where the Commonwealth/Renegade armies had been trying to beat back TOG forces for over a year. The Eradicators they piloted were the best antiaircraft grav vehicles in the Renegade arsenal, equipped with the most advanced detection, targeting, and communications equipment of any vehicle not specially designed for reconnaissance. The Grav Drive, which warped the gravity field of a planet, would allow the Eradicators to "fall" parallel to the ground at speeds up to 900 KPH.

Canaxthantin's eyes flicked across the screen looking for intruders, those little yellow dots that would indicate the presence of unidentified craft in the area. Though the SCDT circuits were programmed to give warning when an intruder entered the range of his scanners, he had decided long ago that it was a good idea to have his own look-see.

Nothing. That wasn't too surprising, because it was not standard procedure for reinforcements to be dropped from space into the middle of a battle while under attack. But from what Canaxthantin had heard about this 2567th Infantry Legion during the weeks of training on New Janos, anything might happen. Only recently cobbled together from the fragments of the various Renegade units that had survived the fighting on Caralis for the past year, the Legion already had a reputation for bad luck. Canaxthantin wasn't sure why, though, for he hadn't seen more than the usual minor glitches during the recent training and refit on New Janos. He sighed, wondering if he was about to find out about the unit's bad luck the hard way.

"Fly Swatter, this is Mother." The communications system crackled as the Transport Loading Officer prepared to deploy. "Announce readiness status prior to launch."

Canaxthantin made one last visual sweep of his display, which still showed only blue squares for his command and blue dots for the other ships in the convoy. All Eradicators showed secure and ready for pressurization. "Fly Swatter ready for departure."

"Fly Swatter announced as ready for departure. Open outer doors."

Canaxthantin saw puffs of dust like miniature whirlwinds race across the floor of the loading bay as the outer doors slid back. Atmospheric pressure was dropping, and the dust storms showed the flow of air toward the almost airless void of the troposphere. The pressure seals of the Eradicator popped as they inflated, and Canaxthantin yawned to regulate the pressure in his ears. The blue boxes went red, then blue, on the data display, indicating that the other Eradicators were fully pressurized. The observation bubble that covered the command hatch provided all-around visual contact with his unit. It was an archaic device, but a seasoned tanker rarely relied only on electronic devices for sight.

"Status blue. Open inner doors."

The huge duralloy doors of the inner hull slid back to reveal the dark void ahead. The transport was in a slight "nose-up" attitude to the planet, pointing toward space, and so the rim of the surface was not yet visible. The transport would not roll over until all the grav generators of the reinforcements were fired up and declared operational. The craft's commander did not want any of his charges hurtling out of the bay before they were ready.

"All Fly Swatters, engage grav drive now." Canaxthantin spoke calmly but forcefully into the lip communicator to the other vehicles in his command. No response was necessary, for the data display would indicate grav-readiness. He watched his panel indicators blink red as the grav engines sprang to life and then returned to blue, showing readiness on all vehicles. "All Fly Swatter gravs engaged. Continue launch countdown."

"Roger. Launch countdown continues. Three-zero to launch."

The nose of the transport swung down slowly, and Canaxthantin felt his driver take control of the vehicle, bringing it to a standard hover as the deck dropped away. The rim of Caralis appeared in the access doorway, a straight line of green and white across the open maw of the transport. Canaxthantin always expected to see a curve, but at 90 kilometers, they were too close for such a view. The planet filled the opening as the transport went into a standard ten-degree launch configuration. The Eradicator's own engines now held them in place, warping the ship's artificial gravity to control their fall.

Canaxthantin always got butterflies at the moment of launch. At this altitude, there was not enough planetary gravity for the Eradicator's Marshman Drive to control the vehicle. Leaving the ship's gravity for the wisps of upper atmosphere was like jumping out of a plane, except in a 143-ton vehicle. Though it took less than two minutes, Canaxthantin could hardly wait to fall from 90 kilometers to 15 kilometers, where the gravity was stronger and the tank's grav drives could fully function.

"Mother, this is Fly Swatter. Launching now. Fly Swatter, Fly Swatter, follow me." Canaxthantin switched to internal-only communications, "O.K., driver, take her down." He would rather have piloted the Eradicator himself, but Duncan Spint, the young Triarii assigned as driver of the command vehicle, needed to know that the Centurion had confidence in him. This would be Spint's first live launch at 90 kays, and though he would have had many hours on the launch simulator and been rated as an acceptable pilot, the first time was still the first time.

The Eradicator moved gingerly toward the open doors, sliding forward in a ten-degree dive. The vehicle would only be completely under its own power for the few moments more it took to pass through the access doors. Then the Eradicator broke into the clear and began its fall toward brightside, slowly accelerating.

Canaxthantin checked the data display, watching the other Eradicators as they cleared the transport and followed him into the 90,000-meter free fall toward Caralis. He glanced behind him, though he knew it was impossible to spot the other vehicles at this range. The bulk of the transport, 400 meters long, dominated the dark to the rear, but even its shape was rapidly diminishing. The display showed that the vehicles were forming two ragged vees as they rushed toward the planet, and Canaxthantin saw his wingmen forming 500 meters to the right and left. The distance would narrow as the grav generators became stronger, dropping to 200 meters as they neared the surface.

He looked toward the on-rushing surface of the planet and felt a charge running through him. Being only a passenger for the descent gave him time to observe the planet and the landing zone. Normally, he would have been in control of the vehicle, but one of the privileges of command was not having to drive. Unlike his countless other drops, this time Canaxthantin could sit back and take it all in.

At 15 kilometers, the drives kicked in and the twin-vee formations tightened as they approached the surface. Spint knew the location of the landing zone, which gave Canaxthantin nothing to do until the formation touched down. He didn't even have to remind the others to stay close and follow him in. He was well-pleased with the performance of his men.

Training had been tough, because he had wanted it so. Long hours in the simulators and on the ranges had brought the unit to high—he was almost willing to call it "peak"— efficiency. Their targeting control was good, and the two platoons had scored well on the gunnery ranges. Under his command was a Century Headquarters unit and a platoon of Eradicators to replace those lost in previous engagements on Caralis.

Once contact was made with the Legion, he would take control of the entire Air Defense Century, his first full command of a unit that size. On the one hand, he was looking forward to that command and the chance to take on TOG aircraft. But like any normal soldier, his stomach knotted with the all-too-familiar tension preceding first contact with the enemy. It was the eternal fear of the unknown. How would he act? How would they? Until it all happened, who could say for sure?

2

Caralis, Shannedam County
The Commonwealth
6 January 6829

Dawn of D + 1. The Antiaircraft Century was at stand-to on the planet Caralis, all vehicles up and ready. Rubbing the sleep from his eyes, Canaxthantin wondered about the tradition of having everybody awake and ready at dawn. It was done, or so he was told, because this hour was the best time to attack. The enemy might still be in their racks, half-asleep and stumbling to counter the surprise thrust. What Canaxthantin didn't get was that if everyone stood to at dawn, and if everyone knew that everyone stood to at dawn, why was it such a good time to attack? He had been performing the ritual every morning for the past seven years, and never once had he experienced an attack at that hour.

He glanced down at his Data Display Panel, checking for intruders. The DDP screen glowed back, blue squares and dots marking the location of the Century Headquarters and the platoon of Exterminator vehicles in the area. He flipped the scan to wide-image. Most of the Legion was now visible, a host of blue dots scattered like freckles across the screen. Everything seemed tranquil and safe, with not an enemy unit in sight.

Four kilometers away, the rocket-launching Century was deployed in a shallow valley, its orbital rockets pointed at the recent track of a Thor satellite. From conversations overheard on the commlink, Canaxthantin knew that the satellite appeared to be dead, and so the rocket battery did not want to engage with its limited supply of high-altitude, long-range weapons. They were tracking the Thor carefully, though, watching for that first glimmer of activity. Only when that happened would it become a viable target.

The air-defense vehicles could engage the Thor as well, but there was no need for that if the satellite were dead. Firing a long-range missile would only give away the unit's location to no avail. Better to wait until the satellite showed signs of life before knocking it down.

With his finger, Canaxthantin traced the Renegade "R" symbol in the dew speckling the accordion panel holding an AA missile to the rear of the turret. The moment the SCDT and DDP spotted an intruder, the panels would snap open. He could also open the panels on command, but he saw no need to expose the sensitive missiles to the morning damp.

Just then, the soft crump of a distant explosion shook Canaxthantin from his revery. Looking toward the rocket Century's position in the east, he saw a column of smoke rising over the trees. Glancing back at the computer DDP, he saw one of the blue dots representing a rocket launcher fade out. Accident? Attack? He scanned the horizon again.

There, just at the limit of vision, he saw a silver shape climbing over the horizon. Then another. And another. He picked up his personal monocular and scanned the distant horizon. He locked on to one of the silver shapes and increased amplification. Slaved to the Satellite Communications and Data Transfer circuit, the monocular analyzed the shape and speed of the target, then flashed the information to the right viewpiece of the monocular, where it appeared as an overprint.

"Name: Martiobarbulus (Marty)," it began, then gave additional data on the performance, armor, and armament of the heavy fighter. A *Marty*, he thought. What was a *Marty* doing here? He glanced at the end of the document, but already knew what he would see there. "Alignment: TOG."

What the devil were TOG fighters doing over the Legion's rocket artillery? And why hadn't the SCDT picked them up? Through the monocular, Canaxthantin could see pinpricks of light springing from the bows of the *Marty* as they swooped over the rocket Century. And still the DDP showed no enemy or unidentified craft.

Canaxthantin felt his stomach knot so violently that bile rose in the back of his throat. His equipment had failed, and now he would fail the Legion. It was a repetition of the same hard-luck stories he had heard so often about the 2567th. Sweat poured from his body, and he felt tears of frustration and rage well up in his eyes. Not this time, you bastards. Not this time, he thought. You're not going to get those vehicles without a fight from me.

"Fly Swatter, Fly Swatter, this is Fly Swatter Six. The rocket battery is under attack by TOG fighters. Bearing one-six-hundred mils. Maximum thrust. Treetop flight. Engage targets of opportunity. Weapon control loose. Follow me. Move."

Canaxthantin switched to internal-only communications. "Did you get that, Spint?"

"Got it, sir."

The Exterminator shuddered as it turned to the south. Canaxthantin felt the surge of the grav thrusters as the vehicle accelerated toward the distant valley. At full acceleration, it would take the Exterminator a little over two minutes to reach the rocket unit's location, because it would have to climb to treetop flight. He dropped down inside the turret to scan the DDP again for signs of the enemy. Still nothing.

"What the hell is wrong with my sight?" he growled as the range to the target closed. There was still no indication of enemy in the area. He reached down and switched the sight from automatic to manual. Now it would, or should, pick up all vehicles in the area. They would not be designated as enemy or friendly, but at least they would be visible. The screen flared briefly and then went blank.

Canaxthantin pounded on the controls in rage. "Damn machine! What the hell's wrong with you?!" He looked out the command hatch. They were right in the middle of the fight. Rocket vehicles were burning on the perimeter of the valley, their ammunition igniting in spectacular fountains of fire and smoke. Darting through the treetops and smoke pillars came a *Marty*, its mass driver cannon winking.

The painting laser warning buzzer sounded in the turret of the Exterminator, a raucous "whoop, whoop, whoop." "Oh shut up," snarled Canaxthantin. A painting laser marked a target so that a missile or artillery munitions could home in on it with an accuracy approaching 100 percent as long as the laser held on to the target. Canaxthantin knew that fighters didn't usually carry painting systems. This *Marty* must be mounted with a ground-attack pod especially for this mission.

The oncoming fighter opened at extreme range. Its mass driver cannon hit the Exterminator's hull with a blast of 5-centimeter slivers of hardened steel, but the lasers were wide of the target. Traveling at 100 KPH, the molten bits of blasted titanium armor swept over the turret in a wave of incandescent light. "A little closer, sucker," growled Canaxthantin as he hit the foot pedal of his own painting laser. Smoke from the ablative ceramic armor filled the turret, but was whipped away immediately.

"Target painted," came the audio cue from the system. "Extended range prevents immediate lock-on." Canaxthantin glanced at the range-to-target indicator on the lower left of the screen: 3,600 meters. Velocity: 480 KPH. The range was rolling downward faster than he could count. It would all be by automatic control now.

With the targeting and missile systems dead, he would have only the Eradicator's 25mm cannon, an exercise in futility. The 25mm cannon was for ground defense, and even then, it was little more than an afterthought. Against fighters, it was hopeless. There was no chance that he'd be able to get off more than one shot, but he did have the deadly hammerhead rounds loaded. He would continue to fire that ammunition as long as he had targets—or as long as he lived. The other Exterminators would have to get their shots in, too. If one could penetrate, there was always the chance that internal damage would drive the fighter away.

"Whoop, whoop, whoop," continued the painting-warning system.

"Gunner, fire when lock achieved. Load hammerhead." That command told the gunner to keep loading hammerhead ammunition rather than a different type of round.

"Roger."

"Lock achieved," said the computer, its well-modulated voice unaffected by the crisis situation in the Exterminator. Canaxthantin felt the 25mm cannon fire, saw the hammerhead round strike flush between the two mass drivers. Then the *Marty* was gone, flashing past, a silver streak against the mottled background.

The Exterminator banked hard to the left as Spint brought it around in a tight turn, the turret traversing in the same direction to speed target-acquisition. Canaxthantin allowed himself a quick smile when he saw his adversary disappearing in the distance, with the other Exterminators firing their 25mm cannon as it went by. The vehicle banked to the left again, climbing higher over the battlefield. The other Exterminators turned to follow in a loose gaggle of vehicles. Another Marty was approaching from the left. He depressed the painting laser peddle again and was rewarded by another audio cue that the attacker had been marked successfully. And still the "whoop, whoop, whoop" of the warning klaxon blared on.

Data-link between Exterminators was unavailable, but a painted target is a marked target, and the ballistic computers aboard the other vehicles were solving the firing data for themselves. Laser painting wasn't necessary for the 25mm cannon, but the ballistic computers could use the target information for range and lead. The tail-end Exterminator fired at the incoming *Marty*, a 25mm round peeling armor from the right side of the craft.

The *Marty* was going after the last of the rocket battery's firing units, disregarding the line of airborne Exterminators. It had to pass down the entire column, taking hits from each of the vehicles in turn, and all on its right side. The other Exterminators joined in, firing as the *Marty* came abreast of their positions. Being on a parallel course, the *Marty* was not moving fast enough to require a complicated solution to the firing data.

Round after round struck the right side of the heavy fighter, peeling away more and more of the armor. It was the Exterminator behind Canaxthantin's that made the killing shot, a 25mm round ripping through the the fighter's right side without interference. The starboard engine flared briefly, a shower of sparks replacing the normal blue flame; the engine was eating itself from the inside out. Then the right wing drooped and the craft turned toward the ground. The pilot had no chance to eject.

Canaxthantin felt his turret shudder from hits. He looked to his right. It was another *Marty*...no, a pair of them, making a run at the line of Exterminators. His right elbow hit the turret traverse lever. The 50-ton titanium box swiveled to the right. More mass-driver rounds struck the turret, followed by the 7.5/3 lasers.

The MDC peeled away armor in showers of titanium droplets, and the lasers tore through the turret like hot, probing fingers. Canaxthantin saw the dormant targeting computer and screen explode in a shower of sparks, choking the turret with the smell of scorched electricity. There would be no more audio cue of "lock-on achieved" from this system. It was open-iron sights and shoot from the hip. "Get these guys off me!" he screamed into the lip communicator.

"Gunner, visual sighting. Fire as you bear."

The turret spun past the first fighter, the 25mm gun silent as it crossed the target. The turret swept past the second *Marty*. "You missed your shot, damn you," snapped Canaxthantin. Then he looked down at the gunner's position.

It was impossible to tell whether the MDC or the laser had provided the killing shot. The upper body had been blasted to atoms, either to be spread in a monomolecular layer around the inside of the fighting compartment or to mingle with the smoke that rose from the ceramic armor, targeting computer, and communications equipment.

The fighting compartment was a shambles, the automatic loader on the right side spewing 25mm rounds into the air. The loading tracks had been ripped from the side of the breech, and the system, feeling no down pressure, assumed that there was a call for more ammunition. It would frantically continue to feed rounds through its chute until the supply was exhausted. Tiny fingers of flame darted like snake tongues through the ruins of the turret deck, getting closer and closer to the missile resupply bins.

"Spint, take her down! Take her down!" Canaxthantin knew that this machine's ability to fight had come to an end. Now all he wanted to do was survive. And to do that, he would have to ground the vehicle at once.

In response to the command, the Exterminator nosed over into a power dive. It was too late. The vehicle had taken damage to the steering vanes as well as to the Terrain Sensing and Reaction systems. Spint was fighting the controls to regain command of the vehicle, but it was a losing battle. The Exterminator rolled to the right, picking up speed as it fell.

By some Herculean effort, Spint was able to regain control of the craft as it crashed through the trees, then brought the tank into a stable flight mode with the bottom armor toward the ground. Trees shattered against the blunt, shovel-like bow of the Exterminator, branches and leaves cascading like water over the upper glacis. The twin Datalink antenna had been wiped off the front.

Thick smoke was pouring from the commander's hatch and from the ragged wounds around the turret. Canaxthantin stood in the turret, flame swirling around him as he fought to see where the Exterminator might land. The vehicle burst from the trees into a field dotted with the smoldering wreckage of the rocket battery, the same battery Canaxthantin was supposed to have protected.

The Exterminator struck the ground at better than 100 KPH, its bottom armor shredding away under the strain of impact. The shield generators, grav drive cones, and helm controls were reduced to slag as the Exterminator careened across the field. Canaxthantin, standing in the turret, was thrown forward into the remains of the ballistic computer. His combat helmet shattered at the force of the blow, and he felt the cartilage in his nose separating from the bone of the skull, then blood pouring over his lips. He staggered to his feet, pushing himself through the hatch. He was dimly aware of Spint crawling down the front slope of the Exterminator, running for safety.

With all the strength he had left, Canaxthantin pulled himself through the hatch, breaking into the clearer air. Safe at last. He paused to look skyward, searching for the other Exterminators of his Century.

He paused too long. The missile ammunition, overheated by the damage as well as the crash, could remain stable no longer. In a great ball of flame and thunder, the Eradicator exploded.

When the smoke finally cleared, only the shattered lower hull of the vehicle remained. Moving cautiously, Spint searched the area for signs of his commander, but he found not a trace. Giving up finally, he stood staring at the empty sky. The luck of the 2567th Legion had claimed another man.

3

Barmash, Wayne County
The Commonwealth
6 January 6829

GENERAL ORDER 6824-223
   Officers' Training Program, Barmash Training Command, Wayne County, designates Second Lieutenant Roglund I. Karstil, 005-997-4242, Honor Graduate, OTP Class 6824-A.
   By order of the Commandant, Hammond B. Glover, Brigadier

SPECIAL ORDER 6824-977
   Second Lieutenant Roglund I. Karstil, 005-997-4242, is hereby appointed Aide to General Gentrund P. Beldarnus, Base Commander, Barmash Training Command, Wayne County.
   By order of the Commander, Gentrund P. Beldarnus
   General, Commanding
   /s/ Quentus F. Foldinus
   Brigadier, Adjutant

   "This will be a great career move for you, Lieutenant Karstil," said Royal Army Major Alicia Corwin. "Very few officers get a chance to be an aide to a General. It will make your future."
   With his smooth, freckled skin and blue eyes, Second Lieutenant Roglund Karstil might have been all of fifteen years old instead of fresh out of the Officers' Training Program. Standing at attention and staring over the head of the seated Major, he shared her opinion that it was a great privilege to win the post of aide to a General in the Commonwealth Forces. The assignment came to him, by tradition, as honor graduate of the Officers' Training Program. He would hold the post for a year, when it would pass to his successor in the next graduating class.
   In Roglund Karstil's mind, this appointment was no fluke. Since his earliest childhood, growing up in a large family on the planet Spalding, he had dreamed of only one thing—to become a part of the Commonwealth's gallant crusade against the oppressive Terran Overlord Government. And in joining the Army's ground forces, he would be following in his father's footsteps, and those of his father's father. From the day he first signed on a year ago, Karstil had worked hard trying to become the best of officer material. All his scores were

good, with some notable successes in grav tank command. Now he had his first assignment. It was a little scary, but exciting, too.

"With the crying need for officers in all the branches," the Major went on, "even Generals have been asked to forego the use of aides. But here on Barmash, General Beldarnus is important enough to do almost as he pleases. Acquit yourself well and you'll be able to go anywhere on your next assignment. Think of all those nice billets just waiting in Magog County if you do a good job. I never did like it here in Wayne County myself—too far away from everything."

Karstil let his eyes discreetly roam the outer office. Beyond the kidney-shaped desk where the Major sat, the wall was covered with shiny plaques and trophies won by the post. The flags of the post command stood at attention against one wall, a leather sofa in front of them. The thick, red carpet muffled any movement and seemed to encourage conversation at a respectful murmur. The office was meant to impress any visitor, and so it did.

"Now that we've outlined your duties, it's probably best if you take any questions to Lieutenant Larper, who you'll be replacing. He'll be gone in two days, so pay close attention to whatever help he offers. He was a good aide, and the General will see to it that he makes Captain as soon as he leaves." Placing her hands on the desk, Major Corwin smiled up at him in dismissal. "You'll be nervous at first, but by the end of the week, you'll fit right in. Good luck."

The first week passed, then the second and the third, the weeks becoming months and yet Karstil did not become at ease with the job. He still tensed, with a tightening in the pit of his stomach, whenever the General's voice came over the control panel. There was really no need for it, for General Beldarnus seemed a reasonable enough sort. He explained what he wanted in clear, concise terms, and Karstil certainly couldn't complain that the work was too hard. After the big build-up about how important new officers were to the Commonwealth and how many positions were open in all the branches, this job seemed less than planet-shattering in its importance.

"Roglund!" Karstil jumped at the sound of General Beldarnus's deep voice. "Come in here."

The Second Lieutenant stood up, ran his hands over his sharply pressed uniform, and stepped up to the heavy door that led into the office. As always, his mouth went dry as he closed the door behind him.

The General's office was even more spectacular than the reception area. The desk was larger, the carpet deeper, and many of the awards on the wall were the General's personal ones. Images of Beldarnus shaking hands with various important politicians, entertainers, and sports figures also adorned the walls. A silver beverage service was displayed on the armoire, along with other presentation pieces the General had collected.

"I've got another reception tonight," Beldarnus said, glancing up from his desk as Karstil entered the room. He was fit and trim, with only the his short-cropped white hair and a few deep facial lines to give away his years. "Take my mess-dress uniform to the cleaners, have it cleaned and pressed, and bring it to my quarters by 1700. Oh, and you can take my vehicle, because I'll be using a driver and official transportation. I'll see you at my quarters, Karstil. And don't forget that I must leave quarters at 1800."

"Yes, sir. Anything else, sir?"

The General had returned his attention to the papers on his desk, and shook his head without looking up. Karstil spun around on his heel and walked stiffly out of the room.

It was rare for the General to drive his own vehicle to the post because an official driver picked him up almost every morning. Today, however, Mrs. Beldarnus had used his grav sedan, a brand new Skyhawk SKE-200 convertible. She had left the sedan at post headquarters while shopping with Deputy-Commander Silitan's wife, who had given her a ride home. Now Karstil had to get the sedan and the uniform back to Quarters Number One, the Base Commander's home, located in a wooded area adjacent to the post's jungball course. Such were the monumental tasks of an aide.

Karstil checked himself in the full-length mirror inside the door of the outer office. He stood nearly two meters and weighed eighty-six kilos, and thought that the working-dress uniform of the Royal Commonwealth Army suited him well. The gray tunic and trousers had been tailored to fit his tall frame perfectly, but he would have to watch his diet to keep from using up his Lieutenant's pay buying new uniforms every year. He centered his cap over his eyes, smoothed his blond hair, and left the office with a grin of anticipation.

Slipping into the elegant interior of the SKE-200, Karstil wiped the sweat from his hands, started her up, and eased the sedan into traffic along Galloway Boulevard. Recognizing the General's coral-colored grav sportster, the military police officer stopped traffic to make way for it.

Karstil enjoyed driving, and he had to resist the urge to take this sporting sedan higher and get it up to speed. By in-putting the coordinates of his destination, Karstil could have gotten there without ever touching the controls, but he was on manual for the sheer pleasure of driving. Traffic was light, and the transit from the post to the main clothing facility was rapid. Just being inside the elegant sedan made him feel more important, more powerful. This was fun.

As Karstil waited for the General's uniform to be pressed, he looked idly out the window. The drab facility was adjacent to the tank trail that surrounded much of the unoccupied portion of the base, and a column of tracked support vehicles was churning up the dust at that very moment. The drivers were swathed in fire-retardant suits, their face-plates lowered against the clouds of yellow dirt. Karstil envied the commanders. Tons of steel under their control. That was the life.

The column passed and Karstil retrieved the uniform, with plenty of time to spare before he had to be at Quarters Number One. Climbing back into the SKE-200, he turned it away from the post buildings, depressing the accelerator hard as the ground-speed indicator glided up to 100 KPH. Pulsing infrared beacons marked the center of the roadway, keeping the vehicle aligned in the correct lane.

On auto-control, the sedan's vector computers would hold the vehicle solidly within its section of the road. On manual control, the sensor across the lower section of the forward windscreen pulsed to show the vehicle's location in relation to the beacons. He had to pay attention to keep the sedan centered over those pulsing beacons. Trees rippled past, a green blur out the side windows. At 200 KPH, individual trees were no longer recognizable, and at 250, the beacons were a single stream of light. Easing off, Karstil let the sedan coast forward, applying negative thrust to bring the speed bar back toward 100.

Just then, the sedan burst out of the trees into a flat expanse of head-high pandor grass. At the relatively controlled speed of 100 KPH, Karstil was aware of soldiers in full battle armor crouched along the edge of the road. He slowed further, aiming to bring the sedan to a full stop and hover. As he did so, a grav tank rose out of the grass to the left of the road. Even through the sealed windows of the sedan, he could feel the thrum of the grav generator.

Karstil had seen Viper light grav personnel carriers from a distance before and had studied them in a standard course on vehicle recognition, but this was the first time he was seeing one up close. Dressed in a silver-gray fire-retardant jumpsuit, the tank's commander slouched nonchalantly in his command hatch, oblivious of the civilian vehicle close by. The slim turret rotated left and right, its 25mm Gauss cannon probing like a finger toward the treeline a kilometer away. The TC spoke into the boom-mike attached to the helmet, the words completely muffled by the sedan's windows.

Just then, another Viper rose from the grass to the right of the road, then another further to the right. Karstil had the SKE-200 at a stationary hover, applying negative thrust to take position between the two closer tanks. He was aware of a line of infantry forming behind the tanks, the sergeants gesticulating to the members of the squads to chivvy them into the proper formation. It all looked quite proper. Karstil was too inexperienced to know that these were reservists who lacked the snap of regular troops.

The line of infantry passed through the row of tanks and began to advance on the distant trees. The Vipers let the infantry gain 100 meters, and then they began to move forward in support. Fascinated, Karstil eased the SKE-200 forward with them, keeping formation with the Vipers to his left and right.

At 500 meters from the trees, explosions erupted from the ground. Karstil knew they were pre-positioned ground charges, placed in the field by the training cadre, but he jumped just the same. The Viper to his right veered away from the road, its turret traversing to pick out some invisible target. He saw the Gauss cannon light momentarily as it engaged, firing toward the opening in the trees where the road entered the forest.

This was only training, and the cannon were firing low-charge lasers that linked with a computer. The computer would record hits, registering "kills" on vehicles and men. If a tank was hit, all its weapon systems would go dead. Being "killed" was embarrassing but not fatal, and it gave a feeling of reality to the otherwise mechanical training exercises.

As he watched, Karstil became more and more wrapped up in the action. The thunderous explosions, the awesome rumble of the grav tanks, the plumes of dirt shooting high in the air became a mesmerizing spectacle for the young cadet. After all the time spent studying in school, it was almost the real thing.

Then his peripheral vision caught the movement of the Viper to his left as it accelerated toward the opening in the trees ahead. Karstil focused on the tank commander, who was hunched down in his command hatch, head bobbing up and down as he consulted the range-finder and painting laser. The other Vipers were falling behind, their commanders either unwilling to support the charging tank or unaware of the movement. What were they doing?

Karstil recalled from his officer's training that a vehicle left unsupported was a sitting duck for enemy infantry. This guy wouldn't have a chance. He had to do something! Karstil slewed the SKE-200 to the right and left, trying to attract the attention of the other vehicles. "Move! Damn you! Move! Move!" he shouted, even though his voice was inaudible through the thick windows of the sedan. "Support him! Support him!"

But the other Vipers were not closing on the leader. In fact, they were falling further behind. Someone had to save him. Karstil accelerated the SKE-200 behind the lead tank, rapidly closing the distance. The yellow dust kicked up by the Viper's movement obscured his vision, and he was only marginally aware that it was creeping into the interior of the sedan. He accelerated more, pushing hard to keep up with the lead Viper. More explosive charges went off, throwing clods of dirt against the side of the sedan and spattering the windscreen. The opening in the canopy of trees was the answer. There they could hide in safety from the observation of the enemy gunners.

Together, the two vehicles, the 90-ton Viper and the 7-ton sedan, raced toward the opening that meant safety from fire. The high acceleration and maneuverability gave the sedan an advantage, but the Viper had a head start and higher initial velocity. The Viper edged slightly to the right, trying to hit the center of the opening; the commander obviously wanted the greatest number of maneuvering angles.

The protective shroud of the Viper is designed to allow the infantry to dismount in safety and secrecy. Though thick enough to stop shell fragments, it is not generally thought of as real armor protection. A 4-kilogram hammer, wielded by a reasonably strong legionary, could dent or bend the ogive, and an experienced legionary could tell how long a Viper had been in the field by the amount of crinkle in the shroud.

Weak though the Viper's shroud might be, it was infinitely stronger than the tissue-thin skin of a civilian sedan. Karstil didn't catch the change in the Viper's vector until it loomed right in front of his windscreen. He applied full negative thrust, swerving sharply to the right. It was, however, too little, too late. The right rear portion of the shroud touched, ever so slightly, the left front fender of the SKE-200. Just kissed it, but that was all it took. Instinctively, he placed one hand in front of his face.

The fender folded up like so much cheap plastic, the glass of the head lamp exploding in a shower of fragments that pattered against the windscreen of the sedan. The impact swung the SKE-200 even more sharply to the right, completely out of control. A giant tree loomed ahead. Somehow Karstil managed to apply full left drive to avoid it, and the sedan slewed away, the right rear fender skirt brushing against the massive trunk. Now the sedan spun to the right, grounding itself with a sickening crunch in the forest duff. Oily black smoke rose from the rear-mounted grav engine. The framework of the sedan was a crumpled mess.

Meanwhile, on the road, the Vipers roared by. The commanders coolly avoided looking at the remains of the civilian vehicle just visible among the trees.

By the time Karstil walked back to the cleaning facility to use its communicator, the building was closed. He was still in a daze when a friendly civilian security guard gave him a ride to headquarters so he could call a tracked recovery vehicle. He was almost in a panic thinking about it. General Beldarnus's own private vehicle. The one he had personally entrusted to his new aide. Destroyed. The casualty of a fierce battle between his own troops in a simple field exercise. If ever there was a fate worse than death, Karstil was sure this was it.

The sedan was so deep into the trees that the recovery team had to cut its way in before they could snap tow cables onto what was left of the rear bumper, wrenching the frame of the SKE-200 during the extraction process. The General's uniform, the innocent object of Second Lieutenant Karstil's mission, was safely rescued from the sedan, only to be accidently run over by the recovery vehicle.

4

Caralis, Shannedam County
The Commonwealth
11 March 6829

Dinnertime on the planet Caralis. Ranked a lowly Triarii, Quentain Podandos grimaced, stepped out into the fading sunlight, and slowly made his way over to the mess area. Stretching out all around him was a full Cohort, six Centuries of combat troops, dug in and on stand-by alert at the edge of the area known as the Farkon Highlands. They were the point in the Renegade Legion's struggle to keep Caralis's crucial continent from falling to TOG.

It was Podandos' first exposure to Alsatia's subtropical zone, and it hadn't taken him long to decide he didn't like it. The weather was uncomfortably humid and the soil chalky and bleached of color. How could anything ever grow here, the former farmboy wondered idly as he slipped down into the mess bunker.

Back at his station, he balanced his mess tin in one hand while trying to operate the access hatch lever on the port side of the Pedden Renegade Artillery Vehicle. The door-like access hatch opened toward the rear of the RAV, and so Podandos had to operate the lever with his right hand while keeping the mess tray steady. The lever required some effort to operate. The harder he tried to turn the handle, the more he felt the tray slipping from his hand. He gave up the attempt and decided to eat outside the vehicle.

The weather was fine and there was no real reason why he should seek cover for his evening meal. There was barely enough room in the cab for the three-man crew as it was, and he knew that his seat, the driver's station, had been folded up to make more room. He would have to erect his seat before he could eat anyway, and that would mean another balancing act.

The Pedden was grounded in a deep crater, placing the upper deck no more than a meter-and-a-half above the flat, unforgiving surface. Quentain pushed the mess tray onto the deck and then hauled himself up beside it. He contemplated his meal. The food served by the battery's mess section did not compare, in any way, with the meals provided during training. Those meals had been well-prepared and in sufficient quantity to fill the bellies of the recruits. This one, although probably nutritious and filling, was not nearly as appetizing.

Podandos bet that the officers didn't have to eat this stuff. Lumps of solid food were hidden by some kind of gray sauce that turned gelatinous as it cooled. He briefly considered letting the whole mass cool until it became semi-solid. Maybe the whole thing will come off the tray in one piece, he thought. In the end, he decided to just go ahead and eat. Whatever it was on his plate turned out to be better than it looked.

Podandos leaned back against the mount for the GPA5 artillery tube and looked over the other pieces in the battery. The three gun-launcher systems were deployed in a wide triangle, far enough apart that an incoming artillery round would not destroy all of them at one time. The battery commander's vehicle was snuggled against the treeline 300 meters to the rear, while the flanking pieces were more exposed in the open field to the front. Behind the trees were the supporting vehicles and the rest of the Cohort. The unit's other two firing batteries were ranked in the maintenance area, their cannon being zeroed and bore-sighted.

Zeroing and bore-sighting were archaic tasks that no amount of technology could overcome. They involved aligning the tube with the sights and then making sure that both were aimed at the same point. Firing the weapons would knock the target alignment off with each round, and eventually the accuracy of the round would be outside the acceptable limits of probable error. The troops in the field became more than a little angry when the rounds landed outside the designated impact pattern, especially when they fell short.

There was a real love-hate relationship between the front-line troops and the men of the artillery, the so-called "red-legs." When fire support worked, the front-line troops loved it, but when the rounds went wild, the troopers threatened to come back to the rear and take care of the gunners themselves. Considering the hell-or-high-water fighting nature of these men, it was a threat not to be taken lightly.

All in all, being a part of a Renegade Legion was not quite what Podandos had expected. The 2567th was a Provisional Legion, meaning it had been formed ad hoc from various other units, only to be disbanded once its specific duty was completed. Despite the designation, it was still every bit a fighting Renegade unit.

Quentain had imagined that the other men of his battery would become like a band of brothers, his "comradres in arms," but that had certainly not come to pass. In fact, his introduction to the other members of the battery had been underwhelming. Sergeant Bolan, the vehicle commander, had barely acknowledged Podandos' presence when he first reported to the vehicle. Bolan grunted once, nodding his head toward an open place on the floor. Podandos had assumed that this was where he was to store his gear. He dropped it there, and when no one objected, decided that would be his place.

The gunner, Triarii Angus Secunda, had been slightly more communicative, showing Podandos how to erect the driver's seat in the cramped confines of the cab. Quentain was getting ready to occupy the seat when Bolan hit the release lever and dropped the station to the floor, where it would remain. A warm welcome this was not.

The crewmembers took their meals alone, either because that was SOP for the battery or because they wanted it that way. His other questions about battery operation were greeted with monosyllabic responses from Secunda or by further grunts from Bolan. There had been no training on the GPA5 or any of the secondary weapons controlled from the cab. Podandos was an expert with the AP laser, controlled from his combat station, and he assumed that Bolan was equally efficient with the Vulcan IV anti-missile system that was his secondary responsibility. Both weapons could be controlled from the gunner's station, but his primary function was to operate the firing system for the main gun.

When the RAV had been moved into the maintenance area for bore-sighting and zeroing, it was Bolan who moved the vehicle. Without saying a word to either of the other crewmembers, he just fired up the grav generators and moved. Secunda had been leaning against the side of the Pedden when it rose from the crater, and the starboard side would have caught him if he hadn't leaped aside in time. Though he probably wouldn't have been seriously injured, he seemed somewhat rattled afterward. But as far as Podandos could tell, Secunda had said nothing about it to Bolan.

Basic training had given him the impression that being a member of a Renegade Legion meant becoming part of a huge family. That's what had drawn him, the idea of comradeship with many other soldiers dedicated to overthrowing the hated TOG, whose troops had attacked his home village on Holloway years ago. All during his training, Podandos had eagerly anticipated the time when he would face actual combat. But now he was less enthusiastic because it was hard to tell what it would be like fighting alongside Bolan and Secunda. What was worse, all the other crews in the battery seemed to operate in much the same cold, indifferent, uncommunicative way. Indeed, the battery commander, Centurion Wickersham, had said not a word to him in the week since Podandos arrived.

It was as though there was a virus of silence in the Legion, a sense of impending doom. Perhaps, thought Podandos, it was because of the bad luck that seemed to stalk the Legion ever since its creation. In its very first day on the field, one of its antiaircraft platoons had been destroyed while defending the Legion's orbital rocket battery. Only one of the vehicles and half a dozen crewmen had survived, leaving the Legion's protective umbrella spread thin. According to the rumors, those unlucky antiaircraft vehicles had been caught with their equipment down and hadn't even seen the enemy fighters until they were on them. From the very beginning, nothing but bad luck.

There was another rumor, spoken of only softly at the replacement station, that the platoon's destruction was part of a plot. But everyone tried to behave as though that were sheer craziness. To admit the possibility that someone in the 2567th wanted to see it fail was too dangerous to ponder. But still it was there, a nagging doubt about those around you, about those on whom your life depended. Podandos shuddered, thinking it better to have bad luck, at which a man could curse, than an invisible enemy against whom there was no defense.

Quentain reached inside his combat suit and pulled out the novel he had been reading. If the others in the battery wanted to ignore him, fine. To keep himself company, he had picked up the book in the Legion Exchange and was now deeply immersed in the adventures of Natos Durbal as the hero tried to solve the riddle of life in the Skuttarra Dukedom.

The novel would not go down as one of the greatest pieces of literature ever produced within the Commonwealth, but it had been the best of a limited selection. Most of the light reading material came on computer chips, acceptable by the majority of the work stations in vehicles and other equipment. But a chip-book would have required that Podandos use his station inside the Pedden, and that was obviously not an alternative, based on the current situation. There was no place for him to sit, and the chill from Sergeant Bolan was enough to make a man shiver. The top of the vehicle was fine, and even after the light faded, he would be able to use the head-set illumination device to see the pages.

The character Durbal was trying to establish a hydroponic farm in the barren soil of Koblos IV. The soil was rich enough, but the viral strain kept wiping out the crop as soon as it reached maturity. And then there were the Barrakan Rock Rats. The rats didn't attack the crops, but they did eat the flouropanels Durbal had rigged to supply light during the dark time on the planet. They could be fearsome predators when challenged, and Durbal had to guard the station during the night. His personal laser was sufficient, but he needed a better source of replenishment power. The rats were closing in again, and Durbal fired into the darkness. One of the rats exploded under the laser, sending a shower of magnesium sparks into the darkness. Magnesium sparks? The rats were silicon-based, not magnesium.

Podandos looked up from his book. A magnesium flare was still burning in the darkness, illuminating the field and the battery position. He shielded his eyes, dropping the flare guard on his battle helmet to dampen the effects of the brilliance.

The whole battery position stood out in the glare, the hulls and cannon of the vehicles reflecting the light. Quentain could see men running, recognized Secunda sprinting toward the Pedden. Then, from the edges of the flare light, the first of the fighters roared overhead, the sonic shock wave coming close behind.

The attacking fighters did not need artificial illumination to engage ground targets, but with the battery shut down, there were no emissions to track. The flares allowed visual identification of the ground targets until the RAVs fired their own generators. And the light was used to terrorize the victims. There was something about the unnatural glare that temporarily froze men in their tracks.

Podandos caught a glimpse of a flat-nosed, delta-shaped craft with twin ventral fins in the reflected light of the flare. He tried to get the insignia as the craft roared by, but it was too fast. Did it really matter, though? They had to be TOG fighters. The nose and leading edges of the wings glowed from the heat of atmospheric flight, the four probing weapon mounts almost incandescent from the heat. The sonic wave followed almost at once, the shock flattening the men in the field and throwing Quentain off the top of the RAV. As he spun through the air, he caught sight of his book disintegrating under the pressure.

The fall, even in a combat suit, was enough to knock the wind from his chest, and he lay on the ground, face up, panting for air. As another fighter roared overhead, he tried to cover his face against the ensuing blast. He felt his eardrums pop, then screamed to release the pressure from his lungs, afraid that they, too, would burst from the over-pressure. The flare guard on the helmet exploded in a cloud of shards; he shut his eyes against the tiny needles and felt them sting his face and neck as they penetrated the skin. He was gasping for breath now, his lungs sucking in huge amounts of dust from the clouds churned up by the passing fighters. He staggered to his feet, reaching for the Pedden's access port handle.

The handle wouldn't move. The port was locked from the inside. He beat on the hatch with his fists, his face pressed against the vision block. Inside, by the dim light of the combat lanterns, he made out Bolan in the driver's seat, could see him engaging the grav drive. He stumbled backward from the side of the vehicle as it began to rise from the crater, more dust spewing from the sides of the depression as the vehicle came free.

Angus Secunda pushed past him, knocking him forward onto the lip of the vacant crater. In one leap, Secunda launched himself onto the side of the rising Pedden, grasping the thermal fins in front of the directional vane. He screamed out in pain when his hands hit the red-hot fins. Having fallen back into the crater, Podandos watched Secunda pull himself onto the Pedden's upper deck.

Another flare burst overhead, directly over the crater. Even through the combat suit, Podandos could feel the heat. Dust from the crater clogged his nose and mouth. He crawled to the lip and looked over the field. The Number Two Pedden was rising from its crater at the far end of the field, and he could see the anti-missile Vulcan laser tracking ineffectually against the incoming fighters. It did not have the range to engage, but the gun captain was doing what he could to drive away his attackers. Through the chaos, Podandos again caught sight of the blunt delta shape as it streaked over the arena. The thermal glow had gone from the wings, the craft having cooled down from its violent re-entry. The twin probes on the nose of the craft blinked, bolts of searing light reaching toward the ground.

Both shots struck the port side of the Number Two Pedden as it staggered from its protective crater. Quentain saw shards of titanium armor, incandescent from the heat, peel away from the side of the RAV. The Pedden slewed to the right in an uncontrolled turn, the front of the vehicle gouging the ground as the driver struggled to maintain control.

The battery commander's vehicle fired the GPA5 artillery tube, the projectile streaking into the upper darkness. What type of ammunition could they be firing? Podandos wondered. He knew that RAVs carried no real antiaircraft weapons. He attempted to rise from the lip of the crater and was immediately knocked backward by the blast of a mass driver cannon projectile striking the rear of his own crater. Huge gouts of dirt flew into the air, the tortured ground glowing red at the point of impact. He fell again, shielding his face from the flying soil and felt the searing dirt burn his hands.

The injured Pedden was trying to make it to the cover of the woods, the battery commander's Pedden giving what covering fire it could from its position by the trees. It was hopeless.

Podandos could see the damaged left side of Pedden Number Two; it was only 50 meters away. The armor had been penetrated, with the ceramic base armor still glowing from the passage of the mass-driver hits. The Terrain Sensing and Reaction circuits had been destroyed on the left side of the vehicle, the wiring hanging like severed entrails from the damaged hull. The second fighter was making his pass now, and the exposed Pedden was an easy target.

The right side of the Renegade vehicle, undamaged from the first attack, was savaged by multiple hits from mass drivers and heavy lasers that winked from the nose and wings of the attacking aircraft. Great chunks of metal that had been the thermal fins spun through the air. The right directional vane vaporized in a puff of blue light.

Podandos saw the vehicle reel from the hits, the nose striking the ground as the driver, centered in the forward cab, fought his frozen controls. The portside access hatch flew open, the vehicle commander clearly illuminated by the flare and the bright ruddy glow from inside the vehicle. He grasped both sides of the opening as though to leap from the mortally wounded vehicle. Then the roaring inferno of the burning ammunition swept over him and he vanished in the blink of an eye.

The roar of an approaching Pedden made Podandos turn. His own vehicle, up to speed now, was making for the woods, was going to cross directly over the vacated cater. He hesitated, momentarily wondering if he should dive out of the way, burrow into the crater, or try to leap aboard the hurtling RAV. He could see Secunda atop the craft, hanging onto the GPA5 mount with one hand while shaking the other in rage at the diving fighters. The glare of the twin flares illuminated every corner and crevice of the compound, and both vehicle and rider stood out in stark contrast to the night blackness.

Mass-driver bolts churned the ground in front of the Pedden as the attacking pilot adjusted the strike of the rounds, waiting for a confirmed hit before he fired his wing-mounted lasers. The first MDC hit struck the exposed GPA5 tube, tearing the cannon from its mount and hurling it upward into the darkness. The attacking pilot, seeing his MDC score, thumbed the laser firing switch. The Pedden was bathed in iridescent light as the shields turned aside the laser hits, but the two MDC bolts passed through the flickering shields to impact on the titanium armor. The metal vaporized in an instant, opening the ceramic ablative armor to subsequent attack. Then the first fighter was gone and the second was making his run on the wounded vehicle.

Dust spewed from the underside of the vehicle and the grass of the field was pushed aside like the bow wave from a speeding boat. The blunt prow of the approaching RAV charged on toward the woods beyond its crater. The second ship made its firing pass over the field. Podandos saw the ceramic armor vaporize under the pounding of MDC hits, saw the left shield go out as its generators disintegrated. Unimpeded now, the lasers tore into the cab.

One laser struck the GPA5 mount at Secunda's feet. In an instant, the Triarii vanished, all the water in his body explosively rendered to super-heated steam.

The nose of the Pedden began to rise. Bolan had given up all hope of making the treeline and was trying to reach Low-Altitude Flight to escape his attackers. Podandos could see the grav coils glowing red on the underside of the hull, deeply shadowed in the glare of the flares. Smoke was pouring from the side. The Pedden roared over the crater, and Podandos ducked involuntarily to avoid the lower front glacis. The whine of the grav generators at maximum thrust pierced even his ruptured eardrums, and Podandos covered his helmet with his hands.

The vehicle rose into the darkness, into the safety of the velvet night. There was a single, brilliant flash at the point where the Pedden had disappeared. Particles of titanium armor, ceramic slag, components, and grav coils pattered to the ground around the crater.

Above the field, the flares guttered out, their final moments marked by floating embers like evil red eyes peering out from the dark. Podandos rolled to the rim of the crater and peered across the position. The wreck of the Number Two Pedden glowed through the tall grass. Behind the treeline, he could see the light of other burning vehicles, caught in the maintenance area when the air strike had come in. Darker against the trees loomed the battery commander's Pedden, the GPA5 cannon still glowing softly from its firing efforts.

It was only then that Podandos noticed that his face and hands were covered with blood. The backs of his hands burned from being rasped by the shards of plastic and earth that had torn all the skin. His eyelids were sticky, his right eye clouded. He could hear nothing, and he beat the side of his combat helmet with the heel of his hand to clear his ears. Nothing. His ruptured eardrums transmitted no sound.

Podandos staggered through the trees, past the battery piece, to what was the Cohort position. Wreckage lay scattered everywhere. Six Peddens, lined up for bore-sighting, were now nothing more than heaps of slag and glowing parts. The targeting and fire control radar vehicles, hidden against the trees, had not found safety there. The wreckage pulsed with the fires that still shot from the gaping holes in their torn armor. A body, or part of a body, blocked his path. He bent to examine it and found only the trunk; arms, legs, and head were missing. He rolled the body over, catching sight of the insignia on the left breast of the combat suit. Centurion Maximus. It was the Cohort commander.

He looked again across the shattered remains of the Cohort position. There was no other movement visible in the light of the burning vehicles. Only stillness and deafening silence. Podandos rose, lurching slightly as he tried to gain his balance. The battery commander's vehicle was behind him through the woods. Somewhere to the north was the artillery Manus headquarters…if there still was a Manus headquarters.

His whole body was trembling as he tried to collect himself. His first thought was to rejoin the rest of his unit, but that didn't make much sense. His unit didn't exist anymore.

Clark, Wayne County
The Commonwealth
21 May 6829

SPECIAL ORDER 6824-428

Second Lieutenant Roglund I. Karstil, 005-997-4242, is appointed Assistant Administrative Officer, Wayne County Financial Command.

Above-named officer will report at once to this command. No delay en-route is authorized. No advance/travel pay is authorized. Officer is not authorized to travel by civilian vehicle.

By order of the Commander, YaTakas Q. Labidinius
General, Commanding
/s/ Opilina J. Farbinator
Colonel, Adjutant

Ceiling-mounted illumination panels cast shadowless light over the vast space of the Wayne County Financial Center. Row upon row of computer work-stations disappeared into the distance. Before each computer hunched a gnome-like figure, quietly keying in information on each of the millions of legionaries, active and reservist, who operated in this sector of the Commonwealth. Each record was updated, checked, cross-checked, referenced, re-referenced, and annotated. The only sound was the occasional squeak of the automated canteen carts as they made their rounds down the endless rows.

Around the perimeter of the area, raised above the teeming mass, were the enclosed offices of the administrators who checked, cross-checked, referenced, re-referenced, and annotated the already checked, cross-checked, referenced, re-referenced, and annotated records supplied by the workers down below. Silence hung like a blanket over the assemblage. When conversation was necessary, it was carried on in the hushed and reverent tones engendered by the vastness of the operational area.

"I'll go over it again for you, Lieutenant." Warrant Officer Sardan VenVentor leaned forward over the pile of computer print-outs and went on with his lesson in droning monotone. "The Multi-plex 400/GHF/3/A program is designed to rapidly locate anomalies in pre-designated financial data. In order to correctly operate within the system, the operator need only locate the serial sending system of the host unit. By referencing the DIP switching function on the guest station to the opposite settings of the host station, a loop-back test can be run prior to the inputting of data from the host. With the command TRXD, you may then receive the data from the host. The Multi-plex 400/GHF/3/A frequency tolerance allows both the RD-200 and HK-900 to operate through the same serial interface. This is all based in the permissive interconnect specifications of both units. The override protocol is never to be used during the inputting function."

Despite the importance of this information, Karstil began to feel his eyelids getting heavy. There must be something in the air of this place, he thought. Or maybe he wasn't getting enough sleep. How else explain the fact that none of what the other man had just said made any sense?

After two months at the Finance Center on the planet Clark, Karstil was tired in every muscle, tendon, and joint. The work was not physically taxing, but it was an effort to drag himself to it. He hated it. He hated the hours of sitting at his desk, a human clerk, an anachronistic anomaly in a computer-driven world. Basic Training and the Officers' Training Program had been something new all the time. Even being a General's aide had presented different problems every day. But this, this was boredom personified. Karstil marveled at the ability of some men to come cheerfully, even expectantly, to work here.

Why had he fouled up so royally with General Beldarnus? He might still be riding around in the grav sedan from time to time if he hadn't behaved so impulsively when he ran into the training exercise. The only thing he could hope for here on Clark was that he'd have a chance to redeem himself.

VenVentor stared at the new Second Lieutenant. The Lieutenant's face stared back, but there was no recognition in the eyes. VenVentor, with 35 years of experience in the financial section, had seen officers come and go. Most of them never really grasped the details, the fine sense of accomplishment possible in the intricacies of Commonwealth Military Finance. Luckily, this Lieutenant had arrived just as a new subsystem was about to be initiated. The young man could learn the new system from the ground up, instead of encountering all the problems of the older program. VenVentor looked on his assignment as a rare challenge.

"Don't worry, sir. You'll get the hang of it. Let me set you up on a trial program with limited data input. You'll be able to work it through yourself. You'll be crunching the data in no time." VenVentor knew how to deal with officers. The motto of the Warrant Officers' Protective Association (WOPA), an unofficial, but nevertheless very real, organization was "Minimize the Risk." Minimize the damage that a commissioned officer could do the system. Officers came and went at the facility. They were usually cheerful, anxious, and hopelessly inept. The task of the professional Warrant, then, was to keep to a bare minimum any damage they could do to the system. "Minimize the Risk."

Karstil stared at the Warrant Officer, blinking several times as though trying to focus on the man. VenVentor was like so many of the others here at the Finance Center, dedicated to the computers that ran his life. He may have been a tall man at one time, but years of sitting hunched over a terminal had rounded his shoulders. He walked in that strange, mincing way that came from years of wearing felt-covered slippers to reduce static electricity. "Static will play holy hob with a terminal," Karstil had been told on his first day. And every day thereafter. The air was kept dry. The temperature was a constant 22 degrees Centigrade. The light intensity of the overhead panels was kept constant. It seemed as though everything possible was done for the sake of the computers.

That wasn't quite true, however, and Karstil knew it. The computers, powered by a standard AI bio-system, were immune to heat, dust, and static. The creation of such a strictly controlled environment was intended more to impress the gnomes with the awful responsibility of their task. It was a way of saying, in no uncertain terms, that the computers were the important component of the finance center.

For the past five weeks, Karstil had been trying to fathom the intricacies of the Multiplex 400/GHF/3/A, as dutifully explained by VenVentor. The Warrant Officer certainly knew his stuff, but it just wasn't getting through. Karstil would just have to try again, would have to concentrate harder. Perhaps a walk through the area would clear his mind. As soon as VenVentor left the office, Karstil stood up and stretched. Then he headed for the computer bay; it would be a good idea to show the troops down below that the administrators were at least aware of their existence.

The hunched operators didn't even look up as Karstil walked the aisles. The pale overhead illumination and the green glow from the consoles gave the operators a deathly pallor. A mortician would look on this place as a real challenge, thought Karstil. Trying to make these people look alive would be a tough job. He studied the operator at one of the terminals. The man hunched intensely over the keyboard, his right hand on the numeral pad, the left holding a light pencil. By moving the pencil across the screen and keying in commands from the number pad, the operator was updating some legionary's financial record. Somewhere in the vastness of space beyond the center, credits were being added to or deleted from his next pay voucher.

The system was superb. The data was stored on a serial well, and all the legionary need do was insert his payment record card into an electronic teller to receive part or all of the pay due him. He could use the card to buy anything, from clothing to a personal vehicle. The computer deducted the amount required and even kept track of credit purchases. The steady pulk, pulk of the terminal keys and the sibilant wisp of the pencils across the screens were the only sounds in the cavernous room.

A canteen cart, a little more than one meter high, moved slowly down the aisles, stopping on command at the terminals that had indicated, silently, a request for some refreshing or stimulating drink. One operator inserted his card, pressed the button for the desired beverage, and waited for the computerized drink-droid to produce the result. Thunk, whirr, grind. Out came the container with the ordered refreshment. The droid moved on.

The machine was now creeping up the aisle behind Karstil. He stood waiting until the canteen came abreast of his location and then inserted his card. The "unauthorized terminal location" light flashed just as he slipped it in the slot. He had inserted his card while the droid was in transit between terminals, but now it had stopped. He figured that if something were wrong, the machine would just spit out the card and tell him the correct terminal location.

No such luck. Instead, the machine thunked and whirred away as though it couldn't decide what to do. Then it seemed to pause, as though thinking. With a final thunk, it apparently decided to keep the card and give nothing in return. Slowly, it moved on up the aisle to the next station that had indicated a need for refreshment, the captured credit card now deep inside the access port.

The terminal operator inserted his card and pressed a series of buttons. Karstil watched intensely, wondering all the time what he had done wrong. His order had been complex: Coffee, cream, sugar, extra cream, extra sugar. There wasn't either cream or sugar in the machine. For that matter, there wasn't any coffee in the machine either. It was really a chemically tailored drink, artificial whitener, and artificial sweetener, but it was called "coffee," "cream," and "sugar" to assuage the sensibilities of the consumers.

The machine thunked away, inputting the commands. It paused. The machine had a problem it was trying to solve. It had too many cards in the ready slot for the commands it had been given. It whirred away again, its on-board micro-processor evaluating the possible responses. It was ready.

The access door snapped open, and the empty drink container popped out from the machine, striking the terminal operator point-blank on the left temple. The operator leaped to his feet, turning to face his antagonist. The drink-droid continued its assault by next firing a cloud of powdered whitener, extra whitener, and sweetener, extra sweetener, clear over the keyboard of the terminal.

The operator flung himself over the keys like a mother protecting her child from harm. When the machine sprayed steaming hot coffee onto his back, he leaped away in pain. His foot caught on a conduit to the right of the work-station as he staggered into the terminal of his immediate neighbor, falling backward into the other operator's lap. The machine doused the now-exposed keyboard with the last of the coffee and then subsided into contented silence. The keyboard gave off an hysterical squeak, sparked once, and died. The terminal screen flashed momentarily and followed its keyboard into blank death.

The drink-droid, eminently satisfied with its work, moved on to the next work station.

"Lieutenant Karstil," sighed the Warrant Officer, "you must be very careful while on the work floor. The canteens are programmed to serve the terminal operators. Any inputting of additional or extraneous data or deviation from their work schedule can present problems."

Karstil smiled sheepishly, not knowing what to say.

The drink-droid's assault was due to Karstil's insertion of his card while the machine was not at a commanded work station. Now the Senior Warrant Officer, VenVentor's immediate superior, was explaining the results of Karstil's actions to the Second Lieutenant. "This facility has been designed to maximize through-put on the part of the operators. Deviation from the scheduled program is not allowed. In the future, you should monitor work-station activity by becoming a host station to the terminal in question. Warrant Officer VenVentor should have explained all this to you earlier. Since he has been remiss in his duties, I will take on that task for him."

VenVentor squirmed slightly, his shoulders drooping under the verbal lash of his superior. Karstil out-ranked both of the Warrant Officers, but he knew better than to respond. VenVentor would say nothing more about the incident. Karstil hung his head in embarrassment, intently studying the nap of the carpet as it sprang back from the pressure of his toes.

Back at his own cubicle, VenVentor explained the system yet again. "The Multi-plex 400/GHF/3/A program is designed to rapidly locate anomalies in pre-designated financial data. In order to correctly operate within the system, the operator need only locate the serial sending system of the host unit. By referencing the DIP switching function on the guest station to the opposite settings of the host station, a loop-back test can be run prior to the inputting of data from the host. With the command TRXD, you may then receive the data from the host. The Multi-plex 400/GHF/3/A frequency tolerance allows both the RD-200 and HK-900 to operate through the same serial interface. This is all based in the permissive interconnect specifications of both units.

"Although the data on the terminal in question has been lost, it can be retrieved from the database on the serial well. All that needs to be done is to pull the latest well-saved material from the serial and cross-reference it with the current input loading on the station-top terminals. It is a manual process that takes some time. And remember, the override protocol is never to be used during the inputting function."

VenVentor went over the steps of the program several times until Karstil finally began to grasp the system. All right, he thought, this time I think I know what I'm doing.

"Since you seem to have learned how this works, I will leave you to the task." VenVentor rose from his chair. It was shift-termination time, and VenVentor was about to depart for his quarters. The second shift had been notified that Karstil would be uploading all previous financial records for Wayne County and they were to deal only with current data. Karstil would have the records and the serial well to himself for the next ten hours.

Fortified with a thermos of coffee he kept on the small table across the room, Karstil went at his task. He didn't drink the coffee near the terminal, having seen what kind of accident that could cause. Besides, going to the coffee allowed him to stretch his legs.

The task was not difficult, just long and tedious. He had ᴐ pay close attention to what he was doing so that the current records and the previous data agreed in every case. Dates of birth, entry to Commonwealth Forces (called Basic Pay Entry Dates), current marital status, and other information had to be cross- referenced and checked. He was astounded at the number of mistakes he found. Obviously, there had been no cross-check for several years, and the current data was lacking a number of important entries. He found the name of one man who had inadvertently not received his full pay for seven years. That legionary would have a pleasant surprise the next time he checked his credit balance. Then there was another legionary who had been double-paid every year on his anniversary of entering the service. That man would not be happy when his next pay voucher showed zero pay allowed. He wouldn't be paid for more than a year.

The time actually passed quickly. Karstil became more confident as he worked the program. This stuff was easy. The system automatically saved itself every ten minutes, the machine whirring away even as he used his light pencil and command keys to move entries to their correct locations. The terminal would also take voice commands, but Karstil did not feel comfortable enough with the system or his diction to rely on that too much. All this time, he was only dimly aware of the gnomes huddled at their terminals in the vast bay below his windows. And they, in turn, paid no attention to the lone Second Lieutenant laboring above them.

Some eight hours into the task, he was beginning to grow groggy. He stopped using the light pencil and began to rely more and more on the control keys. To keep his speed at the former rate, he engaged the override protocol. This allowed him to use his hands on the number pad as well as the main keyboard. Finger dexterity was less important when using the keys, and he didn't have to lift his hands from the keyboard to update the entries.

Almost ten hours into the job and the last entries were being made. Karstil swept through the few remaining legionaries on the list. At one point, he caught himself almost missing an address in the Home of Record entry. All planet abbreviations had been changed from a two-letter code to a three-letter code some years before. The planet Wrangby in Magog County had been changed from WR to WBY. Any standard correction program would have noticed and changed the designator. Why let the machine do it? Karstil thought. He hit the shift key and quickly typed WBY.

On many computer terminals, the shift key is very close to the control key. For any experienced typist, this was no problem. For less-experienced operators, however, some care was needed. For all his good intentions, Karstil was not much of an experienced typist. As the little finger on his left hand dropped toward the shift key, his ring finger struck the control key instead. Control "W" produced no result, but Control "B" produced the question: "Erase current file in serial well? (y) (n)."

Karstil saw the question flash across the screen and all his senses snapped to attention. He didn't need to read what it said to know that he had hit an incorrect key, so he lifted his left hand from the keyboard. Unfortunately, the right hand was already moving toward the "y" key. Faster than thought, his index finger struck the answer key.

At 299,792.5 kilometers/second, the erase command streaked toward the well. Karstil knew what had happened. He moved his finger toward the "Cancel" key as quickly as he could. But no human muscle response can outrun the speed of light. The screen went ominously blank. For Karstil, it felt like a rock had just fallen on top of his stomach. The light panels in the outer room dimmed. The screens in the bay shimmered and recovered.

With a thin veil of sweat breaking across his brow, Karstil sat motionless and stared at the empty screen. Nightmare visions of the General's sedan flashed before him as he picked up the manual and frantically opened it. He scanned down the table of contents, searching for help. He opened to page 267.

"In order to prevent permanent loss of data, save your material at regular intervals. Never use the 'Erase current file in serial well' command unless you intend to clean the entire file of current material. The override protocol is never to be used during the inputting function."

There it was. Clear as could be. All under the appropriate heading of "How to Save Yourself From Disaster."

Caralis, Shannedam County
The Commonwealth
10 October 6830

Veteran Sergeant Lucifer K. Mullins shrugged his thick shoulders against the rain. It was not a proper rain, one that pours down, punctuated by brilliant flashes of lightning. This was more like a heavy mist, one of those insidious rains that tempts a man into thinking it will soon end. And then it doesn't. The rain had been falling for three days now, and the leaden skies showed no sign of clearing. "As if things weren't ugly enough on this rock..." he muttered.

The continent of Rolandrin, base of operations for all Commonwealth and Renegade forces on the planet Caralis, actually consisted of a group of large islands stretching from the equator all the way north to the arctic tundra. Mullins, by nature, would have much preferred being stationed further south, where it was warm. But that was life in the Legion.

The Sergeant walked toward the line of fighting vehicles, Liberator Medium Grav Tanks and Viper APCs, that were the teeth of this Century detachment. There should have been three tanks and six armored personnel carriers, but battle losses had reduced the strength of the Century to one tank and four APCs. Those vehicles that remained showed the scars of recent combat, and all of them would need some repair.

Great chunks of titanium armor had been scoured from his own Liberator. He had been lucky that the last hit from the TOG 100mm Hammerhead round hadn't taken them all out during the recent action at the Kemmlar Basin. The armor on the flank of his turret had been scaling away when the round hit. A micro-second later and the shot would have peeled its way through the ballistic protection and exploded inside the turret. Either the gunner or the commander would have died. Mullins shrugged. That was why tankers got the big credits.

A trickle of water found its way into his combat suit. He felt the cold drop accumulating at the base of his neck. It got larger and larger, and then coursed its way down his spine. Because their combat suits were as comfortable as fatigues, tankers tended to wear them all the time. Though designed to give protection from the searing flash that accompanied a direct hit, it was too bad they couldn't do much to keep out the rain. They were cleverly designed to funnel all the water down from a man's head and shoulders into his boots, however. Mullins tugged at his trousers, pulling the suit away from his skin. His boots were beginning to squish.

He walked between the protruding arms of the hull of his Liberator and climbed over the empty TVLG missile rack. There was no real reason why he should be in the motor pool. There was no work going on, but he felt more comfortable here than in the barracks. The platoon of nine men, three combat crewmen to each vehicle, had been reduced to three during the last campaign. His own driver had been wounded and evacuated, and the other tanks of the platoon had been destroyed, with only one crewmember surviving out of the six. The platoon personnel bay was empty, too, filled mostly with the memories of those who had shipped out for combat and not returned. Until the next draft of replacements arrived, it would remain filled with their ghosts. Of course, this was a reality of combat life, a reality no one knew better than Lucifer Mullins.

The new draft should be in at any time, he thought, hoping that the platoon would get at least some good men. He had served in various Renegade Legions for sixteen years, and it seemed to him that the quality had gone down steadily. Especially in the last few years. Maybe I'm getting too damn old to be a platoon sergeant, he thought. At thirty-four, I should be looking for a job at Cohort staff, or maybe even at the Manus level.

Replacements didn't mean all that much to him; he had no emotional attachment to them. He was going out as a replacement himself. The survivors of the platoon, along with survivors from some of the others, were being evacuated to a distant planet where they would serve as the cadre for the formation of a new Manus Primus unit. He would be saying good-bye to more than just his tank.

Mullins broke open the front of his battle suit and reached inside for his smokes. He found the pack in the inside pocket, but when he withdrew it, it was soaked with water. The smokes had dissolved, the paper and tobacco mixed in a grainy mass. There was no hope of salvaging the pack. He squeezed it slowly in his right hand, watching dejectedly as brown water oozed between his fingers. Years of training prevented him from dropping it to the ground; someone would have to pick it up later. He put the pack back into the inside pocket and closed his suit.

He preferred the thick, black cigars he rolled himself, but the supply of tobacco and papers had been lost in the battle damage from the last engagement. The materials were kept in a locked box he had welded to the deck of the turret fighting compartment of his Liberator. He had the only key. The box had taken a hit from a light laser after the turret armor had been destroyed, incinerating the tobacco in an instant. That was one more thing TOG owed him. Tobacco of that quality was difficult to come by, and Mullins had found no resupply as yet.

Mullins pulled himself onto the top of the turret and spun the wheel that secured the commander's hatch. The hatch had been scored by a 7.5/6 laser that had grazed it from behind. The damage wasn't serious, but it made the wheel grind as it pulled the dogs of the hatch. The spring-loaded hatch popped up, and Mullins lifted it full open, securing it in the upright position. Full open there was no way the hatch could shut by accident, but years of training made securing it a reflex action. He had seen an unsecured hatch drop on the fingers of an unwary tank commander while the tank was maneuvering. That man wasn't commanding tanks anymore. Even with advanced bionics, an artificial hand was not an asset inside a tank.

The odor from within the tank filled his nostrils, and instantly a small grin creased his hardened face. There was something about the way tanks smelled. Whether they were brand new, right from the rebuild yard, or combat veterans, they all smelled the same. It was a combination of circuitry, hydraulics, crystalline titanium armor, and sweat. He would recognize that smell anywhere, even in his sleep—even if he were dead. Tank-smell. He loved it. It was the scent of power and speed, violence and death. For Mullins, climbing into a tank was like coming home through the front door.

The tank was cold inside. With the fusion power packs removed, the tank was an inanimate object. Just 273 metric tons of titanium, steel, ceramic shields, and circuits. Clammy steel at that. The rain had penetrated the fighting compartment, and the interior was covered with a fine layer of mist. Mullins eased his solid 110 kilos through the narrow hatch into the turret. He wiped the telescopic sight reticle with the cuff of his right sleeve. With all the sophisticated sensing systems in the Liberator, visual sighting was not vital, but open sights still worked when all else failed. As long as the tank commander or the gunner were functional, visual sighting was possible.

Mullins traversed the sight, spinning the sighting wheel to turn the telescope mounted on the turret top. Manual control was another anachronism in a high-tech world. But like visual sighting, it was soldier-proof. Mullins scanned the motor park, watching the other vehicles swim through the misting rain. Suddenly he froze, then spun the wheel to bring the sight back along its traverse. Something had been moving out there among the vehicles. He hadn't seen it clearly, and for a moment, thought it could only have been his imagination.

He traversed slowly, straining to see anything and everything. Move the sight. Examine the foreground. Examine the middle ground. Examine the distance. Move the sight. Repeat the process. There was movement out there. Almost at the limit of visibility, there was someone else moving in the area.

The lens of the sight was protected by a metal shroud, but the rain had reached it, distorting the image. Mullins screwed his eye against the reticle. Someone was on top of a Liberator well down the line. The Sergeant couldn't see who it was or what the person was doing, but someone was definitely there. He checked the azimuth indicator so that he would be able to find the target when he rose from the commander's hatch. 1650 mils.

His head popped out of the hatch, and he looked to his right. The long line of Liberators and Vipers stretched into the mist, disappearing in the gloomy distance. At first, he couldn't find his target. He went through the search procedure: foreground, middle ground, distance. He made himself do the search, to not look for a particular target.

There it was! Just visible through the rain and fog, a figure was squatting on the turret of one of the Liberators.

Mullins rubbed the mist from his eyes and peered into the darkness, his heavy jaws clenched tightly.There should not be anyone on the line at this time of day. Certainly not at that end of the line. Those were the tanks that had been fully serviced, ready to be returned into action. Once that was done, the tanks should have been secured and protected until their commanders could sign for them again.

Mullins rose from his hatch, keeping his eyes on the distant figure. He knew that he would lose sight of his target when he dropped to the ground, but that couldn't be helped. He closed and secured the commander's hatch, feeling his way through the operation. Then, watching his prey as long as he could, he moved down the right front sponson.

As soon as his feet hit the ground, he darted away from the line of tanks, clearing their bulk from his line of sight. He'd lost his quarry. He wiped the moisture from his eyes and began to jog down the line of vehicles. No one. He couldn't be sure on which tank the figure had been, but it had been pretty far down the line. He looked back at his own Liberator, trying to judge the distance through the chilling mist. This is about right, he thought. He moved back two tanks, just to be sure, and then climbed to the turret.

Mullins tried to position himself at the location he had seen the other man. He looked around the turret, not sure of what he was looking for. It seemed all right, and he jumped the meter separating it from the next tank. Another search, and again there was nothing visibly wrong. The third tank was the same. And the fourth. It was not until the fifth tank that something was different.

Even before his boots hit the deck, Mullins could see the footprints of another pair of boots, though they were fading under the steady rain. He stood quite still, examining the deck and turret side. There were imprints of knee pads where the man had been kneeling on the hull roof beside the 50mm cannon.

Mullins stood still and examined the gun mount with his eyes. After seven years of living in a Liberator, he knew what should and should not be there. He did most of his own maintenance, not trusting others to fiddle around with his tank. At first, he saw nothing and turned to go. Wait. Something caught his eye. He looked back, sinking to his knees to get a better look. He saw nothing wrong. Carefully he turned his head, taking his eyes off the 50mm mount, trying to recreate the attitude from which he had noticed something.

There it was again. This time, he was sure of it, and he knew where to look. There, at the base of the mount, where the accelerator coils connected to the elevating mechanism, was a hair-thin copper wire. Mullins bent down to examine it. The wire led into the restraining cap at the base of the upper accelerator coil. That was not right.

Mullins tried to loosen the nut with his fingers, but it had been torqued down tight. He kept a set of tools, unauthorized, in his tank, and he retrieved them to crack the nut. A fine copper wire had been wound around the base of the accelerator coil. It was a devious act. The cannon would fire, perhaps many times. But sooner or later, probably in combat when the gunner went to rapid fire, the copper wire would heat up and melt. When the molten copper hit the accelerator coil, the coil would fuse solid, rendering the cannon inoperative.

There was the possibility that the malfunction would be fatal, but if the crew survived, there would be no evidence of what had triggered the fault. The copper would have melted into the coil, and only a skilled technician who knew what to look for would be able to trace the accident to a different source.

Mullins felt a cold knot in the pit of his stomach. His own 50mm cannon had failed in the last battle. He had survived, but only barely. He returned to his own tank and disassembled the accelerator coils for the 50mm cannon. The coil on the upper accelerator was fused solid. He lifted it out and examined the knurls of the coil. In the fading light, he could see no evidence of tampering. He examined the inside of the retaining nut. There, crushed in the threads of the nut, he saw a faint wisp of copper. His cannon had been sabotaged as well. A slow rage boiled within him, as he imagined what he would do if he ever got his hands on whoever had done this.

He glanced quickly around the motor pool. He could see no one, but he felt the hair on the back of his neck rise. Who can I tell? he thought with sudden alarm. Who can I trust? He would have to be careful, very careful, about what he did. The best thing, he decided, was to check everything himself, first on his tank and then on all the other tanks in his platoon. It would have to be done quietly after the Century had been re-equipped, They had training time ahead of them. There would be time to do the job. But would he recognize sabotage when he saw it? What else might there be?

Mullins replaced the 50mm cannon parts and left the motor park. The platoon personnel bay was dark when he returned, the soft grumble of a sleeping man the only sound. That would be Mastati Franklin Grouse, the gunner in his tank. Grouse was a skilled gunner and a good worker in the field, but in the barracks, all he seemed to do was eat and sleep. Perhaps he was like the legendary camel, stocking up on nourishment and rest so he could use both when the time came.

Mullins lay down on his own bunk and stared at the ceiling. He could hear faint music coming from the Cohort snack bar down the street, even occasional laughter. He needed to think. Danger lay all around him, and the uneasy feeling in his gut would not go away. Whoever was doing the sabotage, they were probably not acting alone. There had to be a bigger system than one man breaking 50mm cannon. The new draft would have, should have, new men who were above suspicion. Perhaps they were the ones he could trust.

Then another, more terrible thought hit Mullins. If it wasn't safe here on base in Rolandin, what did that say about conditions elsewhere on Caralis?

He was still wearing his damp combat coveralls when he finally fell into troubled sleep nearly an hour later.

7

Windsor, Wayne County
The Commonwealth
14 October 6830

SPECIAL ORDER 6824-663
    Second Lieutenant Roglund I. Karstil, 005-997-4242, is hereby appointed Assistant to the Administrative Officer, Wayne County Public Affairs Office.
    Above-named officer will report at once to this command. No delay en-route is authorized. No advance/travel pay is authorized. Officer is not authorized to travel by civilian vehicle.
    By order of the Commander, Follansbee L. Paternoster
    Colonel, PAO, Director
    /s/ Jovannus A. Glabinus
    Major, Adjutant

    "This office," the man said grandly, "deals in those public matters that do not fall under the venue of any other department. As a result, we are the leading edge of what the public of the Commonwealth knows about its armed forces. Although Commonwealth Forces are a branch of the government, and although our budgets and operations are controlled by the Cabinet, there are times when it is in the best interests of the Royal Army to impress the members of the Cabinet with the needs of our service. Whether we like it or not, we are in competition with the Royal Navy for relatively limited funds. If the Navy had its way, the Army would be relegated to a minor service under the control of the Naval Grand Marshal."
    Colonel Follansbee Paternoster, Commander of the Public Affairs Office for Wayne County, stared out his office window, his back turned toward the newly assigned Second Lieutenant. "It really doesn't matter what is true," he said, turning to face the officer. "It is the image that counts. And we deal in that. If the Cabinet sees us as active, intelligent, prepared, and professional, we will get the discretionary funds. And that, Lieutenant Karstil, is what you will be doing. You will help us get those funds."
    And so it was. In a few months time, so many press releases had rolled off Karstil's desk that he eventually became expert enough to get one approved on the first rewrite. The job was not as boring as the work at the Finance Center, and not as strict as being a General's aide. All things considered, he kept telling himself, this might be the right job for him. It just might.
    Now the big show was coming. There had been debate in the Cabinet and Parliament

about finances for the next year. The Navy had put on a demonstration that impressed some of the members, and the discretionary funds hung in the balance. Now the Royal Army had its chance to impress the powers-that-be, for a large group of VIPs would attend the upcoming Basic Training graduation ceremony. Though there were Basic Training programs all over the Commonwealth, Wayne County's program had been chosen as the showpiece.

Roglund Karstil had taken part in military ceremonies during his short career as an officer of the Commonwealth. Graduation from Basic and Officers' Training School had been impressive affairs, and he had seen the taped coverage that appeared on the news after the events. He had marveled to have been a part of those impressive programs. Now he was finding how much work there was in creating the visual impressions.

Making a big impression was as much for the troops' morale as to influence the visiting dignitaries. It helped foster pride among the ranks. Karstil wasn't of high enough rank to care much about the dignitaries, but he did care about the rank and file. He remembered his own intense pride upon graduation from Basic as the blocks of troops marched past the reviewing stand, the colors snapping in the breeze, the bands playing the Royal Army March.

After graduation, the recruits would be sent to their branch specialization schools or to the Officers' Training Program. Among the graduates designated for OTP was the daughter of Cabinet Member Cobalatus Drango. Even having a daughter in the Royal Army was not enough to make Drango a staunch supporter of either the Army or the Commonwealth Force. But he sat on the Defense Appropriations Committee, and he was a big man in the Cabinet. This was exactly the type of good-will opportunity to which Colonel Paternoster had alluded.

Part of the post facility was the brand-new visitors' center and its twenty-five story hotel. A thermoplex structure rising eighty meters above the surrounding post, it was easily the tallest building in the area. From its upper floors, reached by transparent grav-elevators, the parade ground and the demonstration ranges could be clearly seen. The twenty-first floor, designated for special VIPs, had a single suite occupying the entire floor. The central room spanned the length of one wall, and a special thermoplex panel had been developed so that there were no breaks in the window-wall. It was like floating 60 meters off the ground.

Every visiting President, Count, or Cabinet Member who had used the suite had glowingly praised its facilities. Though Cabinet Member Drango was not the highest-ranking member of the visiting party, Karstil thought it strategic to assign the suite to him.

A reception dinner was planned for the night before the graduation ceremony, and Karstil was assigned to the planning as a special detail. He huddled for hours over the menu with the mess steward of the reception facility. It was going to be spectacular, and Karstil was confident that everything would be perfect. No more foul-ups here. The mess steward and his staff had outdone themselves by creating a special recipe for appetizers of imported Bansi mushroom tops stuffed with bread dressing, onions, peppers, and tiny Lubin shrimp. Karstil spent the entire food budget for the quarter to bring in these little delicacies, and he decided to follow it with a green root cream soup, broiled side of Staedler's ox, roasted potatoes, entwhistle beans, and a green salad with hot ginseng dressing. The dessert was a frozen concoction of exotic ices and cream, covered with sprinkles of nuts and Peltan fruit. Not only was the meal a taste treat, it would also be visually enticing.

He made sure, too, that there would be extensive press coverage of the reception and dinner. Though some news stations were moderately hostile toward the military and its continued expenditures, Karstil thought they would find it difficult to say anything bad about the Royal Army if he invited them to the reception. He figured the boys at the top would like that. Of particular importance was Judith Westover of GHTY. She was the leader of the anti-Army faction. From her vantage point near the reception line of smiling dignitaries, she would surely find it difficult to be negative in her reporting.

The day arrived. As a minor member of the staff, Karstil was not among the officials designated to meet the dignitaries. He stayed in the background, watching his handiwork unfold before him. The column of escort vehicles wound its way to the reception center without a hitch. Karstil, feeling an unusual sense of accomplishment, returned to his office.

Two hours later, he was back in his office, eagerly planning for the upcoming review of graduates. He was filled with the intoxicating certainty that he had finally done a job well. The holovid cameras would be placed at strategic locations in order to prominently feature Sedgia Drango as she marched past. Because she was a rather large, perhaps even portly girl, it was important to show her at just the right angle and range. As Karstil began to jot down some notes, he whistled cheerfully.

Suddenly becoming aware of an unpleasant odor, he looked up, seeking the source. Someone had been sick, very sick, nearby. He shrugged it off and went back to his notes, but the smell got stronger and stronger, filling his small cubicle. It was too much, and Karstil decided that the sergeant in the outer office should do something about it. He rose from his desk and moved toward the open door.

At the same instant, the imposing figure of Colonel Paternoster filled the doorway. The man was a ghastly mess. His whole body shook. His face was bright red, his eyes bulging from the sockets, his lips spattered with flecks of foam. His uniform was disheveled. Great stains of vomit were spattered over his blouse. Karstil's eyes widened with horror as he saw what looked like a partly chewed piece of sausage clinging to the Colonel's collar. Paternoster had wiped his face, but some grayish-green liquid still hung from his left ear. Purple claw marks stood out lividly against his throat.

"You imbecile!" Paternoster screamed. "The only reason I don't throttle the life out of you right now is because I may still have a career left to me. Six months to retirement, that's all I have left. I could kill you where you stand!"

Karstil was speechless. Flushed hot with color, he retreated back into his office, careful to swing the door full open as he did so. The sergeants in the outer office would provide some security from this obviously raving man. He glanced quickly around the room, searching for some heavy object with which to defend himself if necessary. "Sir, sir, I don't understand…"

Colonel Paternoster stepped forward, legs rigid, fists clenched at his sides. As more foam rose to his lips, his heavy breathing sprayed bits of it down the front of the already soiled uniform. "Ac, ac, ac," sprayed Paternoster, his Adam's apple bouncing. "She was all over me like a wild cat." The words came out as one long spurt. "She walloverme likeildcat."

Karstil noted that the Colonel's eyes were tracking independently.

"What is it, sir? What are you trying to say?"

"Acr, acr, acr. Dame Drango was sick all over me."

The Colonel waved his arms wildly like a berserk bird attempting to get airborne. The face of Sergeant Connor, pale with fear, appeared in the doorway behind the Colonel.

"What, sir? What?"

Karstil continued to retreat, putting the desk between himself and the Colonel.

"Acrophobia!" The word sprayed out of the man's mouth, spittle flying past Karstil just as he ducked out of the way.

Paternoster couldn't speak, couldn't move. His body was completely rigid. His eyes, each one following its own course, rolled upward. His head tilted back, then the shoulders, then the body, and he collapsed into the arms of Sergeant Connor.

For a long moment, Karstil and the Sergeant stood frozen, too stunned to move. Finally, Karstil crouched to unloosen the Colonel's tie. The room was suddenly quite hot.

"What the hell was that all about?" Karstil begged to know as two medical orderlies came rushing through the door to tend to the stricken man.

"Acrophobia, sir. It's a fear of heights. Cobalatus Drango's wife has a fear of heights. It says so right in his dossier."

Karstil felt the pit of his stomach drop down to his shoes. He brought his hand up and rubbed his brow furiously. The dossier! He had never looked at it, never even considered that it might be available. He swung the computer terminal around so that he could see it himself.

"Yes, sir. We've got one of these on every VIP in the system," Sergeant Connor offered matter-of-factly. "Either our own copy or one that's accessible on the serial well. There's all kinds of nifty stuff on the lot of them."

Karstil shot a quick glance at the Sergeant, his face strained with anger and frustration. Sure enough, the Sergeant was right. There it was on the computer screen—all kinds of background information about Drango, his wife, their children. He scrolled rapidly, amazed at the detail available. Staring blankly, he could only watch as yet another assignment rolled right on by.

When he did stop scrolling, it was at a huge section on the family's medical profile. "Julianna Drango (neé Sobitor); Acrophobia." Just below it was the entry: "Cobalatus Drango; Anaphylactic reaction to *C. vulgaris* and similar."

"Sergeant, what's 'Anaphylactic' and 'C. vulgaris'?"

"I don't know, sir. There *is* the dictionary."

Karstil's blood boiled further at the man's smug tone, but under the present circumstances, what could he say. Quietly, he went to the dictionary reference in the computer.

"An-a-phy-lax-is *n. Pathol.* Violent susceptibility to toxic agents after a primary dose has been received into the blood. Treatment requires immediate action. A high percentage of the victims die so promptly as to preclude treatment..."

That sinking feeling returned to Karstil's stomach and burned inside him. Then he tapped "C. vulgaris" onto the screen.

The computer digested the second request and then cued, "More information required."

Karstil thought for a moment. He had no idea what *C vulgaris* was, but he thought it could have something to do with food. He entered "Food" as an additional prompt.

"C (Crago) vulgaris *n. Biol.* Any of the many small, long-tailed, principally marine, crustaceans (genus *Crago*), including the edible shrimp (*C vulgaris*)."

"Shrimp! He's allergic to shrimp!" Karstil leaped to his feet, glancing toward the chronometer on the wall.

"Sir?"

Karstil rushed right by Sergeant Connor on his way to the door. "The banquet! My God! It'll kill him!"

The receiving line was to have started at 1800 hours. That would mean they would be sitting down to dinner at any moment. He raced down the long hall.

"Officers," Sergeant Connor said, slowly shaking his head while he helped himself to a cigar from the box.

The visitor's center was only some 100 meters away from Karstil's office doors. He sprinted the distance, pushing his way through the milling crowd of newspeople at the door. One of the commentators was speaking into her camera as Karstil rushed passed.

". . . and that concludes the news from..." She never had a chance to finish the sentence.

Holovid viewers, watching live throughout the planet, saw the newscaster flattened by a hurtling officer. The reporter staggered backward against a potted plant. She struggled to regain her balance, clawing and grasping at the branches until she was almost standing again. Then the plant, pot, and reporter all tumbled backward into the reflecting pool in front of the reception center.

Karstil, meanwhile, burst into a banquet hall that shimmered with crystal and rich draperies. At the head table, a number of generals and their ladies were just settling down to the lavish feast. Dressed in full formal regalia was a tall, stern-looking man, none other than Cabinet Member Drango. Beside him sat the pale woman who was his wife.

The waiter carrying the hot soup never had a chance. As Karstil crashed into him, he saw the tureen of soup turn over in a graceful arc toward a woman's head. Karstil glanced at her upswept hair, the curve of her neck, the string of jewels, knowing it was too late to warn her.

He careened past.

At the table, he could see Drango lifting something toward his mouth. As the guest of honor paused to say something to the General at his side, the fork moved closer and closer to his mouth. The mouth was open, ready to take the dainty, ever-so-expensive morsel.

With a screech, Karstil launched himself across the width of the table. The mouth was closing on the food. Karstil saw the face turn toward him, shock and dismay registering in the eyes. With one last, desperate swing, Karstil slapped the fork from Drango's hand, not even seeing that it was a mushroom.

Karstil crashed headfirst into the ornate wine glasses, silverware, china, and floral displays. Out of control, he slid down nearly half the length of the long table, past open-mouthed officers, dignitaries, and ladies. A large potted plant marked the end of the table. Unable to slow his progress through the debris, he went headfirst into the china vase. Then, mercifully, everything went black.

Windsor, Wayne County
The Commonwealth
15 October 6830

Stiff and proper in their silver dress uniforms, the five Commonwealth Royal Army officers gathered around the serving table, bathed in the soft white lights of the Senior Officer's Mess. The silver tray held snifters and a decanter of Napoleon brandy salvaged from a disabled and captured TOG battleship. There were some things that the Commonwealth could never reproduce, no matter how hard it tried, and Napoleon brandy was one of them. The officers picked up the snifters and moved to the overstuffed chairs near the wall-sized thermoplex viewing plate.

Windsor's short night was beginning, its blue star descending behind the rim of the barrier mountains. The plain below was long with shadows, purple against the ochre landscape. Gusts of wind whirled wisp willows across the parade ground and between the low buildings around its perimeter.

"This meeting—off the record and unofficial, of course—is to determine what action, if any, should be taken regarding Second Lieutenant Roglund Karstil." General Wastun FelFarnuth gestured the other four officers to their seats as he spoke. "The man's actions are beginning to strain the credibility of the Royal Army. All of you have had some association with him. You have copies of the report of his activities, and I'm sure you've had a chance to read it. I think the best way to handle this is to cover the material chronologically. Brigadier Foldinus, you were the first to encounter Karstil. Do you have anything to add?"

Brigadier Quentus Foldinus, who had recommended Karstil as an aide to General Beldarnus, squirmed deeper into his seat. The General was usually a forgiving man, but he had never let Foldinus forget about Karstil. Every so often, when the Brigadier was pressing some recommendation, Beldarnus would look up and inquire about the career of his former aide. Foldinus was never quite sure how Beldarnus felt about Karstil, but his own memories of that young man were far from pleasant.

"Karstil's a menace, General. Plain and simple. And if I never saw him again, it would be too soon." Foldinus stared through the thermoplex panel at the gray-blue clouds that dotted the evening sky. His words came flat and clipped. "If I could bring him up on charges, I would. But it wouldn't be in the best interests of the service.

"The young man lacks what it takes to be an officer in the Royal Army." Foldinus held the snifter in the palms of both hands, letting his body heat warm the amber liquid. The heady scent of the brandy rose, filling his nostrils. He liked brandy, especially Napoleon brandy, and he wanted to savor the moment. One of the advantages of associating with Generals was the perks that came with the job. Napoleon brandy was one of them, and he didn't want to lose it. "Let's be rid of him quietly but soon."

"Thank you, Foldinus. Your views are duly noted." General FelFarnuth knew all about the incident that had triggered the dismissal of Karstil as Beldarnus's aide. Beldarnus was married to the General's sister, and Nordine kept her brother well-informed. The General knew that Beldarnus had liked his aide, despite his problems, and that it was Nordine who couldn't stand the sight of him after the incident on Barmash.

True, Karstil had wrecked her grav sedan, but that could be put to youthful exuberance. A more experienced officer would not likely have gone chasing after tanks, but Karstil's folly also showed his enthusiasm. FelFarnuth remembered the look on Nordine's face when she told him about the incident. She just couldn't see the humor in the situation, yet Nordine had hated the SKE-200. Its destruction had given her an excuse to get a different sedan.

"General Green," said FelFarnuth, "you are aware of Karstil's activities at the Finance Center. Give us your opinion."

Leonard Green had succeeded YaTakas Q. Labidinius as chief of the Finance Center when that officer had retired. Although Green had never met Karstil, he had been apprised of his activities. Labidinius had spent the last four and a half months of his career undoing the damage caused by the Second Lieutenant's momentary lapse of attention. He stretched himself out in the chair, the highly polished toes of his boots catching the light from the dim overhead panels.

"I don't know that much about our subject, but he certainly seems to be a threat to anything mechanical. The Royal Army is so dependent on electronics that I don't see how we can keep him." Green spent a moment pondering the shine on his boots. After thirty-five years in the service, he had seen all kinds of officers pass through. Some good, some bad. None had ever been a complete disaster. But there was a time when you had to cut your losses, and this might be one of them. As a new officer, how often he had wondered what it was that Generals did. Now he knew, and would have preferred the problems of a junior officer. The decision he made in this case would have a permanent impact, for better or worse, on a young man he had never met.

"Maybe we could still find a place for him somewhere," Green offered. " He was honor graduate from the Officers' School, so there must be something to him."

There was silence in the room. Not even the rising wind outside the vision panels disturbed the moment of contemplation. Green's words seemed to have made an impression.

"I can, to a degree, understand the Second Lieutenant. He must have quite a low threshold of boredom. The ability to stay with a task that seems meaningless or mundane is an acquired trait in most of us." Leonard studied his shiny boots again. How he had hated administrative tasks in his own days as a Second Lieutenant. Luckily, he had never been responsible for their accomplishment as a junior officer. By the time those tasks had become a part of his career, he was high enough to understand their necessity. And he had had a good supervisor. But perhaps Quentus was right, the man had to go for the good of the service. He lowered his eyes, unwilling to actually recommend terminating the officer in question.

"Colonel Melisander," FelFarnuth broke in, "you are the officer in charge of the reception center, the scene of our officer's most recent and perhaps most damaging incident. The whole episode is not completely clear to me. Perhaps you could fill us in."

Lieutenant-Colonel Xerxes Melisander, twenty years in the service of the Commonwealth and holder of sixteen commendation medals, pursed his lips and slowly eyeballed every man in the room. "We can be as easy on this young man as we want, but he is, apparently, a menace."

The four men senior to him stared at Melisander. One of the officers cleared his throat. Melisander had been involved in the handling of VIPs for most of his career, having learned very early how to become indispensable to those of higher rank. For eighteen years, he had run the hotels of the Royal Army, and he had the commendations to prove it. But he had never been able to break through into the ranks of the Colonels and above. This was his chance. Now, seated among this conclave of officers, he had the opportunity to make an impression as a decisive man.

Melisander could feel his blood pressure beginning to rise even as he spoke about the incident. "To place an acrophobe in a transparent elevator for a ride to the twenty-first floor, a floor that is all windows, is either the height of lunacy or decidedly cruel. In either case, the continued career of the Second Lieutenant would be contrary to the best interests of the Royal Army. If he is neither a lunatic nor cruel, then we would have to assign ulterior motives to him." There it was, that suggestion that Karstil was acting for some outside organization. The others would not have thought of it, but now it was planted like a deadly little seed that would grow in their minds. All Melisander had to do was water it and watch it grow.

"It would have been a disaster had the Minister been afraid of heights. But the acrophobe was his wife. I think Colonel Paternoster will attest"—he glanced at the Colonel who sat silent and strained near the window—"to the violent reaction of Dame Drango."

The reaction had, indeed, been violent. The Minister had remained in the reception area, while his wife retired to their rooms. The elevator had just cleared the entrance hall level when the woman began to break down. There was no way to stop the ascent before reaching the twenty-first floor, and she had fastened herself to the Colonel—by the throat. By the time they reached the fifteenth floor, she had become violently ill, and the Colonel would never be able to wear that uniform again. He had wrestled her off the elevator and into the room, only to find that the entryway was as open as the elevator had been.

Holding her down with one arm, he cried out for security and medical assistance. The Minister, security, and the medical orderly arrived together, and it had taken all of them to sedate the stricken woman and carry her off to bed. Drango himself had been in little better shape, and he had been sedated as well.

"The unprovoked attack on Grand Minister Deman at the banquet was equally inexplicable," continued Melisander. "It was as though Karstil were trying to complete the destruction he had begun. The added blunder of dumping Judith Westover, the most influential reporter in the system, into the reflecting pool, needs no comment." Melisander looked at the other officers, his thin tongue darting over his lips. Colonel Paternoster, close to nervous collapse himself, had also been sedated after the incident.

Melisander actually knew very well why the Second Lieutenant had tackled the Grand Minister. Fearing that Drango would poison himself with the shrimp, Karstil was attempting to save his life. There was no way the Second Lieutenant could have known that Drango was not at the banquet. He had seen the guest of honor about to eat a shrimp-filled mushroom, assumed that it was Drango, and attempted to intervene. But there was no reason to assign noble motives to Karstil. That would only complicate the decision-making process.

"Perhaps the whole incident was part of a plan to deny the Royal Army the discretionary funds it needs. Seen in that light—and I'm sure Colonel Paternoster will agree with me—all of the the Second Lieutenant's actions become quite explicable." Now the seed of doubt was carefully being nourished. "That being the case, we should act decisively against any further occurrences." There. The assumption that it was true would make it so. Melisander was on a roll. He watched the other officers nodding in agreement. Melisander prepared himself for the punch line of his proposal. He was going to finish Karstil once and for all.

"Colonel Paternoster will, I'm sure, also agree with me that this man needs to be disciplined in the strongest manner. A court-martial, held quietly on some out-of-the-way planet in an adjacent county, would not attract attention. We could ensure that the officers of the court as well as the defense attorney were apprised of the situation and what the General desired as the outcome. It would all be very quiet and legal. There are penal colonies, I think, within TOG space, and I'm sure they would take our young man."

Melisander leaned back in his chair and took a long, satisfying sip of his Napoleon brandy. That, he thought, should set the tone for the rest of the evening. He knew Karstil would not, could not, be sent to a TOG penal colony, but the thought of the ultimate punishment would make anything less seem reasonable. Not only had he solved the problem before this little conclave, but he had shown himself to be a man of strong views and direct action. The Generals and Colonel Paternoster, his immediate superior, would see him as a person who was honest, fair, and willing to be assertive. A slight smile crossed his lips as he looked at the Colonel.

Paternoster had just been released from the hospital where he had been under mild sedation for the past twenty-four hours. He had been kept sedated until after the graduation review and the departure of the Drangos. The doctors had felt, and probably rightly so, that any contact with the Minister or his wife would have an adverse affect on the Colonel.

Paternoster took a deep breath. "Even I think that you are too harsh on our young man, Melisander. Although I was sedated, that did not impair my brain. I have been thinking about the incident as well as the history of the officer. I was aware of his record when he came to us, and I wanted very much for him to succeed. Unfortunately, that has not been the case."

Colonel Paternoster studied the half-empty snifter of Napoleon brandy in his hands. He didn't like Xerxes Melisander, having always considered him smarmy, power-hungry, and self-serving. Now here was the Lieutenant-Colonel obviously trying to make points at the expense of a Second Lieutenant. After the incident at the banquet, Karstil would never be one of Paternoster's favorite officers. But this devious effort by Melisander to use the young man's misfortune for his own personal gain made the Colonel resolute in his defense.

Paternoster looked at the other officers. FelFarnuth was watching him intently, leaning back in his chair, his arms supported by the soft leather bolsters. Foldinus was swirling his brandy, but Paternoster could tell by the tenseness in his position that he was hearing every word. Colonel Green was leaning forward, his elbows on his knees.

Paternoster looked Melisander in the eyes. "The idea that Karstil may be an agent for some outside organization is either foolish or malicious. There is no evidence of it, and the interjection of such a concept into these proceedings is unwarranted." He saw Melisander recoil as if struck. "Making such a suggestion casts aspersions on an officer who is defenseless. If there are ulterior motives, perhaps they are in this room and not with the Second Lieutenant." Melisander was sinking further and further into his chair, retreating from Paternoster's attack.

"I think we can eliminate any thought of outside direction from our thoughts."

"The concept," continued Paternoster, "that we can discipline the man on another planet and then hand him over to TOG for incarceration is as craven as any I have ever heard. Even if it were meant as a joke, and I assume it was, it is a very bad joke. The mere mention of it tarnishes the concept of honor. If laundry needs doing, we should do it ourselves."

It was as though each chair had been illuminated, the lighting becoming more intense as the occupant spoke, dimmer when the man was thinking. The light on Lieutenant-Colonel Xerxes Melisander's chair blinked out. He ceased to be a part of the discussion.

"No, I think we misjudge the young man. There is nothing malicious or evil about Karstil. All he suffers from is youth, excess enthusiasm, and more than a little clumsiness. Perhaps, as a matter of discipline, a reprimand is in order. But I think he deserves another chance. Unfortunately, I don't think he can be given that chance in Wayne County. And perhaps not even in the Royal Army."

Paternoster left the obvious answer hanging in the air of the room.

GENERAL ORDER 6824-668
Second Lieutenant Roglund I. Karstil, 005-997-4242, is hereby laterally promoted to

the rank of Optio and transferred to the forces of the Renegade Legion.
Above-named officer will report at once to this command. No delay en-route is authorized. No advance/travel pay is authorized. Officer is not authorized to travel by civilian vehicle.
By order of General Wastun FelFarnuth.

RLS Maiestas, In Transit
The Commonwealth
31 October 6830

Renegade transport *Maiestas*, registration number KNA44732BT, rattled slightly as it broke out of Tachyon-space, the dimension that allows for travel faster than the speed of light. The ship was on its way to Rilus V, where units were being trained and reformed to join in the desperate fight to keep Shannedam County from falling to TOG. The blinding flash of transition back to rational space penetrated every corner of the ship. Optio Roglund Karstil, former Second Lieutenant of the Royal Commonwealth Army, felt the momentary sensation of falling that accompanies the transition. He gripped the arms of his seat to steady himself. No matter how often he experienced the transition, he never got used to it.

There was something strange and queasy about the whole Tachyon, or T-space, experience. The void of space went white, the distant stars black dots against the milky nothing. Unreal. Unacceptable. People who liked it joined theNavy. Karstil would never like it. He wanted solid ground around him. Grav tanks were fine, even though they didn't touch the ground. At least solid ground, with its feeling of safety, was nearby. If man had been meant to venture into T-space, thought Karstil, he would have been given . . . Well, he would have been given something.

The voyage from Windsor in Wayne County to Rilus in Shannedam County had taken seven days in T-space. At breakout back into normal space, a computer-voice had dutifully advised them, "All personnel set perscomps for 148 hours." Karstil didn't have his own perscomp to measure the time spent in T-space, only the one he had been issued upon boarding. No one could spend more than 30 days at a time in T-space. After that, the friction of molecules from the tremendous speeds of travel would cause matter to instantly disintegrate—a horrible death. This friction or disharmony was known as Shimmer Heat, and had to be "burned off" before one could make further T-space journeys.

Karstil would turn in the perscomp when he reported to Legion headquarters, but he wasn't worried about Shimmer Heat. It wasn't likely that he would venture back into T-space for quite some time after he reached his new posting with the Renegade Legion.

The journey had given young Karstil plenty of time to think. Three serious "mishaps" and a reprimand in his personnel jacket wasn't exactly how he had envisioned the beginning of his career in the Commonwealth Royal Army. In fact, he had been one dejected man upon leaving Windsor. But after a quiet day or two aboard ship, his outlook had begun to change.

Maybe being transferred to the Renegade Legion wasn't such a bad twist of fate. The Legion was every bit the fighting force that the Commonwealth was, and many said it was even better. Karstil knew that a lot of troopers thought it an honor to serve with the Renegade forces. Anyway, no more banquets or computer work for him. Here, now, in the Legion, he could finally prove himself the only real way a soldier can—on the battlefield.

Life aboard the *Maiestas* had been pleasant enough, except that there was so little to do. The only way to tell time was by the chronometers posted at various locations throughout the ship, and that added to a sense of aimlessness. First call came at 0600, followed by breakfast an hour later. After that, passengers were not allowed to return to their rooms until 1300 hours, which meant spending the morning in the lounge reading or playing cards. The library on board was well-stocked with both books and electronic fare, but Karstil liked being with the action, even if it was only a game of chance. He'd never been one to go off by himself for hours on end. He enjoyed the company of other people too much.

By the end of the second day, Karstil and a group of five other young officers got together and spent the rest of the voyage constantly playing Pendulos, a complicated game of cards and dice. It involved two or three two-player teams competing against one another in bidding for, and then taking, tricks. Karstil was not a champion-level player, but he had a good grasp of the basics and usually finished the evening on the plus side of the ledger.

Durban Collis was the best player and usually won. A tall, handsome man only a year or two older than Karstil, he carried himself with the self-assurance of the nobility. He hadn't said a word one way or the other about his heritage, but he had dropped enough hints to let everyone know he was better than the average Renegade. Collis had plenty of spending money, too, and his pearl-gray uniform was obviously well-tailored. He had been assigned to the General Staff section for the region headquarters and was looking forward to seeing "old friends" again. He never mentioned who those "friends" might be, but he spoke of the Generals in a most familiar way. Karstil couldn't tell if Collis were just name-dropping or if he actually did know these people. He finally decided on the former explanation; no one could know that many Generals.

Durban had a sharp tongue that he used with stinging effect on the other players when their card sense lapsed. His favorite target was Holton Bard, an unfortunate young man who became flustered at almost any occasion. Durban was all over him like a blanket, scathing him with polite comments about his perception and his play. The tongue-lashing finished, he would then explain the correct play, doing it in the simplest and most insulting manner.

Karstil rose in Bard's defense occasionally, especially when the young victim was on the verge of tears. It was this defense that made Collis keep his distance from Karstil and grant him a grudging respect. Bard was a particularly unlikable young man of receding hair line, pendulous lips, and watery eyes. His slight stature and soft appearance made him an obvious target for barbs and slights. He reminded Karstil of a garden slug. That image was particularly disturbing because Bard was assigned as an infantry platoon leader. The terror of combat would have strange effects on a man like him.

As long as Karstil drew Bard as a partner before the other man had played with Collis, he was acceptable. Bard would dither and whine over the cards, but his play of the contracts was average. If, on the other hand, he had played with Collis, and been badly beaten, the unfortunate young man would be reduced to a lump of quivering jelly by the vicious verbal attacks. Then he was hopeless as a player, retreating into a shell of mindless confusion.

Lawrence ("Just call me Larry") Stone was a hulking brute whose bulging shoulders gave the impression of a man with no neck. He held his cards in both hands, his body hunched over the table like a huge bear. His bidding and play were hesitant and slow, as though his brain processed the information and possible responses at a speed slower than the average person. Collis had sent a few verbal barbs his way, but Stone had not reacted except for some grunts. The one time his eyes had flared red was enough to silence Collis's attacks for the rest of the voyage. On his uniform, Stone wore the branch designator patch for psychological warfare and intelligence. Karstil could only guess at how a man of his limited imagination could have joined such a branch of service.

Karstil liked Stone as a partner, though. The man was slow but steady. He bid cautiously, usually underbidding the hands, his play correct, if unimaginative. He scored few bonus tricks, but he was never set back many, either. Karstil could always count on a decent score when it came time to play with Larry Stone.

Bently Frew was a pleasant chap who didn't seem to take anything too seriously. He was the same age as Karstil, but unlike the new Optio, he was without experience in the military. Instead, Frew seemed to view his allotted time as something of a lark, expecting to serve in some rear area and then get out. His assignment was in transportation and supply facilities management. It would, as he pointed out on many occasions, give him a head start in the real world when his time was up. He scorned the "poor idiots" who had been assigned to the combat arms, seeing them as nothing but well-trained pawns in the scheme of the military. He could not understand, and said so on a number of occasions, why anyone would willingly want to serve where he might get shot at.

Frew bid his card aggressively, happily playing doomed contracts, forgetting the defeat immediately, and then moving on to the next hand. When the cards were with him, he did well; when they were against him, he crashed in flames. Karstil always shuddered when it was his turn to play with Frew.

The sixth member of the table was Julianna Pope, she of the blazing red hair, shapely body, and flashing green eyes. Karstil found her strangely unsettling, and the other players seemed to as well. Perhaps it was the lack of social contact with females that often went with being a member of the military. Maybe it was her hair, her skin, her sweet and delicate scent that was so captivating. Whatever it was, Roglund Karstil couldn't keep his eyes off her.

There were women in the Renegade Legions, just as there were in the Commonwealth units. There was no discrimination in the military and women were encouraged to join. Karstil had encountered women instructors in Officers' Training School, and they had been accepted because of their rank and obvious professionalism. But Julianna was different. She was the first female officer he had dealt with on a continuing social basis. In that way, she was the first "real" woman he had come in contact with since joining up.

She was designated as an armored air defense artillery officer, and that meant that she would be in grav tanks near the front. In conversation, she had mentioned turning down the chance to be an installation air defense officer because it was her duty to serve up front with the troops. The thought, she said, of being stationed on some out-of-the-way planet for years was enough to send her 'round the bend. She and Frew exchanged barbed remarks about their separate views of spending time on some quiet post in some backwater system. The banter had stopped after Julianna looked Frew in the eye and said, "When the six of us walk into an officers' club wearing our branch designators, five of us will be proud." Karstil cheered her silently, deathly afraid of appearing to be too forward with the lady.

Juliana was a good card player, treating each hand clinically and shrewdly. She never took undue risks with the contract, bidding what could be made and playing the hand in the best manner. At the table, Karstil was uncomfortable when she was his partner, distracted by his own thoughts. *What will she think if I play the wrong card? How should I react if I do play the right card?* Then, when she was partnered with someone else, he was even more uncomfortable. *Why is she smiling at that guy? Does she prefer him as a partner?*

He tried to concentrate on the cards, but all he could think about with Julianna was the softness of her voice, the charm of her laughter, the playfulness in her eyes. More than once he had to snap himself out of a hard stare. Yet, in all the time on board ship, he had never mustered more than a quick nod and a casual, "nice game last night," whenever he ran into her.

And so the voyage had passed, one long game being played out, broken only by the adequate meals served aboard the *Maiestas*. The stewards and mess attendants were obviously trying to please the passengers, and the meals were served in the main dining room by uniformed waiters. There was breakfast at 0700, followed by a coffee break at 1030. That usually consisted of hot buns, coffee cake, fruit popovers, and any number of different beverages. Dinner, the biggest meal of the day, was served at 1230. It usually consisted of an appetizer, soup, salad, main course, and a sweet.

At 1600 came afternoon tea, with its light sandwiches, cakes, scones, cookies, and more beverages. Supper, for which dress uniform was required, was usually buffet-style. The line opened at 1830, and the meal could be taken at any time until 2000 hours. A late snack came at 2300 and consisted of cold cuts, cheese, fresh vegetables with cream dip, fresh bread, cakes, and pies. The bar was opened at 2100 so that passengers could take the final meal of the day with beer, wine, or other, stronger libation.

Karstil liked the service and the meals, but by the end of the fifth day, his dress uniform was beginning to bind at the waist. The lack of exercise and the fulsome meals had put some weight on his frame, and he wondered if he were being fattened for the slaughter.

"All passengers prepare for debarkation." The sound of the loudspeaker brought Karstil back to the present. "Officers report to the 100 Deck with personal equipment. Enlisted personnel report to the 400 Deck with personal equipment."

The 100 Deck was the location of all the officer cabins as well as the lounge. The 400 Deck was actually a cavernous bay three decks tall that housed the racks of enlisted bunks. The men were stacked twelve-high, and Karstil wondered what kind of man could sleep in the top bunk.

The transport was too large to go planetside, and so debarkation was accomplished in orbit, either through a space station or through smaller transports that would take the passengers to the surface. In this case, no orbital station was available, and so the smaller ships would be used. Access to the smaller ships was through transparent gangway tunnels that extended several meters from the side of the *Maiestas* and hooked up to the smaller craft.

Karstil felt his stomach lurch as he stepped out onto the walkway between the two ships. It was perfectly safe, he knew that, but there was something awesome about stepping out and walking through space as simply and easily as one would walk down the hall of a large building. Halfway across, he felt himself pass from the artificial gravity field of the transport to the field generated by the smaller ship.

It felt good to finally be off the *Maiestas*. Now that he had completely adjusted his thinking with regard to the Legion, he couldn't wait to leave the transport and get in on the action. Walking the transparent gangway was like crossing the gulf between his past and his future. The space transport was linked with what had been. The smaller transport was the future. Karstil strapped himself into his seat, noting that all the card players had found seats far separate from one another. Perhaps they, too, felt as he did about the transition to the surface. Ties with the past were broken. It was time to look to the future.

54

10

Rilus V, Shannedam County
The Commonwealth
31October 6830

The military port on Rilus was a bustle of small ships landing and taking off for orbit. The air was filled with the high-pitched whine of grav generators, making conversation almost impossible. Arm-waving NCOs herded the incoming troops toward cavernous hangars that lined the perimeter of the landing field. Over the enormous doors were signs that designated areas for officers, NCOs, and enlisted personnel. Seeing these areas further broken down by alphabetic designators, Karstil made his way toward the long line designated for "Officers: Di-Lo."

Inside the hangar were rows of tables separated from the main body of the hangar floor by metal stanchions that channeled the incoming troops into lines. Seated at the tables were Renegade enlisted men with long, computer-generated lists. Behind the tables were grim-faced Sergeants who eyed the boiling mob of men with marked disdain, their arms folded across their chests, feet spread. Behind them was another row of tables with computer displays operated by other enlisted men who checked the data if there were a problem in the first row.

The receptionists at the tables looked at their lists and handed each newcomer a card that was color-coded for yet another reception area. Karstil saw clusters beginning to form around the hangar under brightly colored signs. Those were probably unit markings for the various Legions and supporting regiments stationed in Shannedam County. The men gathered under the signs were joking and laughing, cheering each new addition as he joined the group. Good-natured banter passed from one cluster to another, but Karstil could not decipher the words amid the communal babble.

One would never guess from the jocular, casual atmosphere that these men were about to be thrown into the midst of a pivotal struggle with the TOG forces. For more than 20 years, the Commonwealth/Renegade forces had been frantically defending the industrial and mineral-rich Shannedam County against increasing TOG inroads. Set smack in the middle of the other thirteen counties in the March, Shannedam was the seat of the Alaric March, one of twenty-one Grand Dukedoms comprising the Commonwealth. If it fell, that would all but seal the fate of the entire Dukedom.

Karstil noticed one unit, larger by twice than the others, under a blood-red indicator. They did not banter, either among themselves nor with the other groups, but stood in sullen silence amid the general uproar. The only thing Karstil could imagine was that this was some kind of penal legion, as in TOG, but he knew that neither the Commonwealth nor Renegade forces had such units. His idle reflections went no further as the line crept steadily forward each time an officer was assigned.

At last, it was Karstil's turn at the head of his line. Before him was an harassed-looking young woman who had obviously been at her task since early that morning. Coffee cups and broken pencils littered her desk, and the neat piles of routing cards had fallen over. The sheaf of computer paper draped itself across the table, most of the names on the list having already been marked with a purple highlighter.

"Karstil?" she asked. "Is that spelled with a kay or a cee?"

The question made no sense, because Karstil was in the line clearly marked as "Di-Lo."

"Kay," he said, deciding that anyone who looked that tired didn't need additional grief.

"Karstil...Karstil," she murmured, flipping through the computer list. He could feel the pressure from the line behind him as others tried to peer over his shoulder, hoping to catch a glimpse of their own names on the sheaf of paper. It was no use, of course. Karstil had tried it himself while standing behind the man who preceded him, but the paper moved so quickly that there was no chance.

"Ah. Here it is." He noticed that he had become an "it" rather than a "you."

Her next words should have been the number of the unit to which he was assigned, followed by the admonition, "Take this card and stand over there." This would be followed by a general cheer and back-thumping as the new man left for his station.

Strain creasing her forehead and making her whole expression sag, she looked up from the table. Silently, she proffered a blood-red card and indicated the sullen group at the far end of the hangar bay. The men around Karstil stepped back. There was no cheer, not even a murmur of approval.

Holding the card out before him as though it were some dead animal, Karstil moved away from the table. The crowd parted, the other officers moving back as soon as they saw the red card. It was as though he had stepped into a transparent bubble that isolated him from the rest, carrying him toward the others of his new unit the way the transparent gangway had moved him from the transport to the shuttle. The members of the group did not even acknowledge his approach, much less welcome him. Displayed in neat block letters at the bottom of the red indicator was, "2567 RIL (P)." So, Karstil thought glumly, this is home.

Hours later, the ground transport came to a halt before a long brown building. It was a standard barracks like so many other Commonwealth and Renegade post facilities. Their modular design allowed them to be constructed from indigenous materials or transshipped across the Galaxy. The building's age was indeterminate, but that, too, was typical. Karstil had begun to believe that a paint called "Aged Decay" was sprayed over all such buildings as soon as they were constructed. They all looked the same.

The replacements were herded into the building by somber, almost funereal, sergeants. Funereal, thought Karstil, would be a good descriptor for the entire process; condemned men awaiting their final destination. Hardly a word had been spoken by any of the replacements during the hour they stood in the hangar while transports for the other units arrived to collect their new men. His group had been the last to depart. Even the functionaries making unit assignments had left before they did. Only the maintenance crew, silently driving their vacuum vehicles through the detritus, remained. The men under the red sign had no choice but to accept the situation without question.

The building held a large theater, but it was too small to hold all the people being pushed in. Officers, as was their due, got the chairs in the front-center of the room, the enlisted men finding seats where they could. The rest stood. No one spoke. Glancing around the assemblage, Karstil noted that several among the crowd showed obvious plasto-skin, as though recently released from the hospital. One legionary's face and hands were still swathed with protective white bandages over the pink, regenerated skin. The man didn't look too happy to be here.

"Attention!" The audience rose to its feet with an echoing crash.

"At ease. Be seated." Another rushing sound as the assembly sank back into its seats.

"Welcome to the 2567th Renegade Legion. My name is Prefect NaBesta Kenderson. We have a long way to go, and it is you men who will take us there."

Prefect of the Legion NaBesta Kenderson stood at the edge of the stage, staring out over the auditorium filled with officers and enlisted men. His pearl-gray dress uniform was expertly tailored to reveal his superb musculature and imposing bearing. The deep purple cuffs highlighted the triple gold knots of a Prefect, and his left breast was adorned with the medals of an apparently heroic career.

Optio Roglund Karstil was immediately transfixed by Kenderson, the very image of a fighting officer. Young, handsome, of heroic lineage, and with a reputation of his own, Kenderson was the type of man often described as a "natural leader." As the Prefect's piercing blue eyes passed over the crowd, Karstil felt himself sitting up straighter, with spine and head crisply erect.

"This legion," Kenderson was saying, "has a reputation for bad luck. I will be the first to agree that there is such a thing, but I don't think luck is something that just waits for a man. Luck is something you make. You make it by checking everything. You make it by being good at your job. You make it by having confidence in the men you have trained. And when you've done that, your luck is good."

Kenderson stood with his hands clasped behind his back, his feet spread. He knew how important it was to impress the replacements with the idea that the 2567th Renegade Infantry Legion (Provisional) was going to be a good unit. Bad morale was an insidious disease that could spread through a unit like the Snow Plague. Unlike a plague, however, there was no medicine to stop it. He hated the "Provisional" tag at the end of the Legion's designation, because it would keep his men from thinking of it as their own unit, their home. That was not good. Kenderson had argued with the High Command to have the tag removed, but they would not deviate from tradition.

The Prefect studied the faces of the replacements. They looked pale and drawn, probably because of the unforgiving light from the overhead fluoropanels and the fact that they had just come from T-space. There were some who might buy into the idea that the Legion could be changed. He could tell by the way they returned his gaze. Many more would reserve judgement till later. And there were others, combat veterans from other units or just hard cases, who would shrug off the briefing as so much hype. His job, as he saw it, was to inspire the cautious and the skeptical with the enthusiasm he sensed among the first group.

"Unlike some of the legions of the Renegade forces, the 2567th does not have a long and glorious history. That can be both good and bad. A unit tends to be what it was. If the past was glorious, like that of the Second Armored Cavalry Regiment, the men fight for the reputation of the unit. They rise to the challenge. That is why the Second ACR continues to be elite even when it has just taken on replacements.

"As most of you know by now, the 2567th was cobbled together from the survivors of other units and various supporting elements on Caralis. That's why it's 'Provisional.' Supposedly, it will be dismembered when the task on Caralis is done, but I hope not. I want us to be good enough to earn the right to become a 'real' Legion. The 2567th went into combat with almost no training as a cohesive Legion. Even the individual Manus units were disorganized and uncoordinated. And that's why it got clobbered. That's not the best way to begin a legend. But we can change all that. Our heritage begins now. What is past, is past. Don't dwell on it. And don't let your people dwell on it. The future is ours to make. We drag no baggage with us if we don't want to. And we *don't* want to.

"I could tell you that you have been specially chosen to turn the unit around, but the truth is, I had no say in who was assigned here. You're just the current draft from the replacement center. So I know nothing of you, but I can tell you something of me. I'm the youngest Prefect in the Renegade or Commonwealth forces. I got this job because someone thinks I can command a Legion, this particular Legion. I think I can, too. And I will.

"We are here on Rilus to create and train the Manus Primus for the Legion, the rest of whom are still on Caralis. It is my intention to build a fighting Manus as an example to all the others. This will be my Manus.

"I will not remain with you while you train; there is plenty for the officers and senior non-coms to do without the Legion Commander peering over their shoulders. I'll visit occasionally, but other matters call me to Caralis.

"You have to understand that Caralis is very important to the Commonwealth." Kenderson raised his hand and a star chart appeared on the screen behind him.

"Over the past years, TOG has been pressing the attack all across Shannedam County." As he spoke, red indicators showed worlds that TOG had seized, while blue marked those worlds still held by the Commonwealth. Kenderson traced a line from the contested planets of Gustaviv's Regret across to Caesar's Folly and Defiance, then his finger seemed to follow a jagged path up to Wuj, then sharply down to Ku Crassus, Caralis, Messana, and sharply up again to Rolonitru.

"The Commonwealth is defending along this front, and Caralis lies at a strategic point of this large bulge that cuts into TOG advances. If we lose Caralis to TOG, it will give them a stranglehold on the planet Messana. The loss of Messana's crystal mines would be a disastrous blow to our military effort in Shannedam County.

"If we can contain TOG on Caralis, or take back all of Caralis from them, then the Commonwealth will be able to mount its own offensive. We can retake the entire County. And once you've completed your training and rejoined the rest of the Legion, that's what we will be fighting for!"

As Kenderson turned to go, the command "Attention!" set the theater rocking. The assemblage came to its feet with a thunder that resounded against the walls. The Prefect began to stride across the stage, then stopped and looked at the men. When he spoke again, it was more softly than before, but his voice carried to the very edges of the packed hall. It was as though he were speaking to each man individually.

"In my book, there are two ways to motivate a man—either you light a fire under his ass or you start a blaze in his heart. Believe me, I'm familiar with ways of lighting and feeding that fire. But you can't always count on someone being there to do that for you. You need to have the blaze of glory, honor, and pride burning within you. Then, and only then, can you become the best fighting force in the field. We of the 2567th can do that. And we will do that. Or we will die trying."

58

11

Rilus V, Shannedam County
The Commonwealth
3 November 6830

A thin wisp of smoke rose from the command hatch of the stationary Liberator grav tank. Anyone unfamiliar with the commander might have assumed that the vehicle was on fire. Those who knew him, however, would know that the smoke came from a thick, black cigar clenched between the grav tank commander's yellowed teeth.

Lucifer K. Mullins, Sergeant and Acting Platoon Leader of the Second Platoon of the Second Medium Grav Century on Rilus V, elbowed his muscular bulk through the narrow hatch. His shaven, bullet-shaped head reflected the early moonlight as he surveyed the formation of the other platoon vehicles. Marks left by his combat helmet stood out red against the skin of his skull and he rubbed them to help increase the circulation.

The other Liberator Medium Grav Tanks occupied the points of a roughly equilateral triangle on the hilly terrain common to this region of Rilus, their turrets pointed away from the center of the formation. This was not the standard defensive formation, however. The Century was deployed, as was the rest of the Manus, on line. The vehicles at the far corners should have been moved forward to provide interlocking defensive fire for the rest of the Century, but Mullins had changed the platoon SOP. He was more concerned with all-around defense for the platoon, not trusting the deployment of the other platoons or the ability of the Centurion, Cobaro Freund. He had quietly spoken to the drivers of the other grav tanks and told them how this platoon would deploy at every halt. His distrust for the rest of the Century was contagious, and the men had been quick to respond. Now, in the silver light of the moon, he could see the other vehicles at their assigned stations, silently protecting the full 6400 mils that comprised the platoon's perimeter.

Mullins tugged at his right ear, a typical mannerism when he was deep in thought. The platoon was still dangerously short of men, with only five of the nine positions filled. There were just enough men to drive all the vehicles, with a gunner in one tank and a commander, himself, in another. That meant that one tank had neither a gunner nor a commander, and none of them was at full strength. The first replacement draft had filled two positions, and both new men had been assigned as drivers.

Grouse, he of the camel-like ability to sleep and eat in barracks, had been assigned as the gunner/commander of Tank Three. A new man, Triarii William Umbartis, was his driver. Umbartis was proving to be a good man, and Mullins planned to promote him to the rank of

Principes as soon as possible. Umbartis was a qualified gunner and would become the gunner for Number Three when the full draft was accomplished.

The other survivor, Triarii Sedgwick Abul, was the temporary driver of Tank One. Another good man. Mullins would transfer him to his own tank when a third driver appeared. Triarii Graff Kloun, temporary driver for Mullins' tank would move to Number Three. That would put the most experienced driver in his tank, and when Umbartis moved up in Tank Three, Grouse would return to Mullins as well. Mullins intended to have the best men in his tank and the best chance of survival in the next battle. To hell with the others.

Three men were approaching the tank laager, coming from the direction of the Century Headquarters and heading straight for the wide circle of strategically encamped vehicles. Mullins could tell from the men's fresh-looking gear bags that they were replacements. The two in front were advancing at a good pace, while the third, some distance behind, was having trouble figuring out the best way to carry the bag. Finally, he ended up dragging it on the ground. That, thought Mullins, was probably the new platoon leader. Just what he needed, a wet-behind-the-ears officer. Typical, he thought, just typical. Well, he'd dealt with young Optios before, and he could deal with this one now.

The officer stayed well back while the other two replacements checked into the platoon. The first to report in was a Sergeant, Hampert Farwell, whose primary experience was in tanks. Farwell was slender and wiry, with a thin scar on his chin. Mullins was glad to see him, because it would give the platoon a little more experience. Farwell's original unit had been the 1717th Renegade Legion, recently transferred to the Commonwealth command. Farwell, like some of the other members of the Legion, had opted to retain complete Renegade status. Now assigned to the 2567th, he was not a happy man.

The second man was Duncan Spint, formerly of the Legion Antiaircraft Century. The deceptively short but strong Spint had been one of the survivors of the disaster on Caralis and had been transferred, not at his own request. It was the policy of the Renegade forces that people who were sole survivors, or close to it, not be sent back to their old unit. Spint didn't seem to care. He was a driver, and would drive whatever he was assigned. Mullins decided to put him in as the driver of Tank One. With the new officer still hanging back, that would leave only the gunner's spot open in that tank.

Abul, the current driver of Number One, would move to Mullins' tank, and Grouse, the gunner in Three would also become Mullins'. That would put Kloun as driver in Three, with Umbartis as gunner. Farwell would be in command.

The formalities over, the new officer approached. Mullins was expecting youth, but this was unreasonable. A wet-nurse job if ever there was one. Officers were officers, however, and must be treated with the respect due them.

"Good evening, sir. This is the Second Platoon." Mullins dismounted from the turret where he had been sitting during the reception of the other replacements.

"Good evening, Sergeant. I'm Second Lieut...sorry, Optio Karstil. I'm your platoon leader." Roglund Karstil examined the Sergeant who stood, almost at attention, before him. The man was shorter than him by about seven centimeters, but much heavier, probably by fifteen or so kilos. His smooth, rounded skull was completely bald, but Karstil could see stubble on the surface. The Sergeant apparently shaved his head. That practice was common among tank crewmen because it allowed for a better fit of the combat helmet. At least the man hadn't put a tattoo on his head.

"I'm Sergeant Mullins, sir. The Platoon Sergeant."

They saluted each other simultaneously, then shook hands. Mullins liked to measure a man by his handshake. Karstil's was soft and weak.

Karstil took a deep breath and held it, letting himself go slightly light-headed. He had been told that this was a way to control nervousness, and he was nervous now. He could feel his heart pounding in his chest, while he mentally scrambled for all the things an Optio should say upon meeting his command for the first time. He should say something about being glad to be here, about not changing things until he had had a chance to look around, about how he would work with the Sergeant of the platoon. All that had seemed so reasonable in school; none of it did now. Karstil's stomach growled, reminding him that he had not yet supped.

"I thought you might take Tank Number One, sir," said Mullins, not waiting for the Optio speak. "It's over there to the right." Mullins pointed into the falling darkness where the right-flank Liberator was hull-down in its crater. Mullins could see Abul already leaving the tank and the new driver taking over. At least there would be no need for lengthy explanations about who was assigned to what vehicle and why. "Is there anything else, sir?"

Of course there was something else, and Mullins was well aware of it. The Optio should be asking questions about the deployment of the platoon, about the latest recon reports, about the combat readiness of the platoon, who was assigned, platoon vacancies, the standard of maintenance, and on and on. The Optio should say something like, "I'm going to the tank now, Sergeant. Join me there in about five minutes to brief me on the platoon."

"Why don't you go to your tank now, sir," prodded Mullins. "I'll join you there in about ten minutes to brief you on the platoon's status." That would give Mullins just enough time to grab a quick meal of combat rations and then finish his cigar.

"Right, Sergeant." Karstil was thankful that the Sergeant had cued him to to his next series of actions. The ten minutes would give him a chance to reach the vehicle, settle in, and get ready for his interview. It would also give him a moment to check the Officers' Guide Manual about what to do next. With an audible grunt, he shouldered his duffel bag and turned toward the barely visible tank.

When Karstil reached the vehicle, he climbed up to the turret of the Liberator Medium Grav Tank. He had trained on grav tanks during Officers' Training School and during the Renegade Transition Course, but he had never been on or in a Liberator. All its weapons—the 150mm and 50mm Gauss cannon, the 5/6 laser, and the Vulcan III—were mounted on the exterior of the turret. That made them easy to maintain but a little fragile in combat. The Liberator had a reputation for being both quick and fragile, necessary attributes, considering its relatively light shielding and armor. But the turret was roomier than most, one of the Liberator's endearing qualities.

No matter how violent and deadly the combat, a soldier spent most of his time not shooting at the enemy. The Liberator, with its large interior fighting compartment, was a livable machine. A story—probably apocryphal—had passed around Transition Course about one tank commander who had built a complete wet bar inside the hull. True or not, there certainly was enough room for one.

All three hatches on the turret were open, the luminescence of the interior battle lanterns showing as a soft glow in the exterior darkness. There was enough light to make out the driver rummaging around his hull center-line seat. In contrast to many Armored Fighting Vehicles (AFV), the driver sat in the rear of the hull, behind the gunner and commander. He drove by means of vision screens and terrain displays, never actually seeing where he was going. It was a safe system as far as the driver was concerned, but it was terribly claustrophobic.

Karstil crawled through the right-hand forward hatch, and pulled his duffel bag in after him. The driver glanced up, a look of relief passing over his features.

"Good evening, sir. I'm Duncan Spint, the driver."

"Evening, Spint. Karstil. Making yourself at home, I see."

Spint grinned sheepishly. He had, indeed, been making himself at home. Believing himself the only man in the vehicle, he had spread out his gear over most of the turret deck. His own cubicle in the rear of the vehicle was cramped as the designer's largess with interior space did not extend to the driver's compartment. He began to collect some of his gear.

"That's all right, Spint. Leave it where it is," said the Optio. "There are only two of us so far, and I don't need that much room for my gear." He regretted the statement as soon as it passed his lips. Spint would now consider the turret deck as his own, and Karstil wanted the place clear when Mullins arrived. He would either have to get Spint to clean up or give the Sergeant the impression of sloppiness. He was still not good at giving orders. He resolved to do better in the future.

It took Karstil only moments to stow his heavy bag on the right side of the turret. Deciding against digging out his personal kit until after his interview, he pulled out his pocket notebook and jotted down some quick notes. "Personnel" was the easiest subject, followed by "Situation" and "Equipment Status." His stomach growled again, which sent him rummaging through his duffel looking for an emergency ration. Then he though better of it and wrote "Rations" in his logbook.

"Evening, sir." Mullins' round head was illuminated in the command hatch, the unlit stub of a cigar jutting from the corner of his mouth.

"Come on in, Sergeant. I have a few questions."

12

Rilus V, Shannedam County
The Commonwealth
3 November 6830

Through the open hatch of his tank, Roglund Karstil stared up at the unfamiliar star patterns of the night sky and let his thoughts wander back over the interview with his Platoon Sergeant. It had been a good, if slightly tentative, meeting, each man probing gently to discover the soul of the other. Mullins seemed competent, if a little willful. The platoon formation, which Karstil hadn't changed, was a mark of the Sergeant's self-confidence and also showed a distinct lack of confidence in higher authority. It was as if Mullins didn't believe official reports that had Rilus a pretty good distance away from the front-line fighting. Karstil would have to mull that one over in the future. The best thing to do would be to maintain the triangle formation at night, but he would put two tanks on line with his own in the rear. That would give better observation and fire to the front, with his tank providing rear security.

The platoon strength was good, being short only one man. The decision to place the shortage in the leader's vehicle was reasonable as his would probably be the last tank to fire in any action. The job of the platoon leader was to control the movements and fire of the other tanks in the unit, not to become engaged himself until absolutely necessary. The tank commander could fire the weapons in a pinch, and so the lack of a gunner in the command tank was not an insurmountable problem.

The other tanks were at full strength. Mullins had chosen to place all the old hands in his own tank. It was, again, understandable, but really not the best use of the original people. Mullins wanted people he knew and trusted in his vehicle. That showed his judgement being a little hard on the other members of the platoon, but Karstil was sure that future training would weld the unit into a solid command.

His own driver, Duncan Spint, was an unknown factor. He had formerly driven an Eradicator, a much newer and more sophisticated vehicle than the aging Liberator. Spint would have to learn some things about his new assignment, but a driver was a driver. The only drawback with Spint was that the man might consider himself, and the 2567th, an unlucky unit. That was something Prefect Kenderson had mentioned in his briefing, something to be guarded against.

Farwell, Umbartis, and Kloun, the commander, gunner, and driver, respectively, of Number Three were all new men. Farwell was a veteran, as his rank indicated, and he could be counted on to do the right thing. The 1717th Legion, his old outfit, had a fine reputation, and he couldn't have made Sergeant without being good. Umbartis, according to Mullins, was competent as well. Moving him to the gunner's chair in Number Three was a reward for hard work in the week he had been with the platoon. That would bear some watching. Kloun had reported at the same time as Umbartis and had been Mullins' driver. Again, according to Mullins, there was nothing to say against him.

The current situation had two different meanings. True, the Platoon was part of a Century, which was part of a Cohort, which was part of a Manus, which was part of a Legion. And the Legion was conducting marches to test the condition of the tanks and communications equipment. That was straightforward enough, but there was another, concurrent situation. Each night the platoons would occupy a different defensive posture. Tonight they were supposed to be part of a Manus on line, defending the rest of the Legion to the rear. There was a definite "direction of the enemy" in all of this. But Mullins had placed the platoon in an all-around defense, as though he were part of a patrol deep in enemy territory. That showed a lack of trust in the ability of the Century to defend itself. But if each platoon decided to defend itself rather than the Century, it would become a self-fulfilling prophecy. The Century was the sum of its scattered parts, and then had to become a whole greater than the sum of the parts. Which was exactly the reason the unit had been pulled back to Rilus for retraining.

Karstil wanted deeply to believe that the Century was a viable unit. He wanted to be able to trust the other tank platoon and the organic infantry platoon. Wanted to trust the command and control of the Century Headquarters. But it was obvious that Mullins had no trust in any of the Century formations. He had muttered something about the situation on Caralis and let it drop. There was something about the actions on that dreary world that lurked like a virus in the veins of anyone who had been there. Karstil decided to check that further.

Equipment had been another sore point with Mullins. There was an obvious lack of trust between Mullins and the maintenance people. When Karstil had asked when the vehicles were due for their monthly status check by Legion maintenance, Mullins had growled, "We do that ourselves. We know the tanks better than those wrench-jockeys." Further questioning had elicited the impression that the higher the maintenance facility, the less Mullins thought of it. Century maintenance was all right as long as the tank crew went to the shop with the vehicle. Cohort maintenance was a doubtful entity, and the Legion's Maintenance Cohort was to be avoided at all costs. "We have to check their work," Mullins had said. "And when I say check, I mean check. We have to pull the whole tank apart after it comes back from them. There's no telling what those ham-handed slobs might have broken or screwed up while the tank was in their tender care."

That was going to be a problem, and Karstil didn't know how he would handle it. The "band of brothers" concept that was supposed to be part of the Renegade Legion was not operative with this Legion. Karstil had always liked working on vehicles, having tinkered with the family grav sedan as a youth. He would be perfectly happy to tear the Liberator apart, but he didn't relish replacing the two-kiloton Gresham Coils with the organic platoon maintenance equipment. "How many men does it take to change a grav coil?" "Twelve. Eleven to hold the coil and one to turn the tank." Even that old joke was too much. He had only nine men in the platoon.

The Liberators were an old design, adapted from the TOG Opprimos that had come with many of the Renegades almost a hundred and fifty years ago. It had been upgraded and modified countless times, with new armor and shields added as combat showed the weaknesses in the original. There were just too many Liberators in service, needed too desperately for combat against TOG, to pull them out for major re-design to fully correct the weak shields and armor. They would have to soldier on, doing their best with what they had.

Some problems could be solved in the field or by Legion maintenance. The delicate turret ring problem could be alleviated, to a degree, by the crew stacking their duffel bags around the outside of the vehicle. It wasn't really much additional protection, but it gave the crew the illusion of security. They had to be careful not to restrict the side-mounted weapons by encumbering the traverse with gear, however. After all, the first mission of the tank was to shoot, not to be protected. Legion maintenance could replace the antiquated J-04 Vulcan III AntiMissile Defense System with the newer J-11 or J-12 systems, but that would require leaving the tanks with a group that Mullins distrusted. Karstil wondered if the newer Vulcans were worth the price of the struggle he would have to wage with his platoon sergeant.

The Liberator did have its advantages, though. It was quicker by 50 percent than the Catapult, and unlike the newer Scorpion, Spartius, and Trojan Horse, it mounted kinetic energy weapons as well as a deadly long-range laser. At 3,000 meters, it could savage an enemy Romulus with its 150mm Gauss cannon while its adversary was still trying to paint the Liberator's hull.

The TOG Horatius was a worthy opponent, but its main gun, also a 150mm Gauss cannon, was mounted in the hull. The Liberator, in open terrain and moving fast, could get alongside the Horatius to take full advantage of its turret-mounted weapons. Trying to slug it out with an Horatius in a head-on fight was foolish because the Liberator's turret was too fragile for such combat. Survival of a Liberator required that it move fast and shoot straight.

A heavy grav tank like a Trajan was a different matter. To score a kill against one of those, the Liberator's 150mm cannon would have to hit the enemy repeatedly. The cannon was good, but it had to chew away 100 centimeters of armor before there was any chance of a penetrating kill. The fact that the 5/6 laser used the same targeting system as the cannon was an advantage. If the gunner could make a solid hit with the cannon, firing High Explosive Armor-Piercing (HEAP) rounds to open the external armor, he could follow up with the 5/6 laser. If the gunner was either good or lucky, the laser would find the same hole. Any hit to the HEAP scar would at least penetrate to the ballistic protection, and if the laser followed the same path as the round, the effects could be spectacular. Two hits like that were sure to take out weapons systems, hit the gunner, or wound the tank commander. And it would leave a gaping hole in the turret. That was enough to give any TOG Centurion pause for thought.

All during his interview with Mullins, Karstil's stomach had continued to growl, but the other man never mentioned rations for the evening. Karstil had decided that tomorrow would be time enough to deal with food. The fat he had put on aboard the *Maiestas* would tide him over until the morning. Maybe he'd even lose some of the weight he'd added during transit.

He rolled onto his side, pulling the sheet over his head. Tomorrow was another day, he thought, the first day. He would pore over his Officer's Manual, burning every rule, every regulation into his brain. To use Prefect Kenderson's words, he would do whatever it took to be the best officer in the field, or he would die trying. He fell asleep filled with plans and hopes.

Mullins lit his cigar again, snapping the match out with his forefinger and letting it spiral down into the fighting compartment. Grouse and Abul were asleep below, curled up like a pair of cats. Mullins would let them sleep a while longer before he awakened Grouse to act as security for the platoon. He hadn't mentioned night-watch to the Optio, and the young officer had not thought to ask. Fine. Mullins would run the platoon, seeing to the internal functioning while the Optio took care of the big problems.

He was satisfied with his first meeting with Karstil. The Optio may not have asked all the right questions, but he had asked enough. When the subject of maintenance came up, Mullins almost mentioned the wire he'd found in the accelerator coil of the 50mm cannon. Then he thought better of it. Let the Optio settle in first. Mullins wanted to get a better feel for the young officer before he dropped something heavy on him.

The memory of the little wire haunted his thoughts, even though he had checked all the weapons in the platoon and found nothing wrong. He tried to reassure himself with the certainty that at least they were starting off right. The Optio had prodded him about sending the tanks to Legion Maintenance for their status check. Mullins decided he would have to inspect each vehicle after it came back, but he could accomplish that under cover of a showdown inspection. He didn't know what he would tell the Optio if he did find something. Well, he would cross that bridge when he came to it.

A glance at the faint light of the Data Display Panel showed him the location of the other vehicles in the platoon and Century. His was the only unit in all-round defense, but he could justify it because theirs was in one of the Century's flank platoons. The other tank platoon was on the right flank, the century's infantry platoon deployed around the Century Headquarters. Mullins snuffed. There were enough people in the Headquarters platoon to provide their own security. They didn't need the infantry as well.

Mullins didn't like to have all the infantry at the Headquarters. Grav tanks were impressive fighting machines, but they were vulnerable to infantry. He believed that the best defense against enemy pedes, or foot soldiers, were your own. It was always more comfortable to have an infantry squad bivouacked with tanks, especially at night. They provided extra security and could keep the enemy legionaries at least 600 meters away. The enemy was still dangerous at that range, but at least they couldn't close-assault the stationary tanks. No tanker in his right mind wanted enemy soldiers crawling over his turret. Not ever. Especially at night.

He lit his cigar again, watching the dying match spin into the semi-darkness of the fighting compartment. The scattered stubs told him he was smoking more matches than tobacco, a sure sign that the cigar had passed its useful life. He thought about digging out another one from the locked box in the fighting compartment. That would mean at least another hour on watch. He ran his tongue across the roof of his mouth and tasted the sourness of too many combat rations, too many cigars, and not enough sleep.

Franklin Grouse was his watch relief. Mullins deftly lowered himself into the fighting compartment, careful not to step on the exposed hands and feet of the sleeping crewmembers. Seeing Abul's thermal sheet fallen from his shoulders, Mullins tucked it back up before awakening his relief. He gently shook Grouse by the shoulder.

"You're on. Wake Abul in two hours, and tell him to get me two hours after that." Mullins waited for Grouse to come fully awake, waited for him to put on his boots, rub his eyes, and stretch. Then, looking straight into the eyes of his gunner, he repeated his instructions. "I'll take your rack. You take his. No use having bed rolls all over the place."

Grouse mumbled something in response.

"What?"

"I have the con," joked Grouse, as though aboard some ancient naval submarine.

"Right. Maintain current course and speed. Call me if anything happens."

"Roger, Sarge. Roger, roger."

Mullins crawled into the still-warm thermal cocoon. Like all good soldiers, he needed no decompression time. He was asleep as soon as his head touched the titanium grate of the fighting compartment floor.

13

Rilus V, Shannedam County
The Commonwealth
10 November 6830

The training program for the 2567th rolled on. The last replacement, Quentain Podandos, joined Karstil's platoon after being held for a week at Century Headquarters. He had reported direct from the hospital, and the Centurion had held him on light duty for a week before sending him to Karstil. The man still had plasto-skin on his face and hands, evidence of wounds he had suffered in recent battle. The pink replacement skin would take on normal coloring after a few weeks, but until then, the man had to be careful about exposure. Karstil often wondered at the advancements of medical science. They were good enough to make synthetic skin that the host body would eventually accept, but they weren't good enough to make it look real on the first application.

Karstil did not question the Triarii about his wounds, instead checking his records at Cohort to find out what had happened. While serving as gunner on a Pedden artillery vehicle, Podandos was wounded when his Cohort was mauled on the planet Caralis. By the time he was out of the hospital, another gunner had filled his spot and Podandos was assigned as a "casual" to the Manus, a soldier not yet given specific duty. He had drifted down the replacement chain until he arrived at the Century and eventually the platoon. Karstil didn't really need another driver, but Podandos' record showed him qualified with the AP laser. There were no weapons of the type within the platoon, an omission that the Optio regretted, but any weapons-qualified soldier was an asset.

For some reason Karstil could not ascertain, the man had been shunted off by every command so far. Karstil shuddered at his own memory of the chain of failures that led to his current assignment. Maybe this Podandos was a kindred spirit. He also thought that having two "sole survivors" in his tank might be a good omen. The fact that Quentain and Duncan were both survivors might bring the command tank luck. With the way training was going, Karstil felt he was going to need all the luck he could get.

The platoon was good enough, but there was an uneasy feeling just below the surface. Karstil could sense it in the way the men went about their duties. It wasn't lethargy, exactly. His men were competent, yet it seemed as though nothing mattered to them. Mullins and Farwell were professionals who took pride in their work, but Karstil couldn't put his finger on what might be amiss among the others.

When the tanks came back from Legion Maintenance, Sergeant Mullins had made the men inspect every part of the vehicle. Communications systems, targeting computers, and weapons were torn down and inspected. It was, said Mullins, good training for the troops to see it all laid out. They would become familiar with the components and gain confidence in both the equipment and themselves. As he told his men time and time again, "To know your tank is to love your tank."

It was true. While the other platoons suffered minor failures that sent vehicles to the Century or Cohort for repair, Karstil's platoon never failed to bring all its tanks into the night laager. Once Mullins had to ride on the side of Number Two, holding a component of the Marshman Drive in place so that the tank would not have to drop out of the column. Mullins and the crew spent the night repairing the drive with parts obtained from some unknown source. Karstil didn't ask where they came from, and Mullins didn't volunteer the information.

The Cohort was much like the Century. Activity went on, but there was a definite lack of cohesion. According to Mullins, a source of information and opinion on all matters military, it was because the Centurion Maximus had "gone 'round the bend." The Sergeant wouldn't expand on the subject any more than that, but each time a directive from Cohort reached the platoon, Mullins would shake his head and mutter something under his breath.

Karstil took note that he was also busy with other matters. For one thing, he was only now getting familiar with the Renegade rank system. They used an organizational system that harkened back almost six thousand years to the First Roman Empire. Both the Commonwealth and the Renegades used the legion as the basic large unit, but below that, the names changed down through the command. Where the Commonwealth had a Brigade, the Renegades had a Manus. Where the Commonwealth had Battalions and Companies, the Renegades used Cohort and Century.

Ranks were equally archaic. The Renegade Century (a Commonwealth Company) was commanded by a Centurion rather than the Commonwealth Captain. The Cohort (Battalion) was commanded by a Centurion Maximus instead of a Lieutenant-Colonel, and a Legatus rather than a Colonel commanded the Manus (Brigade). The Renegades dropped certain ranks that the Commonwealth used. There were only two junior officer grades, Optio and Centurion, for the Renegades, where the Commonwealth had Second Lieutenant, Lieutenant, and Captain. Among the senior commanders, there were Centurion Maximus and Legatus, while the Commonwealth used Major, Lieutenant-Colonel, and Colonel. The Renegades did have a Legatus Maximus to designate the senior Legatus as the commander of the Manus Primus, or First Manus.

Karstil liked being a platoon leader, liked the fact that Century Headquarters didn't interfere in what he was doing. Centurion Alanton Freund inspected once a week, but by and large, he was noticeable by his absence. The Centurion Maximus, Tartus Nollen, had come by only once in the early stages of training. The visit had been perfunctory, at best, but had left Karstil disturbed.

That day, the Century had pulled into some trees for the noon rest. Mullins, as usual, had the crews out of their tanks and burrowing into the grav drives. It wasn't that there was anything wrong. It was just Mullins' obsession with checking everything at every halt. The men ate their noon meal while they worked, and Karstil pulled maintenance right along with them. It was only when he stepped back from the hull of his Liberator and trod on the toes of his Centurion that he learned of official visitors in the area. The man he'd bumped into was Nollen, venerated hero of the Rift County campaign and Centurion Maximus of the Cohort. Karstil snapped to attention and saluted, raising a grease-covered arm. His combat coveralls were open to the waist, with the upper part peeled back and the sleeves tied around his middle. That might not be regulation for wearing the uniform, but it did prevent lubricants from staining it.

"Is that the way you've been taught to wear your uniform?" Centurion Freund bit the words out carefully, obviously angry. Behind him, at a correctly respectful distance, stood

Sergeant Justine Gortos, the Senior Sergeant of the Century. She was making notes furiously with a metal stylus on her electro-pad.

Karstil was confused and felt his burgeoning confidence beginning to wilt. He knew that the presence of his superiors required some action, but, at the moment, he had no idea what. If he were in barracks, he would call "Attention!" In the field or while the men were working, he should call out something else. He thought that "At ease!" was the correct order, but to shout that out with the commander standing directly in front of him might seem as though he were ordering the commander to be silent. He chose the third solution to any problem: do nothing. He hoped that Mullins had spotted the newcomers and would take the correct steps.

Freund had not yet returned his salute, nor had Nollen. This presented another small problem. Karstil felt like a fool, standing before his superiors with right arm raised at a forty-five-degree angle, palm open and outward. How long does a man hold a salute if the superior does not return same? The manual covered this situation, but again, Karstil could not remember the regulation. If he dropped his arm too soon, he might cut off Freund or Nollen at the moment they were ready to return his salute. While he debated thus inwardly, his arm was getting tired; he could feel the shoulder muscles becoming strained.

"You're a disgrace to the uniform," continued the Centurion. "And officers are not supposed to pull maintenance on vehicles. That's why there are enlisted men."

Karstil couldn't see the other crewmembers, but he could feel their eyes and those of the whole platoon on him. Where the devil was Mullins? His arm, still raised in the salute, was beginning to burn from fatigue. Behind Freund, he could see Nollen bending over to pick at something on the ground.

"All right. All right." Freund returned the salute, allowing Karstil to drop his arm. Meanwhile, Centurion Maximus Nollen had begun to stare up into the treetops as though unaware of the little drama taking place before him. He was holding a small flower to his nose as he scanned the woods.

"This is an administrative halt. Why are all your vehicles in the woods? We could hardly find you," Freund snapped. The Sergeant continued to take notes. Karstil knew that all this would probably appear in his fitness report.

"Cock robin," said Nollen, still entranced by the action in the trees. He stood tall and rail-thin, his body swaying slightly as though wafted by the dusty breeze.

The Centurion hesitated, then rushed back into his diatribe as though eager to cover up Nollen's strange words.

"Tell me, Optio, is this your idea of leadership—letting your men run around without uniforms on, while you…"

"Cock robin. No doubt about it. I can see it from here," Nollen went on.

Still standing stiff and rigid, Karstil stole a glance over at Nollen just as a heated rush came over him. What was this? A new secret code, maybe?

Freund was working himself up into a rage. He had been embarrassed that the platoon was not where he had told the Centurion Maximus it would be. Now he wanted to cover his own tracks by making sure that the Maximus knew whose fault it really was. Out of the corner of his eye, Karstil could see the other members of the platoon getting back into proper uniform. At least Mullins was squaring away the others so there would be no additional cause for anger.

The Centurion Maximus was busy cleaning his ear with the fingernail of his little finger, carefully examining the residue he extracted. Forgotten, the tiny flower lay where he had dropped it.

"We follow certain procedures in this Century, Optio, and you should know that. One of them is to inform our headquarters of our whereabouts *and* our activities." Freund was leaning forward slightly at the waist, his face getting closer and closer to Karstil's. "That allows headquarters to know what's going on. No matter what you think, Optio, you are not running your own show here."

Karstil could feel the "if-I-had-the-chance-you'd-be-gone" speech coming. He had heard it before, more than once. This time, he could feel the fury beginning to rise behind his eyes. It was not his fault. No one had told him that this was an administrative halt, and hiding in the trees was the right thing to do in any case. He was exactly where he was supposed to be. Perhaps he should not have stripped off his uniform, but it was understandable. The idea that officers were not supposed to pull maintenance was true, but with three vehicles and only nine men in the platoon, it was ridiculous to leave better than 10 percent of the force off maintenance because of a technicality like officers' privilege. If he were to go, at least he'd go with all guns blazing. He took a deep breath, preparing himself for something he would later regret.

"Ride a cockhorse to Banbury Cross, to see a fine lady upon a white horse."

"Sir?" Karstil said, utterly baffled. He tried to think back to what the manual said about codes. The Centurion Maximus was half-turned away from the other two, his glance wandering through the woods. Karstil and Freund looked at each other, the young Optio grasping for an explanation, while the senior officer simply refused to acknowledge that there was a problem.

"What did you say, sir?" asked Freund, shifting uneasily.

"Rings on her fingers and bells on her toes, she shall have music wherever she goes." Nollen finished the nursery rhyme, obviously satisfied with himself. "What we need is music when we move."

"Music, sir?"

"Yes. I've always liked music. Not necessarily military music, though we should have some of that. But ballads, too."

"Yes, sir," the Sergeant said.

Nollen was staring past the two junior officers, hardly acknowledging their presence.

Karstil's jaw dropped as a thought suddenly hit him. This senior staff officer, this decorated war hero of the Renegade Legion, wasn't talking codes. He was talking gibberish.

Freund and the Sergeant with the notepad exchanged weary glances, as though they had been through this before. The Centurion Maximus had not been listening to their conversation. The rage seemed to drain out of Freund. He looked directly at Karstil. "Forget what I said, Optio. Forget everything about this incident. Carry on."

"Yes, sir. I will, sir.""

"First Sergeant."

"Sir?"

"The Centurion Maximus and I will be leaving now. Arrange transport for him back to Cohort."

"Yes, sir."

As the party turned to go, Freund reached over and took the electro-pad from the Sergeant's hands. He hit the "Erase" button on the pad. In an instant, the interview was lost to history.

Karstil slowly turned around, and there was Sergeant Mullins pulling out a well-chewed cigar from the breast pocket on his suit.

"Did you see that?" Karstil asked. "That guy's completely nuts."

"Yes, sir, as a matter of fact he is," Mullins replied flatly as he lit his cigar and turned back toward his tank.

The marches and mock battles continued on the wide, rolling plains of Rilus, as the Century became integrated into the Cohort, and the Manus. Though Karstil and his unit were growing in confidence, he still felt something lacking in coordination. The infantry platoon of the Century always deployed around the Century Headquarters at night. That allowed the grav tanks to operate on the perimeter without fear of grinding one of the unfortunate pedes into the ground by accident. Renegade doctrine called for infantry to be deployed with the tanks, but the Standard Operating Proceedure (SOP) of the Century didn't follow that.

All units, from Manus to Century, had to practice the deployment from column of march to hasty attack. The principle here was to apply mounting pressure to the enemy formation as the unengaged units in the column maneuvered to attack. In order to be successful, communications had to be kept to a minimum, with each subunit commander following his instincts in responding to the situation.

As soon as contact was established by the leading elements of formation, the enemy was taken under fire and assaulted. The commander of the forces in contact made a quick estimate of the enemy's strength, which he relayed to the column commander. With that information, the next-higher unit deployed its forces for an immediate attack while the commander notified his superior of the situation. The process continued until either the enemy was broken or the column ran out of troops of its own.

All this required that commanders be able to make rapid and accurate estimates of enemy intentions and strength, to deploy their forces to deal with the perceived enemy capabilities, and to inform their commanders of the ever-changing situation. Dependable subordinates, well-trained troops, and an accurate eye made the system work. That and training, training, training.

Karstil loved the drill. Roaring along over the open terrain at one meter off the ground at better than 240 kph, his faceguard down, the wind tearing at his coveralls, gave him a feeling of power and invincibility. When in the position of lead platoon, he usually took the center point, with Farwell and Mullins on either wing in the form of a flying V. He preferred Farwell and Mullins out front. Farwell was a good navigator and could be expected to attack at once, while Mullins was ever the competent professional.

Placed behind them, Karstil could see any situation developing and take appropriate action. This also meant that he wasn't immediately plunged into the chaos of battle by being the very lead tank, and he could use the additional time to advise Century Headquarters of the situation. If his platoon were not the lead platoon, he deployed his tanks in either echelon right or echelon left of the advancing unit, listening to the communicator, making his own estimate of the situation, and preparing to deploy in a flanking maneuver should the lead platoon come into contact with the enemy.

The problem with the technique was the constant traffic on the commlink. Even with multiple bands and synchronous receivers, it was difficult for Karstil to sort out the reports from the other platoons, the commands from Century, his commands to his own tanks and their replies, and the intra-tank comunications. On some occasions, the talk rose to an incoherent babble. Mullins let the Optio stew with the problem before he suggested a solution for the lower command link: using hand and arm signals.

Hand and arm signals were touched upon at Officers' Training School, but the wealth of other communications equipment rarely made them necessary. That was fine at school where distances between tanks were kept to a minimum and instructors limited the number of units using the frequencies. In the field, the commlink system soon became clogged with voices shouting commands or reporting to superiors. Distances between tanks increased to 400 meters or greater. Being available for visual communications also meant that the vehicle commander had to ride into battle exposed in an open turret. This last did not promote long life on the part of TCs.

On the other hand, as Mullins pointed out, it was easier to command from where you could see rather than to rely on the electronic, thermal, and seismic sensors in the command station. Mullins was a great believer in his own eyes, distrusting and disliking electronic gadgets. Karstil couldn't tell whether the dislike came from something visceral or from experience. He was hesitant at first to go with the hand and arm signals, but he tried it and it worked. One great advantage of the system was that the other tank commanders had to pay attention to the Optio and what he was doing. After some practice, the platoon became proficient with the system, and commlink traffic was reduced to manageable proportions. The other platoons did not institute the same system.

The actual use of signals over great distances was easier than some critics believed. Each tank commander was provided with a laser signaling device. This pencil flasher could send a tiny beam of light great distances, and the combat helmets were equipped with an all-round laser sensor. When an individual wanted to send, all he had to do was point the laser at the receiving station and flash the light. The sensor alerted the receiving station that its attention was desired. After that, it was easy to communicate with the light or with hand movements.

Karstil wondered if Mullins pushed the hand and arm signal system because it was better or because it gave him the opportunity to smoke his foul-smelling cigars. It was hard on the other crewmembers to have a smoking cigar in a tank that was buttoned up for combat. The DDP and sensor displays gave 6400 mil observation, but humans do not like being cooped up in a steel box.

Visual signals gave the platoon a secure link that normal sensing equipment could not detect. In an environment filled with electronic sensors, the ability to communicate without electronic pulse was an advantage. It was difficult for the enemy to detect a shut-down tank. The use of the standard commlink gave the enemy a chance to "see" the sending unit with their electronic eavesdropping equipment. Hand signals left no trace.

But there was another, more subtle reason for the hand-signal system. It made the platoon think and act as a unit. It gave them something the others did not have. The sense that they were a unit, acting on the commands of a central figure began the process of the band of brothers. The tank commanders became more aware of the locations and actions of the other tanks. That reaction became automatic, and commanders did not have to "look for" the other two tanks of the platoon. Because they had been paying attention during the slow times, when the action accelerated, they still "saw" what the other tanks were doing.

The Century also practiced the deliberate attack, the hasty defense, and the defense of a prepared position. The hasty attack was an exhilarating experience, but the others were dull as dirt. Tedious planning for movement and fire marked the deliberate attack. The units approached the Attack Positions and waited while the simulated artillery and satellite fire was brought down on the enemy positions. Once the enemy was hurt and confused, the attack rolled forward and over them. These attacks were slower, and Karstil felt naked and uncomfortable even as he drove forward at 120 KPH. The attack would have to wait until the flanking units cleared the phase line, eliminating all enemy resistance. This meant that the successful attackers had to slow their movement while the laggards caught up. This was not being a tanker.

The defense was even worse. The tanks sat in their craters while the mock artillery exploded around them, the umpires shooting any destroyed and damaged tanks with their "God Guns," the small lasers that temporarily disabled any vehicles eliminated from wargame maneuvers. The first tank knocked out in every defense was that of the platoon commander. Though this was supposed to sow confusion among the survivors, it didn't. In the first defense, it was Mullins who planned the platoon's deployment and its actions in the defense. When Karstil's Liberator was declared dead, nothing about the command structure really changed. Because Karstil was always dead, the other two tanks learned to do without the instructions of the Optio. And Karstil never had the chance to deal with the problem of being attacked. Mullins did a good job, and Karstil would sit on the top of his "dead" Liberator and watch his Platoon Sergeant move the tanks from one prepared position to another to "destroy" the oncoming "TOG" vehicles.

Training continued. Karstil faced each new day, each new challenge, with growing confidence. The end of training was in sight. Gunnery qualification and final operational test and inspection would mark the First Manus' completion of the re-training cycle. After that would come the greatest test.

Combat.

14

Rilus V, Shannedam County
The Commonwealth
14 November 6830

"Morning, sir. Nollen's gone," said Mullins.

Karstil had just started to climb down the front slope of his tank when Mullins greeted him with the announcement. He was standing beside the port sponson on the left of the tank, his well-muscled arms folded, the habitual cigar clenched in his teeth. The statement had been just that, a statement. Karstil could detect the indifference in his Sergeant's voice.

"Nollen?" Karstil squinted in the brightness of day.

"Yeah. The fun guy who talked to the birds and wanted music as we moved. He's gone. They took him away to the rubber room late last night."

Karstil felt no surge of emotion at the news. Nollen had been a cipher as far as he was concerned, and their one and only meeting had been less than overwhelming. It was strange, however, for a Cohort Commander to slip away in the night. Usually, there was a party and a suitable gift presented by the officers and men. As a General's aide, Karstil knew all about squeezing money out of the command for a gift to the departing colleague. As the commander left, his honorary baton clutched in his hands, the officers of the unit lined the road for a last salute. It could be an impressive ceremony.

Karstil also knew from his experience with General Gentrund P. Beldarnus that it was unusual to change commanders at the end of a training cycle. It was normally done *before* a unit began training so that the new man had a chance to get a handle on things before having to take the unit into combat. There had been no touch for a gift, no going-away bash, and the relief of command had taken place at the end of the cycle. Very strange.

"I guess they just slipped the body over the side and let it float away," Mullins said.

"He wasn't really that bad, Sergeant," said Karstil, feeling obliged to rise to the defense of a fellow-officer. It was just a knee-jerk response to an NCO's criticism of an officer. Better, he thought, to have said nothing.

Mullins raised an eyebrow at his Optio but kept silent. Further comment would only strain the situation, and he liked Karstil. The young Optio was learning quickly, and it was difficult not to be caught up in his enthusiasm. The one thing Mullins really liked was that Karstil did the Optio's job and let him do his. Most officers, junior officers, had been trained to be Sergeants. When they got to their units, they continued to be Sergeants and tried to do the NCO's job. Karstil didn't.

"How'd you hear that he was gone?"

"Got it from Uva, the head shed top puke."

"The what?"

"Top puke. You know, sir. The Mess Sergeant in the headquarters."

"Ah," Karstil answered. Better to say "Ah" as though you had forgotten than to admit ignorance. Let the Sergeant make his own guess as to what he knew.

Mullins leaned forward, resting his elbows comfortably on the starboard sponson of the Liberator. "Do you think it will change anything?"

Karstil noted the lack of a "sir" at the end of the question. Though it was becoming more common when they spoke in private, Mullins never forgot it when they were in public.

"I don't know, Mullins. It's not my problem." Karstil mounted the front of the tank. "Time to get started. Saddle up. Today's the day we start to qualify these beasts."

The air around the tank gunnery range was hot and thick with the dust coming up from vehicles of all shapes and sizes. The 2567th entered the range just as a battalion of Sterling Heavy Ground Tanks was leaving. Karstil wondered where the Commonwealth Sterlings would have come from. Perhaps they were part of the planetary militia, as he had never encountered them during training.

The Sterling was the biggest of the Commonwealth ground vehicles, a throw-back to a bygone age when ground tanks were the main line of defense. The monsters came grinding past the Century, rooster tails of dust churned up by their giant tracks. Even at a standard, one-meter hover, Karstil could feel the ground shaking. The turret hatches were open, with both gunner and commander exposed from the chest up. They waved at the grav tanks, shouting something that was drowned in the din of their creaking treads.

Karstil watched them make the final turn and disappear down the trail. He waited for the dust to clear a bit before ordering his platoon to make the turn into the complex of ranges. The sensors in the Liberators would have allowed them to operate on the trail even in zero visibility, but other tanks, not sensor-equipped, could be on the track.

Even with his faceshield down, Karstil could feel the yellow dust penetrating his combat gear. His mouth began to dry, his lips turning ochre as he licked them to retain moisture. The fine powder built up on the horizontal surfaces of the tank and even clung to the sides of the turret and hull. The weapons were covered, and more of the talc-like dust crept into the fighting compartment. Karstil knew that the vehicles would be clean by evening, because Mullins would see to that.

The range was designed to work from small to big. The lighter the weapon, the earlier it would be tested. The final test was on Table VIII, Range 42. At that time, all the weapons and communications systems would be integrated into the whole. Passing or not passing the test was not a ticket to the front. Everybody was going to deploy with the unit, no matter how they did on the final range. If a vehicle failed the earlier tests, technicians checked it to ensure that failure was not due to an equipment malfunction. If the equipment passed, the tankers would have another chance to take the test. Pass or fail, they would move to the next Table.

The concept that a failed tank should be sent into combat was strange to Karstil at first. Mullins explained it. If a crew knew that failure would keep them in the training cycle, the failure rate could increase, as crews might blow the tests on purpose. On the other hand, knowing that they would deploy with the unit, they tried as hard as possible to pass. Passing not only gave the crew a sense of accomplishment, it also fostered a sense of confidence and pride. Knowing that all the other tanks in the platoon/century/cohort had qualified diminished the fear of meeting the enemy. It would be terrible to go into combat in a Cohort whose vehicles had not qualified.

At the Range Safety Area, technicians in white helmets swarmed over the tanks, carefully checking weapons and removing the safety wires that kept them permanently disarmed. All during the previous training, it had been impossible to fire full charges from the laser weapons or slugs from the Gauss cannon. Up till now, the vehicles could not fire live ammunition. Training was dangerous enough as it was, and tanks able to fire live rounds by accident would make it even more hazardous. From now on, however, all AFVs of the Manus would have the ability to expend real ammunition.

Even the old hands were affected by the change in the Liberators. Knowing that the tanks were now armed made them seem more worthy of respect. More lethal. More real. Closer to combat.

Karstil could feel the perspiration under his combat coveralls. The weather was not so hot that he perspired heavily, so he knew it was nerves rather than the climate. Just knowing that live rounds were loaded made his heart race. At a single word from him, Karstil's gunner could send a deadly shell flying.

He eased the Liberator over and into the prepared crater on the 50mm cannon range. To his right and left, the other tanks of the Century were easing into position, directed into place by Range Control NCOs who used colored wands to direct the giant tanks. The controllers stood to the left of the tanks, where the commander could see them clearly. Even though the cannon were on "safe," the range personnel took no chances by standing in front of the tanks. Their obvious caution added to the tenseness of the situation. The Liberator shuddered as it settled into the permanent crater and waited.

A Range Control Sergeant climbed up the side of the tank and placed a warning beacon on top of the Vulcan III laser housing. He passed the control wires through the commander's hatch. Podandos took the end and plugged it into the master fire control panel of the tank. From now on, it would be impossible to activate any of the weapons without having the warning beacon blink to life. It would also be impossible to disconnect the warning beacon. To do so would automatically activate the beacon, and the siren built into the base could howl until a Safety Officer turned it off with the appropriate key. The range was going to be as safe as humans could make it.

The first range consisted of pairs of two-meter square targets: one at 500 meters, the other at 1,000. The targets were mounted on swivels so that they could turn, exposing themselves to the tankers on the firing line. The first exercise was to fire three rounds at each target, checking to see that the sights and cannon were aligned. The second part of the test presented the two targets in random sequence. The gunner identified the target and fired two rounds from the cannon at each target. The tank commander had nothing to do except sit in the turret and watch the 50mm shells scream down range.

"All tanks, arm your weapons." At the command from Range Control, the gunners in the tanks activated the master firing panel. The warning beacons on the tanks began to flash.

"We can do it," Karstil whispered into his headset microphone, more to convince himself than the others in the tank.

A tense pause followed as the Safety Officers ensured that all tanks were "hot." Then came the words from the control station: "Ready on the right. Ready on the left. The firing line is ready. Prepare to engage targets as they appear. Commence firing!"

Karstil stood in the turret of the Liberator and and felt his body shudder as Podandos fired at the distant targets. His first round missed low, but after a quick sight adjustment, the others struck the center of the target panel. Quentain Podandos was proving to be a satisfactory choice for the gunner of Number One. Karstil watched the platoon's other two tanks as they shredded their own targets. To his right, Mullins's tank was pounding the target. Grouse, Mullins' gunner, put his four rounds into the center of the target panels on the first try. As the targets appeared for their second sequence, he sent the 50mm slugs into the stanchions that held the frame, one round into each. The target frame exploded under the impact of the depleted uranium projectiles. That wasn't bad shooting. The frames were no more than five centimeters thick, and to hit them at 1,000 meters was quite an accomplishment.

"Tank Seven, Tank Seven. What the devil are you trying to do?" The Range Control Officer was calling Mullins's tank.

"Sorry. My aim was off just a tad."

"Well, 'sorry' doesn't cut it, Tank Seven." Karstil could tell that the Range Control Officer, an officious Commonwealth Lieutenant Colonel, was angry. Now he'd have to send some of his crew down-range to fix the target. "You can just sit there until all the others have finished. No more shooting for you on this range."

Mullins rose from the commander's hatch, stretched, and lit the cigar stub he held between his teeth. That task accomplished to his satisfaction, he leaned back against the Vulcan III housing and smiled defiantly.

The third sequence of targets began to appear, greeted by the sharp "whang" of the 50 mm cannon of the remaining tanks. Karstil felt his own Liberator recoil as the cannon fired.

Almost as if on command, the other tanks followed Mullins' lead.

"Cease fire! Cease fire!" screamed the commlink. "What do all of you think you're doing?"

Karstil glanced down-range. Not a target frame had survived.

"You did that on purpose. I know you did!" If the Lieutenant Colonel had been angry before, he was apoplectic now. "That is wanton destruction of Commonwealth property." Karstil could see the Range Control Officer waving his arms and stomping his foot as he shouted into the commlink microphone, a comical sight to behold.

"All of you, get off my range! Just get off my range! This will be reported to the appropriate command!"

Everyone else on the range was giggling and laughing now. Especially Karstil. To hell with your little firing range, he thought. This outfit is ready for battle.

As the Liberators moved away from the firing line, Karstil looked down the column. Even with the visors down on the command helmets, he could sense both the tension and excitement among the other commanders. They were going to catch it now, sure as God made little green apples. Welcome to the Second Cohort, First Manus, of the 2567th, thought Karstil of the new Cohort commander. Whoever you are, wherever you've come from, we are all about to meet you.

15

Rilus V, Shannedam County
The Commonwealth
14 November 6830

The Cohort stood on the wide parade ground, the men lined up silently in front of their tanks. A column of three medium Centuries stood to the right of the formation, the three light Centuries to the left. Each Century was on line. Centered in front of the two columns of Centuries stood the Headquarters. The Cohort had been summoned here from bivouac in the field to meet the Commonwealth Brigadier in charge of gunnery qualification. Rumor had it that many heads were going to roll.

The call to report to the parade ground had been so soon after the incident on the gunnery range that the men had no time to clean the tanks or to change uniforms. Now they stood in the bright afternoon sunlight, their combat helmets at their feet, waiting for the axe to fall. From Karstil's position in the second platoon of the Second Century, he could just see the figures of the Cohort Headquarters, but could not make out the Cohort commander among the mass of men.

A wheeled sedan entered the parade ground from the right, driving swiftly toward the front of the formation. A large reviewing stand with flags whipping in the wind occupied the ground directly in front of the Cohort's formation, and the sedan was obviously headed there. Instead of approaching the stand from the rear, the sedan came to a stop directly in front of the Cohort Headquarters, covering the staff with dust as it screeched to a halt. The driver dismounted, ran around to the far side of the vehicle, and opened the door for an officer.

Karstil lost sight of the newcomer as he made his way to the steps on the side of the reviewing stand. Then the figure appeared on the stand, alone. Even at 35 meters, Karstil could see the rank badges of a Commonwealth Brigadier glinting from the shoulder flashes, could see the rows of service ribbons on the left breast. The Brigadier strode to the front of the platform and surveyed the assembled troops.

"Never in my thirty years of service have I seen such a blatant disregard for the property of the Commonwealth." The voice of the Brigadier was flat, high-pitched, whining. "The lack of discipline that would lead to the wanton destruction of a range at this facility is indicative of the poor attitude that pervades this unit. Because you are Renegades does not in any way relieve you of your responsibilities to the Commonwealth.

"I, unfortunately, have no control over the actions of a Renegade Legion unit. Were it within my power, I would have this Cohort, indeed, the entire Manus, dispersed throughout the Commonwealth to prevent you from having any influence over our forces. But I do not have that power.

"Your Legion has the reputation for being a collection of misfits. Certainly your combat record speaks for itself. The 2567th has been a failure since its birth, and I am sure, based on what has been reported to me, that you will continue to uphold this reputation.

"From now until you leave this facility, you will be confined to either your bivouac area or to the range. You will be allowed no access to any of the extensive post facilities. These restrictions will be enforced by the Military Police assigned to this post. They will work in concert with the Military Police assigned to your Manus. Any violation of this injunction will lead to immediate arrest, confinement, and trial by court-martial.

"In addition, any destruction of ranges or other equipment of this post will be made good by the offending unit. All individuals in such a unit will have their pay garnisheed until the damages have been paid. If the individual cannot be identified, then the unit's officers and men will accept the responsibility for the damage on a pro-rata basis.

"You are a disgrace to the uniforms you wear. If your commander were not newly assigned to the unit, I would hold him personally responsible for the conduct of the unit. Since he is new, assigned today, I will not place blame for this incident on him nor report it in my after-action report to Commonwealth Headquarters. Any other incidents, will, however, be placed in his permanent record, as it will for all officers in this command."

The Brigadier spun about, and Karstil noted that the about-face was not very sharp. The Brigadier's arms swung outward from his sides as he executed the turn. That, thought Karstil, would have driven the instructors at Officers' Training into a fit.

The Brigadier stamped across, the platform and down the stairs. The driver stood at attention beside the open door of the sedan until the Brigadier was seated, shutting the door with a resounding "thunk" as if to emphasize the Brigadier's words. The sedan roared away, showering the Cohort Headquarters with more dust. Silence fell over the assemblage.

The troops stood, waiting. The formation was not over. Every man, from the lowest-ranking Triarii to the senior Centurion who served as the Cohort Executive Officer, knew that the Centurion Maximus was going to have something to say. And that something was probably going to be as bad as the Brigadier's words.

There was a stirring in the Cohort Headquarters area. Karstil could not see the man who left the formation until the figure began to mount the platform. He was short, probably no more than 1.7 meters, and slender, less than 60 kilos. And he was old. Karstil could see his white hair reflecting in the afternoon sunlight. The Centurion Maximus walked to the edge of the platform and gazed out over the Cohort.

"At ease." The voice cracked with authority, and the formation shifted. "Give me your attention."

"My name's Harras. Milton Harras. I'm your new commander." Karstil watched Harras. The man, even though small, certainly had command presence. More presence than the Brigadier who had occupied the same space just moments ago. The voice was strong enough to carry over the troops, yet the man wasn't yelling.

"I had hoped to meet you people under different, less formal circumstances. But one of your Sergeants seems to have more or less called this meeting on his own, so here I am."

Karstil could feel heads turning toward Mullins. For once, the focus of attention was not on him. He glanced in the direction of his Platoon Sergeant, and saw Mullins's skull redden under the glances of his neighbors. It was obvious that Harras knew exactly who had done the first shooting. Karstil glanced up at the commander and saw that his eyes were locked onto Mullins as well.

"That Sergeant, who shall remain forever nameless, has gathered you all here under less than optimum circumstances." Harras's eyes never left Mullins, and Karstil could see his Sergeant becoming redder and redder. At least he would not be mentioned by name, thus preserving official anonymity. "So we will let that drop." Harras took his eyes off Mullins and let them roam over the formation.

"I am new to the Renegade forces. I spent the last twenty years as a member of the Commonwealth, and during that time, I heard many things about the Renegades. Most of it indicated that you are somewhat individualistic in your approach to discipline. That seems to be true. But I also heard that you are fighters. I hope that reputation continues as well.

"I have been studying the history of this Cohort and the Legion. We seem to have been plagued by bad luck, but I think a unit makes its own luck by being professional about what we do. We can do that by checking everything—twice. We can get this Cohort qualified on the tank ranges. We can keep away from the Brigadier.

"If we do all that, most of us will still be around when we rotate back from Caralis again." Harras paused and let his eyes sweep the crowd. "By the way. Let's see if we can't improve our shooting while we're here. Try to hit the targets, not the frames."

A collective sigh of relief ran through the ranks as they realized no additional punishment would be forthcoming. But then again, the man's mention of Caralis did serve to remind everyone that there was a war going on out there, that TOG's superior numbers were not all that far away.

Evening was falling over the bivouac site. Mullins lit his cigar and spun the match into the soft darkness. He reached inside his coveralls and withdrew the clear cello-pack he had kept with him since that day in the motor pool. Inside was the fragment of copper wire he had found in the accelerator coils of the 50mm cannon. He examined the wire as he had done so many times. In the last light of the setting sun, the wire glowed warmly through the transparent packet.

He was debating, as he had so often, the question of whether to tell someone about the sabotage he had found. He made his decision. He would tell his Optio, trusting him to do the right thing. He replaced the packet and dismounted from the turret of his Liberator.

Karstil was just finishing his meal as Mullins approached, and the Optio looked up as the Sergeant emerged from the gloom.

"Evening, Sergeant."

"Sir? Can we talk, sir?"

Karstil sensed something about the Sergeant. Perhaps it had been the two "sirs" in one sentence that made him sit up straight and pay attention. Mullins has something important to say, he thought, or he wouldn't be so formal in private.

"I have a problem I need to talk over with you, sir."

Karstil felt a weight land on his shoulders. Here it comes, he thought. Mullins is going to dump some family problem on me. Now is when I find out that he has a sick wife and an injured kid on some forgotten world somewhere. "What is it, Mullins?"

Mullins fumbled inside his coveralls, digging for something in the inside pocket. Probably looking for family pictures, thought Karstil. The Sergeant found what he was looking for and held it out to Karstil.

"Take a look at this, sir."

Karstil took the plastic envelope and stared at the copper wire. "It looks like a piece of copper wire, Sergeant."

"It is, sir." Mullins squatted down beside the Optio. "But where I found it is the interesting story."

"Go on."

It was full dark by the time Mullins finished his tale, and Karstil was glad that the

Sergeant couldn't see his face. The thought of someone out there willing to destroy the unit made his stomach churn. His face contorted into a grimace. He hadn't a clue about what to do with this information, so he remained silent.

"Do you think the new Centurion Maximus should be told?" Mullins had dropped the "sir" from his speech. "I think we can trust him. He sounded pretty straight today."

"You may be right, Mullins. This is a bigger problem than either you or I can take on."

Milton Harras listened silently to the full story, which Karstil initiated and Mullins finished. He sat inside his personal van surrounded by the paraphernalia of command. Maps, charts, graphs, documents, and reports were stacked everywhere. He held the offending wire, still listening to the two men who stood in front of him. When they were done explaining it, he looked up into their faces, as though he could penetrate to the truth or falsity of the story. Then he opened the top drawer of his desk and dropped the envelope into it, and snapped the drawer shut.

"I'm glad you reported this to me. I'll take care of it." Harras rose from behind the desk, indicating that the interview was at an end. "Say nothing to anyone."

The two men saluted and left the Centurion's command quarters.

Leaving the van, Mullins and Karstil walked in silence back to their unit. Neither spoke until they reached Karstil's Liberator.

"Think we did the right thing, Optio?" Mullins asked.

"If you can't trust your commanding officer..."

"I know. Then who can you trust?"

It was a question both would have to sleep on.

16

RLS Tacitus, In Transit
The Commonwealth
24 December 6830

Roglund Karstil stared into the shadowy gloom of the equipment bay of the *RLS Tacitus*. Despite the numerous fluoropanels mounted along the sides and in the overhead bulkhead, the cavernous space seemed to absorb all the light. Unlike the *Maeistas*, with its numerous decks, the *Tacitus* was filled with a series of long hangars and grid-like catwalks suspended overhead from stanchions. The ship was designed to move very large loads over long distances and that was exactly what she was doing now—carrying most of the First Manus of the 2567th Renegade Legion.

After two months of hard training, Roglund Karstil was glad they were finally on their way from Rilus to Caralis. Like an intricate piece of machinery, the 2567th Legion had been methodically disassembled, rebuilt almost from scratch, and put back together again. Now it was time for them to enter the fray.

The *Tacitus* had none of the amenities of the *Maiestas*: no dining room, no lounge, no privacy. Troops were billeted in tube-like pipe berths down each side of the bay. The officers were quartered on the lowest transverse deck below the layers of equipment. Latrines were located centerline at 100-meter intervals on the lowest deck as well as in the bow and stern. The mess facility was located dead amidships on the same deck. The mess was constantly in operation, feeding troops on a continuous basis. With an entire Manus on board, the line never ended. Some men, getting in line for breakfast, found that the meal had changed to dinner with no perceptible pause.

When not standing in the chow line, Karstil spent as much time as possible on his own Liberator. The vehicle didn't really require any work, but it provided him some privacy amid the general chaos of the transport. Indeed, the tank was beginning to seem like home. It gave him the space to think. To think about the coming combat. To think about his own past. To think about the meeting with Mullins.

In the seven weeks since their talk about the wire, neither man had ever mentioned it to the other again. In Karstil's mind, however, the event loomed so large that he always thought of it as "The Meeting with Mullins." Perhaps it was the utter silence now surrounding the whole thing that seemed to set it off and heighten its significance. No one at Cohort had mentioned their report to Karstil, nor had Harras attempted to contact him. As he walked through the hangar toward his Liberator, Karstil had reason to again ponder what Mullins had told him about finding the copper wire.

The air inside the hangar was stale and cold and reeked with the stinging smell of fresh paint. The last task the tankers had been assigned on Rilus was to paint all the Manus's vehicles with white camouflage—an obvious preparation for landing in the arctic zone of Caralis. But then yesterday, one day after entering T-space, the order had come down to repaint the vehicles jungle-green. Why do the painting while aboard ship? Why the switch to jungle-green? It could only mean that someone at the top suspected a security leak within the Legion. Now that the *Tacitus* had entered T-space, no communication from the ship was possible, and that meant no leaks could get out. Maybe these guys know what they're doing after all, Karstil thought.

The equipment, tanks, artillery, personnel carriers, transports, and cargo vehicles were strung out in long, double columns the length of the cargo bay. They were stowed bow to stern, side by side and with no room between vehicles. Each double row was less than a meter away from the adjacent double row. To reach any particular vehicle required that a man walk down the length of an access-way to a position opposite the vehicle. He then had to climb onto a piece of equipment and move across the tops of the vehicles, leaping over the meter-wide spaces between each double column.

Karstil walked through the nearly deserted holding area, down the long rows of vehicles toward his Liberator. The bow of the *Tacitus* was loaded with three combat-Cohorts, then the supporting combat vehicles, and finally the administrative vehicles. His Cohort was part of the reserve for the landing, and so the tanks were at the rear of the transport. No one really expected opposition during the landing nor on the ground, but neither did anyone in a war want to be taken by surprise.

The vastness of the cargo bay and the constant murmur of the troops that seeped through the walls dampened the sound of Karstil's footsteps. The ship was never really silent, never really noisy. Occasionally, he heard an outburst of laughter or shouting, but it was impossible to establish a bearing before the empty space and the murmur engulfed the sound. Here in the womb of the *Tacitus*, Karstil was alone among thousands of men.

It was just at that moment of lonely silence that Karstil suddenly heard a sharp, metallic clank. He stopped short, his senses alert. It was not a loud noise, just different from what he was used to hearing. He waited in the semi-darkness for the sound to come again. It had come from the direction of his right front, he thought, from somewhere deep within the cargo bay. There! He heard it again.

Moving carefully and quietly, Karstil climbed onto the top of a Chuckwagon grav ammo carrier. The vehicle was built on a Viper hull, with the infantry compartment open to accept ammunition pallets. The ammunition system permitted an armored transport to carry various munitions virtually to the front lines. Though the Chuckwagon was only lightly armored compared to most combat vehicles, it was proof against most light missiles and infantry weapons. As the newer grav tanks were equipped with a quick-loading automatic feed system, a Deliverer grav tank could be resupplied with a full load of ammunition in less than a minute. Liberators, unfortunately, still required manual loading, and the entire crew had to be involved in stowing the 150mm and 50mm rounds.

From the top, Karstil had a reasonably good view of the stowage space. Light filtered down from the pierced decking that formed the rack above, casting a patchwork of illumination over the area. It was difficult to accurately identify shapes, but any movement would become obvious. He shrugged off the noise and was about to turn away when he heard it again.

This time, it came more as a grating squeak than the solid clanking he had heard before. As he searched the gloom for a better fix on the sound's location, he tried to remember where he had heard a similar noise. It sounded, he thought, like someone removing a large nut from rusted threads, and trying to do it quietly. It seemed to be coming from the rear of the bay.

Moving slowly and trying to keep out of the larger patches of light, Karstil crossed the

Chuckwagon to one of the smaller command vehicles. A large section of grav-modified administrative vehicles before the next section of ammo carriers would keep him completely hidden from anyone beyond the bulk of the carriers.

He crossed the valley, jumping from the top of one vehicle to the next, careful to examine the landing spot before launching himself across the intervening space. He didn't want to step through a canvas cover or stumble on a laser. He could have dropped to one of the access-ways between the rows of vehicles, but he felt that any movement there might alert his prey.

At the second section of Chuckwagon carriers, he stopped again, waiting for the sound so he could get a bearing and possible range. After what seemed an interminable wait crouched beside a command hatch, he heard the sound again. It was still the screech of threads on threads, but the direction had changed slightly, and it was closer than he had estimated. Alarm systems were going off in his head. He dropped on all fours and crawled carefully across the deck of another Chuckwagon.

Reaching the side of the carrier, he stretched down for a hand-hold on the vehicle to the rear. Grasping the central lifting shackle welded above the full-width cab, he crossed onto the roof. He looked down through the clear ceramic armored vision block to be sure there was no one in the cab looking up. I should have done that all along, he thought grimly. Well, too late now. A look-out in one of the vehicles will have spotted me by now.

He crouched on the cab and slowly lowered himself to his belly. For a fleeting moment, he had a feeling that whoever or whatever he was stalking was quite close. He could feel the hair on the back of his neck begin to rise, could feel perspiration breaking out under his coveralls. What am I doing here? he asked himself. There's probably nothing to it, and I should just go about my own business instead of snooping around.

He rejected the thoughts as quickly as they came, however. He had initiated the spy business by listening to Mullins and reporting it to Harras. That had made it his concern. He couldn't wash his hands of the affair just because it had passed on to higher authority. It was his duty to check this out. He inched his way to the crest of the upper hull and examined the clustered vehicles beyond.

He first scanned the entire area to be sure no one was standing close by. There was nothing immediately visible, much less threatening. He then started a careful search of the area. Close-range in sectors, sweeping from left to right. Again, nothing. He increased the range of his search, again doing it by small sectors, examining anything visible in the patchwork light. But he could not fully penetrate the gloom of the cargo deck, no matter how hard he tried. For almost five long minutes, he lay motionless on the top of the Chuckwagon with his eyes and ears wide open. His imagination began to play tricks on him. Huge figures seemed to loom in the eerie darkness; raucous screeches and heavy thuds filled his ears. But there was nothing there. Whatever that noise, it had stopped now.

"Come on, Karstil, get a hold of yourself," he muttered, sliding down slowly from the top of the carrier. Retracing his steps, he went back to his own tank.

He never saw the shapes of two men huddled on a Liberator tank in the gloom. Speaking to one another in low tones, their voices were almost lost in the vastness of the bay. One man seemed small, perhaps because of the significantly greater size of the other. The smaller man was kneeling on the front glacis of the tank, the larger man hunched down beside him. They kept below the left side of the turret in order to remain out of sight of anyone beyond. The larger man was curled over the rear of the 50mm cannon-5/6 laser mount.

Their work, whatever it was, was finished and they turned toward one another. They were dressed in special uniforms rather than the standard combat coveralls. The fabric was covered with varying dark splotches to break up the outline. The clothing covered the head, leaving only a small portion of the face exposed. The men had also applied camouflage to their face and hands. A large wrench, glinting softly through its own camouflage paint, moved over the gun mount. It was the sound of that movement that had attracted Karstil's attention.

The two men sprang softly to the last Liberator in the bay and stealthily worked their way around the front of the turret to the cannon-laser mount. The larger man applied the torque wrench to the rear of the mount and began to turn. The nut resisted, emitting the soft screech that Karstil had heard before. The nut removed, the large man extracted one of the accelerator coils from the breech of the weapon and handed it to his companion. He, in turn, examined the coil, using a small, pencil-thin beam of light that came from a hand-held torch. The examination complete, he handed it back to the first man, who replaced it and withdrew the other coil.

As the smaller man examined the second coil, the larger man rose slowly and scanned the other vehicles, searching for intruders. The search complete, he sank back down next to the weapon mount. He took the accelerator coil from the smaller man and replaced it, securing the locking nut.

The two men squatted close together, whispering. The smaller man seemed quite insistent, shaking his head and gesturing rapidly. The other man, squatting bear-like beside the turret, was unmoved. As he listened, he occasionally shook his head, as though in disagreement. The larger man said something, his deeper voice in marked contrast to the softer speech of the smaller.

Then the men parted company, moving off in opposite directions. The smaller man scuttled away across the tanks to the left, his form quickly lost in the gloom. The larger man remained for a moment, as though covering the departure of his accomplice. Then he, too, left the Liberator. His path took him alongside the Chuckwagon where Karstil had been standing only a moment before. The man continued toward the forward portion of the ship, no doubt well satisfied that his mission had been accomplished without detection.

17

For the last three days of the transit to Caralis, Karstil was seldom away from his Liberator. He even began to skip meals in order to spend time on or near his tank. Quentain Podandos was often there, too, preferring solitude and his novels to the gambling, which was the way most of those aboard spent their time. Karstil encouraged Podandos to sit on the top of the turret while he read; he even rigged a small light on the Vulcan III mount to provide the needed illumination. Meanwhile, he kept his nagging suspicions about the noises in the cargo bay to himself.

The fighting on Caralis, now centered on the planet's central continent of Alsatia, had been sporadic for the past ten weeks, while both TOG and the Commonwealth had pulled back for refit of Legions savaged in earlier combat. The Manus Primus, or First Primus, of the 2567th had been disbanded, with veteran elements shipped off-planet to distant Rilus for extensive refit after the devastating casualties they had suffered at the hands of the 3241st TOG Strike Legion.

Now both sides were attempting to reinforce the units still in combat on the planet's surface. Big battles were shaping up, and both TOG and the Commonwealth were rushing forces to the threatened area. The side that gained the initiative would secure the planet.

The Terran Overlord Government had first invaded Shannedam County nearly twenty years earlier, and had taken half its worlds. Among the currently contested planets, Caralis and Messana created a salient into TOG-controlled space. For that reason, both sides were intent on holding Caralis. TOG, because they wanted to clean up the area, and the Commonwealth because the planet served as a strategic link to the TOG-occupied worlds of Mysia and Tarraco.

The Commonwealth had been trying to keep the arrival of the 2567th's First Manus under wraps. After the *Tacitus* left Rilus, it made a short jump toward New Janos, but then broke out of T-space to make a sudden course-change for Caralis. The intention was to deceive TOG agents on Rilus about the Manus's actual destination, but rumor was that TOG was reinforcing Caralis and that there would be fighting as soon as the fleet broke into rational space near the planet. The Commonwealth was rushing a battle fleet to the area to cover the deployment of the First Manus. Life was going to become quite interesting.

On board the *Tacitus*, the gambling stopped, and the lines on the mess deck became shorter. The men spent more time with their equipment, checking what they could in the confined space. It was impossible to inspect the grav drives, but turret systems were checked and re-checked. Mullins and Karstil dismantled the cannon and laser systems, glad that the Liberator's weapons were externally mounted. It was impossible to inspect the well-protected weapons of the newer tanks in the cramped equipment bay. Their crews could only hope that nothing had gone wrong during the eight-day transit from Rilus.

The transition from T-space to rational space had to be carefully calculated. If it occurred too close to a planet, the ships might not have sufficient maneuvering space at the moment of breakout. Neither could the transition be made at too great a distance, for that would give the defenders an opportunity to detect the ship and to prepare and launch a counterstrike. A transport the size of the *Tacitus* and her destroyer consorts were splendid targets, and enemy fighters would be quick to swarm over them. No matter how fiercely the escort vessels protected their charge, they would not be able to stop all the fighters if the enemy were determined enough. The *Tacitus* had some weapons for her own defense, but they were no match for a squadron of fighters.

If the outer and inner hulls of the *Tacitus* were breached, the cargo bay would depressurize in minutes. Because of the bay's enormous size, however, it would take at least ten minutes to fully depressurize the hull from a 10-meter breach. That gave those well away from the breach plenty of time to prepare for the event. Those close to the opening, on the other hand, had better be well-prepared for depressurization.

Each of the fighting and support vehicles could be sealed against depressurization, the carplexy dome of the commander's hatch providing visual observation. For the administrative vehicles, each crewman was issued a battle suit that was completely closed, except for the neck and wrists. Carplexy helmets and special gloves could seal the suit, and the recirculation system built in could supply oxygen for fifteen minutes. The suits were similar to those worn by the crew of the *Tacitus*, except that the latter could recirculate air for up to two hours.

The transport was too large to land on the planet's surface, so the Manus would deploy from space some 90+ kilometers above ground. Special shuttles provided by the *Tacitus* would shuttle supplies to the planet. That was the most dangerous part of the launch. Grav tanks could be expected to survive a combat launch, diving for the surface. The shuttles, however, would be sitting ducks for enemy fighters as they waddled toward the planet.

All this was, of course, pure rumor. Though the men of the First Manus had yet to be briefed on the real situation on Caralis, horror stories about other launches began to circulate among them. Listening to the rumors, Karstil tried to evaluate them for possible clues about what to expect. The thought of battle at 90 kilometers above the planet's surface was not the way he had imagined his first introduction to combat. The idea of being caught in a disabled transport was especially unnerving. Karstil's Cohort was crammed into the rear of the *Tacitus*, with almost no chance of escape if the giant took disabling hits prior to launch. He could imagine the transport, its drives and control shot away, falling toward the planet. In his mind, Karstil saw the cargo doors blown open, the surface of the planet clearly visible through the jagged opening.

Falling from 90 kilometers would give everyone plenty of time to contemplate death on impact. He could almost hear the screams of the men as they tried to drive their vehicles toward the opening. The rush of atmosphere through the cargo bay would be deafening. Grav tanks would try to make the opening, but only the first few would make it. The others would become a mass piling up near the front. Damaged tanks would drift back through the bay, crashing into others that were trying to make the doors. The fall would take long minutes. Better to die in an incandescent flash during reentry than to crash on the surface.

"All personnel prepare for breakout." With a start, Karstil found himself back in reality. The communications system of the ship was received by all equipment as well as being broadcast on the repeaters throughout the bay.

Karstil swallowed hard as his stomach began to churn.

The brilliant white flash of transition from T-space to rational space penetrated every part of the giant cargo area, and Karstil felt the momentary falling sensation that always accompanied breakout.

"All personnel record 192 hours of T-space on their perscomps." Karstil had heard that command before, and he wondered at the men having to keep track of such information. He thanked his stars that he need not be concerned about it. Soon he would be planetside, where real was real, and he needn't worry about the deadly effects of too much time in T-space.

"Standard orbit will be accomplished in zero-eight minutes. Manus personnel prepare for launch." Karstil squirmed in his seat while waiting for more information on the situation. He wanted to know if he were going to make it to the planet safely.

He thumbed the platoon communications channel. "Report status."

"Two O.K." That was Mullins reporting in that he was locked and ready.

"Three O.K." Farwell in the rear tank was also set to go.

Karstil switched to the Century frequency and waited for Centurion Freund to request his status check. The reports were mostly unnecessary, though, because the Data Display Panel showed the current status of each of the tanks and APCs in the Century. They showed as bright blue squares for the tanks, triangles for the Viper APCs. Brilliant red triangles at the bottom of each mark showed that the vehicles were still secured to the transport's loading decks. As the inner doors came open, the restraining devices would be released in sequence from the front. It would not do to have vehicles floating around inside the cargo bay prior to the scheduled launch.

"Platoons report status. Roger in turn as I call your units." Freund's voice was calm over the speaker. He had been through this before and knew that a calm commander made for a calm command.

"Headquarters."

"Headquarters. Roger." That was the smooth yet firm voice of Sergeant Gortos reporting the administrative and support units ready for launch.

"Infantry."

"Infantry. Roger."

"First tank."

"First tank. Roger."

"Second tank."

Karstil pressed the push-to-talk switch on the joystick of his command seat and practically shouted into his headset, "Second tank. Roger."

"O.K., second tank, take it easy. We're not there yet. All commands have reported status O.K. Listening silence. Out." There would be no more chatter on the Century frequency until listening silence were lifted or contact with the enemy made.

Karstil settled back in the command seat and tried to relax. He glanced around the inside of the fighting compartment. Podandos was crouched over his gun sights, staring intently into his gunner's DDP. Feeling it his duty as team leader, Karstil reached over and tapped his gunner's shoulder. "Relax, Quentain. We're a long way from launch." Podandos smiled back, but the smile was strained and crooked. The gunner knew full well what combat was, and the disaster he had survived could not have left fond memories. I hope he pulls through, Karstil thought. Hell, I hope we all pull through.

Duncan Spint was almost invisible in the driver's station to the rear of the turret fighting compartment. Karstil could see his hands on the control-stick, the gloved fingers slowly clasping and unclasping. Spint was another survivor. Karstil knew he had been through a live—but not "hot"—orbital drop into a combat zone. He would be all right once he got the Liberator out the launch doors.

Karstil felt the *Tacitus* shudder, and he hoped it was only normal deceleration. Perspiration covered his body. He turned away so the gunner could not see his face.

"Launch point reached. Condition blue. Open outer doors." The *Tacitus* had made it to standard launch orbit at 90 kays, just in the fringes of Caralis' atmosphere. No enemy in scan range. Karstil felt some of his nervousness dissolve. His ears popped slightly as the pressure in the cargo bay began to decrease. The seals on the Liberator inflated with a satisfying thud. The transport ship shuddered again as the bow of the ship began to climb into its pre-launch attitude. "Condition blue. Open inner doors." Three hundred meters away, Karstil could see the giant clam-shell doors of the hull swing open to reveal the blackness of space. The nose of the *Tacitus* dropped slowly toward the planet, and the line of the horizon crept upward into the opening. Karstil felt the decks move as the hydraulic stanchions maneuvered to keep the rear areas level, while allowing the forward areas to point toward the planet. As each section was launched, the succeeding units would creep forward until they reached the seam between the level and the tilted decks. Once across the joint, launch would commence.

"This is *Tacitus*. Hand-off to Little Fish complete. Begin launch."

"Roger, *Tacitus*. Little Fish on internal control. Market Crowbar begin launch sequence." The Manus commander, or his designated representative, had ordered the First Manus to leave the *Tacitus* under its own control. As it cleared the doors, the other units would be launched. "Rendezvous at Navis Regal Kilo Ferax Three-Two-Four-Five." Karstil tapped the coordinates of the landing zone, NRKF3245, into the on-board navigational computer. Now, even if the entire crew were rendered unconscious during the launch, the Liberator would find its way home.

Far above the loaded decks, Commodore James Elwin prepared to launch his cargo. Time was the enemy now. The run from breakout toward the planet had been acomplished. All he had to do now was to kick the tanks out into space. And that was his problem.

The interface between space and atmosphere was 90 kilometers above the surface. The highest operational altitude for the grav-powered vehicles and the transports, the point at which their grav drives could bite the forces of gravity, was closer to 15 kilometers. (Launch could thus be acomplished at any altitude between 15 and 90 kilometers.) It was all a matter of time.

The *Tacitus* could enter the atmosphere and make the run from 90 to 15 at better than 300 kph, but that would put the big cargo carrier and her escorts in the edges of the atmosphere for fifteen minutes on the run in, and another fifteen on the run out. That was a lot of time to be wallowing around. Enough time to get fried by any enemy lurking in the area. Worse still would be to find TOG fighters waiting at 90 kilometers when the transport emerged from atmosphere. She would be moving slowly, a sitting duck for the high-speed interceptors shooting through the void. Better, he decided, to launch the vehicles from a distance, letting them free-fall toward their operational altitude.

As far as Karstil could tell, the launch was proceeding normally, with each of the commands creeping forward to the break in the deck and then sliding down toward the open doors. The lower decks were launched first, then the ones higher up in the bay. He could see light streaming down into the depth of the hold as the upper units ahead cleared their positions. All decks ahead and above had been cleared of vehicles, even the huge grav barges that held the additional supplies and support vehicles of the Manus.

"Barber Donkey, this is Little Fish. Begin launch sequence."

"Roger, Little Fish. Barber Donkey proceeding to launch point." The little red triangles that indicated the restraining gravs blinked out; the vehicles of the Cohort were free of the mother ship. Barber Donkey, the call sign for Milton Harras and his Cohort, was on its own. "Barber Donkey, Barber Donkey. Initiate grav sequence."

Karstil saw the blue squares and triangles turn orange as the grav drives in each of the Cohort vehicles fired up, saw them blink back to blue, showing successful initiation of the grav drives. He scanned the DDP for any sign of unknown or hostile targets. It really wasn't much of a search. The sensors had a maximum range of 50 kilometers, and anything attacking could close that distance in a flash.

Through the mottled darkness of the cargo bay, Karstil saw Centurion Freund's Liberator begin to move.

"Follow him out, Duncan. And stay as close as you can."

"I've got him on my screen, sir. I'll be welded to his butt all the way down."

"I don't need welded, Duncan. Close will do."

"Roger, sir."

With the other two tanks of the platoon following behind, Karstil led his troops out into the blackness of the troposphere 90 kilometers above brightside on Caralis.

Caralis, Shannedam County
The Commonwealth
30 December 6830

Karstil felt his stomach turn over as the tank passed through the outer doors of the *Tacitus* and began the 90-kilometer plunge toward the surface of Caralis. He glanced down and back at Spint, glad that the driver had only sensor screens. He would not feel the change from the comfortable cocoon of the transport to the unlimited view of the troposphere. Karstil, in the carplexy bubble over the command station, had a full view of the transition.

Ahead, the Century Commander's Liberator was sliding downward toward the planet. Karstil looked astern and saw the other Liberators emerging from the darkness of the hull into the brilliant light of brightside. The *Tacitus* was a rapidly diminishing shape that soon merged with the blackness of space.

"Little Fish, Little Fish." That was the *Tacitus* with something to say, probably a good-bye-and-good-luck statement. "Multiple unidentified craft. Four-zero-one-zero mils relative. Range, one-two-zero kilometers. Closing fast. Altitude nine-six and dropping."

Karstil peered over his left shoulder toward the relative bearing the *Tacitus* had given. At 120 kilometers, the intruders would not be visible, but his action was almost a reflex. He glanced back at the DDP, another useless gesture because they were still beyond the 50-kilometer range of the sensors.

"This is Barber Donkey. All units arm. Prepare to engage targets of opportunity."

Were they going to fight it out 85 kilometers above the planet?

Freund's Liberator went into a steeper dive, trying to reach the surface and the protecting umbrella of the Legion's Air Defense Century. Karstil felt his own tank tipping forward as Spint followed their leader down. The problems of gravitic drive were becoming apparent.

The Marshman Drive allowed an object to fall parallel to the surface rather than toward it. To accomplish this effect, the drive system had to be roughly perpendicular to the gravity gradient. As the angle between the drive unit and the gradient decreased, so did the effectiveness of the drive. This was not a problem when vehicles were close to the surface of a planet, as climbs and dives were relatively narrow and of limited duration. When a grav tank was launched in space, however, the problems of the gravity gradient angle became more acute. A dive of 85 to 90 kilometers was possible only at relatively shallow angles. It was the angle problem that made the controls feel mushy and unresponsive at high altitude.

When a grav-drive vehicle went into a dive from 85 to 90 kilometers, a new set of parameters entered the drive equation. The first parameter was the angle of dive of the craft and the relationship of that angle with the grav drive. The gravitics worked well as long as the angle of attack did not exceed 20 degrees. When the craft nosed down to a steeper angle, the grav drives became less and less effective until they became useless. At a dive angle of 45 degrees, the grav drive was only 50 percent effective. By the time the angle reached 55 degrees, the grav drive was ineffective. Grav-equipped spacecraft, such as the *Gladius* or the *Na'Ctka Moquka*, overcame the problem by the thrust of their engines. Grav tanks, on the other hand, had no thrust other than what the Marshman unit provided.

All this meant that the Liberator tanks were confined to a 20-degree safe-dive angle. To reach the surface of the planet at that angle required a horizontal traverse of approximately 270 kilometers. Even at maximum speed of 600 KPH, 10 kilometers each minute, it would require twenty-seven minutes to reach the planet. But to be safe from the attacking fighters, the tanks did not have to reach the surface. Somewhere between the edge of the troposphere and the ground was an umbrella of safety provided by the Legion's air defense units. The attacking fighters could operate at high speeds in the thin outer layers, but as they approached the thicker air below, the turbulence became too great for the structural integrity of their craft. They would either have to decelerate or risk having their wings torn from the hull. If the fighters reduced speed to operate in the thicker atmosphere, they would become targets for the air defense missiles. Speed was their primary defense.

Thus, the grav tanks did not have to complete the full 270-kilometer run to the planet to escape destruction. By the time they reached 10 or 15 kilometers, they were safe. But even a drop from 90 to 15 kilometers required twenty minutes. And that was plenty of time for the fighters to wreak havoc among the diving tanks.

The second parameter of the grav-tank launch was the relationship between the angle of attack, the speed of the tank, and the mass of the tank. It was possible to reach speeds in excess of 900 kilometers per hour while falling from 90 kilometers. But the greater the angle, the lower the safe speed. If a craft entered the lower reaches of the atmosphere at a 20-degree dive and 900 KPH, it would have difficulty regaining level flight before the ship's trajectory intersected the arc of the planet's surface. The result of this inadvertent intersection was severe deceleration trauma: grounding, augering in, crashing. It had a number of names, but the results were equally fatal.

The ideal angle and speed for descent was 10 degrees and 600 KPH. This angle required a run of about 90 kilometers, a distance that could be traversed in nine minutes. An angle of 20 degrees and 900 KPH could be reached, but closer to the surface, a shallower angle and a lower speed became necessary. There were warning systems within each vehicle that notified the commander and driver if the dive/speed parameters were being exceeded.

Karstil scanned the DDP for a sign of the incoming craft. If they were fighters, which was almost certain, they would be closing at speeds of about 3 kilometers per second. Assuming that the sensors picked up and identified the craft at maximum range, they would appear on the screen and cross it in thirty-three seconds. They would be in the 4,000-meter effective range of the 5/6 laser for just over a second. The gunner had to identify the target and lock on at the first opportunity. As the target closed, he had one second to get off a shot before the craft streaked by. There would be no opportunity to traverse the turret for a second shot as the attacker fled.

It would be possible to fire all the weapons except the TVLGs at the fighter as long as the craft were in a head-on attitude. Deflection shots of any kind would be pure luck and probably a waste of ammunition.

It had been only seconds since the warning from the *Tacitus*. Karstil glanced down at the angle of attack indicator and saw it creep past 15 degrees. The angle warning light began to pulse faster and faster as the angle increased. Initial speed had been a comfortable 300 KPH, and that, too, was increasing past the 500-mark. Karstil's eyes darted all over the control consoles as he strained to stay on top of the situation, as any good commander would.

Warning lights suddenly flashed across the DDP, and as the whole left side of the screen became flooded with yellow triangles. The computer identification system was designed to recognize ground vehicles, and so it would take some time before it cycled through all those. They were enemy, and that was all that concerned Karstil. For a few seconds, he sat staring at the approaching blips on the screen. Then he swung into action. He traversed the turret to the left, lining up the weapon systems to coincide with the trajectory of the oncoming fighters.

Well away from the falling tanks, a deadly ballet was taking place. Renegade and Commonwealth interceptors and corvettes, launched by the escort ships or rising from the planet, formed up to interpose themselves between the vulnerable grav vehicles and the enemy fighters. Karstil looked out and saw a momentary bright flare against the black; someone would not be going home. But try as they would, the defenders could not keep all of them from breaking through to the streaming reinforcements bound for Caralis.

"Target identified," the computer called out calmly. "Data follows." Information on the enemy craft scrolled across the targeting computer screen. First came a name: "Pilum." More data on the fighter followed, but Karstil didn't care what it could or could not do. The fact that it was hostile was all he needed to know right now.

A three-view diagram of the *Pilum* followed, the drawings dissolving into a single plan-silhouette in the lower right of the screen. Other information framed the screen, indicating the range to target and the closing speed. The distance was still too great to paint or lock onto the target. Karstil jockeyed the turret, keeping the target centered in the computer screen. As the range closed to firing distance, he would hand over control of the turret and weapons to Podandos.

"He's coming fast, Quent, but it'll be a straight bow shot. He's all yours."

"Roger, sir. I've got him."

"Spint."

"Sir."

"Hold her steady. Keep the angle where it is. As soon as Quent fires, increase dive. We'll try to dodge the others. Be prepared for recoil. I'll keep the turret left-side until they're all past."

"Wilco."

"Quent. Fire everything at the same time. Recoil from the cannon may throw off your other shots."

"Wilco."

Karstil pressed down on the treadle, activating the painting laser. Flicker shields on fighters didn't change, so once painted, the target would be identified forever. The laser reached out beyond the 4,000 meter effective range, probing the shields of the fighter.

The distant targets were in visual range now, and Karstil's heart raced as he watched the slim silhouettes of the *Pilum*s growing ominously larger. The wing-mounted lasers and bow-mounted mass driver cannons on the *Pilum*s winked light as they opened on the falling tanks. There were at least two groups of four or more fighters, strung out in loose columns. The closer column was headed straight for Karstil's Century, the other was higher and attacking one of the units in the rear. The Liberator quivered as a mass-driver slug penetrated the shields and tore a chunk of titanium armor from the left-rear access panel above the steering vane.

"Target painted. Lock achieved," said the steady voice of the computer.

He waited for three seconds. "Let 'em have it!"

Karstil felt the 273 metric tons of the Liberator tremble as three turret-mounted weapons fired together. Podandos had locked the firing switches down so that all he had to do was activate the master fire control. That was not standard procedure, but it worked.

Through the carplexy bubble, Karstil saw the lead fighter glow red across its nose as the shots from his guns struck home. The Liberator dropped precipitously as Spint went into a steeper dive, the angle warning light going bright red as the pitch exceeded the 20-degree safe angle. Then the *Pilum* was past them in a flash, and the others were boring in on the rest of the Century.

Ahead, the Viper APCs were taking hits, and Karstil could see the sparkle of light on the portside armor of the trailing carrier. The Vipers were firing back, but their 25mm cannon was almost useless against the speeding fighters. They were firing more for their own morale and the hope that the 25mm slugs would harass the enemy pilots than because the shots were effective against their adversaries.

When Karstil looked astern, he realized it was the first time he had checked on the other tanks of his platoon. Absorbed in his own Liberator's fight, he had been too busy to try to control the fire of the whole unit. Now Karstil saw that one of the tanks was missing, Farwell's Number Three. He made a quick scan of the DDP and identified Farwell. The vehicle had fallen back during the dive, and rather than try to catch up, Farwell had attached himself to one of the trailing Centuries. Stay where you are, thought Karstil. You'd be a sitting duck all alone if you tried to join us.

More enemy fighters appeared on the screen, at higher altitudes than the swarm that had hit them. They were taking on the rear Centuries, leaving the leaders to plunge into the safety of the heavier atmosphere. The dive warning light continued to glow, and Karstil looked down at the angle indicator. Thirty-five degrees!

"Spint! Level off!" Karstil tried to control his voice, but his shout cracked slightly.

"I'm working on it, sir. I'm working on it."

"Get it under control!"

"She won't pull up."

"She's got to."

The speed indicator went past 850.

Somewhere above and to the rear, a column of *Pilum* fighters was savaging a Liberator. Karstil could see flashes of light against the darkness of space as titanium armor vaporized under the pounding of multiple lasers and mass drivers. His own tank quivered as Spint fought the control stick in an attempt to bring the tons of hurtling equipment under control. Karstil watched helplessly as the angle indicator began to drop in a steeper dive: 34...33...32...The altimeter was rolling downward with alarming speed, past 39,000 meters and still dropping.

The Liberator to the rear was in trouble. The pounding by the *Pilum*s had caught her from the bottom, smashing the grav drives and helm controls. With no power and no controls, the Liberator rolled over and began a vertical plunge toward the planet. From 50,000 meters, the fall would take ten minutes. If the fall were accomplished in a vacuum, it would take just under four, but even a Liberator tank reaches a terminal velocity where it cannot fall any faster. This gave any crewmen still alive plenty of time to contemplate their impending deaths.

The wounded tank plummeted past Karstil's tank. He could see the smashed grav coils hanging from the under-side of the vehicle. The turret had been hit, and the rear fuselage was jagged and glowing red. Scraps from the shattered hull peeled away, leaving a ghostly trail of burning parts as the ship hurtled to certain death. I hope they're all dead, thought Karstil. If I have to go, make mine quick and clean.

Karstil looked back down at his driver. "Any time now, Mr. Spint."

"I...don't...know, sir," Spint said through gritted teeth as he fought with the control stick. "She...isn't...responding..."

Throughout the tank, warning bells were blaring. This is it, Karstil thought and closed his eyes. This is it.

The next thing he knew, the heavy shoulder straps were digging into his shoulders. It felt like a hundred men were pushing him from behind. That could mean only one thing. The tank's boosters had kicked in, allowing Spint to pull out of the dive.

Opening his eyes, he saw that the angle warning light had ceased its steady glow. It was only blinking sporadically now. The indicator showed 20 degrees and decreasing. The speed indicator was dropping through 650 KPH. Spint had gained control. The altimeter showed

8,000 meters, well below the safe altitude and under the air-defense umbrella of the Legion. Karstil gulped in a breath of air and felt the tension drain from his body. He suddenly felt chilled, the perspiration going cold on his skin. His hands began to shake uncontrollably, and he felt his stomach rumble. Glancing up, he saw that the landing-zone coordinates were still posted in the computer, and so he switched the controls to automatic. The Liberator responded with a slow turn to the right as it searched for the designated location and picked up the landing beacon on its way to a smooth, pinpoint landing.

When it was finally over and the tank had come to a halt, Karstil looked at his two crewmen, Podandos and Spint.

Podandos spoke up first. "Congratulations, sir. You just made your first hot jump."

Spint smiled and gave the traditional thumbs-up.

At this, Karstil wiped his dripping brow. "Piece of cake."

The laughter echoed throughout the tank.

BOOK II
POWER UP

19

Alsatia, Caralis
The Commonwealth
2 January 6831

The falling light softened the outlines of the tanks and supporting vehicles that surrounded the open field. The equipment of the Century, like that of the other five Centuries in the Cohort, was dispersed over a wide area, making the unit a less lucrative target to any air or Thor-satellite attack. A meeting of all Cohort officers had been scheduled for 2100 hours, just after twilight, and Karstil made his way from his platoon to the Century Headquarters, where transport to Cohort Headquarters was to rendezvous.

The Cohort was organized for all-round defense, with the five medium Centuries in a roughly pentagonal perimeter around the Cohort Headquarters. The light Century and headquarters personnel were in the center. Each side was 10 to 15 kilometers long, the pentagon itself 20 kilometers across. The Second Century defended in the usual manner, tank platoons on the wings, the infantry centered and to the rear around the Century Headquarters.

The four Manuses of the Legion were ringed around the Legion Headquarters. Because the Manus Primus of the 2567th had twenty-two combat Centuries, compared to twelve in the others, it occupied more ground and was oriented toward the enemy. The Legion as a whole occupied a zone 65 kilometers wide, an area of nearly 4,000 square kilometers. Transport through the Legion zone was provided by the 2567th's Supply and Transport Manuses. To move large numbers of troops lacking their own vehicles, the Supply Manus provided unarmored grav transports, sarcastically referred to as "cattle cars." For moving smaller numbers of men, Asinus grav vehicles could transport six men in relative comfort, ten if packed in, and up to twelve in a crunch. It was in one of these that Karstil would ride.

By the time the Asinus reached Century Headquarters, it held nine men, eight officers and the driver. The four officers of the Century had crammed in as best they could, but one Optio had to ride on the outside. As junior officer of the Century, Karstil won that privilege. Centurion Freund, of course, was in a front seat, while Holden Ventis, Infantry Platoon Leader, and LaTonta Broast, the other Tank Platoon Leader, squeezed into the cargo compartment. Ventis and Boast both had less time in service than Karstil, but had been Renegades longer. Because only Renegade time counted in the eyes of the Renegades, Karstil was what veterans liked to call "the junior balloon." He understood the rules of seniority, and said nothing while climbing on top of the Asinus.

The headquarters tent at Cohort was crowded with other officers by the time the Asinus sled arrived. Karstil's hands were stiff and sore from gripping the stanchions that held the canvas cover on the cargo compartment. The air of the tent was thick with conversation, most of it concerning the TOG fighter-attack on the way in. Harras's Cohort had not sustained any permanent damage, for the lost Liberator was assigned to one of the other Cohorts of the Manus. Some of the vehicles had taken damage, however, and Cohort maintenance personnel had been in a flurry of repairs over the past two days. Still, the orbital drop onto Caralis had given many men a fresh taste of battle, and already the war stories were flying.

There was also a rumor that some tanks had experienced mysterious equipment failures during the drop. The most common was failure of the DDPs to acquire the enemy craft during their run in. All computers were being checked with clones of TOG transponders. Though none had been found deficient, checks were continuing. As the junior of junior officers, Karstil was not included in most of the conversation. Even Holden and LaTonta had friends here from Renegade Officers' Training, and they were quickly absorbed in the crowd of others. That didn't bother Karstil much. He knew his place here and was content to keep his mouth shut and his eyes and ears open.

As the Cohort staff entered the tent, the assemblage fell silent. After a brief introduction by an anonymous Administration Officer, the Operations Officer took over the briefing. Centurion Moldine Rinter was a small, dark-haired, energetic woman who seemed to fix each officer with her sharp gaze. She spoke without recourse to notes, and her grasp of the myriad minutiae that went into an operation was impressive. She began with the facts and figures about Caralis, most of which they had heard before.

Caralis was the third planet in the system and the only one capable of supporting Human life. Its equatorial diameter was 40,900 kilometers, with a circumference of 128,490 kilometers. The surface was 55 percent water, 45 percent land, making nearly half the planet arid. After the fight for Caralis had begun three years before, the world's population had shifted to Rolandrin, the Commonwealth-controlled western continent. The bulk of the 2567th Legion had also been moved to secure bases on Rolandrin while the Manus Primus was being rebuilt on Rilus. Once the Manus was scheduled to rejoin the Legion, the rest of the 2567th had returned to the embattled Alsatian continent. It was they who had secured the landing zone for the drop.

Only scattered farming or mining centers remained on Alsatia, though the great deserts in portions of the interior had kept it from ever being densely inhabited. The population of Caralis's third and easternmost continent, Malthus, had been evacuated long ago. Malthus had fallen to TOG early on in the struggle, and now served as the enemy's base of operations.

The really important part of the briefing discussed Caralis's location in relation to the nearby habitable worlds. The Caralis-Messana salient pushed well into the TOG areas of Shannedam County, almost to the border of Keserdal County. By holding the salient, the Commonwealth and Renegade forces could threaten the flanks of any further TOG expansion into Shannedam as well as Pembroke County. After three years of continuous fighting on Caralis, however, neither side had been able to drive the other offworld.

Currentl / deployed on Alsatia and waiting to square off were, on one side, the Renegade Legion's 2567th Infantry Legion as well as the Commonwealth 2031st Strike and 354th Armored Legions. TOG Legions included the 3241st and the dreaded 13379th, the Harbingers of Death. In addition, unconfirmed reports had the 149th Praetorian Guard, a Theater Reserve unit for TOG, landing on the continent of Malthus and preparing for transport.

Because of the 2567th's hard-luck reputation, it would be committed one Manus at a time to a relatively quiet sector. Each Manus would defend a portion of the front anywhere from 100 to 500 kilometers, where it would carry out limited offensive missions. As the Manus became combat-experienced, it might be rotated back for a rest while another Manus took its place. The Manus Primus would act as the Legion reserve, its Cohorts defending small portions of the front until each Manus had some experience. In this way, the 2567th would gain combat experience before the the the entire Legion was expo. d. From the Manus Primus,

Cohort Harras was to be the first in.

Karstil reacted with pleasure to that news, for it meant the waiting was over. No more sitting around listening to the rumors about what was happening. They would go in to give and get their licks right away.

Continuing with the briefing, Centurion Rinter informed them further about the terrain and the enemy. The area chosen for the Cohort was barren, except for steep ravines, razor-sharp ridges, and scrub brush. There was limited rolling terrain where defensive operations could be conducted with ease. Supply transport was not especially difficult because all the unit's vehicles were grav-equipped. Reports indicated that the terrain was only lightly held. Enemy strong points could be expected in the rolling areas, but with great voids between.

TOG units could be expected to defend fiercely until overwhelmed, then fall back to the next important land feature. The rough terrain meant that there would be numerous, covered avenues of approach to most of the objectives that would hide an attacker. But those same features offered the prepared and forewarned defender the chance for ambush. Attacks would be conducted with "the maximum speed commensurate with safety." Karstil knew that catch-all meant that if you were slow, you'd be chastised, and if you got caught, you were moving too fast. He could see the Century commanders squirming at the statement.

When Centurion Maximus Harras took over the meeting, he talked a different war. Gone were any of Rinter's cautions about safety. It was her job to point out the problems, and Harras's to pump up the troops. He did the job well. There would be no automatic criticism for those whom the TOG defenders took by surprise. Harras said the Cohort would push and push and push, reinforcing the deepest thrusts and depending on speed and surprise to keep TOG elements confused.

With the Centurion's every word, Karstil could feel the excitement and confidence building within himself and among his fellow officers. He was almost ready to cheer when Harras finally took his seat. The conference broke up, with the officers hurrying out to catch transport back to their Centuries. Movement to the front would begin on the morrow, and many plans had to be covered with the troops before dawn. The leaders would sleep very little this night.

Officers and NCOs gathered in small groups all through the Cohort. Maps displaying the current situation glowed from computer screens. Each Century commander had received special chips with geographical intelligence on the sector, and the information would be downloaded to the other vehicles of the command. Soon each tank and APC would have an up-to-date report on file in the fighting compartment. Cohort Intelligence would post new reports as they came in, transmitting them to the vehicles of the command once they had been evaluated. Those not involved in the meetings checked their vehicles and bedded down for as much sleep as they could manage.

The tiny Equus grav sled eased its way out of the Legion Headquarters area and moved slowly across the 25 kilometers that separated it from Manus Secundus. The driver and his passenger did not speak. All active sensors were shut down, with only the passive thermal sights used to navigate the vehicle.

At the edge of the Manus area, the driver slowed the Equus and descended into a gorge. After the vehicle dropped down out of sight, the driver and passenger dismounted and covered the Equus with a special anti-thermal shroud. The transport sled would be invisible to both visual and sensor scans. The only way to find it was if someone stumbled onto it.

Both men quickly donned camouflage coveralls that obscured all but the face and hands. Then they painted themselves darkly to break up the outline of the still-exposed areas. Taking equipment packs from the rear of the vehicle, they strapped them to their backs. Having completed the change of uniform, the two men crept up out of the gorge and headed toward the perimeter of the nearest Century.

As they approached the camp, they dropped to a crouch, then to hands and knees, and finally to a crawl. Using the concealment of every bush and outcropping of rock, they passed through the perimeter, penetrating to the headquarters bivouac site. The men of the Century, crossing between vehicles and command tents, passed within meters of the intruders without being aware of their presence. At last, the pair gained their objective, the Century's command and communications vehicle.

The vehicle was in a shallow crater whose lip had been smoothed to allow access to the vehicle. The intruders rolled down the side of the crater away from the entrance and wormed their way under the external shroud. Once they were under the vehicle, the grav drives and helm control were exposed. Working purely by feel in the dark, the men reached the starboard helm and vane control.

The access panel to the control vane was secured by four spring-loaded thumb-nuts that turned easily. The larger man removed the panel, placing it carefully on the ground next to his compatriot. He then grappled among the mass of control cables and junctions until he found the heavier cable that carried the instrument commands to the vane. The second man switched on a small heat source, sending a pencil-thin beam of thermal radiation into the mass of wires. His companion's special infrared glasses allowed him to see the profusion of cables as though in full light. He carefully separated the bundle, choosing only one. Holding that cable firmly in his right hand, he reached into his equipment shoulder pouch and extracted a finger-sized tube. Using his teeth, he stripped the protective coating from the tube, exposing an adhesive-backed strip.

Holding the bundle apart to keep the selected cable exposed, the man pressed the tube against the cable, the adhesive bonding the two. With the tube in place, and still holding the cable, the man extracted a needle-thin probe from the top of the tube and forced it through the protective covering of the large cable. The tube emitted a soft beep, and a red light in the top came on for an instant. The man carefully pressed the cable back into its bundle, pushed the others back around it, and then replaced the access panel.

The finger-sized tube was a powerful explosive, the probe its fuse. The bomb would sit quietly in the bundle of cables, recording every thrust change sent to the vane. At some future time, the probe would have counted high enough to satisfy the pre-programmed command, and the bomb would go off. The explosion would destroy the vehicle's ability to respond to directional commands. If it occurred during combat, the unexpected loss of control would be disastrous. No evidence of tampering was apparent from either the bottom of the panel nor even inside once it was opened.

The two men retraced their steps to the Equus, where they reversed the procedure they had followed earlier. They removed the paint first, then the uniforms, and finally the shroud for the vehicle. Seated in the Equus, they fired up the grav generators and switched on the active sensors. From now on, if anyone spotted and stopped them, they were just two members of the Legion Maintenance Cohort returning from a spot inspection. To further buttress their disguise, they chose a Century at random and did conduct a spot-check of the sensors systems in three fighting vehicles, just in case they were questioned.

As it turned out, the saboteurs were in and out and no one ever suspected a thing. Having done a good night's work, they were back with Legion Headquarters in time for breakfast.

20

Alsatia, Caralis
The Commonwealth
3 January 6831

Cohort Harras hit its Start Point right on schedule. The Renegade Cohort started advancing in a diamond formation, the light Century leading, a medium Century at each of the other three corners, and two medium Centuries surrounding the Cohort command. This was a formation for use when contact with the enemy was imminent but his strength and location were unknown. Though the Cohort was behind the current front line, Harras had chosen this formation to reinforce the attitude that the unit was now in it for real. Being in friendly territory, the Cohort might just as easily have adopted a column formation for its move. A column was easier to control because it was merely an exercise in follow-the-leader.

With the Cohort diamond formation, the wings spread 20 kilometers from the center, the unit swept the terrain of any enemy. Any Century that made contact with the enemy would turn and attack at once. The Cohort would realign itself on the fighting Century, maneuvering the new flank Centuries around the pinned enemy. The trailing Centuries would then become the reserve. It was a perfect formation for meeting an enemy, and it had been practiced by various armies for over six thousand years.

The march was uneventful, and the Cohort hit the Release Point on time. As the Centuries cleared the RP, they broke out of the diamond formation and moved up to join the 2031st within 5 kilometers of the front lines, the Centuries now under direct command of the Cohort rather than the Legion. Occupation of all forward positions would take place a Century at a time under cover and observation of the trailing Centuries already-hull down in a defensive posture.

To relieve a force in place was a difficult operation because it gave the enemy a chance to take advantage of the normal confusion by a preemptive strike. That was one reason the trailing Centuries were where they were, far enough to the rear not to come under fire, but close enough to engage quickly if needed.

Karstil's Century was on the left of the line, and his platoon, the second tank, was on the left of the Century. He grounded his Liberator behind a slight rise and watched the other two tanks ground 400 meters to the left and right, slightly forward of his position. With this deployment, it was not necessary to fire the digging cannon because the crest of the hill provided adequate hull-down protection. Once the flank tanks were down and set, Karstil ordered Spint to back the Liberator down the slope until it was in full turret defilade. There, he could see and cover both flanking tanks as well as see to the front. But the tank would not be a viable target for anyone attacking from the front. That would allow him room to maneuver if necessary, able to bring his weapons to bear on the threatened sector before the Liberator became a target.

An hour later, one of the trailing Centuries approached Karstil's position, led by a guide from the 2031st. The guide was lounging on the turret of the lead Liberator, a study in nonchalant boredom. He showed mock terror to see that Karstil had rotated his turret to the rear and was tracking the oncoming formation. Karstil waved, and the guide waved back. The tank commander, a consummate professional, took no notice of this exchange. The guide took on the same attitude as the tank moved past, silently mocking the TC's stern appearance. Then he leered a "you'll be sorry" at Karstil as they passed 10 meters away.

The relieving unit included an Armored Personnel Carrier whose smaller bulk occupied the third position in the column of four vehicles. The infantry was riding on the outside of the Viper, acting more like tourists than men about to enter combat. But that was typical of infantrymen, who loved to act as if no danger existed. If a tanker's life was likely to be short and violent, that was even more true for infantry. With only the thin armor of the Viper between them and instant death, they often chose to ride outside their vehicles if possible. Most of them would rather take their chances outside the APC, which they referred to as a titanium coffin, trusting to their own luck and agility to escape hostile fire. They thought of their carriers as armored buses, and didn't like the fact that the driver, gunner, and commander inside actually thought of the Viper as a light tank.

"Think of this as a bus," had commented Ventis when Karstil had first seen the Century's infantry vehicles. "If I had my druthers, I'druther they took all the weapons off the thing. My drivers keep looking for something to kill with the damn thing. Not me. I want to do my fighting on the ground. They bury and decorate infantry pedes one at a time. They bury and decorate tankers in groups of three."

Tankers, Karstil knew, had a tendency to sneer at the infantry: poor, dumb ground-pounders. In the case of the Liberator, the thought of 273 tons of titanium armor and ceramic shielding hurtling over the ground at speeds in excess of 200 KPH was impressive. The poor pedes slogged along at considerably less speed, working their weary way across every bit of terrain. But that had its advantages. Men assigned to grav tanks were never done with the work those iron monsters required. It was a constant round of maintenance and repair, testing and sighting, that took time, and time, and time. The crews would be up all night in preparation for the next day. Not so the pedes.

Once the Vipers were down in a defensive position, the infantry could bed down, too. Cleaning personal weapons and checking the TVLGs or mortars took almost no time at all. Then they could sleep, secure in the knowledge that the APC crew was doing the maintenance on the beast. If the pedes and the vehicle commander were on good terms, they might lend a hand at the maintenance, however. The Vipers were ready to go in one-tenth the time of a Liberator. Infantry had its advantages.

The last of the relieving tanks disappeared over a rise of ground a thousand meters ahead, leaving the landscape as barren as before. The ground was open and rolling, giving way to sharp gorges some fifteen hundred meters to the left. Karstil was worried about that area, and he would have liked to have an infantry squad to stick on his flank. The worry was unfounded because the enemy could not possibly penetrate that far to the rear without being spotted by one of the forward units. But it was good practice to worry. It was what an Optio was supposed to do.

"Hasty Warbler Two-two-six, this is Hasty Warbler Six." The commlink crackled to life. "Hasty Warbler" was the Century call sign. "Six" was Centurion Freund. "Two-two-six" was Karstil. "Hasty Warbler" seemed appropriate for Freund, thought Karstil.

"Warbler Six, this is Warbler Two-Two-Six."

"Two-two-six, this is Six. Commence OPLAN Capto on my order."

"Two-two-six. Wilco."

Operational Plan C called for the Century to withdraw to a night laager 15 kilometers to the rear. There the Century would prepare for tomorrow's operation, probably a passage of lines and an attack. Karstil wondered at the use of phonetic names for letters. They were supposed to reduce confusion so that letters like "cee," and "bee," and "tee" would not be confused over the commlink. Thus, each letter had a name: "cee" became "Capto," "bee" became "Bellum," and "tee" became "Toga." Learning the letters was all part of training— learning military-code. The cynics called it "milspeak."

Karstil reached down and extracted a red flag from its holder to the right of his command hatch. He placed the flag in a socket, an unauthorized modification, on the turret. The other tanks should be watching his, and as soon as he saw red flags flying from their turrets, he would know that they were. The flag system was an idea of Mullins for establishing communications without use of the commlink or the laser torch. It, like the hand signals, showed that the platoon was a unit.

The red flags appeared almost immediately, indicating that the other tank commanders were paying attention to Karstil. He stood in the hatch and flashed a quick code with his hand laser to indicate that the platoon was about to move, pointing in the direction of the new objective and blinking the formation the platoon was to use.

"Hasty Warbler Two-two six, this is Hasty Warbler Six. Execute."

Six, this is Two-two-six. Wilco."

Karstil raised the hand laser over his head and saw the grav drives of the other tanks kick in, bringing the Liberators to a one-meter hover. He dropped his arm, and the other tanks turned to follow him out of the defensive position.

104

21

Alsatia, Caralis
The Commonwealth
3 January 6831

The long night had been filled with activity. Everything had to be checked and re-checked. Ammunition for the main and secondary weapons, power packs and coils for the lasers, racks and tracking systems for the missiles. Grav drives had been powered up and tested, Terrain Sensing and Reaction circuits checked. Everything was checked, and then re-checked. Each tank commander inspected and checked his own tank. Then the platoon sergeants checked the vehicles, then the platoon leaders, and finally the Centurions. No one got any sleep, and if he did, it was only a cat nap. Everyone was nervous. Tempers were short.

For many of the men of the Century, this would be the first time in full combat. Some were silent, deep in thought about what the sunrise would bring. Others were surly, snapping back at real or imagined criticism from their peers and scowling at their superiors. A few were boisterous and full of pep, lending a hand to any task, ever looking for something to do. All were scared.

Umbartis, gunner for Karstil's Number Three, was one of the boisterous ones, his speech filled with "no problem," and "piece of cake." He worked on his own tank and then volunteered to help with the others. At some point in the middle of the night, he wandered into the infantry platoon and gave the Viper crews a hand at loading their 25mm ammunition and missiles. Mullins had to find him and drag him back to the tank platoon. "No problem, Sergeant," had been his response when Mullins chewed him out. "Just giving the poor pedes a hand with their stuff. We're all in this together. No problem."

Mullins watched him disappear into the darkness on his way back to his own tank. That man, he thought, would bear watching. It was the cheerful ones who usually cracked first. He made a mental note to have a word with Sergeant Farwell before they moved out in the morning. Tank crews were too small to have one of the men go bonkers in the middle of a fight. With Umbartis burning off all his energy now, he would have little left when dawn came. Mullins had seen men, keyed up at the thought of combat, fall asleep at the first contact with the enemy.

Graff Kloun, Farwell's driver, was surly. Any suggestion that something in the drive and navigational system needed to be checked brought an instant, violent response. A short, blond man with bulging muscles, he was one of the youngest in the platoon. He loved his tank and the feeling of power it gave him. He would rather drive the tank through an obstacle than go around or over it. He fumed and fretted over the tank, and the "let's-be-happy" attitude of Umbartis obviously rubbed him the wrong way. After one too many replies of "No problem" from Umbartis, Kloun turned on him, grasping a wrench in one massive hand. "Don't 'no problem' me. One more crack out of you, and I'll put a crease in your head." Kloun's hazel eyes blazed, and Umbartis, sensing that there was a fight in the offing, backed away.

Franklin Grouse and Sedgewick Abul, gunner and driver, respectively, of Number Two, were silent. Like Mullins, both had seen tank combat before, and so knew that the best they could do was be prepared. Mullins would take care of the tank and them; they would survive. But even within that sanctuary of resignation, the two men did not sleep. They, like the others in the platoon, the Century, the Cohort, knew that the rising sun would propel them from the safety of the bivouac area into the violent world of the quick and the dead.

Every time he stopped doing something, Karstil felt his stomach churn. Lurking like some fearsome beast at the back of his mind was fear of the morrow. As long as he was inspecting a tank, or loading ammunition, or issuing orders, or talking to a platoon member, the beast remained safely caged in his brain. But when activity stopped, the beast would pounce, wrapping its talons around his stomach. At times, even the flurry of activity was not enough to ward off the beast, and it would strike him in the mid-sentence.

Karstil was afraid of two, completely unrelated things that worked together to drive the cold sweat to the surface of the skin. He was afraid of the tanks. All that titanium and ceramic armor gave a feeling of invulnerability, but he knew it was a false sense of security. At Officer's Training and again in the transition course to the Renegade Legion, he had seen often enough a demonstration of the deadly effect of Gauss cannon and heavy lasers.

The training Sergeants had been proud of the fact that a 150mm cannon could tear its way through huge amounts of armor, spraying the inside of a tank with deadly droplets of molten titanium and shards of fractured ceramic. He had seen holovids of tank combat, in which the armored monsters were reduced to infernos from which there was no escape. In one of these, a crew was trying to flee from a tank that was hit and on fire. The commander was still in his hatch, the figure almost obscured by the great gouts of flame leaping out of the turret. The body hung there, its arms waving in the rising heat. The man was obviously dead, but the heat continued to move the body as if it were alive. The commander was beckoning toward the camera as if urging the photographer to join him on his pyre. Karstil shuddered every time he thought of it.

Make it clean, he thought. Make it clean. Those horribly shattered and charred bodies he had seen at the base hospital so long ago. Those men, stoic under anesthesia and pseudo-skin, that he and General Gentrund P. Beldarnus had visited. They would recover, someone told him, and be as good as new. But at what cost in pain? A quick, clean kill would be preferable. Or would it? Dead was not better than anything. Medical magic could do wonders even to the most horribly mangled body. At least those men had survived. He was only twenty years old; he had so much ahead of him.

Death was not the only fear. He was also afraid of failure. If he had only to worry about himself, Karstil felt he could face the day with composure. But the idea of somehow letting the others in the platoon down terrified him. He was the one making the decisions that would send the other tanks into combat. He had failed to control the platoon during the brief fight high above the planet. Would he fail on the ground as well? And what if he were the only survivor? How could he live with himself, knowing that it was his mistake that killed eight other men? What if his failure caused the whole Century to be destroyed?

He tried to envision the problems that could occur during the attack. For the passage of lines, there was no problem if the others were ready for it. He would form the platoon into a vee, with his tank in the center. He would put Mullins on the dangerous flank nearest the enemy position. It was a hell of a way to treat the Platoon Sergeant, but the job had to go to someone. Better to put the best man at the point of danger. But should he take the flank? There was the philosophy that a commander should never ask a man to do something he would not do himself. Should he take the lead in a wedge, the other tanks to the rear and guarding the flanks? That would put him at the most critical point, an heroic thing to do, but he might lose control of the platoon. No, he thought, the vee was the best. He would be in the center rear.

And what kind of enemy would they face? He hoped for tanks, which was something he could handle. If the intelligence reports were correct, they would outnumber TOG at the point of contact. That meant that more of them would be shooting at fewer of the enemy. He who shoots first, wins. That had been doctrine at school and on the tank range. Get the target painted, and then blow it away. Shoot only at painted targets, no matter what the range. Everybody shoot at the painted target—and hope that you were not painted yourself. If luck rode on your turret, you would survive.

"Shoot the painted target. Shoot the painted target," he mumbled to himself as he walked through the platoon laager.

"Excuse me, sir. What did you say?" It was Quentain Podandos, looming out of the darkness.

"Shoot the painted target, gunner."

"Roger that, sir."

The first faint rays of sun were painting the sky a luminescent pink. Trees, tanks, and men began to emerge from the stygian dark that had enveloped them like a comforting shroud. Grav drives on tanks still hidden among the small trees whined into life. Tank crews rolled up the thermal camouflage tarps that had draped their vehicles during darkness, making them all but invisible to the prying eyes of the orbital stations. Karstil felt the beast grab at his guts once more, his knees suddenly weak, his mouth dry. "Mount up, second tank. Let's go!"

There had been no need for the command, all the other members of the platoon had long since mounted. The grav drives came to life, dust spewing from under Tanks Two and Three as they rose to a one-meter hover. Only his own tank was still grounded, waiting like the armored charger of some knight five thousand years earlier.

Karstil looked around the bivouac area. Where there had been men scurrying about in desperate activity, now there were only hovering tanks and the scream of grav drives powered up to maximum, straining to be let free. A fatigue cap skittered across the ground, propelled by the rising morning breeze and the turbulence of the gravitic forces, unseen but still at work. The full morning sun sent its slanting rays across the far reaches of the plain, illuminating the gray-green monsters that wavered atop their piles of gravitational waves, tons of titanium suspended on an unseen cushion of primeval energy.

The tanks of the platoon rotated slowly to face where the Optio stood. Like giant pachyderms, the tanks slowly turned and bowed to their commander. The cannon, like extended trunks that seemed to sniff at this tiny, insignificant human in their midst, came closer and closer. Karstil turned to his own mount, still calm and docile on the ground. He moved between the twin lateral bow sponsons and mounted over the rack of TVLGs.

As his boots struck the top of the hull, he felt his own Liberator begin to rise as it, too, came to a hover. Spint had been watching him through the driver's sensors. Karstil climbed to the top of the turret and dropped into the commander's station. He raised his arm, signaling the others to form behind him in a column. It was time to face the unknown of mortal combat.

In other bivouac areas, the Centuries of the Cohort came to life. Liberators and their accompanying Viper APCs rotated slowly toward the distant front lines, jockeying into position. The light Century, equipped with Wolverine Light Grav Tanks, jumped off first. It would lead the Cohort toward the lines, establishing clear zones and providing guides as necessary for the mediums that would follow. They would then drop back to provide flank guards for the Centuries as they crossed through friendly lines. The Wolverine was an acceptable tank, for high-speed reconnaissance and raids, but it would be more of a liability than an asset when it came to a stand-up fight. Once contact had been established, the Wolverines would cover the flanks and rear and act as the mobile reserve for the Cohort. The light Century was a good place for the special breed of dashing, slightly undisciplined young men who flaunted death at every turn. They lived fast, fought hard, and died in heaps. Recon Centuries almost always sported a death's head as their emblem, and this one was no exception.

And so the hard-luck outfit of the Renegade Legion moved out to meet the enemy.

Deep in the pit of his stomach, the beast that had held Karstil during the night released its grip on his insides. The beast would hide in his imagination forever, but for the time being, he had banished it to the nether regions. It was time to fight.

22

Alsatia, Caralis
The Commonwealth
3 January 6831

Their orders had come down. "Century Secundus will advance on Axis ZEPHYR to seize Objective REGAL. Century Quintus will support as necessary. Century Secundus will advance and seize Objective SALTUS on order. Century Quintus will be prepared to seize Objective SALTUS on order. Extract OPLAN 2567-34, Milton Harras, Centurion Maximus, /s/ Moldine Rinter, Ops, Official."

Century Secundus advanced in a wide wedge over the dry plain of the Alsatian Flats, two tank platoons making up the points of the formation. Centered and to the rear came the Century Headquarters and the platoon of infantry. The formation was ideally suited for detecting and engaging an enemy of unknown strength and location. Intelligence had reported that the TOG force in the area, the 13379th Legion, would be thinly spread, defending in a series of strong points. These elements of the famed TOG Legion were equipped, said Intelligence, with Aeneas light grav tanks and Lupis APCs. The Lupis was a scrappy dog in a fight, relying on its speed and armor rather than weaponry to save it. The Aeneas was another matter. Its 1.5/4 laser made it a worthy opponent for the light Wolverines, but it was no match for the medium Liberators.

The 13379th was also equipped with Horatius medium grav tanks, a worthy opponent for the Liberators when the Horatius was on the defensive, but no contest in a maneuver fire fight. Intelligence was reporting, however, that the Horatius Centuries had been beaten so severely in recent weeks that few of them were operational. Beyond all this, there were still the heavy Cohorts of the Harbingers of Death to consider. Again, Intelligence placed them and their Trajan and Octavian tanks well to the rear.

Karstil's platoon, the left flank of the Century, was also in a wedge, with Mullins on the left, Farwell on the right, and his own Liberator centered and to the rear. The entire formation was some 800 meters wide and 400 deep. The terrain was open, rolling, and barren but for an occasional scattering of Acalaba bush. With sensors on maximum, Karstil could see 50 kilometers in all directions. He would know about anything using power at that range long before it came in range of his lasers or main gun. Passive targets would be harder to detect.

It was over almost before he knew it. There was a slight rise in the ground where a well-camouflaged Liberator sat hidden beneath a thermal shroud. Once past that, the platoon was through the friendly lines. From now on, anything seen or sensed would be TOG.

Karstil felt the fear-beast stir in his imagination, its claws reaching for his stomach. Its grip was less strong than on the night before, but it was still there, awaiting a chance to strike. Karstil willed the beast away as he watched the flank Liberators rolling over the terrain. Perfect tank country: open terrain, no steep valleys, no woods, no enemy...

No enemy. No enemy. No enemy. Where was the enemy?

Trickling under his helmet and breaking out on the palms of the hands, perspiration began to spread along his arms and down his back. He wiped his hands on his thighs, but the sweat kept coming back. Most of the moisture seemed to be concentrating on his buttocks, producing "butt-weld," a common ailment among those who must sit for extended periods. He squirmed, trying to spread his cheeks, but it didn't do much to keep them from sticking together. Karstil was frantic to scratch, but he didn't dare. Glancing down and to the left, he checked to see if Podandos were aware of his commander's problem. The gunner was bent forward, eyes glued to the sights, taking no notice of Karstil.

Suddenly, the sensor flashed red light. Karstil stared at it and felt his heart leap up into his throat. *The enemy.* Information appearing around the sensor screen indicated an unknown enemy emission at 30 kilometers. He looked at his other tanks. Both Farwell and Mullins had their laser torches aloft, indicating that they, too, had picked up the reading. Both TCs turned back toward Karstil, waiting for orders. He pointed toward the emission and pumped his arm. The heads turned back, and Karstil saw the Liberators begin to accelerate.

"Spint, follow them in. Gunner, possible target, bearing six hundred relative, range thirty kays."

"Got him." Karstil felt the Liberator turn and surge forward under maximum thrust, felt his back pressing against the support. The other Liberators were kicking up rooster tails of dust as they roared across the open ground. The sensor screen continued to show an unidentified intruder, now at zero relative, with the range diminishing at 3 kilometers a minute. The Liberator steadied at 170 KPH, well within safe speed for normal flight mode.

The ground flashed by, a yellow blur under the charging Liberator. The other tanks in the platoon were weaving through the Acalaba scrub and occasional scrawny trees that dotted the land. Karstil watched them on his sensor screen, twin blue squares that remained stationary against the moving terrain. The targeting computer was attempting to solve the incoming emissions, searching through its TOG-recognition memory. As the range closed, more and more data was fed to the computer, narrowing the possible choices.

At 10 kilometers, the computer was sure: Aeneas Light Grav Tank. As statistics for the TOG vehicle flashed across the screen, Karstil hardly noticed the information. He knew the Aeneas, knew what to expect. The computer was 70 percent-satisfied with the resolution but kept grinding up the data. At 8 kilometers, the warning lights flashed again. A second Aeneas was active in the same location.

Karstil glanced at the terrain analysis on his command screen. The TOG tanks were behind a long, narrow ridge, probably in a hover at turret defilade. In three minutes, his platoon would be in range of the 1.5/4 lasers. That was not a deadly weapon as far as the Liberator was concerned, but no sense confronting them head-on.

"Three, this is Six. Maintain heading. Reduce to one-twenty. Break, break. Two, swing left to flank that ridge. We'll rally on their position"

"Two, wilco."

"Three, wilco."

"Spint." Karstil flipped the commlink controls to internal-only. "Reduce to one-twenty as you come abreast of Three."

"Roger, sir." The Liberator began to slow, closing the gap between it and the right flank Number Three. Karstil saw the blue indicator of Mullins' tank break to the left and head for the crest of the ridge. The Aeneas tanks were sure to have seen him go, and Karstil waited for them to react. He glanced over the top of his turret, trying to see the lurking enemy. The range was falling toward 4 kilometers, and he still hadn't achieved visual acquisition of the target. Like most commanders, he was more inclined to trust his eyes in the heat of battle than the computer screen.

The slim turret of an Aeneas appeared on his target screen. "Got it," shouted Podandos into the internal commlink. Karstil hit the painting laser treadle, saw the indicator light flash to show that the laser had fired. No "Lock-On Achieved" cue came on the screen, and Karstil hit the treadle again. The Aeneas tank had good forward shields, and there was little chance that painting would be successful at 4 kilometers. In thirty seconds, it wouldn't make any difference; the 150mm cannon would be in range. Even a hull-defiladed tank was a viable target once inside maximum range.

He thumbed the seat control and dropped inside the protective armor of the turret. From the command station, he had 6400 mil observation, and the vision-enhancing devices allowed him to see clearly at extended ranges. The next operation should have been to close the hatch, but Karstil, like most tankers, felt claustrophobic with a closed turret, even on a vehicle the size of the Liberator.

The control radar screen flashed momentarily red; the painting laser warning klaxon began blaring its "whoop, whoop, whoop." A painting laser was reaching out for the Liberator, trying to decipher the flicker shields on the tank's front. The klaxon would switch to a high-pitched scream if the enemy were successful. So far, so good, thought Karstil.

As the range dropped toward 3 kilometers, Karstil saw the 100mm cannon on the tanks flame up, a pulse of blue light expanding around the muzzles. What are they doing? thought Karstil. We're still beyond their maximum range. The answer to his question came almost immediately when twin puffs of smoke burst directly in the paths of the charging Liberators.

A great defense! thought Karstil. This smoke was more than visual screening. It was a cloud mixed with metal vapors impenetrable to sensors that cast a sensor shadow to anything behind it. No driver in his right mind would charge into smoke; he would be completely blind.

"Break left! Break left!" Karstil felt the Liberator turn, his body swinging hard to the right in his seat. He braced himself against hatch coaming to keep from tumbling into the fighting compartment. He had not strapped himself in before combat and there was no time to do it now. Number Three vanished beyond the smoke to the right. The Liberator, clear of the smoke screen, turned back to the original course. The painting laser warning whooped once and then began to scream. Damn! thought Karstil. Damn! Damn! Double damn! He stepped down on his own laser treadle, hoping that it had maintained its orientation on the targets through the violent evasive action. Still no confirmation.

"Target confirmed. Lock achieved. Range one-five-double zero," cued the ballistic computer.

"Shoot! Shoot!" shouted Karstil into the internal commlink. There had been no need for his command. He felt the Liberator buck and the 150mm cannon spat out its 40-kilogram HEAP round. Karstil saw his right sponson glow red as the enemy 1.5/4 laser struck through the flicker shields. A neat hole appeared in the upraised portion of the protruding arms, molten titanium spewing from the opening.

Karstil felt the turret swing to the right under the gunner's control. "There is a painted target within the firing arc. Lock achieved. Range one-five-double zero," cued the ballistic computer. The soft, female voice seemed to purr with satisfaction in the headset. She sounds pleased, thought Karstil. Still too far for the 50mm cannon and TVLGs, but the other weapons would reach. The recoil of the 150 was matched by the high-pitched "whing" of the 5/6 laser. The Gauss cannon didn't need a painted target, but the theory was to "shoot the painted target," and that's what he did.

Karstil could see the two Aeneas tanks hovering 600 meters apart. Both had their turrets pointed at his Liberator, the one successful paint having attracted all their weapons. The TVLG weapon packs grafted to the right sides of the turrets were open and in launch configuration. As soon as he passed within the 1200-meter range, both tanks were ready to let fly. The far tank had been successfully painted, undoubtedly by Farwell, who was somewhere off to the right. That paint had attracted the ballistic computer as well as Podandos, who had swung the turret a few mils to the right to bring the 5/6 laser to bear.

Karstil was stunned at how large a 100mm gun appeared from the front end. It was as though he could see all the way down the barrel to the breech of the weapon. The barrel was as large as a trash can. He braced himself for the shock of a 100mm slug.

The Liberator's HEAP round struck the far Aeneas flush on the gun mantlet, sending a shower of incandescent armor over the turret. An instant later, the 5/6 laser struck centimeters to the right of the HEAP round, boring its way into the turret. Gray-green smoke spewed from the wounds.

In an instant, the stricken Aeneas was hit again on the left side. Farwell had worked his way around the flank of the formation, and at less than a thousand meters, he had fired his full complement of weapons at the painted target. Karstil saw the double flash of a TVLG launch, saw the missiles arc across the intervening space to strike the Aeneas flush on the left-side armor. The 150mm and 50mm had fired first, both weapons loaded with HEAP. The side armor, fragile as it was, peeled away in a golden blossom of molten titanium and ceramic droplets. With the flank laid open, the TVLGs bored in, exploding inside the light tank. The heavy laser weapon added damage. The Aeneas staggered, shedding pieces of titanium plate like a leper shedding skin.

The Aeneas wasn't dead, a surprise to Karstil, but it was done as a fighting machine. Its only hope of survival was its acceleration and speed, and the fact that the other tank would now become a target for the closing Liberators. The range between Karstil and the functioning Aeneas was down to 1,000 meters and dropping. He pressed the treadle for the painting laser, and this time the female voice indicated success: "Target painted. Lock achieved. Range ten-double-zero." He felt the turret swing a few mils to the left as Podandos switched targets.

The healthy Aeneas was not calmly waiting the same fate as its consort. The double flash of launching TVLGs erupted from the box-like weapons housing on the right of its turret. Karstil watched in fascination as the twin missiles roared across the hot open ground that separated his Liberator from the Aeneas. They came so slowly, the red ogives of the nose cones clearly defined by the halo of the rocket engines. There was no doubt that he would be hit, for the "whoop, whoop" of the warning system indicated the enemy's successful paint. Closer and closer they came.

Karstil felt panic grip his throat. This can't be the end, he thought. Not like this. He held his breath, waiting for the searing heat and flash that would mean penetration. He clenched his teeth, his eyes squeezed shut, arms braced against the computer station.

A high-pitched scream filled the fighting compartment. The Vulcan III antimissile system had engaged both TVLGs. The radar and primary ballistic computer link had evaluated the threat, seen that the other Aeneas was not going to fire its TVLGs, and engaged both incoming missiles. Karstil glanced up in time to see fragments of the destroyed missiles rain down around the Liberator, some of the bits sparkling on the flicker shields. "Yes!" he screamed into the lip mike, the breath exploding from his chest. "Yes! Yes! I love it!"

He looked at what remained of his adversary and almost pitied him. The Aeneas was taking a terrible pounding. While Karstil had been bobbing and weaving in a panic-stricken frenzy to avoid the TVLGs, Quentain Podandos had been pounding away at the Aeneas with everything the Liberator had. He had struck the bow mud-guard and upper glacis of the Aeneas repeatedly with the 150mm, 50mm, and 5/6 laser. The titanium armor was scaling off in great slabs, the ceramic under the metal skin fractured and scored. The TS&R systems had been destroyed, the circuits hanging like entrails from a wounded beast.

The Aeneas was rising from its position, trying to turn its undamaged side to Karstil, but it was too late. Mullins, coming up from the left, had a clear shot at the crumpled bow armor. The ballistic computer in the Aeneas, faced with the threat of Karstil's Liberator at close range and Mullins' tank closing from the side, could not decide on a target. That moment of hesitation sealed its doom. The 150mm, 50mm, and 5/6 laser of Karstil's Liberator struck the Aeneas on the rear of the hull, smashing through the steering vane access doors and peeling off the crew ladder. Simultaneously, Mullins engaged the battered front with his own long-range weapons. Karstil had an instant picture of the Aeneas flash through his brain. He could see it all quite clearly: the tank hanging in the air, the circuits dragging on the ground, a 150mm round suspended directly in front of the glowing wreckage.

Then it all dissolved in a blue-white flash that seared his eyes. The turret flew up through the ball of flame, its slim profile clearly etched by the light below. The main gun began to glow in the heat from the explosion, finally melting away in the scorching heat. As if relieved of a great weight, the turret rolled upward, turning over and over as it crashed to the ground. There must have been a round in the chamber of the weapon. As the turret struck the ground, the breech exploded, shattering the piece like a broken egg. Only the broken remnants of the turret remained of the Aeneas. The rest had vanished in the molten conflagration.

The shock of the explosion stunned Karstil. Even the Liberator's 273 tons were not immune to the effects of the blast, and it swerved wildly even as it continued to charge the former location of the vanished tank. The Liberator plowed through the cloud of gases that had marked the spot of the Aeneas, the caustic fumes swirling into the turret, making Karstil gasp for breath. As he cleared the haze, he activated the painting laser again, more by reflex than because of any observed target. The vaporized tank had blanked the sensors to anything that lay beyond, and there was at least one other Aeneas still in the area.

"Target painted. Lock achieved. Range one-seven-double zero," came the response. "Target speed two hundred and accelerating. Range increasing at ten-double-zero per minute." The other Aeneas was attempting to flee, using the death of its consort to cover its own withdrawal. A quick glance at the targeting computer confirmed the information. The Aeneas was just reaching maximum missile range, and it would be outside of 150mm range before very long. Then Karstil noticed that the Aeneas, in an attempt to reach higher speed, had risen to treetop level to avoid a small cluster of trees. That meant there was still a chance of hitting the soft under-belly.

"Quent. Load APDS. Shoot. Spint! Maximum thrust!"

"Roger." Karstil heard the ammunition loading system whir in response as Podandos indexed the change of ammunition into the weapons system. The nose of the gun dropped slightly to make up for the increased muzzle velocity of the new round as well as the surging acceleration of the Liberator. The Liberator trembled as the 150mm Gauss cannon spat out the hyper-velocity shot, the laser firing an instant later.

Karstil knew that there was a better-than-even chance that both shots would strike the under-side of the retreating Aeneas, and the probabilities were on his side. Caught square in the center of the bottom armor, armor so thin that it must have been applied as an after-thought by the designers, the armor-piercing round punched a clean hole in the titanium. The heavy laser struck as well, but any damage it did was secondary to the devastating effect of the shattering depleted uranium slug. Its molten fragments ripped through the drive and helm control of the Aeneas.

Those on board the Aeneas must have experienced an instant of heart-stopping fear at the realization that they were doomed. With the drive and helm destroyed, the Aeneas skidded into the ground. It rolled over once, great slabs of armor and circuitry spewing from the gaping hull. Then it crashed again in a cloud of dust and sparks, the ground scraping away enough of the hull to reach the ammunition. Like the first Aeneas, this one was enveloped in a blue-white flash of light. Not even the turret survived. Not even momentarily.

At 190 KPH, Karstil's Liberator was at the site of the contact in seconds. This time, Spint had enough time to avoid the opaque cloud of debris that blanked the sensors and spattered the ground with minute fragments of what had once been a viable fighting vehicle. Nothing remained of the Aeneas. It was gone. Atomized. A rapidly thinning cloud of gases. For Optio Roglund Karstil, his first kill.

23

Alsatia, Caralis
The Commonwealth
3 January 6831

Karstil returned to the platoon position. Even at range, he could tell that Mullins was scowling. The Platoon Sergeant was sitting on the turret of his Liberator, his communications helmet cradled in his left arm, a cigar planted between his teeth. His eyes were fixed on Karstil. Duncan Spint brought the tank to a stop and hover 20 meters from Mullins' vehicle, letting the Liberator sink gently to the ground. Mullins continued to watch his Optio.

The flush of victory was too great for Karstil to be cowed by his Sergeant. That the platoon had been victorious with no apparent losses was almost too good to be true. Karstil bounced down and swaggered over to Mullins; all he needed was an eye-patch to complete the illusion of a latter-day pirate.

"Fine day for a war, Sergeant."

"Did you enjoy your little escapade, sir?"

"Why not? Did you see the way Quentain bloomed that little sucker? Poor slob never had a chance. Once I got my sights on him, there was no place for him to hide. He juked just as I fired, but he never had a chance. If the rest of the Century does as well as we did, this is going to be a piece of cake. I thought the Toggies would put up a better fight than they did. Great day for a war, Sergeant. A great day for a war."

"Speaking of the Century, sir, did you tell them that we'd made contact? Have you reported our location?"

Karstil felt his spirits drop. One of the first lessons a junior officer learns is to keep his commander informed. He should have reported contact with the Aeneas tanks, should have given a status report after the action, should have kept the platoon together, should have checked the ground around the tank's positions for intelligence, should have...should have...

"No problem, Mullins. I'll do it now. By the way, why are we stopped?"

"Don't worry, sir. I've already talked to Century, given 'em a status report, and searched the area for TOG indicators. I found two infantry TVLG packs near that stand of brush over there. I told Century about 'em." Mullins gave Karstil a look that was as close to a "dim view" as a sergeant could give his commander. "Cohort," he continued, " has ordered a temporary halt while the rest of the Centuries close up ranks. And Century would like to speak at you. When you have the chance, sir."

"I could have done that when I got back."

"Yes, sir, you could have. But Century saw the action on their sensors. They called me."

The sinking feeling struck Karstil again. He had been too busy to switch his commlink back to the Century push. He hadn't even placed it on monitoring, so how could he have heard it when Century had called? Stupid mistake number…number…Well, another stupid mistake. He had been too busy getting the last kill to worry about the rest of the platoon. Now he had Mullins to deal with.

"I'll get on the link and give them a call."

"No need to, sir. I think that's 'turion Freund on the way over now." Mullins indicated a cloud of rapidly approaching dust to the rear of the platoon position. As if on cue, Sedgwick Abul, the driver of Number Two, lifted the Liberator from the ground and let it drift away from the Optio. By the time Centurion Freund's Liberator reached Karstil, the Optio was standing completely alone.

Freund's tank grounded beside Karstil in a cloud of dust and fragments. Even before the dust cleared, Freund was on the ground beside the hapless Optio. "Good morning, Karstil. Have any plans for the day? Any plans that I should know about, that is?"

"No sir. I mean, yes, sir."

"Fine. Fine. When you have a moment in your busy schedule, perhaps you'd like to let me know what they are."

"Yes, sir. I'm sorry for not reporting that contact. I guess I forgot."

"'Sorry?' 'I forgot?' Well, 'sorry' don't pay the bull-dog, Optio," Freund erupted. "And 'I forgot' has no place in this Century. Around here, officers are supposed to be in command of units, not individual tanks. Do you have any idea what you've done?"

Now Karstil was sitting on the horns of a dilemma. If he admitted that he did know, he would seem a self-centered egomaniac intent on personal glory. If he pleaded ignorance to his actions, he would be unfit to act as a platoon leader. Such thorny dilemmas had certainly not been covered at Officers' Training School. He hesitated, weighing the correct response.

Evidently Freund did not need or want a reply. "While you were off gallivanting around looking for personal kills, the rest of the Century was sitting still, awaiting the outcome of your joyride. How was I supposed to know that you had encountered two Aeneas tanks? How was I to control the rest of the Century when my platoon leader in contact didn't bother to report? Do you have any idea what this has done to the movement of this Century? This Cohort? By your self-centered actions, you have jeopardized the entire Cohort operation. Leaving your position exposed our flank and made everyone stop. Didn't they teach you anything while you were with the Commonwealth? That'll teach me to take a re-tread officer from the Commonwealth. Get your brains out of the seat of your pants and put them back in your helmet where they belong!"

Karstil could feel himself withering under the blast from his commander. He could also see, in his mind's eye, the comments that would go into his Efficiency Report. Deadly words like "self-centered," and "no sense of loyalty to his superiors." That was all it would take to end his career with the Renegades.

"You will never, I say again, never, ever, make contact with the enemy that you don't report it to me. Do you understand?" Karstil nodded dumbly, the words of reply stuck in his throat. "Now get back on your tank and get this circus you call a platoon back into the operation." As Karstil raised his hand in salute, Freund spun on his heel and climbed back aboard his own Liberator. Karstil was still holding the salute when Freund turned back. "And one more thing, Optio. If I weren't so short of replacement officers, I'd relieve you on the spot. Don't stand there like a moron. Get on your tank and get out of here." The Centurion dropped inside his tank without another word or glance. The Liberator rose from the ground, did a tight turn, and swirled away, leaving a squad of dust devils in its wake. Karstil dropped the unreturned salute.

As the dust cleared, Karstil was aware that Mullins was standing next to him.

"The old man didn't seem happy, sir," Mullins stated matter-of-factly.

Karstil turned on his Platoon Sergeant. There was no satisfaction in Mullins' face, and the tone of his voice did not indicate that he was taking a jab at his platoon leader. "One of the things we've never gone over, sir, is contact reports. And who should make them."

Karstil felt the blood rising in his face. "I know how to make sit-reps, Sergeant, and I know who is supposed to make them."

"Yes, sir. I wasn't thinking that you didn't, sir. It's just that you have a platoon to run, and there are times when that is more important than reports to the head-shed."

Karstil stared at his Platoon Sergeant, trying to decipher the meaning behind the suggestion. He couldn't tell whether Mullins was trying to be helpful or sarcastic. "What do you mean?" He tried, unsuccessfully, to take the whine out of his voice. Either Mullins didn't hear it or chose to disregard it.

"The next time we make contact, sir," continued Mullins, "I'll monitor the Century frequency. If I don't hear your report, I'll cue you on the platoon network. If you're too busy to make the report, and you probably will be, just tell me to do it. Farwell and I can make the reports just as easily as you can, sir. That way, you won't have to worry about it. If they need to talk to you, I'll hand-off the commlink to you."

Again, Karstil tried to deduce the man's motives. But Mullins' expression was completely open. Either the Sergeant was setting him up in a devious and convoluted way, or he was actually trying to help. Karstil decided to take the suggestion at face value. "Sounds like a plan whose time has come, Sergeant. We'll do it that way in the future."

"Roger that, sir. I think it's time to move." Mullins raised his arm, circling his hand above his head as an indication to Abul to bring up his Liberator. Karstil did the same thing, and both Liberators, like war horses responding to their knights, moved closer.

As the Liberators grounded for the commanders to mount, Mullins turned to his Optio. "By the way, sir. It wasn't all that bad. And nice shooting on the part of Podandos." Mullins winked and gave him a thumbs-up' signal. "When we halt for the night, you might want to check the bore-sight of the 5/6 laser against that of the main gun. Your laser hit was a little off-center."

Karstil felt pride rush over him. Mullins had not been getting ready to shoot him down. He was even giving him some advice about his shooting. He climbed onto the turret. Freund, he thought, could stuff it. He could, and would, run the platoon. He hadn't screwed up so terribly.

Mullins slipped into the commander's hatch of his Liberator and reached down to the locked box welded to the inside of the fighting compartment near his station. From it, he extracted a new cigar, biting off the end and clamping it between his teeth. He cracked a match alight, waiting for the initial mini-explosion to die down before he applied the tip of the flame to the end of the cigar. He inhaled deeply, letting the smoke escape ever so slowly until he was shrouded in a blue-white cloud. His Optio had screwed up, and perhaps only he knew how badly.

The lack of a sit-rep to Century was enough to get Karstil royally chewed out by Freund; he had deserved it. The way Karstil went off after the TOG Aeneas on a wild chase boded ill for the platoon. If he continued to run his tank like that, he could jeopardize a lot more than just his career. Mullins had intended his "nice shooting" tag line as a compliment as well as a warning. A compliment that the gunner had done well, and a warning that the Optio hadn't. Mullins was afraid that Karstil had heard the compliment and not the warning.

Well, he thought, if things don't go too far wrong for the rest of the day, perhaps a little talk in the evening would set the problem right. Wet-nursing Optios was one of the things platoon sergeants were supposed to do.

He saw Karstil make the hand-and-arm signal for a platoon vee. He would be on the left again. "Move it, Sedge. We're on the left again."

"Right, sarge. You got the Optio squared away?"

"That's not your problem, Triarii. You drive this thing. Let me worry about the platoon."

"You got it."

24

Alsatia, Caralis
The Commonwealth
3 January 6831

The platoon continued to move forward under the blazing sun. Gone was the high-speed advance of the morning. Century Tertius, on the right, was meeting opposition, and Karstil, monitoring the Cohort command frequency, could hear reports of the action. Their supporting Century, Quartus, pushed through the combat and continued the advance. It was impossible to tell how much damage Tertius had taken, but from the talk on the commlink, the unit was hurting.

Secundus continued to advance, but there were numerous halts when the Liberators had to ground behind low rises, watching and waiting for the word to move again. Karstil was just as happy for no additional contact. He felt he had done his bit, and been roundly chewed for his success.

The warning light on his sensor display blinked red. "Target of unknown size. Bearing 800 mils relative. Range 30 kilometers. Target approaching." The voice of the sensor computer sounded a little exasperated, as though it, too, thought that one combat a day were enough. Karstil glanced at his flanking Liberators. The flash of their laser torches indicated that they had also picked up the intruder.

"Atlas Snapper Two-six, this is Snapper Two-two-six," Karstil called. Freund was going to get all the information this time. The call sign for the Century changed every six hours. The change was supposed to confuse any enemy intelligence who might be listening. Karstil wondered if it really worked. Mostly, it confused the using stations more than any listener, and on numerous occasions, a transmitter would use the old call sign, then correct himself, and use the new one.

"Snapper Two-six," Freund acknowledged.

"Two-two-six. We have intruder at 800 mils relative. Range 30 kilometers and closing." The Optio spoke as calmly as he could.

"Roger, Two-two-six. He's entering your sector. Advance and engage."

"Two-two-six. Wilco. Out"

Karstil raised his arm, waiting for the others to acknowledge his orders. The two Sergeants lifted their hands in response. He pointed toward the oncoming target and pumped his arm. The Sergeants dropped their hands. Orders understood. Karstil flipped the internal-only switch on his commlink. "The hunt is on. Maintain formation, Spint. Quent, look alive down there." Both crewmen grunted acknowledgement, and Karstil felt the Liberator begin to accelerate as Spint maneuvered to maintain the formation.

The open, rolling terrain they had crossed this morning had changed to the deep ravines and knife-edged ridges described in the commander's briefing. It was no longer possible to charge forward at a 1-meter height. The rocky spines rose 60 meters to narrow tops no more than 2 meters wide. The valleys between the ridges were narrow and twisting, in places no broader than 50 meters, gouged out by some long-forgotten deluge that had riven the surface into myriad wrinkles. Some of the valleys doubled back on themselves so violently that any speed over 60 KPH would have put the Liberators straight into the sides of the cliffs.

The choice was either to slow down to a safe speed while deep in the chasms, or to rise above the surface of the tortured landscape to hurtle over the tops of the razor-edged spines. Both actions brought with them their own dangers. Operating deep in the gorges meant that the platoon had to slow down to an unacceptable speed, but also that the vehicles would not be able to support one another when the action began. Operating above the ridges would allow mutual support, but enemy infantry hidden in the crevices would have a clear shot at the soft belly armor of the Liberators. A dilemma.

The TS&R systems clearly showed that the terrain got worse rather than better. Multiple brown contour lines appeared on the sensor screen, the sides of the gullies showing red as the computer sensed excess speed for the terrain. Karstil watched the red intruder square, trying to judge its altitude based on its speed. The target was obviously doing better than 150 KPH, so either the terrain was better there, or they, too, were above the ridge lines.

"Two-two, this is Two-two six. Climb to Toga Toga Ferrax. Speed one-nine-zero."

"Two, roger."

"Three, roger."

The Liberators climbed out of the valleys to skim across the tops of the ridges at Tree-Top Flight mode. There were no trees around here, but the called-for altitude would put the tanks above the razor-sharp ridges that webbed the terrain. It was a gamble Karstil was willing to take. Centurion Maximus Harras had said that speed and surprise were the watchwords of the operation; caution was for the TOG units. At 190 KPH, the Liberators crossed gorges every two or three seconds, the whine of the grav drives echoing down the valleys in roaring thunder that reverberated and swelled in a staccato beat.

The red square on the sensor screen got closer, dividing into two squares at 10 kilometers distance. The sensor and ballistic computers were processing information on the unknown targets, waiting for the 70 percent accuracy that would allow them to announce the enemy as "Identified."

"Target identified. Two Lupis light grav Armored Personnel Carriers. Flight mode: Toga Toga Ferrax. Speed: 120. Range: five-zero-double zero. Personnel doors closed." Information on the Lupis carriers rolled across the sensor screen. Karstil didn't need to check the information. It was junk from the computer recognition files that he knew by heart.

Lupis carriers? Lupis carriers? This was going to be an easy kill. The light APCs carried 25mm cannon and SMLMs. All Karstil needed to do was stay outside the 2,000-meter range of the SMLMs and shoot at his leisure. His 150mm cannon and 5/6 lasers would tear them apart before they had a chance. The Lupis APCs were probably fleeing the contact with the right flank, seeking protection in their speed. But they had stumbled onto the left flank of the Cohort; now they would pay for their cowardice. And the fools kept coming closer! It was a dream come true. Obviously, they hadn't spotted the Liberators. Karstil resolved that he would let Mullins and Farwell do the shooting this time. He would be merely a spectator.

"Snapper Two-six, this is Snapper Two-two-six." This time, he would tell Freund exactly what was happening.

"Two-six."

"This is Two-two-six. Targets identified as Lupis carriers. Am moving to engage and destroy."

"Roger, Two-two-six."

"Two-two-six out."

Karstil switched to the platoon frequency. "Two, break. Three, this is six. You shoot. I'll watch."

"Three, wilco."

"Two, wilco." Karstil thought he heard worry in the voice of his Platoon Sergeant. "Two. Sit-rep?"

"Six, roger. Sit-rep sent. Good hunting."

"Two. Roger."

Damn, thought Karstil. The Lupis carriers had sensed him. They were turning away. Turning away, but too slowly. And they weren't accelerating. "Bearing 6,300 mils relative. Range 3,600 meters. Range decreasing," came the voice of the ballistic computer. Karstil could see that the Lupis carriers were taking evasive action, weaving back and forth across the tops of the ridges. Indicator lights on the sensor showed that both Mullins and Farwell had opened with their painting lasers. Moments later, he saw the blue glow surround the muzzles of the 150mm cannon as both tanks fired at their fleeing adversaries. Indicator lights blinked on the screen indicating hits on the rear of both APCs.

It was a chase now, and the higher acceleration of the Lupis carriers should have saved them. They had better speed than the heavier Liberators, but their evasive maneuvering quickly cut the distance between them. They should have blown the doors off the Liberators, been out of range in a minute or two, but the commanders were obviously panicked. They forgot that speed was their primary ally.

A double square blip appeared over the right-hand Lupis, indicating that it had been painted, even at 3,000 meters. Farwell was having good luck with his painter today. It was only a matter of time now before the Lupis was nothing but a heap of slag at the bottom of one of the gullies. Karstil saw Farwell's 150mm cannon glow again, the superheated gases at the muzzle expanding as the shot left the tube. Even with the hyper-velocity of the projectile, Karstil was at an angle to track its flight to the target. The round struck the rear of the turret, covering the Lupis in a shower of white-hot sparks. The laser must have missed because there was no pinpoint glow to indicate a strike.

Mullins had not changed targets to hit the painted Lupis. Evidently, he assumed that Farwell could finish off his number without help from the Platoon Sergeant. When he did kill it, it would not have to be a shared kill like the Aeneas tanks earlier. He kept after his own target, his driver holding the tank steady on course to give the ballistic computer a better chance to lock onto the Lupis. Panicked or not, the Lupis driver or commander was a skilled soldier. He would wait until Mullins had locked and fired, then he would juke to the right or left. Only a dead-on hit had any chance of real damage, but the Lupis was not escaping clean. Karstil saw a 150mm round score the right side of the light APC, peeling off a huge chunk of armor in a glowing scar that extended across the four infantry access doors.

Both Lupis APCs were spewing smoke, either from damage or from burning smoke grenades still in the launchers mounted on their diminutive turrets. Launching smoke as a screen was hopeless. The tanks' speed and the constant movement of the enemy APCs made smoke ineffective as a shield. But there was no doubt that the rounds in the smoke dischargers had been hit on the left tank. A white cloud enveloped the turret, and it was a good thing that the TS&R circuits were mounted in the hull. Otherwise, the tank would have been completely blind.

Spint was holding the command Liberator between and to the rear of the other two. From that position, Karstil had a ringside seat for the combat. There was no real doubt as to the outcome. It was only a matter of time before the two Lupis carriers were destroyed. Karstil pounded on the top of his turret. "Smoke 'em! Smoke 'em!" he shouted to no one in particular. He could feel his heart racing, his breath shallow and rapid. The adrenaline rush poured through him, bringing a high flush to his face.

"Whoop, whoop, whoop, wheee!" The painting laser warning klaxon went off in Karstil's turret, indicating an attempt to paint and then a successful attack. Why paint me? he thought. They don't have the range to shoot, and I'm not the main target. Stupid. Hardly something to worry about. If the fleeing APCs wanted to waste their painting on an impossible target, that was all well and good. They would die that much more quickly under the hammer blows of the 150mm cannon.

"Go ahead," he shouted. "Shoot at me, you idiots. Shoot at me!" He leaned back and gave a shrill laugh of nervous satisfaction. He had never had so much fun before. It was not necessary, he realized, that he do the shooting; there was just as much satisfaction in seeing the other two tanks of the platoon make the kills.

"Targets identified. Two Horatius tanks. Bearing five-two-hundred mils relative. Range two-four-hundred meters. Targets stationary." The soft voice of the ballistic computer purred in his ear. Two Horatius tanks? Where had they come from? Then it was all crystal clear. The Lupis carriers had been a decoy to lead the platoon into an ambush. He had fallen for it like a load of bricks. His platoon was all spread out, involved in a stern chase against light vehicles. Now the real enemy, hidden in the ravines, grav drives shut down, had sprung their trap.

25

Alsatia, Caralis
The Commonwealth
3 January 6831

"Targets. Bearing Five-two-zero meters. Break contact. Engage left." Karstil switched to internal. "Take her down. Take her down! Smoke!" Karstil felt the Liberator drop away as it dived for the doubtful security of one of the narrow valleys. A 150mm round cracked overhead, just where the turret would have been if the tank had continued. Smoke from the launcher bloomed behind him, and then the tank was below the level of the ridges, hurtling along between the spines.

The sheer sides of the cliffs flashed past in a blur, their sharp protrusions lost in the blinding speed. Ahead, the valley took a sharp turn to the left; too sharp for the Liberator to make at its current speed. The far wall approached inexorably; it would be a final resting place for the plunging tank.

"Get her up! Get her up!" Karstil screamed into the headset. There was no need for him to shout. Duncan Spint had no intention of becoming a statistic in the combat record of the 2567th Renegade Legion. He had seen the wall, knew that a head-on collision at 200 kilometers would splatter the tank like a piece of overripe fruit. He had both hands on the control-stick, pulling back with all his strength to control the tank. Slowly, almost impercep-tibly, the nose of the tank began to rise. Then the bow cleared the edge of the cliff, and the tank rocketed into the air high above the terrain in an uncontrolled climb.

Below him, he could see Mullins in a hard left turn, his turret already tracking onto the new targets. Farwell's tank was nowhere to be seen, his line-of-sight blocked by his own hull. "Wheeeeeeeeee!" The painting laser warning klaxon went off again. If nothing else, those TOG bastards were persistent.

The Liberator staggered as a 150mm APDS round struck square on the left side, just to the front of the turret. At least the enemy hadn't been firing HEAP, which would have burned a huge hole in the Liberator's side. He ducked, involuntarily, from the hit. A laser blast vaporized the Vulcan III dome to his left rear, shards of molten plastic spattering his combat helmet and sticking, smoldering, to his suit.

In the rear of the fighting compartment, Duncan Spint was struggling with the controls of the careening tank. The hit on the left side had been lucky; at this high altitude, most of the shots should have hit bottom armor. Unlike the Eradicator, whose crew was housed high in the turret, the driver of the Liberator was in the virtual bowels of the hull. That made the combat station safe, but there was little chance of escape if the tank took a hit. Spint threw his 85 kilograms against the control stick, forcing the nose down. He lifted off his seat, the tank dropping away from beneath him. His left foot came down on the negative thrust pedal. If he couldn't get the tank under control, subsequent hits wouldn't make any difference.

Above him in the turret, Karstil whipped back and forth as the tank bucked to Spint's efforts. He was losing his orientation. With the tank moving in one direction, and with the turret traversed 1600 mils to the left, he was moving sideways. He stamped repeatedly on the painting laser control. The ballistic computer, immune to the gyrations of the tank, had been feeding information through his headset on a continual basis. "Target identified. Target locked. Target painted. Range one-nine-double zero meters." Karstil almost believed he detected surprise in the electronic voice. Impossible, Karstil reminded himself, knowing he had to get a grip on his thoughts.

A blue globe appeared at the muzzle of the 150mm cannon. Karstil hoped Podandos was in better control than he was. The gunner's station was braced with arm and foot rests so that he could maintain a steady seat even in a wildly twisting tank. The commander, needing more latitude of movement, was not so lucky.

He forced himself not to look over the top of the turret; the screens inside gave a better picture of what was happening. Spint had been able to get control of the Liberator, which was now speeding over the tops of the ridges at right angles to the two Horatius tanks. He glanced at the Data Display Screen, but the picture made no sense. The screen was designed to show the terrain and vehicles relative to the direction of the tank hull, not the turret. With the turret traversed to 4800 and still turning left, his screen was 1600 mils out of line with the tank's direction of movement. Karstil noted that there were still three blue squares on the display, which meant that the platoon was at least still intact.

Karstil's Liberator shot past the stern of Mullins' tank, so close that he jerked back involuntarily as though to avoid striking the other vehicle. Number Two cut away and Karstil felt his own tank begin a hard turn to the left. The 150mm cannon fired again, and he heard the high whine of the 5/6 laser fire right behind. As the tank steadied on course, Karstil finally had a chance to orient himself to the terrain and the battle.

The two Horatius tanks were still at a hover above the edges of the ridges. Both had been tracking Karstil, but when he passed behind Mullins, they had switched targets to the Platoon Sergeant's vehicle. Karstil saw that Mullins' Liberator had sunk down behind one of the ridges, placing itself in hull defilade. The protection offered by such a position wasn't much at 1,800 meters, but it was better that sitting full in the open like the two Horatius tanks. Karstil saw the 3/6 lasers from both enemy vehicles hit low, scouring their way through the ridge in bursts of incandescent slag.

"Spint. Close them. Keep to the right." He treadled the painting laser.

"Target painted. Target locked. Target stationary. Range 1,600 meters and closing." A slight tremor in the voice, perhaps. The computer was getting excited? The 150mm and laser fired together. Karstil could see the turret of the near Horatius swinging away from Mullins' tank and onto his own. The 50mm cannon was still out of range, as was his own, but the 3/6 laser and SMLM systems weren't. The constant "whoop, whoop, whoop" of the warning klaxon indicated that the Horatius was trying to paint. The enemy gunner must have decided that any shot was better than none, and Karstil saw the SMLM pod snap open to disgorge one of its long-range missiles. The laser struck the front of the Liberator just below its own missile racks, but the TOG computer had been unable to decipher the flicker rate of the tank. The aligned light of the laser splashed over the flicker shields, glowing in iridescent colors as it spent its energy. The SMLM round hit the front glacis, and Karstil blinked. That hit also indicated the TOG painting laser's inability to penetrate the shield. The flicker shields caused the missile to detonate prematurely, its blast swirling over the tank.

The main guns of both Horatiuses continued to pound on Mullins' tank, the 150mm rounds bursting on the glacis and turret mantlet. Indicator lights on the DDP inside Karstil's turret showed that critical tolerance levels for both the hull and weapon systems were being reached. Mullins would not be able to stand much more of it. He treadled the laser painter again, and was again rewarded with the "target painted" notification. The range was down to 1200 meters, opening distances for the TVLGs and 50mm cannon.

Karstil winced as a pair of missiles left their compartment between the side sponsons. Both cannon fired together, the 150mm using HEAP, the 50mm firing APDS. He saw the Vulcan antimissile system on the near Horatius track the incoming missiles, but that system was not of the same quality as the Liberator's. One of the missiles shattered into microscopic fragments under the multiple-laser pounding of the Vulcan, but the other got through along with the 150, the 50, and the laser. All four rounds struck square on the front of the turret, gobbets of molten titanium and chunks of ceramic armor cascading from the front of the compartment. The turret stopped tracking almost at once, its targeting computer reduced to glowing embers and popping circuits.

Beyond his original target, Karstil saw the other Horatius swing its turret toward him. The tank was rising slightly to fire over the top of its partner. The huge 150mm main gun tracked through the arc. Inside his turret the piercing, shrill "wheeeeeee" of the painting laser warning told that the enemy had been successful this time. At this range, even the damaged tank, its targeting systems crippled, would have a chance. A thousand meters was once a significant distance, but with the new acquisition systems, high-velocity cannon, lasers, and guided missiles, that was virtually point-blank nowadays. Karstil lowered his head and muttered the age-old prayer of the British soldier: "Dear Lord, for that which we are about to receive, make us ever thankful."

The SMLMs from the Horatiuses were launched first, one from each tank arcing across the azure sky on brilliant tails of fire. The 50mm slugs then struck home, as did the HEAP shells. The Liberator shuddered under the multiple hammer blows of four hits. The fighting compartment filled with the acrid smoke of immolated ceramic armor and the crisp smell of burnt circuits. The ballistic computer winked as its power supply was cut, glowing again as the secondary circuit took over. Karstil looked down at his gunner. Podandos was bathed in sweat, his face a contorted mask of rage. Rivulets of perspiration coursed across his cheeks, digging furrows in the grime caking his features. He saw the gunner's fingers tighten on the firing switches, felt the Liberator buck as the weapons fired.

There was no hope now. Only the main gun found its target, the HEAP round exploding on the right upper sponson glacis of the Horatius. Both enemy tanks were lined up for the kill. Karstil glanced at the terrain ahead, looking for a nearby fold in the ground into which the tank could dive. Nothing. In all the area they had crossed, among all the knife-edged ridges, this particular place was perfectly smooth under his tank. A level plain separated the damaged Liberator and its adversaries. The painting laser warning continued to scream itself to death. That, thought Karstil, was probably the last thing he would ever hear.

When the Horatius tanks had sprung their trap, Sergeant Farwell and Tank Number Three had been well to the right of the battle. He had heard his Optio call out when the trap was sprung, but his experienced eye told him that he was 5 kilometers away, out of range of the enemy. And he still had two damaged Lupis APCs to deal with. He made the instant decision that the APCs were a dangerous factor requiring his attention. A parting shot at his primary target sent the Lupis into the wall of a ridge, its grav and helm controls shot away.

The other Lupis, knowing it was supported and probably assuming that all the Liberators were engaged with the TOG medium tanks, had turned toward the distant battle. That assumption became its undoing. As the Lupis swung to the left to bring its feeble weaponry to bear, Farwell had unloaded his laser and 150mm cannon into its flank. The 5/6 laser had followed the HEAP round into the same hole, burrowing through the titanium armor, the ceramic shielding, the vane control, and finally into the ammunition storage area itself. The Lupis had dissolved in a blue-white flash of light that seared the eyes even at 1,200 meters.

Having taken care of those enemy, Farwell turned back toward the main battle. He saw

Mullins, hull-down behind a ridge, trade shots with the two Horatius tanks as Karstil crossed behind him and made his charge. A head-on assault was out of the question. Quickly posting the last-known coordinates of the TOG tanks on the ballistic computer, he took the Liberator into the maze of gullies that filled the area off to the left of the battlefield.

Creeping through the valley, he emerged well to the flank and rear of the enemy just as they began to pound Tank Number One into a marble. He saw the ballistic computer recognize the near tank, the one that had risen to point at Karstil, as laser-painted. Swinging his turret to the right, he took careful aim at the broad stern of the enemy. His computer purred lock, range 1100 meters, and he fired every weapon on the Liberator. William Umbartis, the man Mullins had marked for the next promotion to Principes, was as good a gunner as the platoon had. All weapons hit the target. The 150mm HEAP round scoured away a great chunk of the metal armor, burning its way into the ceramic shield. The 50mm APDS round hit close by, tearing away even more. But it was the TVLGs and laser that finished the job. The stern shield systems vanished in a blazing instant, grav drives reduced to molten bits. The 5/6 laser, finding nothing to impede its fiery course, bit through the embers and struck into the vital heart of the tank.

For a moment, the Horatius continued to hover, as though it had survived the savage attack from the rear. Then its bow began to rise, the tank sliding backward into the gully from which it had first emerged to spring the trap. As it reached the mid-point of the arc between level and vertical, the tank was shattered by an internal explosion that obscured its more fortunate ally.

In Karstil's tank, the "wheeeeee" of the warning klaxon ceased its dismal wail. The only sound in the vehicle was the sudden thud of the 150mm cannon firing another HEAP round into the turret of the damaged Horatius. That tank, its turret damaged to the point of destroying its targeting and communications systems, could take no more. The commander and the gunner died in a flash of light. Parts of the hull exploded outward, the turret disintegrating into bits of weapons pods, cannon, and laser mountings. The grav coils went crashing into the gully to become part of the conflagration of their sister tank. The battlefield was silent at last.

Spint let the Liberator coast to a stop beside the gully, unwilling to take the tank over open space until he had determined whether or not his drives and helm still worked. Farwell's tank came to a stop in the same area, its hull wreathed in smoke that drifted up from the gully to its rear. Karstil, leaning across the turret of his tank, stared into the silent face of Farwell. Then both men turned toward the last known location of Mullins.

From deep within a gully, the damaged Liberator crept to the surface. The left side of the turret had been stripped clean, the 50mm cannon and 5/6 laser mount ripped from the side. Great strips of armor hung from the sponsons, twisted by the heat of the exploding rounds. As they watched, a head appeared from the commander's hatch, followed slowly by the blackened body of a man. They watched in awe as the figure reached inside the turret and extracted a small, cylindrical object. He put it to his lips, spat, and placed it there again. Then a match flared in his hands, and he applied the flame to the end of the object. Smoke wreathed the figure, which leaned back in the turret, both hands braced against the coaming. Then the man smiled.

Seeing his Platoon Sergeant and his tank damaged but alive, Karstil felt his legs wobble as his knees gave out. A feeling of relief swept over him. Now it was time to send his sit-rep.

Karstil couldn't help but smile as he spoke. "Atlas Snapper Two-six, this is Atlas Snapper Two-two-six. Sit-rep. Over."

"Snapper Two-two-six, this is Two-six. Roger, send your sit-rep."

26

Alsatia, Caralis
The Commonwealth
3 January 6831

Technology is grand. Computers are able to sense and recognize objects that are beyond the range of human vision. Modern armor is impervious to most weapons. Laser and Gauss cannon can strike a target that is moving at high speed, protected by flicker shields, or is hull defiladed. Technology is grand. But when all is said and done, it is still stoop labor that makes the systems work.

Stoop labor, that back-breaking, muscle-straining labor, was what Karstil and his platoon now faced in the chilly air of night. The breath-stopping, heart-pounding excitement of battle had given way to the labor of repair and replacement. A quick survey of the platoon showed the cost. Karstil's tank had been hit in the side and front. No shots had penetrated, but huge sections of titanium armor and ceramic plating had been blasted from the hull. These would have to be replaced before the tank would be combat-worthy once more. Farwell's Number Three had been hit by light weapons and could be patched with little difficulty. But Mullins' Number Two was a wreck. The front armor was not worthy of the name, and so many shots had penetrated the ceramic shielding that it was possible to see into the fighting compartment. One of the TS&R circuits had vanished along with both forward shield generators. The 50mm cannon and 5/6 laser mount had been torn from the side of the turret, and the Vulcan III anti-missile system was gone. The tank was a candidate for either depot maintenance or the boneyard.

Mullins accepted the situation with resigned equanimity. His Liberator had seen him through many actions, and he looked on it as an old friend. But the friend had served its purpose. He broke the cigar case from the inside of the commander's station. That task accomplished, the Liberator ceased to be "his" and became just another wreck awaiting disposal.

Meanwhile, the rest of the platoon went to work on the remaining tanks. High intensity oxy-torches carved away the titanium armor damaged in the day's action. Once the men had removed the damaged sections, they lifted new armor panels into place and tack-welded them into position. Razor-thin deep probes were inserted between the plates. By drawing the probes around the patch, the patch and the original hull were bonded together.

Repair of the ceramic armor was a relatively simple but time-consuming task. The interior damage was removed by hammering away the fractured and charred residue on the inside. This was close, difficult work requiring that the man with the hammer work from the inside of the fighting compartment. Kloun and Umbartis were the strongest men in the platoon, and so it was they who spent most of the time inside Karstil's tank. The ceramic shielding on Number Three had not been damaged in the action, so bringing that tank to full fighting effectiveness was not difficult.

Karstil and the rest of the crew of Number One took turns wielding the 5-kilo hammer inside the cramped compartment. Though neither Karstil nor Podandos were strong enough to do much of the pounding, they were small and lithe enough to reach areas where the bulkier men were at a disadvantage. Karstil spent an hour inside the right sponson, battering away at the rock-like ceramic. While Karstil was still wedged inside the sponson, Centurion Freund arrived at the platoon to check on its progress. Knowing the commander's philosophy that officers do officers' work and enlisted men do enlisted work, Mullins covered for his Optio. While Freund was inspecting Number Three, the man pulled Karstil from the sponson so he could greet his commander when he returned.

"Let's snap it up, Karstil. You're holding up the whole Century," Freund said as he approached. "Broast took almost no damage, and Ventis is ready to go."

They also had seen almost no action during the day, Karstil thought. His platoon had been through two encounters, one of them against long odds, and had emerged victorious. And with no crew casualties. "Yes, sir. We'll be ready as quickly as we can."

"You'd better be ready sooner than that," snapped Freund. "Getting a tank reduced to a pile of garbage is not the best way to stay ready for combat. I had to beg for a replacement from Harras. It'll be here in an hour. It should take a 'competent' crew less than an hour to check it out. Be ready to move in two hours."

Two hours? thought Karstil. That was a virtual impossibility. "Yes, sir. We'll be ready an hour after the tank arrives."

"No, Optio. You weren't listening. I told you to be ready in two hours, and two hours is what I meant. I'm not going to have the Centurion Maximus all over my ass because you can't deliver. I told him two hours, and I'm telling you two hours. I expect you to do your job."

"Yes, sir. Two hours it is." Even in the chill of the darkness, Karstil could feel his face flush with the anger rising in his chest. His platoon had done well that day, had done better than could reasonably be expected. They had destroyed six TOG armored vehicles at a cost of one damaged tank. He didn't consider his and Farwell's as really damaged, just nicked up a bit. He hadn't lost any men, either.

"You Commonwealth types," continued Freund, warming to his theme, "have got to learn how real fighting men do things. In the Renegade Legion, we don't do things at half-speed. I know all about your record. In my book, serving as a general's aide doesn't count as having served in the real world. Here we do it the Renegade way. And that means getting the job done on time."

Karstil felt the flush on his face fade away. Now, at least, he understood why Freund was all bent out of shape. He didn't like retreaded officers who joined the Renegades. Harras was a Commonwealth re-tread as well. There was no way for the Centurion to take a shot at the Cohort commander, so he simply took it out on Karstil.

"Get this circus of misfits squared away, and do it now." Freund turned on his heel and vanished into the darkness.

"We can do it, sir." Mullins must have been standing very close in the darkness, must have heard the entire conversation. "We can put one man on security, and the rest of us can get on your tank. Abul will be the man so he can pick up the new Liberator as soon as it arrives and bring it into the laager." Mullins put his hand on Karstil's shoulder. "We'll do it."

"Right, Sergeant." Karstil wanted to thank Mullins, but the words stuck in his throat. He was afraid Mullins would hear his voice crack from the suppressed emotions. Officers didn't cry, no matter how much it hurt.

The platoon members pored over Karstil's tank, taking over when the maintenance crew asked for a break. Tankers usually didn't do the work of "wrench jockeys," but this was different. Even the maintenance people got into the spirit of things, letting the tankers pour the ceramic matrix into the open spaces that had been hammered out for it. While Podandos and Kloun filled the holes in the ceramic plating, Spint and Karstil replaced the damaged TS&R system in the left hull. Mullins and Farwell disappeared into the engine compartment, checking the circuitry and control cables for the grav drives and steering vanes. The job was not especially taxing, but it required a fine sense of electro-mechanical wizardry. Mullins had that sense, and he was pleased to find that Farwell was a kindred spirit. The young sergeant was proving to be a real asset.

Creeping through the innards of the left grav and vane system, Mullins traced the intricate maze of cables and tubing. He burrowed deeper and deeper toward the fusion coil, making sure that nothing had been dislodged or broken from the shock of combat. Feeling along with his right hand, he traced the vane control from its exit on the power coil back toward his left hand. The hands were about to touch, completing the task, when he felt a slight bulge in the cable. Probably a fault in the cable, he thought.

"Gimme a little more light in here, Willie." Umbartis pushed the light probe deeper into the bowels of the tank. With the greater illumination, Mullins was able to see the abscess on the vane control cable. He suspected that the violence of combat must have shaken something loose, and that it had rubbed the cable until the covering had ruptured. That wasn't really a major problem. The interior of the cable was shielded by a second skin of flexible metallic around another layer of insulation. Unless there was some additional damage in the area, the cable would be all right. He ran his fingers over the rupture one more time, routinely checking to see whether the second shielding layer was still undamaged.

He stopped in surprise. Where he had expected to feel a hole in the cable wall, he found a bulge instead. Obviously, his original assumption was not correct, for this was no rupture in the cable. He craned his neck to see directly into the abscess, prying open the crack to get a better look at the inside.

"Umbartis! Get Optio Karstil. Have him crawl inside here. I have something to show him."

Umbartis departed, returning moments later with a slightly disheveled Karstil. "What's the problem, Sergeant?"

"I want to show you something about how this system works, sir. I figure that since we've got this thing ripped open, it might as well be now."

"Good idea, Sergeant, but I'm not sure this is the best time."

"Would you mind crawling in here, sir? I think you'll find it interesting."

Karstil had no intention of crawling into the lower hull of the Liberator. There was enough work to be done by all hands without taking time off for a tour of the inner hull. But something in Mullins' tone gave him pause, made him refrain from telling the man that he didn't have the time. "Is it really important, Sergeant?"

"Sir, I really think you should come in here."

Karstil shrugged. If it were that important to Mullins, he might as well go on a guided tour of the cables. He wriggled through the access door on the rear hull and squirmed into the crowded interior. He found Mullins' feet in the semi-darkness, the Sergeant's body silhouetted by the glow of the light probe. He had half-expected the Sergeant to meet him rather than wait for him to crawl all the way in.

"I thought you ought to see this, sir." Mullins' voice was low.

"What is it?"

"Take a look, sir." Mullins held open the vane control cable, letting the light from the probe fall full on the gash in the line. Karstil stared. There, tucked into a slit in the cable, was a finger-sized tube. A thin wire extended from the top of the tube and was buried in the cable.

"Well, well. And what do we have here?" That, thought Karstil, had to rank with the most inane questions in the history of man, but the words had just popped out.

"What we have here, sir, is a little unauthorized modification of your steering."

"Can we get it out?"

"That, sir, is a question I have been asking myself. And there is another question. Who do we tell?"

"If we can't get the thing off, we won't have to worry about telling anyone. Do you think it's an explosive?"

"Without a doubt, sir. Someone is trying to knock out your steering. I would guess that wire is some kind of a counter. The whole thing may be set to go off if anything happens to it. If we cut the wire, it may be all over."

"Give me a little more light." Karstil examined the tube, a thin, white object the size of his index finger. "It looks like score marks around the other end. Maybe we can pry off the end." Karstil realized that the use of the plural personal pronoun had something to do with being only centimeters from a small chunk of powerful explosive. The whole platoon had become a "we" rather than a "me" and "them."

"Sir?" It was Umbartis calling from the outside of the tank. "The new Liberator is here. They want someone to sign for it."

As though he didn't have enough on his hands already. "Have Farwell accept delivery. Have him begin the systems check with Grouse and Abul. Mullins and I will be out of here as soon as we can." He turned back to his Sergeant. "If you hold the cable steady, I'll try to pry the back end off with my fingers. I think I can get my thumbnail into that groove. I don't want to use a metal object on the tube. You never know how these things work."

"Go for it, sir."

With Mullins holding the cable as steady as possible, Karstil drove his thumbnail into the groove around the base of the tube. Applying gentle force, he pried the end off the tube, working around the perimeter. The cap gave slightly under the pressure of the thumb, slowly lifting away from the body of the tube. Karstil didn't want to have the thing break open too violently; there was no knowing what would be attached to what. The cap came away, and Karstil held his breath in anticipation. Nothing happened.

"Hold it up a little bit more, will you, Sergeant." Mullins elevated the head-end of the tube. "There's something loose in there. Give me the light."

Steadying the cable and tube with his left hand, Karstil moved the light probe until the beam of light struck the open end of the tube. Inside, Karstil could see a gray-green object that almost filled the tube. Two wires, one yellow and one green, were stuck into the object. Karstil described what he saw to Mullins.

"Probably composition-M, sir," said Mullins. "It's a pretty powerful explosive. Has a burn rate of about 10,000 meters a second. Faster than we can run if it decides to go off. Those wires probably go to the primer."

"And what we want to do is cut the wires. Which one first?"

"An interesting question, sir. If it makes a difference, and we guess wrong, it won't much matter to us. If it doesn't make a difference which one we cut first, then . . ."

"I'm not going to try to remove the primer before I cut. Let me have your nippers." Mullins twisted, reaching for the tool pack he had strapped to his waist. He handed the small nipper to Karstil. "Well," said the Optio, "here goes." He placed the jaws of the cutters around the yellow wire. Wondering whether it was the right thing to do, he looked up at Mullins' tense face. Without taking his eyes of Mullins, Karstil squeezed.

The wire separated with a soft, metallic tink. Karstil looked down, moving the cutters to the other wire. It cut as well.

"Good thing you cut the green wire first, sir. The yellow one was probably the trap."

Karstil looked up at Mullins. No need to tell him that he had cut the yellow one first.

"I'm going to try to extract the wire from the cable. If we can get the whole thing, it will be better for the Intelligence people." A tug brought the needle-sharp probe clear of the cable. " Let's get this thing off the cable. I'll keep it until we have a chance to get to Harras. I don't trust anyone else with it."

"Nice work, sir. It's a pleasure doing business with you."

27

Alsatia, Caralis
The Commonwealth
4 January 6831

Karstil and his men met Freund's two-hour deadline, but only with great difficulty. Removing the little explosive device had taken valuable minutes from the maintenance of the vehicles. Though the crew from Legion Maintenance was still securing a new cover on his Vulcan III antimissile system, Karstil reported in by commlink that the platoon was up and ready to travel. Karstil wondered how he could get the platoon on the move with the workers still atop his Liberator, but he needn't have worried. Freund acknowledged the report, but no movement orders followed. Instead, Karstil was told to stand by at maximum readiness and await orders.

One last item remained, though it was not on any of the work orders submitted by the platoon. Karstil had no idea why welding was necessary on the interior of a brand-new tank, but Mullins insisted that his new Liberator needed some repair. He got the Platoon Sergeant of the Maintenance Contact Team to lend him an oxy-torch for the work in his fighting compartment. It was unusual for an ordnance sergeant to lend a torch to a tanker, but it was part of the payback for the platoon members' help during the night. Whatever it was Mullins had to do, it didn't take long.

Karstil put the platoon into a full-perimeter, 6400 mil defense and awaited orders. The platoon had been on the go since the previous dawn. There had been no time for sleep, and they had only eaten on a catch-as-catch-can basis. The inside of Karstil's tank was littered with food wrappers, dropped where they'd been torn from the dried emergency rations. He had assumed that Century would feed the platoon during the night, but no chow had been forthcoming. A discreet inquiry to Century brought the response that Century had not sent any food down because he had not requested any. Another mistake on the part of the young Optio.

"That's just another lesson for you," Freund told him. "In the Renegade Legion, we try to make reports to our headquarters as they come due. You should have reported your status during the night. Now you'll have to wait until this evening to make the next one. Try to do better in the future." The response had come on the Century command frequency rather than on the administrative one. Karstil knew that the other platoons had heard it, and that Cohort was probably monitoring the network as well. "If you can't take command of your platoon, Two-two-six, try to find someone who can."

Exhausted and frustrated, Karstil felt the tears welling again in his eyes. There was, he thought, no justice in this Century. The two-hour deadline had been unreasonable, and now to be ripped for not mentioning food was too much. There had been no need to make that report, and he knew it. Rations were supposed to be delivered on time by the Century's supply people. They knew the status of the platoon because he had reported no casualties when he went into the night laager. It was just Freund taking another poke at him for public consumption. Well, he would not give Freund the chance to tear into him for having a sloppy Liberator; he put Spint and Podandos to cleaning the inside of the fighting compartment.

Dawn is probably the worst time of the day for a man who has not slept for twenty-four hours. Karstil could feel his eyes burning as he checked the DDP in the tank or scanned the fading darkness in his sector. He could see Podandos nodding at his gunner's station, also fighting fatigue. Though not an especially strong young man, Podandos had spent a good bit of time hammering at the fractured ceramic armor. Now he was paying for it. Karstil let his foot "inadvertently" nudge Podandos each time he saw that the young man had fallen asleep.

It was not as though Karstil didn't have enough to occupy his thoughts. The finger-sized explosive device was carefully wrapped and secured inside his combat coveralls. He would keep it there until he had a chance to deliver it to Centurion Maximus Milton Harras. He debated whether to give it to Dixon Quail, the Maintenance Contact Team Sergeant, for delivery to Harras, but then thought better of the idea. Quail seemed a good man, but who knew what would happen if he gave it to him. Karstil wanted to trust Quail, but how could he trust anybody in this matter?

At the moment, the Century was deployed in a wide triangle, 10 kilometers on each leg. That wasn't really a great distance because the other platoons could rally on anyone under attack in less than four minutes. But Karstil could feel the physical separation. There was no one to talk to other than the members of the platoon, and he felt isolated, alone in the withdrawing darkness. He snapped himself awake. One of the bushes to his front had moved. He was sure of it. Then his brain took over, telling him that it was the darkness and fatigue making him see things. He watched the bush carefully, but it didn't move again.

By full light of day, the platoon was still deployed in its circular defense on a small, scrubby mesa, the tanks facing outward. The anti-thermal camouflage tarps draped around the vehicles made them all but invisible to the prying sensors of orbital stations. On top of each turret, just below the 150mm main gun, was a helmet, and under the helmet, the head of the tank commander. Virtually all tank commanders ran their tanks from a heads-up position, adding one more set of sensors to the ones the vehicle designers had given them. Eyes were an archaic device, as any good designer would say, but men still trusted them more than they did a glowing screen. But not these eyes, and not at this time. Every tank commander in the platoon was fast asleep.

The combat sensors and ballistic computers, never tiring in their search and analysis of the terrain, kept updating the information of the DDPs inside the fighting compartments. Tirelessly, the computers analyzed the information, flashing blue squares and triangles onto the screen. Occasionally, the sensors would detect an intruder at maximum range and prepare to warn the human occupants of the approach. Then additional information would enter, establishing the visitor as friendly, and the warning klaxon would not sound. The platoon slept on, undisturbed. An Equus light grav sled approached the platoon in the semi-darkness before dawn, saw the main guns covering the 6400 mils, saw the tank commanders at their positions, and seemed to think better of approaching. The sled vanished without the computers giving any warning, without any member of the platoon even seeing it.

A shaft of sunlight reflecting from the finned muzzle-brake of the 150mm gun penetrated the eyelids of the sleeping Optio. He snapped his head back, startled to see full day where before there had been only vague shapes and half light. Realizing that he had been asleep, Kartstil glanced at the other tanks, saw the commanders at their stations, and was ashamed of his frailty. A quick glance around the interior of the tank showed him that none of his crewmembers had noticed his nap, however. Podandos was face-down on his display screen, eyes shut, breath coming in long, deep gasps. Spint's head was tipped back against the head-rest of his driving chair, his legs stuck out into the turret basket, completely relaxed.

Karstil reached over and shook Podandos by the shoulder. "Break's over. Back on your head."

"'Ust-resting-my-eyes, sir. Really I 'as." Quentain's speech was slurred, his tongue refusing to perform the necessary movements to make the words distinct.

"I know. Make sure Spint's awake. I'm going to check the other tanks." He glanced at the DDP to see if anything were happening. A blue square blinked back, indicating a friendly intruder approaching from Century. Probably Freund, he thought, coming down to check on him again. Karstil climbed down from the turret, rubbing the sleep from his eyes. He moved quickly to the other tanks, calling out to Farwell and Mullins as he approached. If they were asleep, he didn't want to embarrass them more than necessary. When his two sergeants responded, it sounded as though they'd just been awakened from a doze.

The entire platoon was awake when Freund's Liberator came into sight, its bulk dominating the Equus grav sled that accompanied it. The sled bore the hull number of the Cohort commander, and Karstil smiled to himself. He wondered what Freund's attitude would be in the presence of the Centurion Maximus. Both vehicles grounded beside Karstil's tank.

Freund looked as though he had had a good night's sleep, his uniform immaculate and freshly pressed. The combat coveralls were not supposed to be pressed, meant to be worn just as they came from the cleaners. Some officers who wanted to make an especially neat appearance had their uniforms pressed privately. Harras, on the other hand, looked suitably wrinkled, but clean. Karstil was acutely aware of how bad he must look. His coveralls were stained from the previous day's battle, and they had suffered further during the night of hard work. He was also aware of a certain ripe-smelling ambience about his body.

"This is my combat platoon," explained Freund to Harras. "They were in pretty rough shape when they came in last night, but I've managed to get them ready. It was a tough job, but we all pulled together on it."

"So I notice, Centurion. So I notice." The unpainted patches on Karstil's tank bore mute proof of the severity of the action as well as the amount of work required to get it operational.

"Let me show you what we had to do, sir," continued Freund. "This tank had some major damage that had to be repaired. Oh, I think you've met Karstil, the platoon leader."

"Yes, I have, Centurion." Harras turned to Karstil. "You seem to have been pretty busy, Optio. Why don't you show me around."

Karstil looked at Freund. The Centurion's lips were compressed in a thin line, his eyes glaring at Karstil. This should be fun, thought Karstil, but I'll probably pay for it later.

"Have you had a chance to bore-sight and check the weapons on your new tank?" asked Harras.

Karstil glanced beyond the knot of officers to where Mullins was standing in the distance. The Sergeant had heard the question and shook his head.

"Not yet, sir." Karstil thought it was better to tell the truth first. "I planned to do it in daylight. Mullins was about to start when you showed up, sir." Karstil caught the wry smile on Mullins' face. The Sergeant nodded and moved toward his tank.

"Optio," broke in Freund, "that was something you should have done as soon as the tank was delivered." Freund looked pleased with himself. "You've had plenty of time to do it by now, and you've reported the platoon ready for combat. If you weren't ready, you should not have reported yourself so."

Karstil refused to look his commander in the eye, fearing that his face would give him away. He just nodded and spoke again to Harras. "We did a lit 'le additional maintenance on my tank. Seems that there were mice at work in the control tier."

"Mice, Optio? How so mice?" Harras was interested.

"Nothing major, sir. Just a little gnawing at the control cable for my vane."

"Oh, really? Find anything else?"

"No, sir."

"Show me where you found it. I'm interested in the work of rodents, just in case they have a taste for my other vehicles." Harras turned to Freund. "Excuse me, Centurion. Would you mind monitoring the command net for me? I'll go with Karstil for a moment."

"Wilco, sir," responded Freund, shooting Karstil a you'd-better-be-careful-what-you-say glare as he turned to the Equus sled.

As the two officers reached the side of Karstil's Liberator that blocked Freund's view, Harras turned to Karstil. "What have you got for me, Optio?"

"This, sir." Karstil reached inside his coveralls and produced the finger-sized explosive device. As Harras examined it, Karstil opened the access panel on the side of the grounded tank.

"An interesting little toy. Any idea how long its been there?"

"Quite a while, sir. At least that's my guess. It was pretty well covered with grime, which probably means it was there when we left the transport."

"Well, I'll pass it along to some interested friends. They'll have a look at it. Who knows about it?"

"Mullins found it, sir. We haven't told anyone else."

"Good. It can be our little secret."

Karstil closed the access panel, and both men moved back toward the two vehicles. Freund watched them suspiciously, as though sure Karstil had been telling tales out of school. But Harras gave no indication that anything was wrong. "Get that weapon bore-sighted, Optio," said Harras. "You have an hour before we move, so that should be time enough. We aren't scheduled to move until mid-morning." Harras turned to Freund. "Let's saddle up, Centurion. I have places to go and people to meet."

The two men mounted their respective vehicles. By the time they were out of sight, Mullins had joined Karstil.

"Bore-sight accomplished, sir," said Mullins. "And I had the chance to check the 50mm gun for something unauthorized. It was O.K."

"I gave the Centurion Maximus a little present."

"How did he take it, sir?"

"Very interested. I guess this means that all the control cables have to be checked."

"Yes, sir. I don't know how we're going to do that without telling the platoon."

"If we tell them, how long will it be before everyone in the Legion knows about it?"

Mullins tugged at his ear. "We'll just have to do it one tank at a time." He stared off into the distance. "And just pray that any more little gifts from our friends don't become active until we find them."

Karstil nodded. "And by the way, Sergeant," he said. "I did cut the yellow wire first."

Alsatia, Caralis
The Commonwealth
4 January 6831

Movement on the second day of the Renegade Legion offensive was slow, the Second Medium Grav Century just creeping forward behind the lead elements. TOG defense of the Alsatian continent was becoming stronger and stronger, and the lead Century on the left had a tough fight trying to dislodge a rather stubborn group of infantry behind one of the open ridges. In desperation, they had to commit the Century Headquarters personnel and the last infantry squad to dislodge them. But the advance continued.

As Karstil's platoon passed over a portion of the battlefield, a burning Lupis APC sent a column of smoke into the brazen sky. The ground around the wreck was torn and gouged by hits from a mortar, the circular craters making a neat, dotted line from the crest of the ridge across the hull of the Lupis. Discarded weapons littered the area. A pair of TVLG launchers, their tubes empty and crushed, lay behind the Lupis. To the right and left of the carrier were crumpled bodies in TOG armor. Karstil was surprised at how small and pitiful a man looked, even in power armor, when he was dead. It was as though some of the bulk left the flesh when it died. He didn't stop to examine the bodies, afraid of what he might see. They didn't teach you about this part of the battle, Karstil thought morosely.

The sun was low on the horizon when they closed on the position of the leading Century. The scars on the Liberators and the wrecked turret of the accompanying Viper bore mute testimony to the day's violence. The infantry were hunkered down in craters around their vehicle, probably relieved to be outside their mobile coffin. Karstil's platoon grounded as soon as it arrived at the position, and the infantry began to mount. They and their tanks showed an obscene haste to be away, with little communication between the two tank platoon leaders. All that took place was a quick explanation of who was where and what could be expected of the Toggies. Then the battered platoon was on its way to the rear.

Karstil looked over the position, which occupied a broad ridge that ran across the front. The hill was 8 kilometers wide, broad on the rear slope but scoured with steep ravines along the forward edge. A kilometer beyond the spine to the front, the open terrain gave way to a dense stand of Carnob trees. The tall growth reached up some 20 meters, their branches intertwined into a thick canopy. Beneath the branches was enough open space to make vehicular movement at 70 KPH a reasonable speed.

Both flanks of the ridge were covered by arms of the forest that encircled the ridge.

Century Headquarters and the infantry platoon would be 10 kilometers away, with the other tank platoon some 5 kilometers beyond that. Karstil didn't like what he saw. The platoon was well to the left of the bulk of the Century, out on a limb. The woods provided excellent avenues of approach for infantry, and the trees were tall enough to block observation and fire to the front. He would have liked a squad or two of infantry to cover the woods, but his request was denied. The Centurion told him that the unit had other missions than to support a nervous platoon leader. "Just defend the position with your tanks," had been his reply. "You have more than you need to hold a simple ridge."

There was little enough Karstil could do but take the rebuke. Perhaps the Centurion knows more about the situation than I do, he thought. Maybe he thinks that the right and center are the threatened positions. He thought of asking for an artillery-delivered Anti-Personnel/Anti-Tank minefield but decided against it. One chewing-out a day was enough.

The platoon area was too wide to occupy with the "two up and one back" he would have liked. He had to deploy all three Liberators on line, keeping the normal order he had established on the first day of the advance. Mullins took the left flank, Farwell the right, and his own tank was at center. Once the other two had found good hull-down locations, he had them mark secondary positions with craters. That way they would be able to switch positions in the darkness, reaching previously prepared spots. They would not need to give away the fact that they were in cratered locations. Karstil didn't know if that would help, but it did mean that all the digging cannon would be fully loaded when and if it came time to move.

He still wanted to know what was out front. With no infantry to make the reconnaissance, and with only nine men in the platoon, he decided to do it himself. He had Spint back the Liberator down the rear of the position and then move to the left behind Mullins. The Platoon Sergeant's replacement tank was a marked contrast to Karstil's own scarred vehicle. Everything looked so clean and new. He waved at Mullins as he went by, indicating his intention to circle the front of the platoon position. Mullins waved back happily, a cigar planted between his teeth.

The falling light was almost gone under the arching branches of the Carnob trees. Karstil brought the sensors up to full power, short range. He wasn't too worried about anything at 50 kilometers, for the other tanks of the platoon would see that soon enough. He just didn't want some laggard TOG infantry squad, lurking under the trees, to get in a quick shot with TVLGs or mortars.

The trees were more widely spaced than he had assumed from the hilltop. Movement in them would be faster than he had thought, probably something like 90 to 100 kilometers an hour. He made some quick calculations: If an enemy tank approached through the forest at, say, 90 kph, and began to accelerate as soon as it cleared the trees, say with an additional acceleration of 86 kph, they would be doing around 180 when they crossed the ridge. At that speed, the enemy would be covering a kilometer every twenty seconds. That was pretty fast for his three Liberators. With their hull- and turret-mounted weapons, the tanks would get six targets. But the painting lasers could only acquire three targets, which meant that either the lasers or the TVLGs would have to fire blind.

That was why an infantry squad would have been a bonus. By breaking the eight-man squad into three sections, they would have a chance to paint the approaching vehicles, and the squad would also have had TVLGs or mortars of their own. Even if they didn't spread out, they could cover, paint, and engage part of the advancing enemy force. Karstil shrugged. He didn't have any infantry. He shook his head. For all the supposed contempt tankers had for the pedes, here he was wishing for some. Infantry, in the words of one ancient historian, were like lice. They hid in the folds of the ground and were difficult to dislodge.

The Liberator worked its way slowly through the Carnob forest. Karstil was perfectly willing to move slowly. A tank moving at maximum safe speed in the forest took a lot out of both the driver and the commander. He wanted to save his energy reserve for later. There was no point in wasting his resources. The deep ridges marking the forward slope extended well into the trees, perfect for a stealthy approach by enemy infantry. Again he wished for infantry or an artillery-delivered minefield.

There was another solution available, but he tried not to think about it. There was little room to maneuver in defense of the position, and all the gunner's controls were carried in the commander's station. It would be possible to dismount either the gunner or the driver, or both, to provide the forward security. With a communicator, the outpost could at least give a warning. With a target identified, artillery could be called onto the location. But that meant reducing the effectiveness of the platoon. He'd think about that later.

Farwell's tank was well-positioned, and even though Karstil knew where he was, the tank came as a surprise. He saw that Number Three's turret had been tracking him through the trees, just in case. Farwell was lounging at his station, his right hand below the hatch ring on the controls of the turret. Umbartis and Kloun were outside the tank, their small ration-heater sending up a thin column of steam. Farwell was seeing to it that his crew had a hot meal. Good idea, thought Karstil, and he gave his Sergeant a thumbs-up sign as he passed behind him. He hadn't had anything but a ration concentrate all day, and it was sitting like a brick in the pit of his stomach.

Unlike the standard combat rations, emergency rations were designed to be eaten cold or hot, but hot was better than cold anytime. Karstil wondered about those rations. They were certainly full of nutrition to supply energy, but the only bulk was that of the inedible wrappers. The food turned to ash in the intestines, becoming mere pellets. A diet of combat rations, either emergency or regular, made a man constipated beyond belief. By the time he reached a latrine, his lower digestive tract was loaded with rock-hard slugs that were capable of breaking the bowl. But Karstil hadn't needed to find a latrine very often—not since they had dropped from the transport.

Karstil grounded his tank in the center of the position. He decided against bringing his sensors back to long-range. If the flank tanks kept theirs at full, long-range power, that would be enough to cover the width of the position. His short-range sensors could cover the near approaches, and unless the TOG infantry were very cautious, he would be able to see them at two kilometers.

"All right, you two," Karstil told Podandos and Spint. "Brew up some food. You must be tired and hungry." The two crewmen needed no further encouragement. They scrambled out of the Liberator and immediately set up the heating unit behind the tank. Karstil was about to break open another emergency pack when Duncan Spint mounted the turret.

"It's not really much, sir," he said, proffering a plate filled with a steaming, fragrant substance. "We just mixed up what was left from two or three packs. It was Quent's idea."

Karstil looked at the brown, lumpy mixture on the plate. "It looks good enough to me. My compliments to the chef."

"I'll tell him, sir. But first you'd better have a taste."

"Is there enough for the two of you?"

"Yes, sir. Quent's already eating, and there's plenty left. He said he learned the recipe from one of those books he's always reading."

Karstil tried the mixture. It certainly had an interesting flavor, a cross between any number of main course selections offered in the ration pack. He didn't really care; it was hot.

The meal produced a warm glow that spread from his stomach outward into his limbs. Along with it came the thought that things were not so bad after all. With any luck, the platoon would be able to get through the night without interruption. Standard security, one man on watch in each tank, should be enough. It wasn't like the bad old days before sensors when the troops had to rely mainly on their eyes and ears. The DDPs had performed faultlessly; they could be trusted. He called the other two crewmen to the interior of the turret basket.

"We'll break the night into ninety-minute watches," said Karstil. "Podandos, you take the first watch, Spint the second, and I'll take the third. We'll reverse the order after that. I'll take the fourth, Spint the fifth, Podandos the sixth. That way we'll each get at least three hours of uninterrupted sleep at least once. Sleep near your station. The two of you can sleep inside the turret. I'll sleep outside, on top of the hull behind the turret. Whoever has the watch, be sure I'm awake before you rotate the thing. I'd hate to get caught under it."

The two men nodded assent, Spint sticking out his tongue in mock derision at Podandos who would have to stand the first watch. The driver ducked the hand that jabbed in riposte, scrambled into the turret, and curled himself across the floor of the fighting compartment. One hand below his head like a pillow, the other in front of his face, Spint was already breathing deeply even before Podandos took his position at the commander's station.

"I've set the sensors on short-range," said Karstil, giving his gunner final instructions. "Leave them there. We're on listening silence with the commlink, but if you see anything, be sure to announce it over the communicator. I'm going to visit Mullins and Farwell before I turn in. They're 800 meters to the right and left. You can see them on the screen. With the sensors set on short-range, you'll be able to see me make the trip to both."

Podandos nodded in acknowledgment and then repeated the instructions of his Optio. Not bad, thought Karstil. Quentain might be young, but he certainly remembered his training. Karstil knew that he had forgotten to ask the young gunner to repeat the orders for the night.

The transit of the position took nearly the full watch. The walk of almost three kilometers, down to Mullins, back to the center tank, over to Farwell, and back to the command location took more time than Karstil had estimated. It also took more energy. Both tanks had been alert, Mullins and Farwell expecting a visit from the platoon leader. He told them about his sensor setting, just in case they assumed that no one else had established short-range surveillance.

Karstil could feel the burst of energy from his meal beginning to drop. His legs felt like lead. The last portion of the march, from Farwell to his own Liberator, was all he could do. By the time he reached the hull, he was almost too tired to climb the glacis over the TVLG mount. Podandos was alert at the command station, monitoring the DDP and staring into the darkness. He had been staying alert, Karstil noticed, by wadding up pieces of the ration wrappers and throwing them into the fighting compartment. Spint was surrounded by little bits of wrapper.

"Watch this, sir," said Quentain. He wadded up a piece of wrapper and flipped it at the sleeping driver, hitting Spint square on the nose. The driver wrinkled his nose and swiped at the offending wrapper with his free hand, but did not awaken.

"You can probably knock that off, Quent. Remember, the payback's a bitch."

"Right, sir. You going to sleep now, sir?"

"Yeah. Remind Duncan where I am when he relieves you."

"Yes, sir."

Karstil debated whether or not to dig out the thermal blanket that was part of his kit. The thought of having to climb into the turret, burrow through his gear, and then climb back out was more than he could face. He picked his way around the turret and stretched out on the rear hull. He knew there were things he had to think about, but he was asleep before could remember what they were.

136

29

Alsatia, Caralis
The Commonwealth
5 January 6831

In the chill of pre-dawn, the bear-like man hunkered down in a small depression surrounded by bushes. He had been doing this for three nights, silently watching the surrounding terrain. Pulling the thermal cape over his head, he made sure it covered his feet as well as the bulk of his body. He set up the passive sensor unit at the edge of the hole, adjusting the ambient glow to the point where it nearly vanished. Any intruder would appear as a faint light, while the screen itself would not betray his position to any but a very close watcher. He set the scan on all-round program. It would not do to have someone approach from the rear and inadvertently stumble onto his position.

The position set and cleared, he placed his 2mm needle pistol on the brow of the depression. The weapon held thirty rounds of ammunition and could be set either on semi- or full-automatic. The 2mm flechettes produced almost no recoil, and the weapon could deliver all thirty rounds in just under two seconds. The watcher had two additional magazines. Next to the pistol, he placed two hand grenades. Both were Mark 9 Flash grenades. They did no real damage, just exploding in a blinding flash of light. Anyone wearing a night observation device would be blinded and the device burned out by overload. If the eyes were unprotected, they could be permanently damaged. In either case, the victim's night vision would be gone for at least twenty minutes. An unwarned individual would be at a significant disadvantage. The one-second fuses gave no warning. Just pull the pin and throw.

His tasks completed, the watcher settled down to observe. He remained motionless, his metabolism slowing down until his heartbeat and breathing were almost undetectable. But his eyes never left the dark screen in front of him. The ability to reduce his heartbeat and breathing was a useful talent that he had developed. In this manner, he was able to "sleep" on the job, and yet remain alert. It had taken years to perfect the ability. Now the watcher remained awake while the other members of the 2567th Renegade Legion slept, or worked, or worried, or watched around him.

And there were those in the area who did not have the best interests of the Legion at heart. These too, worked, or worried, or watched. Few of them were asleep.

The man had been motionless, watching, for more than an hour when the DDP screen showed a faint blue light. His head didn't move, but his eyes concentrated on the light, watching it slowly cross the screen. The light showed that the intruder was getting closer, moving in a direct line between Legion trains and one of the Centuries laagered down 5 kilometers away. The intruder, an Equus light grav sled, came to a stop 100 meters from the watcher. He opened the ambient night observation device to get a better look at the sled. There were two men on it. They hid the sled in a fold of the ground, carefully covering the vehicle with a thermal canvas and pulling bushes around the lip of the depression. The blue square on the DDP winked out, and if the watcher had not known it was there, he could only have discovered the sled by accident.

The two men from the grav sled carefully applied black camouflage makeup to their hands and faces and then donned dark clothing that covered them from face to wrist. They did not hurry, performing their task with studied care. Almost invisible against the night sky, they extracted their tools from the sled and departed toward the sleeping Century.

The watcher waited for them to go, carefully marking their track in his mind. Then he rose from his hiding place, leaving his own thermal shroud in place, and moved to the hidden sled. He took the 2mm pistol and both grenades with him.

It took no time at all to discover the hull markings on the sled; it was a repair Contact Team from the 2567th Maintenance Cohort. A brief search uncovered equipment not authorized to repair teams. A small box of finger-size explosives as well as several transponders were hidden under the regular tools. In addition, the searcher also found a small probe designed to test DDP circuits. At first glance, it appeared to be a standard probe, but further examination revealed an additional electronic chip in the main board. There was no telling what the chip was designed to do, but the watcher extracted the thin silicon device with a pair of tweezers and placed it in a thin cello pack. He would study it later.

The watcher placed his NOD on the rim of the small depression that hid the sled and scanned the ground toward the Legion. By bringing the power up to near its maximum, he could discern the two men as they approached a Deliverer that was hull-down in its crater. Unless the men of the tank had their sensors on short-range, full-power, they would never detect the intruders. No matter how good was security around a tank, there was always a way to approach it. With a three-man crew, only one man was on watch at any one time, and that soldier could not be looking everywhere at once.

The watcher saw the men crawl under the camouflage net and disappear. That was all the watcher needed. He was sure now that these two men, and probably others, were responsible for some of the "unfortunate accidents" that had befallen the Legion. The problem was what to do about it at the moment.

The easiest thing, and the one that would cause the least uproar, was to depart, taking with him evidence of his night's work. If he did that, the saboteurs were sure to realize that the chip was missing and realize that they had been discovered. That would only make the others engaged in nefarious activity more alert. It might very well make them lie low for a while. That, of course, would solve some of the Legion's problems in the short run, but the problem would still exist.

The watcher had a pretty good idea who was responsible for the sabotage within the Legion and had tracked his suspect halfway across Commonwealth space to the surface of Caralis. To allow two small fish to queer the whole program would be counterproductive. It would be better if the TOG agents never knew they had been discovered. That was the only way they could lead him to the bigger fish.

To prevent giving away the game, the watcher would have to replace the chip he had extracted from the DDP test probe. That would eliminate vital evidence of what the TOG agents had been doing, prevent the counterespionage agents from correcting the damage. Correction would be easy. Once the type of sabotage were known, the DDP probes of the other Contact Teams could be checked and a counter-chip placed in the main circuit. Then, any check of the DDPs throughout the Legion would reveal damage, and that damage could be corrected. He had to have the chip.

And if he had to take the chip, he would also have to eliminate the saboteurs. The only difficulty with that task was to make it look like an accident. He had to work quickly, for there was no telling when the enemy agents would return.

He slid back down the ridge, into the depression that hid the grav sled. Using the tools left in the vehicle, he removed the access panel that covered the fusion core that powered the grav drives and directional vanes. The explosive devices left behind by the agents were perfect for the job. Any enemy agent who checked the wreckage of the sled would discover only "authorized" explosive fragments. Better to hoist the agents on their own petard than to bring in something new. Anyway, it was poetic justice.

With the explosives in place, he bolted the access panel back into place, bringing the lead wires from the explosive charge out through the opening. The primers for the charges were internal to the devices themselves so there was no need to search for something to make the package go "boom." What he did need was a timing device so that the sled would be far enough away that the explosion destroyed only the Equus sled. That was a simple matter. He wrapped the lead wires around the steering column. By setting the sled to make a wide turn, the column bearing would rotate, finally bringing the two bare wires in contact. Bingo!

There was no way of telling just how far the sled would have to travel before contact would be made, but the watcher tested the mechanism. There was 1,000 mils of play in the bearing before contact was assured. That, he thought, would take the saboteurs between 500 and 1,000 meters away from the current location before ignition took place. That should be enough. His task accomplished, he waited for the intruders to return.

There was a sudden flurry of activity in the Legion laager. It looked as though there was some trouble with one of the Centuries deployed further forward, and this Century had been called to action. The watcher saw his quarry crawl out from under one of the Deliverers and move stealthily into the surrounding darkness. They remained stationary while the Commonwealth tanks rose to a 1-meter hover, formed, and moved off toward the flashes of the distant fighting. That would make the accident easier, for no one would be present to witness the destruction of the Equus sled.

When the area became quiet and desolate again, the two intruders rose from the covering Acalaba bush and returned to their sled. They came with the easy gait of men who felt safe and alone, who had accomplished a good night's work. The watcher pulled the pin on one of the M-9 grenades, careful to keep the arming lever pressed into the palm of his left hand. With his right hand, he thumbed the safety lug on the pistol to the "fire" position and waited.

The men were so confident that they approached without stealth, walking upright, even talking to one another. The watcher continued to track them with his NOD, their bodies showing up as soft blurs on the screen. For the first time, he noticed that both men were armed with standard 5mm needle pistols stuck in their waist bands. As long as they didn't reach for their weapons, this would be easy. But as soon as he thought about it, they drew their guns.

At 100 meters, the men slowed their pace, beginning to move more carefully and search the ground around them. The watcher was sure they hadn't seen him. They were probably taking the usual precautions when approaching their sled. Both men's strides became more tentative, more cautious. The weapons were at their sides, hanging from their hands. Interesting, thought the watcher, one is left- and the other right-handed. And they walk so that the weapon-hands are on the outside. Very good practice. These men are professionals.

A sense of pride swept over him. Three professionals engaged in a deadly hunt. The quarry did not know the horrible danger they faced, but they were taking instinctive precautions against the unknown. These men were not amateurs, hired by TOG for money or glory. They were well-trained agents. At 50 meters, the watcher could see that the men had turned slightly outward, away from each other. They were quartering the ground, dividing up the terrain and looking for anything suspicious, anything that triggered a warning bell in the brain. They kept coming.

The watcher gauged the range to the target. He could throw the grenade with accuracy at least 30 meters, but that was with the right hand. With the gun in his right hand, he would have to throw with the left. Most of his left-hand throws had been at shorter ranges, more of a lob at ten meters or less. Added to the difficulty was the fact that he was lying at the lip of the depression and would have to rise to get any distance at all. That would alert the agents. He would have to wait until they were almost on him before he made his move.

The targets grew closer: 25 meters, 20, 15, 10. He moved his hand to bring the grenade to the lip of the depression. The man on the left, the taller of the two, froze in his tracks, bringing his right arm up to warn his fellow conspirator. At the moment the watcher saw the man's mouth open to shout a warning, he tossed the grenade over the lip of the depression, dropping his head to the ground as protection from the blinding flash of light.

Even with his face pressed against the ground, the searing light penetrated through the lids. He had used these grenades before, but never at night. He had been trained to enter a lighted room, throwing the grenade in just before he cleared the door. Even in a lighted room, the explosion was enough to blind an unwary man. At night, when pupils dilated to let in what little illumination the stars provided, the brilliance of the explosion was devastating.

He rolled to his right, his firing arm extending as his body stabilized. He opened his eyes and was greeted by a series of tiny, green dots floating across his vision. Around the dots, he could vaguely make out the shape of a man staggering backward. Instinctively and without thinking about aiming, he fired the 2mm pistol.

The pistol had been set on full automatic, and the one-second burst released fifteen of the deadly projectiles. The 2mm flechettes, as big around as a pencil lead and 25mm long, have a muzzle velocity approaching 1,500 meters per second, almost the speed of sound. The designers of the pistol had kept the velocity that low, even though they could have increased it, so that the projectiles made no sonic boom when the weapon was fired. But even at that "low" speed, the damage to a human body was incredible. The round hit with such force that the body all but disintegrated, like shooting a standard slug into a grapefruit. When fifteen slugs hit the body, there was no chance of survival.

The watcher's target exploded under the impact, the intruder's chest and abdomen ripped open by the tiny needles that scoured away layers of flesh, bone, and entrails. Even in the darkness, the watcher could see the head and shoulder section separate from the hip girdle, only the thin column of the spine continuing to make the connection between the two. The upper portion toppled backward, the spine finally pulling the legs with it.

He looked to his left, searching for the other target. He saw his man, almost completely blinded by the flash, down on his knees. The muzzle of his 5mm pistol was searching the ground to his front, firing repeatedly into the area the watcher had just vacated. The man was blind, firing on instinct and the tenacious will to live. The watcher felt one of the slugs graze high on his upper back where he crouched, the bullet tearing through back and shoulder muscles. He raised the 2mm pistol, pointed it at the center of the swarm of green dots he saw before him, and released another half-second burst.

The blind man had no chance. Many of the rounds missed their target, the watcher's aim pulled off by his own wound. But those that hit struck high on the target, raking across the shoulders and face of the adversary. Headless, the body crashed backward onto the ground. Not pretty, thought the watcher. Not pretty.

The bear-like man staggered to his feet, blinking against the green dots that still danced in his eyes from the explosion. To protect his cover, he now had to tidy up the mess and make it all look like some kind of accident. The second man was relatively easy, for the hit had been so clean. The first man was more of a problem. The watcher was amazed at how much there is inside a body once it has been released. It took him some time to find the larger pieces of evidence and store them on the grav sled. Parts of the body looked like deviled ham.

He could feel his own blood running down his back, making the camouflage coveralls stick to his hips. There didn't seem to be any bone damage, for his legs worked. But he was afraid that he would lose consciousness from the loss of blood. The problem with a back wound, aside from having to explain it, was that there was no way to treat it himself. He would have to find help, and that could create problems if the helper were not one of his own. He worked quickly, the fear of failure rising in him.

He could feel himself becoming light-headed as he placed the last of the intruders on the sled. No need to be neat, just get the job done. He reached into the control box, hitting the master switch, feeling the fusion core spring to life. He held his breath, waiting for the flash and explosion that would tell him he had wired too well. Nothing. He was safe so far.

He stuffed one of the dead feet against the thrust pedal and felt the sled lurch forward. Some protruding piece of the sled caught in the tear of his coveralls made by the 5mm slug, holding him against the side of the vehicle. He could feel the object, probably a tool rack, probing its way across his back, gouging at the wound. The sled was beginning to accelerate, dragging him across the ground.

The watcher twisted against the metal bracket, tearing flesh and clothing as he struggled. He felt his eyes beginning to go dark, the area of vision shrinking as he neared unconsciousness. In one urgent tug at survival, he wrenched himself free of the mechanical claw that held him, tumbling to the ground as the sled went by.

He was vaguely aware of the sled in the distance, slowly turning to the right. He watched it dumbly as it picked up speed, describing a circle on the terrain. He waited for the explosion that he was sure must come. The sled vanished from his sight, still accelerating as the thrusters propelled it toward its own doom. A brilliant explosion, a white-yellow burst of light against the dark terrain, signaled its end.

The watcher rose to his feet, pushing himself from the ground with his good arm. Cradling his left arm with his right, he stumbled back to his hiding place. Carefully, slowly, he gathered up his equipment, made a mental inventory of everything he had brought. He stored it on his load-bearing web gear, securing the tabs that held it in place. There was a place for everything, and everything had its place. He was momentarily panicked when he found one of the M-9 grenades was missing, then remembered that he had used it. He switched magazines on the 2mm needle pistol. He wanted a full one ready in case he ran into trouble. The gear stowed, he began the 5-kilometer hike back to Legion Headquarters to make his report.

30

Alsatia, Caralis
The Commonwealth
5 January 6831

Karstil looked up at the stars. He was wide awake.

"Time for your watch, sir," Duncan Spint said, looking down at his Optio, not sure if he were awake or not.

"Right. I'm awake."

Spint didn't move, waiting for the Optio to rise from his sleeping spot on the rear deck of the Liberator.

"I'm awake, I tell you. I'm awake."

Still Spint did not move. There was no way he would leave the Optio until he were sure that the young officer were up and functioning. Functioning as well as could be expected from a man who had slept less than two hours in the last forty-eight.

"All right," said Karstil, rolling to his side and rising on all fours. Using the rear of the turret as a prop, he clawed himself erect. Every muscle, bone, and joint screamed out for rest. He felt his knees creak a protest. He had fallen asleep on his side, and he had never moved. He was suffering from "miners' syndrome," the result of remaining too long in one position. He could feel the skin on his left side bearing the creases of the combat coveralls. He peeled the greasy uniform from his torso, letting the night air pour into the top. He was grimy, and gave off an odor that would have been offensive if those around him were not giving off the same scent. He rubbed his face with his hands, massaging the blood back to the surface. "I'm up now. Anything to report?"

"All quiet, sir. It's been like that since you went to sleep."

"Good. Let's hope it stays that way. Good night, Duncan. Sweet dreams."

"I'd settle for no dreams and a good night's sleep."

"Right."

The driver scrambled into the fighting compartment, careful not to tread on Podandos, already sleeping on the floor. Karstil watched him gently push his compatriot to one side and snuggle down beside him. Duncan Spint was asleep almost at once. The human body was marvelous, thought Karstil. If you deprive it of rest long enough, it can sleep anywhere, even on the grid floor of a tank turret.

He scanned the DDP, identifying the other two tanks of the platoon. They had not changed position since he had left them. He wondered if he should call them, tell them to move to a different location just in case they had been spotted. He should do the same for his own vehicle. Then he looked at Spint, sound asleep on the floor of the fighting compartment, and decided against it. There was no use waking him, and if the TOGs were attempting to search the area, certainly his sensors would have noticed it.

A red warning light blinked on and off on the DDP. Karstil stared at the screen, wondering if he had seen it or if his eyes were playing tricks. There was nothing there. Perhaps a malfunction. Perhaps a hyperactive imagination. He looked over the top of the turret, his eyes burning and straining into the dark woods a kilometer to the front. Nothing.

He let his heartbeat steady after the shock, willing it to beat slower, conserving energy. He was not going to be spooked by the fear beast of his imagination. He would play it cool. But the hair on the back of his neck would not allow it. He felt someone watching him. Watching him from the darkness.

There! The red light blinked on and off again. Out there in the woods, 1,200 meters away, the sensors had detected an intruder. It could be only an infantryman, creeping slowly toward the position. So, he thought, you're going to try to sneak up on us. Well, not this time. Just because we have no infantry of our own does not mean that we aren't ready. He opened the commlink channel and raised the lip mike to his mouth.

"Two-two-six, this is Two-two-three." It was Farwell on the right of the platoon position. "Intruders. Range three thousand. Speed one hundred. Targets closing."

"Two-two-six, this is Two-two-two. I have them. Down below the trees. No line of sight." Mullins had them, too.

"Six. Roger. They're in the woods as well." Karstil was going to give some of the bad news, too. He looked down into the fighting compartment, ready to kick Podandos and Spint awake, but Quentain was already buckling himself into his gunner's seat, and he could see Duncan's feet disappearing into the driver's station. They had awakened at the first sound of the radio. Marvelous how a man could sleep soundly and awaken at the screech of the commlink. Training and instinct, the lifeblood of a soldier.

An instant later, Karstil felt the surge of power reach the grav drives. They weren't off the ground, but Spint was making sure that they were ready when the time came. Karstil saw the orange triangles blink under the other Liberators as their grav drives cut in, returning to blue to show that the tanks were fired up. The DDP bloomed with red lights at close range. The TOG infantry had reached the edge of the woods.

"Target identified. Six Lupis carriers. Three Horatius medium grav tanks. Range two-four hundred meters. Bearing one-two hundred mils relative. Speed one hundred kph. Targets closing. No lock possible." The ballistic computer was churning out information on the oncoming TOG forces. Karstil checked his DDP. There were three ovals of red at the edge of the trees: three infantry squads deployed. They were probably from three of the Lupis carriers. The others were probably carrying infantry TVLG squads that would be bounced out once they cleared the forest. Not a bad plan. Three shooting while the other painted.

"This is Six. Engage the carriers first. Disregard the Horatius tanks. It's the infantry who will give us problems."

"Two, wilco."

"Three, wilco."

Both tanks had accepted his orders. Only time would tell if they would be obeyed.

"Conquest Farmer Two-six, this is Conquest Farmer Two-two-six. Flash. Enemy on my position. Three Horatius tanks, six carriers, three deployed squads." Freund, the call sign, and the frequency had all changed at midnight. Karstil had heard no report from the other platoons, could only assume that they weren't being hit.

"Quent. Target the turret on one carrier, the TVLGs on the other. We'll try to paint the TVLG target."

"Target laid on, sir."

"Target identified. Two Lupis carriers. Range eighteen hundred meters. Bearing twelve hundred mils relative. Speed one hundred KPH. Target closing. No lock achieved." The ballistic computer continued to pass on the information.

"Spint. Be ready to move to the secondary position as soon as we shoot. Quent, I'll take the TVLGs. You handle the turret."

"Got it."

"Target identified. Two Lupis carriers. Range, fourteen hundred meters. Bearing, twelve hundred mils relative. Speed, one hundred kph. Target closing. No lock achieved." Karstil felt his heart pounding in his chest, felt his palms moist with perspiration.

"Conquest Farmer Two-two-six, this is Conquest Farmer Two-two." That was the voice of Freund's commlink operator. "Please confirm contact with enemy vehicles. We have only three targets on screen."

"This is Two-two-six. I say again. Three Horatius tanks, six carriers, three deployed squads." Where was Freund? Why wasn't he at his commlink?

"This is Two-two. Negative on your last. Our screens still show only three targets. Check your data and get back to me."

"You and the horse you rode in on, fella," mumbled Karstil. "This is Two-two-six. You have my data. Deal with it."

"Target identified. Two Lupis carriers. Range, twelve hundred meters. Bearing, twelve hundred mils relative. Speed, one hundred KPH. Target closing. No lock ach . . . Lock achieved." Karstil hammered down on the treadle for the painting laser, firing the two TVLG missiles from the upper rack an instant later. He didn't even wait for the ballistic computer to announce whether or not he had been successful. At 1,200 meters, he had a 50 percent chance, more or less, to paint. And even if he didn't succeed, the missiles had the same chance to hit. He felt the Liberator throb as the two Gauss cannon fired together, the thump of the guns pierced by the high whine of the heavy laser. The entire expanse of the treeline rippled with light as the Liberator's shots struck home. Karstil felt his own tank begin to back down away from the edge of the hill.

The TOG forces had known where the platoon was, probably had seen the original occupants move into the area. They had counted on overwhelming the platoon by giving it more targets to shoot at than it had weapons systems. They had been right. With nine possible targets, all of which were capable of taking at least one heavy hit, they were all over the position before the defenders could react.

As Karstil backed down from the ridge to avoid the infantry with their TVLG racks in the woods, the nine vehicles, some of them glowing, but all still functioning, screamed over the position. Even above the roar of the grav drives and the thud of weapons, Karstil heard the distinctive "pop" of bounce infantry deploying from carriers. The Lupis APCs had not even bothered to fire their cratering charges, letting the Liberators find the infantry without a reference point.

"Conquest Farmer. Conquest Farmer. This is Conquest Farmer Two-two-six. Overrun by infantry and tanks." Karstil didn't really care who heard him now. The entire Century might as well know what was going on.

"Back it around, Spint. They're coming back." Karstil felt the tank swerve as Spint gave full forward power to one vane, full rear to the other. He was thrown against the coaming, grasping the edge with both hands. The DDP was alive with red squares and triangles. He hit the painting laser treadle again, hoping that the computer had chosen the correct target.

"Target identified. Lupis carrier. Range eight hundred meters. Bearing twelve hundred mils relative. Speed, ninety-seven KPH. Target painted."

That, thought Karstil, was not the target of choice now. He had tried to knock out the Lupis carriers before they could launch their infantry. No success that he could see. Now that the infantry had penetrated, the real danger was the Horatius tanks. But the computer, having been told to disregard the Horatius tanks in favor of the carriers, was still shooting at the light stuff. The turret weapons fired again. Somewhere in the darkness to the rear of the position, the three weapons struck the side of a Lupis. The Lupis was an armored bus, only slightly better protected than the Renegade Viper. It was not designed to withstand the pounding of heavy tank weapons. Karstil saw the Lupis glow, outlined in fire against the dark sky. There was no accompanying explosion, but the carrier was hurt. He could see the afterglow of molten droplets streaking through the night.

"Whoop, whoop, whoop, wheeeeee!" The painting warning klaxon screamed in Karstil's ear. There was no way of telling if it were a tank, carrier, or one of the lurking infantry squads, only that he had been painted. "Oh Lord, for that which we are about to receive . . ."

"Target identified. Horatius tank. Range, six hundred meters. Bearing, thirteen hundred forty mils relative. Speed, one hundred-ten kph. Lock achieved." Karstil realized he had been pounding the painting laser treadle even as Podandos searched for a tank rather than a carrier. He felt the turret shudder as the weapons fired, waited for the TVLGs to launch. Then he remembered that he had taken command of the missile rack and fired. The front of the tank bloomed in flame as the missiles streaked for their target, the whole bow area bathed in light.

As if in response, the left side of the Liberator was sheeted in explosions as two TVLGs, penetrating the Vulcan III defense, struck home. More hits from at least one 150mm cannon, a 50mm, and multiple laser blasts raked the side. Karstil felt the tank lurch as most of the seven tons of armor that protected the flank of the tank peeled away or were vaporized. A thick pall of smoke filled the fighting compartment as ceramic armor burned under the aligned light of the 3/6 lasers. The DDP flickered, dimmed once, and came on again as redundant circuits picked up the load. The painting laser warning continued to scream in his ear.

An Horatius tank roared over his position at treetop flight to avoid ramming something on the ground. A cratering explosion threw great clods of earth into the air behind it. Podandos didn't even wait for the target to be painted, firing all the weapons under his command into the belly of the tank. Why not? he thought. No use dying with TVLGs still in the rack. Two more on the way.

At less than 200 meters, even an unpainted target was almost a sure hit, and one that shows its bottom at that range is asking for it. As snap shots, there was no way to place one hit on top of the other, but anything, even a 50mm APDS round, will do damage to a thin-skinned bottom. The whole underside of the tank glowed red, grav coils and armor spiraling away under the hits. Karstil didn't even bother watching to see what would happen; the tank was out of action for a while. If it weren't destroyed on grounding, it could be dealt with later.

In the afterglow of the departing tank, Karstil could see a group of TOG infantry hurrying through the gloom. There was enough illumination now to see quite a distance, what with burning tanks and flashing guns. The infantry were carrying TVLG tubes, and Karstil wished he had an AP laser. A 50mm cannon was not much against infantry. When it hit, it killed dead, dead, dead, but it usually got only one man at a time. He realized that he hadn't dropped inside the turret to button up.

The left side of the turret shook from another TVLG hit, all the ceramic armor glowing from the explosion. That hurt, he thought. This thing is so hot I can't even put my hand on it.

He looked to his right. There was a man crawling onto his turret. Now what is he doing? wondered Karstil. Then he knew. The man was carrying a satchel demolition charge. The thing probably weighed 25 kilos from the way he was horsing it up the side. If he gets that planted, thought Karstil, I'm dead.

"Get off my tank!" he shouted. He leaned under the tube of the 150mm cannon and gave the man a push. The TOG soldier looked up in surprise at the shout and the push. He lost his footing on the sloping side of the tank, stumbling backward, twisting in mid-air as he grasped the demolition charge to his chest. The weapon must have been armed, for the charge exploded as he struck the ground. Karstil had the impression of a man completely outlined in light. The body slowly began to unravel, the light eating inward toward the center of mass. Then he was gone.

The front of the Liberator took multiple hits. A round of some size, probably a 50mm APDS, struck square in one of the empty TVLG tubes, the metal shroud and firing rails whirling into the darkness. The right sponson opened like a flower under an exploding 150mm HEAP hit, and the left sponson, held on by imagination more than anything else, absorbed two TVLG missiles. Smoke was pouring from the hatches, and Karstil could hear wracking coughs from the men in the fighting compartment below. From somewhere in the depths of the tank, Karstil could see a flicker of fire. The fire-suppression system hooted into life, and the heavy gases quickly extinguished the flames. The smoke got thicker.

In the command station, the ballistic computer flickered again. Died, came on, and died again. Without a computer to direct fire, it would be open-gun sights at point-blank range.

"Conquest Farmer Two-two-six, this is Conga Whiplash One-three-six. What seems to be the problem here?"

Karstil didn't recognize the call sign or the voice. It could have been anyone, including TOG reinforcements. "Unknown Station, this is Farmer Two-two-six. I'm overrun with TOG tanks and infantry. What the hell does it look like?"

"Roger Farmer Two-two-six. No need to get testy. The cavalry should not arrive before the situation gets critical, else there is no suspense."

Karstil heard them coming. There is something about the throbbing power of a 2500 class grav drive that makes it distinct from all others. Karstil could hear the heavy drives laboring to carry their armored behemoths. In the glow of a burning tank, he saw the bow of a tank come into view, looking for all the world like a three-tined fork. Now that's ugly, he thought, the idea blotted out an instant later as he recognized the incredible bulk of a Deliverer heavy tank. The 200mm main gun, mounted low in the central hull, emitted a huge, expanding blue ball of ionized gas as the projectile sprang from the muzzle.

The 200mm cannon fires a projectile almost twice the weight of the 150, and while the 150mm round makes a distinctive "crack" when it passes nearby, the 200mm shakes the air like a runaway transport. Karstil heard the round pass close aboard as he ducked down inside the turret. Somewhere behind him an explosion shook the ground, followed by the pattering of parts as whatever had been the target disintegrated under the impact. The bow lasers were firing, too, though he couldn't see them except when the light passed through the pall of smoke that covered the battlefield.

Behind the Deliverer came a Spartius medium APC, and Karstil could see the Renegade infantry deploying from the rear of the vehicle. Small, violent firefights were beginning to break out on the rear of the hill as the Renegade infantry began to hunt down the TOG foot soldiers. A second Deliverer rumbled past at low speed, swinging its main gun back and forth as if to clear a path with its own bulk. The fighting drifted down the slope to the front, the TOG infantry seeking the shelter of the woods, the Renegades loathe to let them escape.

A Deliverer grounded gently beside the battered wreck that had been Karstil's Liberator. The commander waved jauntily to Karstil. Karstil stared back, too shocked even to acknowledge his presence. The tank was immense. The 50mm cannon, no small weapon in its own right, was dwarfed by the massive turret. And the hull just went on and on and on. The Deliverer's commander tapped the side of his helmet, questioning if Karstil's commlink were out.

"Conquest Farmer Two-two-six, this is Conga Whiplash One-three-six. That whatever-it-is you're in seems slightly the worse for wear. We seem to have timed our entry in your little brawl to a fare-thee-well."

Karstil felt his Liberator ground. The smoke in the fighting compartment was getting thinner, and he could see Podandos rigid in his seat, his hands still grasping the firing handles. Spint was still invisible in the smoke. "Who are you, Whiplash?"

"Tut, tut, lad. Don't you recognize the call sign and the celebrated panache of your own Cohort Primus? That's the trouble with you medium types. You never get to know what a real tank and tankers can do."

31

Alsatia, Caralis
The Commonwealth
5 January 6831

"Senior Optio Greerson Kane, at your service," announced the platoon leader of the Deliverer tanks after he had dismounted. "I stress the 'Senior' portion of the appellation because I am, to the best of my knowledge, the longest-serving Optio in this 'Provisional' Legion. Now I understand," he continued, "that seniority among Optios is like virginity among prostitutes—it doesn't exist. But since I am about to become a Centurion, with all the privileges that go with such an exalted rank, I thought I should make my position clear. That way you youngsters, those of you still striving to exert your upward mobility within the ranks of the Renegade Legion, can pay me the respect to which I am shortly due."

The smiling young Optio removed his combat helmet as he climbed onto Karstil's Liberator. The morning sun glowed through a shock of golden hair, disheveled from the helmet. Kane wetted his fingers and ran them through his hair. The hair went into place immediately. He cradled the helmet in his left arm, half-sat on top of the 150mm cannon, and offered his right hand to Karstil.

"Glad to met you," Karstil said. extending his hand. "Karstil. Roglund Karstil."

"You seem to have had a busy night," From his elevated position, Greerson scanned the rear of the slope." Our friends from TOG seem to be anally retentive about this piece of real estate you own."

Karstil looked over the ground as well. The remains of an Horatius tank were scattered over the terrain, probably the one that had passed overhead during the combat. An uniden- tified piece of wreckage erupted in intermittent gouts of fire, the ball of flame rising to disappear in clouds of thick, gray smoke. An infantry access door, blown from the side of its carrier, lay forlorn and forgotten on the charred earth, its owner gone and probably not coming back. Debris of all kinds littered the ground. Shell casings, TVLG tubes, helmets, backpacks, mortar rounds, and slabs of armor could be identified. Other pieces were completely foreign.

Behind him, Karstil heard the other two hatches on the turret of the Liberator pop open as Duncan and Quentain came up for air. At least they were still alive. That reminded him of his other two tanks, completely forgotten in the excitement of battle and the depression of its aftermath. He looked right and left along the ridge, rising from his hatch to get a better view of the terrain.

"Ah," commented Greerson. "The cellar-dweller emerges from his valiant tank. You want to know something about your equally heroic friends." Kane reached down to pull Karstil from the hatch to stand atop the turret. "Here they come now."

Both Liberators, having apparently been relieved by Deliverers, were approaching the command tank. A quick glance showed Karstil that his platoon was out of action again. These tanks would see combat only in an emergency.

Mullins, coming up from his position on the left, was riding a 200-ton radio. The TVLG racks were empty and shattered, a gaping hole in the bow just below the mount. The 150mm cannon had been clipped clean off just beyond the first step, the tapered end and muzzle brake a part of the detritus of battle. The Vulcan III mount was gone, melted by a hit, probably from multiple light lasers. The remains were fused to the hull, locking the turret at 5600 mils. The painting laser was still there, but that was it. Mullins rode the top of the turret, cross-legged, his helmet between his knees. He looked grim.

Number Three, with Farwell in the commander's hatch, was dragging something from its damaged rear. A grav coil, still attached to the hull, bounced along the ground behind the tank. Karstil could hear the high whine of the grav drive, which was powered to full thrust in an attempt to move the Liberator. Smoke still boiled from the rear and sides of the tank.

Besides the hull damage, the tank's turret had been reduced to a right side and 150mm gun only. The left side of the turret was completely smashed, showing crumbling ceramic shielding where the titanium armor had been blown away. Even the ceramic shield showed numerous craters, probably an SMLM hit from one of the Lupis APCs. Farwell grounded the tank ten meters away, Mullins bringing his to a stop just beyond. Both TCs dismounted and wearily moved toward Karstil and Greerson. The officers waited while the NCOs reported.

"Umbartis, William," said Farwell. "Gunner in Tank Number Three, slightly wounded in the face and hands. Will not require evacuation. Kloun, Graff; driver in Tank Three, suffering from shock and concussion. Needs rest. Evacuation recommended. Tank Number Three damaged in drives and steering. Not combat-worthy."

Karstil nodded. His own tank was gone, and two others wounded. He turned to Mullins. The muscles in the Sergeant's face were drawn tight, his jaws clenched, his lips a thin line.

"Grouse, Franklin," the words came choking from his mouth. "Grouse, Franklin, gunner in Tank Number Two, dead." His eyes were fixed on Karstil's. They showed neither anger nor reproach, only the 1,000-kilometer stare of a man who had seen violent death at close quarters. "Abul, Sedgewick, driver in Tank Number Two, strained right hand. Will not require evacuation. Tank Number Two, all weapons systems destroyed. Tank not combat-worthy."

"A bit battered, I'd say," commented Greerson. "You don't look all that good yourself. That's a nasty burn on your left arm."

For the first time, Karstil was aware that his left arm and shoulder were throbbing in pain. He looked down. The combat coveralls had been burned away from below his shoulder all the way to the elbow, exposing blistered flesh beneath. The exposed arm was covered by a shiny, sticky liquid that oozed from the skin. He recognized it as secondary burns, probably from leaning against the left side of the turret after the TVLG hits had blown away the armor. He clicked on the commlink; time to report to Century. He opened the external speaker, twisting the mike on his helmet so that he could use it without putting it on.

"Conquest Farmer Two-six, this is Conquest Farmer Two-two-six. Sit-rep."

There was a momentary pause, then, "Conquest Farmer Two-two-six, this is Conquest Farmer Two-two. Send sit-rep."

Freund was still not at the commlink. "This is Farmer Two-two-six. Sit-rep. One dead. Three wounded." He decided not to report himself as wounded. "Two wounded require local treatment. One wounded suggested evacuation. Three tanks damaged. Not combat-worthy."

"This is Conquest Farmer Two-six." At last. Freund had managed to reach the commlink. "That is the second time in twenty-four hours that you have managed to destroy your platoon. Is this going to be a recurring theme with you?"

Karstil looked up at Greerson Kane. The senior Optio looked away, scanning the smoldering debris. Karstil could feel the anger welling up inside again. Now he had to deal not only with his Century commander, but with a strange Optio from another Cohort. He wished he'd left the commlink on his helmet rather than the external speaker. It was too late to change back.

"I will have to report this to higher headquarters," continued the transmission from Freund. "You are becoming more expensive than you could possibly be worth. Your time as a Commonwealth officer does not seem to have done you any good." Karstil saw Kane raise his eyebrows, silent mockery at Karstil's having been one of "them" before joining a "real" outfit. "There is no excuse for your condition. Be prepared to move on my order. This is Conquest Farmer Two-six. End of transmission. No response desired."

"My, my," Kane said with a smile. "Your commander certainly seems to have a wild hair across his backside. I realize," he continued, "that officers, especially junior officers, are not supposed to think or say things like that about their commanders, but once in a while it just slips out. Do you mind?" He leaned down into the commander's hatch and plugged his headset into the open, External-Only receptacle.

Karstil was still too shocked by his Centurion's response to object.

"Conquest Farmer Two-six, this is Conga Whiplash One-three-six." Greerson Kane gave Karstil a conspiratorial grin.

"Conga Whiplash One-three-six, this is Conquest Farmer Two-six."

"This is Conga Whiplash One-three-six. I'm with Conquest Farmer Two-two-six. His recent report was quite accurate. You should listen to the dear boy. He's had quite a fight on his hands, and if he hadn't been either lucky or good, or both, you wouldn't 12be hearing from him. One could suggest, if one were to do such a thing, that you come down here and have a little look-see for yourself. This is Conga Whiplash One-three-six. End of transmission. No response desired." Kane reached into the turret and unplugged the jack of his commlink.

"If your commander does have a wild hair, and I'm not saying he does, that just burned it in. There are some things we "senior" Optios can get away with." He hopped down from the side of the Liberator. "Would you and your people like to join me and my crew for breakfast? My driver fancies himself a chef."

Milton Harras considered the status of the Centuries within his Cohort. Most of the units had been engaged in heavy fighting and many had taken severe casualties. But on the whole, the Cohort had done well. He was pleased, for they had turned back the TOG offensive.

He looked at the combat reports of Century Secundus. Most of the Century had had little work to do, but he noticed that the second tank platoon was reported "Not ready for combat" for the second time in as many days. All three tanks were so damaged now that the Century would have to be withdrawn from the line until the platoon could be refitted. The dead man needed to be replaced, but the wounded would have to stay with the unit. There were just not enough men in the replacement pipeline to take care of the walking wounded.

The Century Commander, Centurion Alanton Freund, had written a scathing report on the platoon leader. Harras knew Karstil, and he had the report of Optio Greerson Kane of Cohort Primus. There was a singular lack of corroboration between the two reports. He opened the communications transcript, that painstaking log of all traffic from platoons and Centuries within the Cohort. The communications platoon at Cohort monitored all traffic, carefully recording all messages. Each day a print-out of the messages was made, each transmission annotated with the date and time sent. He checked the transcript and went back to the two reports.

Greerson Kane's report was a high-spirited rendition of the night's activity, filled with high-toned language and colorful phrases, but it made easy reading. Freund's report had a certain whining cast to it. At the end, he had recommended that Karstil be relieved. The Centurion's report had to be sent on to the Manus headquarters with any comment the Centurion Maximus wished to append.

Harras sighed. What he didn't need was a personality conflict on the frontline, and this one seemed to be brewing up. Freund was a Centurion, after all, and good Centurions were hard to find. But he had the other Optios to think about as well. He rubbed his face. And then there was the report of the intelligence agent about last night. The agent was recuperating in the Legion hospital from a 5mm slug taken in the back. The report had been delivered verbally; there would never be a written record anywhere in the Legion.

He leaned forward in his chair and clipped the report of Greerson Kane to that of Alanton Freund. Taking out his stylus, he wrote under the recommendation for relief:

"My only comment on the conduct of Optio Karstil, Roglund I., 005-997-4242, is one that was given under similar circumstances five thousand years ago: I can't spare this man. He fights."

32

Alsatia, Caralis
The Commonwealth
5 January 6831

The boneyard was a depressing sight. Hectares of fractured vehicles, crumpled turrets, smashed cannon, and twisted armor extended into the distance. Roglund I. Karstil, commander of the nonexistent second tank platoon of Century Secundus stood with the other seven survivors of the unit. They were here to pick up three "new" Liberator tanks.

The maintenance and repair people were hard at work, lifting a turret off this hull, cutting a sponson off that. The salvaged pieces were loaded on huge, grav vehicles for transport to the central facility where they were welded together to make usable vehicles. When they had scavenged everything possible from a vehicle, the remainder was set aside for eventual destruction. From those piles of useless scrap would come brand new tanks and armored personnel carriers.

Tanks have personalities. Those unfamiliar with armored vehicles might consider that a specious thought, but anyone who had spent time with the beasts knew that it was not. Some tanks are docile and manageable. Others are cantankerous. Still others have quirks that could not be eliminated, no matter how much time the maintenance people spend on them. Some tanks drift to the left, others to the right. Some are bow-heavy, others constantly drag their sterns. Some tanks fire up quickly and are ready to go in an instant. Others need to be coaxed into wakefulness. Tanks are as varied as the people who serve in them.

Tank crews get used to their tanks. Sometimes it takes a while to learn all the traits and idiosyncrasies, but sooner or later, the crews do. It then becomes a matter of using the good points and avoiding the bad, like riding a crotchety old horse with a mind of his own. In time, a certain respect develops between the crew and their armored steed.

When this personality is brought to the boneyard to be carved up and grafted on to some other machine, the personality does not die. Instead, it is absorbed, along with the personalities of the various components, to become a new and different psyche. Tanks that come ready-made from the factory have a single soul; those that come from the boneyard have multiple selves. If the crew is lucky, all are friendly, meshing into a compliant whole. If the personalities clash, woe to the crew that gets the monster.

Mullins and Farwell, and to a degree Karstil, understood the problem of having a schizoid vehicle. They contemplated the prospect of a platoon of boneyard rebuilds with little pleasure. The only way to be sure that the vehicle assigned was a friendly one was to test it thoroughly before accepting it. Luckily, they were the only takers for Liberators that morning. That meant that they would be able to testdrive the tanks before they were assigned. They might even have the chance to fire the weapons.

Dixon Quail was surprised to see Karstil. He had recently spent a whole night repairing Karstil's platoon, and hadn't expected to see the Optio on foot and looking for three new tanks.

"Gee, sir, you have to take better care of the stuff," was his comment on seeing Karstil. Quail might have said more, but the bandages on Karstil and other members of the platoon and the grim visage of Mullins brought him up short. These men looked like they could take care of themselves, and they would probably do it in a group of eight. Not the kind of people Dixon wanted to tangle with just yet.

"You people will be wanting to take a look at the new Liberators we've just finished. I'll pass you on to my able assistant, Mastati Lynwood Sparks. He's somewhere out in the yard right now. You can't miss him; biggest man in the Repair and Recovery Century." With that, Quail had waved them off down the lines of "new" vehicles to find either the Mastati or the location of the repaired and reconditioned Liberators.

The platoon walked in silence between the Vipers, Wolverines, and an occasional Pedden or Cincinnatus standing apart from the others. Fresh paint hid the obvious scars of battle, and the hull numbers had been painted over to provide a background for the new owners' personal identification. Karstil stopped at one Viper that bore different numbers on both sides of the front hull and a third number on the turret. One of the hull numbers was from Harras's Cohort, and Karstil wondered who had been the unlucky squad leader of that vehicle.

The twelve reconditioned Liberators stood facing each other across a narrow alley, thick with the scent of new paint. The platoon had been silent as they walked through the yard and now stood in a sullen group at the head of the lines. The attitude didn't last.

Even though the old toy was much loved, choosing a new toy to replace one lost is exciting. Spint, Abul, and Kloun were the first to break ranks, climbing onto the Liberators to search for "their" tank. It became a race as each one tried to pick the best of the litter and avoid the runt. Abul and Kloun examined each tank in order, starting at the head of the line. Spint ran to the far end and started back. But while examining a tank, each kept his eyes on the others to see if they had found one they liked. They soon began to call out comments to one another. "This is a real doggy," "This one will never have me in it," "Not bad for a remake," and such echoed through the lines.

Quentain Podandos and William Umbartis, the surviving gunners, were the next to break. They had eyed the line of tanks, scrutinizing the 150mm cannon and the lighter weapons. Having picked their most likely candidates, they sprinted down the lines to the Liberator of choice. Soon they, too, like the drivers, were crawling over the vehicles, trading comments with anyone who would listen. The three tank commanders watched their "children" go. Karstil could hardly stand it. He was just as excited as any of the other enlisted men. He wanted his own tank again.

The three senior members of the platoon glanced at one another, each man a study in nonchalance. Each knew that the others were anxious to begin the selection process, and none wanted to be the first to break. Mullins knew it would not be him; he had been through this too many times to show unwarranted excitement. Farwell followed his senior sergeant. Finally, Karstil could stand the tension no longer. "I think I'll take a look at this one," he said and moved toward the nearest Liberator. The hunt was on in earnest.

For the next fifteen minutes, the men crawled over the tanks, each immersed in his own thoughts but willing to listen to and comment on the observations of the others. They were so involved that they didn't bother with the young soldier who stood between the lines of tanks, his personal and unit equipment piled about his feet. No one actually saw him arrive. He was just suddenly there, standing in the dust. One by one, the members of the platoon noticed him, stopped moving, and stared.

To say that he was frail was an understatement of major magnitude; emaciated was a better description. His head was supported by a reed-like neck from which shoulders sloped away at a sharp angle. His thin arms were too long for his body, and ended in large, bony hands. He stood knock-kneed and pigeon-toed, looking like he wanted to cry.

Karstil saw him and turned away, hoping against hope that this was not the replacement for Franklin Grouse. Please, he thought, please make him a member of the Rep-Rec Century. But when he looked back the boy was still there, and Mullins was approaching him.

Lucifer K. Mullins stood in front of the scarecrow and looked him up and down from head to foot. We're getting 'em awfully young these days, he thought. Franklin Grouse had been twenty-four. This kid didn't look a day over fifteen. "What do you want, son?"

"Triarii Drinkel Yennan reporting to the second tank platoon, Sergeant." His voice cracked with emotion as he threw back his shoulders and assumed a rigid and exaggerated position of attention. "I've been assigned as a replacement to your platoon."

"What are you qualified to do, Yennan?"

"I'm a trained cook's assistant, Sergeant."

"Cook's assistant? What are you doing in a tank platoon?"

"I don't know, Sergeant. I was assigned according to the needs of the Renegade Legion."

"If they did it for the good of the Renegade Legion, they would have left you at home."

"That's all right, Sergeant," said Karstil, coming up on the interview. "Can you do anything besides cook, Yennan."

"Yes, sir. I am qualified to drive a Pilus APC. Well, not actually 'qualified,' sir. But I did have a chance to drive one once in training."

Karstil turned to Mullins. "Can I talk with you, Sergeant."

Mullins turned to follow the Optio away from where the other members of the platoon were standing in a circle around the replacement.

"What do you think?"

"Young, sir. Young."

"We all had to start sometime. Every platoon gets a greeny sooner or later."

"Yes, sir. They do. A green man in anything but tanks is O.K. In a platoon of nine men, one green man is a lot. I don't mind green, but this kid isn't even dry yet."

"We've got him, and I don't think we have a choice," said Karstil. "We can send him back to Century, but we won't get someone else. If we don't take him, we go back to the line a man short."

"I know. I know."

"I'll take him, Sergeant. You can have Spint as your gunner. Or your driver if you want Sedgewick to move up."

"No," said Mullins. "I'll take him."

"You're too important for that, Sergeant. I'll take him, and that's final."

"'No reply necessary,' sir?" Mullins raised his eyebrows at Karstil. "I don't think so, sir." He looked his Optio straight in the eyes. "You don't seem to understand, sir, that you are the most important member of the platoon. You run the show. And you can't spend your time worrying about fighting and driving your vehicle. If you become your own gunner, you are a very high-priced gunner, indeed. Not only in the pay you receive but in the price the platoon and the Century will pay for that decision. I can wet-nurse young Mister Yennan. You keep what you've got. And that, sir, is what is final."

Karstil stared at his Platoon Sergeant. He had never heard Mullins speak like that before and he wasn't sure he accepted it now. But what the man said made sense, and he knew enough not to continue to argue. "You win, Sergeant." They turned back to what had been a knot of men around the young replacement. Now there was no knot; there were no men.

Karstil and Mullins looked at each other blankly. Then they saw them. The six young men of the platoon, all but Farwell, who considered it beneath his dignity, romping across the tops of the parked Liberators. "He seems to have been accepted," said Mullins.

And so he was. All the men of the platoon looked upon the skinny recruit as their younger brother. They took him under their collective wing and showed him how to survive. It started in the boneyard and continued after they had chosen their tanks. They had no supervision during the choosing, the Rep-Rec people being noticeably absent during the entire process. There was even some doubt as to whether or not they would have to sign for the tanks at all. In the end, they did.

The platoon was moving toward the gate of the motor pool when Dixon Quail stopped them.

"Hold it, boys. Uh, sir, you'll have to sign for those things. Just go in my office. Mastati Sparks will do up the paperwork. Bring the serial numbers from the ballistic computers. Don't worry about engine or weapon numbers."

Podandos, Yennan (he was now gunner in Number Two), and Umbartis scrambled out of their tanks with the information and headed for the office, jostling each other in their high-spirited enthusiasm. The drivers followed the gunners, and last of all came the tank commanders. The TCs smiled at each other, glad that the platoon had shaken off the doldrums affecting it earlier. Even Mullins was no longer grim, the mission of wet-nursing Yennan taking over from his anguish at the loss of Grouse.

The office was a hubbub of voices as each gunner tried to get his data recorded first. Sparks was somewhere beyond the mass of bodies that crowded the tiny office. Karstil could just barely see the top of his head. He must be a big man, thought Karstil. Even sitting down, he is larger than most of the platoon. Karstil was standing behind Sparks, and he could see that the man had his left arm in a walking sling. "He must have dropped a wrench on his pinky," Karstil said to Mullins.

"Yes, sir. And now the biggest man in the Rep-Rec Century gets to fill out paperwork. I'll bet the smallest man is using the heavy pry-bar."

As they worked their way toward the desk, Karstil began to feel uneasy. There was something about Sparks that set off recognition bells in his head. The way the man sat hunched over the desk like a bear holding a pencil. There was something. Karstil tried to remember where he had seen the man before. He went through the maintenance people he had known at school or in the Commonwealth. Not there. Had it been someone at the replacement center? He tried to remember the NCOs who had stood behind the row of tables. No, none of them.

He couldn't remember. But he knew he had seen the man somewhere before. As he got closer and closer to the desk, he noticed a thick pad, like a bandage, that extended from Sparks' left shoulder all the way down his back almost to his waist. The man was not suffering from a wrist sprained by a heavy wrench. He reached the desk. Sparks turned toward Karstil and looked at him. Karstil stepped back, gasping in surprise.

He was looking straight into the eyes of Optio Lawrence ("Just call me Larry") Stone, the huge, bear-like Psychological Warfare and Intelligence officer with whom he had played Pendulos on board the transport *Maiestas* all those months ago. He opened his mouth to say something, but couldn't think of what. What was Stone doing here? And why was he called Sparks? And why wasn't he an officer? All that came out was a strangled, "Aheragh."

The others in the room turned to him. "What's the matter, sir?" asked Farwell.

"Aheragh, ah, er, no. Yes," said Karstil as the platoon members stared. "It's just that..." Then Karstil saw the eyes of Stone/Sparks flare red, the same burning stare Durban Collis had looked into while playing Pendulos. His mouth snapped shut. "Nothing, men. Nothing. It's all right. Let get this paperwork done and get out of these people's hair."

33

Alsatia, Caralis
The Commonwealth
5 January 6831

The Century moved forward as part of the Cohort reserve, which itself was serving as the reserve for the Manus. There wasn't much to think about in this kind of movement, except follow the little blue square on the DDP. Karstil was glad of it. After all that had happened to him over the past few days, he needed the luxury of a simple ride through the countryside so he could review it. His turret was forward, protecting the forward arc, while the guns of the following tanks were herringboned to the right and left. Farwell's Liberator was 400 meters behind him, Mullins another 400 behind Farwell.

The terrain through which they were passing now was open, rolling farm land. Fields of tall wheat and barley filled the large, open, areas with thick stands of both deciduous and coniferous forests to break up the view. Small, neat farmhouses must have stood along the wide road that crossed the area, but most of these had paid the price of war. This area had been occupied by the TOG forces for some time, and the 2567th was rolling the enemy back along a broad front. The Legion was doing very well, ndeed. Better than anyone had hoped.

It did not look as though the farms had been burned in the random violence of combat. There were none of the usual signs of battle: craters, burning wreckage, the detritus of war. Rather, these dwellings had been burned by single, well-placed hits from lasers that ignited the fragile structures. Farm animals lay dead around the houses. There was no sign of the occupants visible to the passing column.

As they moved on through the empty countryside, Karstil was wrapped in his thoughts. Analyzing his actions of the past week, he examined each engagement and how he had behaved. But two questions kept rising to the surface of his brain, both clamoring for some kind of resolution. The first related to the sabotage, both to the 50mm guns and to his vane controls. The second had to do with the presence of Optio Lawrence Stone in the Rep-Rec Century of the Legion.

It was obvious that Stone/Sparks had been operating undercover in the Rep-Rec Century. There were two possibilities that Karstil could isolate: his name was Stone, he was an officer, he worked for intelligence, he was posing as Sparks on a mission on Caralis. Or, his name was Sparks, he masqueraded as the officer Stone on the *Maiestas*, and he was assigned to the Rep-Rec Century of the Legion.

The second possibility was unlikely. There was no reason why the man should masquerade as an officer. And if he had, he would have shown fear when Karstil recognized him at the Rep-Rec Century. Instead, Spark's eyes had telegraphed a warning to say nothing.

So, it had to be that Stone was on Caralis as a spy for someone. But whom? Was he here to watch the Legion? Was he following someone? Had he been summoned here? Was it because of what Karstil and Mullins had found? There were too many questions for Karstil to answer. He would have to wait. But he could not, or should not, trust anyone. He must, he decided, continue normally. He might be being watched. There might be a spy in the platoon. Karstil began to review the records of each of the platoon members; not even Mullins was immune to scrutiny.

Karstil was shaken out of his reverie by the Cohort's sudden change of direction. The rapid advance of the lead Manus had opened a wide gap on the right flank. Cohort Harras had been ordered to fill it and secure the flank. A quick order from Harras, and the Cohort turned 1,600 mils right. The five medium Centuries formed a line, the light Century in the lead, spread across the entire front of the Cohort.

A Cohort in a tactical road march covers an immense amount of ground. A platoon of three vehicles moves at 400-meter intervals, with another 800 meters between it and the following platoon. Thus, from the nose of one platoon to the nose of the following platoon is 1,600 meters. A Century is made up of three platoons (4800 meters) as well as the Century headquarters (1500 meters). Because the distance between Centuries is 2,000 meters, the length from the head of a Century to the head of the following is 8,300 meters. Six Centuries in column as well as the headquarters makes a Cohort column of 45 kilometers, more or less. That was a lot of ground to cover. Added to the equation was the fact that the headquarters must drop out of the line. It would not do to have the Cohort Headquarters stumble on an enemy unit. That meant the Centuries adjacent to the headquarters had to spread out to cover the gap created. It was all very complicated and done at speeds of 100 KPH.

As the platoon made the turn and came on line, Karstil and Farwell swapped places. This put Karstil in the center, with Farwell on the left and Mullins on the right. The platoon boomed along, dodging around trees when possible, rising over them when necessary. This was movement that tankers loved. Nothing ahead but their own reconnaissance unit, open ground, sensors on far scan, the fingers probing out to 50 kilometers, and moving at 100+. The air rushing over the open hatches, the thrum of the grav drives. It was better than walking to work.

They passed a small village, or what had been a small village, which was now a series of empty cellar holes that stared upward like vacant eye sockets. Again there was no evidence of combat, just the systematic, wanton destruction of civilian property.

In an hour, they were on the flank of the Manus, covering the gap that had developed. Now the tricky maneuvering began. The left flank Century maintained contact with the advancing Manus, tailoring its movements to that of the Manus's right flank. The other Centuries maintained contact with the Century to the left, angling their movement to make up for the leftward shift. A good theory, but difficult in practice. Commanders at all levels had to be aware of what was happening, feel the shift in direction. It called for a fine sense and a delicate touch to have the system work without fits and starts.

Karstil put the platoon in a vee formation, his own tank centered and to the rear of the flank Liberators. The flanks moved forward to a ridge or woods, securing the foreground. Then Karstil moved up on line to cover the further advance of the flanks. It was an intricate ballet performed at 100 KPH, the tanks braking to a hover when they reached their over-watch position. And always there was the checking to the left, making sure that the adjacent platoon was still there, still going in the same direction.

As Karstil reached a low ridge between the other tanks, he saw the laser torches in the hands of Mullins and Farwell, indicating a contact at maximum range. As he pulled into the position, his own DDP flared with red indicators at 50 kilometers.

"Mandate Saddle Two-six, this is Mandate Saddle Two-two-six. Contact report." Freund had to be informed of the contact. At that range, it was possible that his sensors had not recorded the intruder.

"Mandate Saddle Two-two-six, this is Mandate Saddle Two-six. Send your report."

"Saddle Two-six. Enemy contact, range 50 kilometers, bearing 6300 relative. Target movement axis 550. Speed 12."

"Two-two-six. No contact here. Advance and investigate. Be advised that Salamander Knapsack is to your front. Break. Mandate Saddle Two-one-six, follow course 2400 compass. Be advised, Two-two-six has made contact. He will be on your left. Break. Saddle Two-three-six, follow me."

The Century was set in motion. Karstil would move forward to investigate with the first tank platoon, Two-one-six, closing on his right rear. Somewhere behind and between the two was the infantry platoon, Two-three-six, along with the Century headquarters. Ahead of the Century were the elements of the light Century, Salamander Knapsack. Freund was leading from behind again, letting his platoon leaders do the work. Usually, a Centurion rode in one of the tanks of the first platoon, directing the Century from there. It meant that the first platoon lost one tank to headquarters, but that was acceptable because it placed the Centurion at the front of the action.

Freund rode in that tank. Against normal practice, he had pulled the Liberator back to the headquarters vehicles and surrounded himself with the infantry platoon as well. That meant the first platoon fought short one tank, and there was no infantry support for the committed tank platoons of the Century. Very irregular.

Karstil stared at the commlink in semi-disbelief. Freund had accepted his Contact report without comment, had set the Century in motion without confirming information on his own DDPs. Maybe things were looking up.

"Saddle Two-six, this is Two-two-six. Wilco. Advancing. Bearing 2470 at one-five-zero kays." Karstil pumped his arm and pointed at the distant target. Mullins and Farwell raised their hands in response. Karstil felt the Liberator surge forward as Spint applied thrust. There was no need to signal either vector or speed; all the tanks had monitored the transmission with Century. The tanks of the platoon would maintain a heading of 2470 mils, compass, at a speed of 150 kilometers per hour. The hunt was on.

34

Alsatia, Caralis
The Commonwealth
5 January 6831

More red circles appeared on the DDP screen as the enemy tanks moved forward. The open and rolling terrain began to give way to low, bald ridges, the valleys between filled with dense stands of trees. The Century was approaching the high rim of mountains that marked the end of the fertile zone. From now on, there would be few signs of habitation.

"Mandate Saddle Two-two-six, this is Salamander Knapsack Three-three-six." One of the reconnaissance units had changed frequency from its own to that of Century Secundus. "We are one-zero kays in front of you. Am dropping unit control to guide on you. Will hand off information on my Debeo Debeo Pando."

"Roger Knapsack Three-three-six. Send data." Karstil flipped the switch on his DDP to allow it to receive information currently posted to the sensors on the Wolverines of the Recon Century. The recon units were equipped with better sensing units than the main battle tanks. The DDP screen blossomed with additional data, including a series of red pinpricks that sparkled across the screen 5 kilometers in front of the detected TOG units. Those red dots indicated active sensors placed 5,000 meters in front of the defender's lines.

Though Karstil had seen active sensors in training, this was the first time he had seen them in the field. According to the instructors at the Officers' Training School, the presence of active sensors usually indicated a prepared defensive position. The sensors could identify, even paint, an approaching vehicle so that it became a target for indirect artillery and Thor satellite attacks. The platoon would be under fire long before it was able to engage the frontline of the enemy. The beast in his brain stirred, reaching for his innards.

"Knapsack Three-three-six, this is Saddle Two-two-six. Form on me. We'll run the sensor screen together."

"Roger, Two-two-six. Awaiting your arrival." Karstil saw the two blue squares that indicated the Wolverines ahead slow on the screen. They were 10 kilometers short of the line of red dots, well out of sensor and paint range. He hoped. The squares began to circle.

"Mandate Saddle Two-six, this is Mandate Saddle Two-two-six. Sit-rep."

"Saddle Two-two-six, Saddle Two-six. Send Sit-rep."

"Two two-six. Active enemy sensors detected. Salamander Knapsack is joining me. We will try to run the sensors together."

"Roger," came the reply from Century. "Keep us informed."

The blue squares of the Wolverines were only three kilometers ahead. Karstil could see them well to the flanks of the platoon formation, circling to fall in behind the Liberators. "Close it up," he ordered over the commlink. "Keep it tight. We'll go through the sensor zone at high speed, say 200. Once through the zone, we'll spread out. I'll lead."

The flanking tanks responded at once, edging toward the center of the formation. The platoon's formation was 200 meters wide as the Wolverines came up behind. Karstil brought his own tank through the formation, allowing the flanks to close behind him. With the sensors clearly displayed on his DDP, he wanted to be the lead tank. Karstil raised his arm, waiting for the other commander to follow suit. Once the four trailing tanks indicated readiness, he pumped his arm and pointed toward the terrain ahead. "Let's go, Spint. Bring her to 200 and hold. I'll direct you." He felt the tank surge forward as Spint applied maximum thrust. He didn't have to worry about waiting for the Wolverines; they had thrust to spare, compared to the Liberators.

Breaking through a sensor zone is best accomplished if the attacker can cross directly over one of the sensors. The constant bearing and rapidly decreasing range can confuse a single sensor, and the additional data from the sensors on both flanks can confuse a computer. Most sensor systems assume that the target is being triangulated by two sources. The third source, rather than confirming the information of the first two, only adds confusion to the problem. Karstil hoped that this theory were true. He used the book solution to a book problem.

Karstil looked back, craning out of the hatch to see the other tanks. They were following behind in a ragged column, their turrets traversed right and left in herringbone style. The two Wolverines came last, the rear tank with its turret pointed to the rear. The Wolverine crews knew what they were doing. At two kilometers from the line of sensors, the laser painting warning began to whoop in Karstil's turret. He pulled himself down into the hatch, only his head extending above the coaming.

"Quent. See if you can detect a sensor on your targeting computer. If we can find one, maybe we can blow it away."

"Searching, sir. No luck yet."

"Switch to high-power, short-range."

"Roger."

Karstil swept his eyes across the DDP. The sensors appeared only because the Wolverines were downloading the information to his display. Should have led with the light stuff, he thought. Too late now. "Quent. With the fifty. Fire. Fire smoke."

"Roger. Up."

"Fire!"

The 50mm gun cracked, its APDS round screaming over the terrain to explode well beyond effective range. Karstil saw "smoke" index in the ballistic computer as Podandos called for different ammunition. The gun would continue to load smoke until a different ammunition was ordered. A moment later, it fired again, smoke blooming 1,200 meters ahead of the Liberator. The DDP went blank beyond the smoke as the cloud shadowed the terrain behind. A mere twenty seconds later, the Liberator whipped around the smoke and into the clear. The laser painting warning went from its high "wheeee" to its standard "whoop, whoop, whoop" and back to a "wheeee" as the tank cleared. Not enough smoke, thought Karstil. "Smoke both guns. Spint, dodge the smoke if you can. Don't drive through it."

Both crewmen acknowledged. Karstil felt the turret jump as the 150mm fired its HEAP round. The easiest and safest way to unload a tank gun was through the muzzle. Then both cannon fired. The high scream of the warning klaxon stopped, whooped once, and then died. The Liberator slewed right and left as Spint ducked around the first smoke cloud and headed for the second.

Karstil saw the DDP fade slightly as the Wolverines lost the sensors in Karstil's smoke. Then a pinpoint of red appeared on the screen directly ahead of the Liberator, flashing to the rear as the tank roared over the spot. Karstil hit the digging cannon. Not much of a chance, but it might shake up the sensor. The explosion rocked the ground around him. He lost track of the sensor.

"Incoming rounds. Vehicle targeted." The voice of the computer, silent until now, spoke volumes in two sentences. "Incoming" meant that indirect artillery had been called onto the column. "Vehicle targeted" meant that either the tank was sitting in the blast zone of exploding shells or that it had been painted and was a direct target. The lack of a warning scream from the klaxon showed that it was area fire.

"Spint, hard right." There was no voice response from the driver, but Karstil caught violent movement out of the corner of his eye. The Liberator swerved hard to the right, the hull dipping dangerously close to the ground. Violent maneuvers at 200 KPH called for significant skill on the part of the driver—or significant luck. Karstil didn't care what Spint had, skill or luck. Whatever it was, it worked. The tank steadied on course.

Karstil glanced under the 150mm tube to see the other tanks follow his lead, breaking to the right in turn. To his rear, the ground erupted in a violent explosion, as an artillery shell landed. A searing ball of brilliant light turned the just-vacated ground to glass. He swallowed hard. Just wait until I can get my hands on those cannon-cockers, he thought. It will be a real pleasure. He felt the tank swerve back to the left, onto the original course.

The terrain flashed by. Clumps of trees were a blur of green interspersed with the gold of dry grass and the gray of lumps of rock. Karstil wondered at Spint's ability to sit quietly in the bowels of the Liberator as it hurtled across the terrain. Spint couldn't see everything; he only guided the tank from the tactical display that appeared before him.

Ahead, a thick forest stretched across the area. A wide slash gave access to the ground beyond. Spint, keeping the Liberator at 1 meter above ground, headed for the opening. It was always better to keep the tank low rather than risk treetop or low-altitude flight. In the gap, Karstil saw a series of small airbursts. The grass wriggled under the impact. "Button up," he said over the commlink, not even bothering to use the prefix code. He dropped inside the turret and felt the armored hatch-cover fall into place.

Inside, the darkness was surprising. The glow of the DDP, targeting computer display, and driving screen stood out starkly in the dim light cast by the battle lanterns. Shadows were drawn in rigid lines across the face of Podandos, whose appearance was like something beyond the realm of normal life. His face was pale green, his eyes glowing in the light reflected from the screen before him.

The DDP showed the gap growing closer. A red warning light blinked on and off as more rounds struck in the area. Across the bottom of the DDP came the notation that HAFE was being fired to close the gap. We'll be through it before it can hurt us too badly, thought Karstil. Just make it quick. He heard the patter of flechettes against the outer hull of the tank like raindrops striking a tin roof. More data scrolled across the DDP: "Area ahead is mined."

"Take her up. Low-altitude flight." Mines could detect vehicles at normal or tree-top flight. Having detected the vehicles, the mines could distinguish between enemy and friendly, tank or APC, and they attacked bottom armor. At low-altitude flight, the targets were beyond their sensor range. Karstil felt the tank begin to rise, felt himself pressed back into his chair as gravity fought to keep him down. The gap appeared on both sides of the DDP, then it was gone and they were in open terrain again. "Down. Get her down." The response was immediate, and he felt himself rise out of the chair, his helmet striking the closed hatch, pressing him upward, forcing his face down on his chest.

He waited for the sensation to stop before popping the hatch. Light flooded in. He glanced at the DDP. One of the Wolverines had dropped out of the formation, the blinking blue square that indicated its progress had stopped. It was located in the trees to the right of the gap, unmoving. A terse indicator below the symbol showed that the helm had been shot away. As Karstil watched it, silently willing it back to life, a red circle appeared over the square, the terse notation "GLAD" appearing across it. Gone. Just like that—gone. If the crew had not bailed out, if they had tried to repair the vehicle, they were all dead. There would be no survivors to search for.

The DDP flared with red symbols. "Targets identified. Two Trajan heavy tanks, three Horatius medium tanks, six Lupis carriers. Carriers are empty. Many infantry targets. Range two-zero-double zero. Range decreasing."

He had found what he wanted to find. This was the front of an extremely heavy TOG force lying on the Legion's flank. Now all he had to do was escape.

"Turn three-two-double zero. Maximum speed!" he shouted. "Shoot!" The Liberator turned hard to the left forcing Karstil against the right side of the hatch ring. He fought to maintain his balance, lest he be thrown from his seat and end up in the bottom of the turret basket. The turret swiveled to the right, the 150 and 50mm guns firing simultaneously. Off in the distance, the rounds exploded, the smoke shadowing some of the red squares.

"Saddle Two-six, Saddle Two-two-six. Two Trajan heavy tanks, three Horatius medium tanks, six Lupis carriers. Carriers are empty. Many infantry targets." He repeated the information from the ballistic computer to Freund somewhere to the rear. "Am withdrawing at high speed."

"Two-six. Roger. Will await your arrival."

He was riding backward now, the tank headed back for the trees, the turret traversed full to the rear. A 150mm round cracked over the tank followed by the deep rush of a 200. The klaxon began its steady "whoop, whoop, whoop" as the tank rose to clear the trees. The rear shields flashed into incandescent light as a heavy laser hit was turned aside. Another round passed under the tank, then the left sponson took a shattering hit that filled the air with molten titanium. The cannon of the Liberator fired again, and again smoke bloomed to the rear. Karstil hit the smoke grenade launcher, the miniature rockets arching from their housings on the sides of the turret. They burst close aboard, and the "whoop, whoop, whoop" of the klaxon died at once.

Below and to the right, he saw the smoking craters of multiple GLAD rounds flash beneath. The live Wolverine circled the crater once and then accelerated to follow the retreating Liberators. Then a thick cloak of natural smoke closed down around him, and he felt the reverse thrust as Spint slowed the tank.

He cleared the safety of the cloud to see Farwell and Mullins waiting for him. To the right, the Wolverine burst from the cloud trailing soft tendrils of mist. "Home, James," Karstil said into the boom mike, "and this time, you can spare the horses."

35

Alsatia, Caralis
The Commonwealth
5 January 6831

The rapid advance of the 2567th Legion had created a huge bulge, 1,000 kilometers wide by 1,500 kilometers deep, in the front line. A bulge is dangerous, for both attacker and defender. For the defender, a bulge can easily crack open to become a break-out. When this happens, the front ruptures, contact with the enemy formations is lost, and before the defender can react, he finds attacking formations deep in his own rear. In such a case, all the defender can do is to withdraw his units as rapidly as possible, trading space for time until he can reestablish continuity along the front.

The attacker's position is not without risk, however. As the bulge deepens, it tends to narrow. Before very long, the entire bulge can be interdicted with indirect artillery fire. This fire, even relatively blind fire, causes disruption at the point of attack. To prevent this narrowing, the attacker must secure, even expand if possible, the shoulders of the bulge. The defender, of course, attempts to hold those shoulders and even attack from them. Attack from the shoulders was the classic tactic for destroying a bulge.

It called for a fine sense of timing. The defender expends assets to hold the shoulders while attempting to establish a coherent front at the point of attack. If he expends too much effort on the shoulders, he will not have the assets to prevent a catastrophic rupture. On the other hand, if he tries to blunt the attack with his assets, he will not have enough material to hold the shoulders and to attack from them.

The attacker must be very careful in his headlong dash forward. If he has tunnel vision about what is ahead, disregarding his shoulders, he may find enemy troops closing in on his rear. If he worries about the shoulders, he will not have the force to continue the push and attain a breakthrough.

This was the situation that now confronted the 2567th Renegade Legion (Provisional) in its attack on the TOG forces on the continent of Alsatia. A large bulge had been created. Cohort Harras, sent to the right flank to secure that opening against TOG incursion, had run headlong into the shoulder and the build-up of TOG units. The decision now was whether to attack at the shoulder or to drop back and defend while the nose of the attack continued. In either case, the forces available consisted of the Cohort and some supporting units. After a lengthy discussion at Legion headquarters, the decision was made that Cohort Harras, supported by limited engineer and artillery assets of the Legion, would attack the TOG defenders in an attempt to seize the shoulder ground or at least disrupt the TOG assault.

All these high-level decisions meant nothing to the men on the frontlines. Flank attacks, deep penetrations, prepared attacks—they were all frontal attacks to the individual soldier. To him, the enemy is active and real, ready to destroy his vehicles and his men. To him, no attack on the enemy is from the flank, it is always head-on. A slugfest. To the Centurions and the Prefects, the blue squares might be striking the red squares in the flank or rear. To the troops on the ground, it was head to head, man to man.

Orders passed from Legion to Manus, from Manus to Cohort, from Cohort to Century: Attack and seize the ground.

Karstil found the Century laagered in 25 kilometers behind the line of active sensors. Either they had dropped back when he had turned to flee, or they had been too far in the rear to support him in his probe. The air at headquarters was sullen. Optio Holden Ventis was busy with his infantry, and LaTonta Broast sat alone under a tree. The "clerks and jerks" of the head shed were silent when Karstil approached, unwilling to meet his eyes.

"Well," said Freund, a smile spreading almost to his eyes, "how did my aggressive platoon leader do?" The Centurion shuffled through a sheaf of papers. "I see you managed to lose one of the Wolverines. Busy reducing the recon people to a non-combat ready unit?"

Karstil had not expected that greeting. The commlink traffic had indicated that things had changed, but he had obviously been mistaken. He looked over at Sergeant Justine Gortos, the senior NCO of the Century, but she averted his eyes. "I ran into more than I could handle. It looks like they're defending in strength."

"So it seems. I've passed your report on to the Cohort. They seemed to like what you said you saw. Anyway, we have orders to attack at oh-six-thirty tomorrow. Tertius will attack on the left, Quartus on the right. We will be the center. If it's not too much trouble, I'd like to have you ready to go by oh-six-hundred. Do you think you can handle that?"

Karstil stared at his Centurion. Of course he could be ready. It was 1635 now. That gave him just less than fourteen hours to resupply and feed the platoon. Both those tasks could be accomplished in thirty minutes. The repair on his damaged stern would take two hours at the most. He could be ready to attack by 1900 today. "Yes, sir. I'll need some repair for my Liberator. I took a 150mm APDS round in the stern."

"That sounds like a self-inflicted wound, Optio." He turned to Gortos, who was studiously busy with a pile of reports. "What do you think, Gortos? Can we break the repair people away to get Optio Karstil's tank repaired?" Gortos looked up, opening her mouth to answer. "Well, we'll see what we can do, Optio," Freund went on, without waiting for a reply. "You've got to remember that the Cohort and the Century have to establish priorities. You'll be placed on the list." He continued with that same smile that almost reached his eyes. "Perhaps you can get your friends at Cohort Primus to give you what you want. You seem to be pretty tight with them."

Karstil saw the Centurion's jaw tighten as he spoke, a slight sneer replacing the smile. It was obvious to Karstil that he would get no more help from the headquarters. Gortos was still watching him, and Karstil thought he saw the Sergeant give a slight shrug as she turned back to her paper work. "We'll be ready, sir."

"I'm sure Centurion Maximus Harras will be glad to hear it. Briefing here at twenty-three-thirty. Try to make it." Freund turned his back on Karstil. The interview was over.

Karstil was still furious by the time he walked the kilometer back to the platoon. Mullins had them laagered in, resupply already completed. There had been nothing else the platoon sergeant could do for the coming attack. Mullins knew all the details of the operation, for the soldiers' telegraph was in full swing. The enlisted people often knew what the officers were going to do before the officers had made a decision. It was a process of "I have a friend who knows this guy in the headquarters, who heard it from an orderly, who works for so-and-so." For all the twists and turns, for all the people who knew someone, it was remarkably accurate. Karstil didn't question the system, but he was often troubled by the apparent lack of security. He shrugged. There was nothing he or anyone else could do about it. And he doubted that TOG would have to work very hard to guess the intentions of the Cohort.

By the time darkness fell, there was still no sign of the repair platoon from Legion. Perhaps, as Freund had said, they had other things to do. The Legion had been in combat all along the front, and there were probably many tanks, damaged far worse than his, that needed their attention. He left the platoon in the hands of Mullins while he returned to Century Headquarters for the twenty-three-thirty briefing.

When he entered the command tent, it was obvious that the meeting had been going on for some time. Ventis and Broast were busy taking notes, and there was an unfamiliar sergeant from the recon platoon there as well. Karstil saw an engineer Optio standing to one side of the room, his platoon sergeant behind him. Another Centurion, wearing the branch designator of the artillery, was pointing out numbered crosses that spattered a terrain display. Everyone turned toward him as he entered.

"Nice of you to join us, Optio Karstil," said Freund, standing to glare at Karstil. "We decided to start the meeting without you. A twenty-three-hundred briefing is expected to start at twenty-three-hundred. We usually don't wait for a junior officer, but your reputation is such that we delayed for fifteen minutes."

Karstil felt his face flush. Being criticized for something was bad enough, but in the presence of others, it was humiliating. He was sure Freund had told him the brief would start at 2330. He was even five minutes early. He wracked his brain trying to remember if he had been told the briefing time had been moved up. There was nothing he could say that would not make the situation worse.

"We haven't got time to start over, Optio," continued Freund. "You'll just have to catch up. I'm sure with your grasp of the situation, that will be no problem." Freund sat down without another glance. Karstil found a place against one wall and tried to listen.

The plan, as far as he could determine, was relatively simple in concept, complicated in execution. There were two ways to attack a defended position: tanks leading or infantry leading. The tanks lead when the anti-armor defenses are considered weak. The tanks would break a hole through the lines, with the infantry mopping up pockets of resistance left behind. The infantry lead when the anti-armor defenses are strong. They would root out the defenders, driving them from cover so that the tanks could bring their heavy weapons to bear. Tomorrow's attack called for the infantry to lead.

Ventis did not look pleased with the plan. No infantry platoon leader ever liked any plan that called for an infantry attack. The Century would roll forward under covering artillery fire until they reached the last secure area short of the sensor line. There the infantry would dismount, moving the rest of the way on foot. The tanks and Viper carriers would provide direct fire support if the pedes got into more trouble than they could handle. An artillery forward observer would go with Ventis.

Broast's first tank platoon would support the right flank of the advancing infantry, his tanks echeloned to the right to maintain contact with Century Quartus. Karstil would deploy his platoon on the left, echeloned in that direction so that he could support the infantry and maintain contact with Century Tertius.

A section of two Constructor medium grav armored engineer vehicles would move in the center of the formation with the Century Headquarters. Although the engineers were specialists, and thus not under the tactical control of the Century, it would be Freund's job to assign them missions based on the recommendation of the engineer Optio.

The engineer Optio leaned against one of the tent stanchions, arms folded, eyes half-closed. There was nothing for him to do except explain what a Constructor could and could not do. That done, he had only to await the developments of the morning. His people were professionals forced to deal with amateurs. Tankers just didn't understand art or finesse that exceeded the mere bashing of targets. He would do his thinking and talking tomorrow.

The artillery Centurion, a nervous-acting man with a lisp, finished his portion of the briefing and passed out chips that would display the fire support plan on the DDPs of all vehicles. When he handed one to Karstil, he averted his eyes, unwilling to make contact with an officer who was obviously below normal standards.

The briefing broke up, the officers departing into the darkness. Karstil delayed his departure, wanting to talk with Freund about the mission, but the Centurion immediately went into conference with the two specialist officers. Try as he might, Karstil could not make eye contact. He left through the double black-out curtains of the tent.

The night had turned cool, the stars standing out in brilliant splendor against the sable sky. It took a few moments for Karstil's eyes to become accustomed to the darkness, even though the interior of the tent had been illuminated by red battle lanterns. He slowly became aware that he was not alone. There were two men standing aside, obviously waiting for him. He stiffened as they drew closer.

"Nice night." Karstil recognized the voice of Holden Ventis. "Sorry about what happened in there."

"Yeah." That was Broast. "Too bad."

Karstil didn't reply. He didn't know if he could trust them, let alone himself, to respond to the implied criticism of the Centurion. Discretion being the better part of many things, he chose silence. The three stood in silence in the dark.

The other two Optios shifted uncomfortably in the gloom. "Ah...Look." It was Ventis who broke the silence. "This is going to be my first time, you know." He had difficulty controlling the flutter in his voice. "I'll be on the left, near your platoon. Watch for me."

"I'll do my job." The reply was sharp and Karstil wished it hadn't come out in quite that tone. Ventis was worried, afraid for the morning.

"It's just that you've had so much more experience than either of us."

Broast grunted in assent.

"I know you can handle yourself," continued Ventis. "Even though Freund has it in for you, we know you're good."

"I'll watch for you," said Karstil, softening his tone. Perhaps these were just young men about to enter violent combat for the first time. Unsure of themselves before the ultimate test.

"Thanks." Both men responded in chorus. "I'm pretty worried," continued Ventis.

"Not to be," said Karstil. "It's never as bad as you fear." He smiled at himself in the dark. For the first time, he felt like a veteran talking to replacements. And these men had been in the Renegade Legion longer than he had. Maybe he was coming of age.

Alsatia, Caralis
The Commonwealth
6 January 6831

The Viper APC grounded gently 400 meters ahead of Karstil's command Liberator. A slight ridge offered some protection from observation and fire, and the Renegade infantry had chosen this point as the last covered and concealed position ahead of the sensor line. Karstil was puzzled and worried. The Wolverine at Century headquarters had not detected the sensors, as it had the previous afternoon. Either they had been removed or they were no longer active. Based on the theory of "better the devil you know," Karstil would rather have had them visible than absent.

The squad spread out on either side of the Viper, 5mm needle rifles at the ready. Like all officers, Karstil had had some basic infantry training. He remembered the adrenaline rush that came, even in training, with the orders to dismount. Then there was no longer the feeling of being a hostage. Each man was on his own, his survival dependent only on his own expertise. Not that being a hostage inside the Viper was all that bad. As a passenger, you didn't have to make any decisions. You could close your mind to everything that existed outside, letting yourself slip away to somewhere else. Once on the ground, however, there was no chance to relax.

The infantry crossed the ridge, silhouetted against the sky. The Viper crept up the slope, allowing its turret to clear the crest. From that position, it could observe the movements of the squad, firing its 25mm cannon or missiles in support. The Viper would remain stationary until the infantry had progressed 600 meters, moving forward while the infantry waited. Then the process would begin again. Bounce infantry, unlike normal, foot-mobile peds, could cover 600 meters in a minute. At that rate, they could, in theory, move at 36 kilometers an hour. The bounce pack, a miniature grav generator, allowed this activity. The packs were not powerful enough to keep the men suspended, but it did reduce the gravitational force. Thus, they could run in long, easy strides that produced a speed of 36 KPH.

The problem with the bounce packs and body armor was the power supply. While a tank could carry a fusion core, the infantryman could not be so equipped. Even the smallest fusion reactor and Marshman Drive unit had a mass of a kiloton. It was the power supply and thrust warps, rather than the anti-gravity generator, that accounted for most of the weight. By eliminating the thrust system and the fusion core, the resulting unit could be carried by a man. Power was supplied by rechargeable batteries. The power source also supplied the energy for the weapons carried by the soldiers.

The batteries were powerful enough for a man to keep up the 600 meters per minute movement rate for an hour; then they would go dead. No soldier wanted to be in a situation where the power supply had dropped that low, for movement would come to a halt and the rifle be unable to fire. The "safe" movement was usually half an hour, and most infantry never wanted to be away from the Viper for more than fifteen minutes. Thus, the advance came to a stop every fifteen minutes while the infantry plugged into the external outlets of the APC and built up the power in their packs.

The option to this creeping movement was to mount the infantry and move. But once the infantry were out of the APC, they were loathe to remount until after the enemy had been found. Being free of the metallic shroud was too intoxicating for the infantry to surrender it for the chance to dream on the inside. Another alternative was to have the infantry ride the outer shell of the APC. The turret top and rear hull of the Viper offered enough flat space for riders. There was also space in front of the turret, but no one, infantry or crew, wanted someone there.

The Century moved forward by bounds for ten minutes without contact or sign of TOG troops. It was all too easy, and Karstil was worried about what would happen when they did find them. The infantry was nervous, too. Karstil could tell by the stiffness of their movements, even with the bounce packs on.

"Flicket Market Two-three-six, this is Flicket Market Two-six." It was Freund calling the infantry platoon. "Advance is too slow. Remount the pedes and get moving."

Karstil had known it was only a matter of time before the Centurion called for a more rapid advance. He could understand the motivation. The Century had been primed for a fight, but nothing had happened. Now the Centurion wanted to get on with it. He had not been prepared for a slow advance against an absent enemy. Karstil saw the infantry scramble aboard the Viper to his front. They chose to ride on the outer hull rather than on the inside. That was to be expected.

The advance moved more rapidly now. With no walking infantry to slow them down, they could move at 70 KPH. That was fast, but bounce infantry equipped with grav packs could dismount at even greater speeds. But 70 was fast enough. With the infantry mounted, there was no reason why the tanks should hang back. Karstil signaled the others to close the distance between the Liberators and the leading APC. He wanted to offer the enemy, when they did fire, the choice of a Liberator or the exposed infantry.

They traversed without difficulty the large stand of trees Karstil had seen the day before without any sign of the TOGs. The more rugged ground beyond was vacant, and the DDPs of the platoon showed no indication of TOG units. Karstil felt perspiration under his coveralls, and his palms were moist against the hatch coaming. His bandaged left arm tingled and he began to get angry. He had found the TOGs here yesterday, had reported their location to Century. He even had a hole in his butt to prove that they had been here. And now nothing. Even the TOGs were trying to make a fool of him.

"This is Tambourine Mistral Three-three-six. Downloading sensor information." The reconnaissance Wolverine had found something and was passing on the information to the other members of the Century. Karstil watched as the DDP sparkled with red points well behind his Liberator. The Toggies had been there all along, watching and waiting. Now the Century was caught between the sensor line and the TOG units.

"Pass the Viper," he shouted into the commlink, and the Liberator surged forward as Spint accelerated. He saw the other tanks of the platoon follow almost immediately, anti-1cipating his reaction. Well, Karstil thought, at least I'm predictable to Mullins and Farwell.

"Incoming rounds. Vehicle targeted." That was to be expected, and the ballistic computer only confirmed it. Probably HAFE, thought Karstil. The infantry must have thought so, too, for they were bailing off the Viper even as the digging charges exploded around it. Poor, damn pedes. Caught in the open, they would be slaughtered by the flechettes.

"Spint. Find some men and park it over them." Karstil twisted to the rear, waving to Farwell who was following. Farwell waved back, acknowledging Karstil's waves. Karstil slammed the hatch shut. The Liberator swerved, then came to a hover. His last impression before daylight was blotted out by the hatch was that of infantry diving under the side skirts of his Liberator. The DDP showed that Farwell was alongside to the left, also stopped. Then the roar of the incoming rounds filled the fighting compartment, followed at once by the ripping scream as hundreds of tiny steel pins drove against the outer hull.

The sound passed and Karstil popped the hatch to look around. The ground around the tank was covered by a thin mist of smoke, the stalks of grass lying in wind rows where they had been scythed off by the flying steel. Infantrymen crawled out from under the tanks, one of them flashing a thumb's-up signal to Karstil as he did so. Karstil responded with his own hand, pointing to where the Viper hovered just beyond. The infantry tumbled through the access doors of the Viper, glad to be inside its titanium hull once again.

"Market Two-two-two, break, Two-two-three. Form a wedge. I'll lead. Three right. Break. Two-three-three, form behind me." The platoon would form into a wedge, with Karstil leading in the center. Farwell would be on the right rear, Mullins to the left. The infantry, mounted inside the Viper now, would follow Karstil's Liberator. With the infantry inside their carrier, there was no reason why the Viper should lead. After a momentary pause while the vehicles shifted their positions, the platoon surged forward, gaining speed.

The DDP showed that the front of the Century had fallen into some disorder. The center Viper, carrying Holden Ventis, had fallen behind the rest of the line, the Century headquarters almost up to its position. On the far right, the first tank platoon was still echeloned behind its Viper and well in front of the rest of the Century. Either they had not been attacked by artillery or they had disregarded it. There was no telling what had happened. Karstil could see that one of the Constructor vehicles had dropped back, moving along the line of active sensors that had appeared on his screen. It was using its mine-clearing attachment to smash the sensors. The Constructor used a massive grav pulse to crush the delicate sensors. The invisible hammer was doing quite a job, and the pinpoints of light winked out as the engineer vehicle passed over them.

Red circles appeared on the DDP, indicating the presence of enemy infantry formations. The ballistic computer noted that the TOG pedes were dug in and bunkered, hard targets for tank cannon to hit and just as hard to damage if they were. Karstil activated the fire-support overlay, and a series of numbered crosses glowed on the screen.

"Privet Sickle Two-six, this is Flicket Market Two-two-six. Fire mission."

"This is Privet Sickle Two-six. Fire mission." Artillery was ready for coordinates.

"Market Two-two-six. From concentration Four-three-three Navis. Add six hundred, left four hundred. Dug-in infantry. Will adjust."

"Sickle Two-six. From concentration Four-three-three Navis. Add six hundred, left four hundred. Dug in infantry. Wait."

The enemy infantry position was still 3,000 meters ahead, and even at 70 KPH, it would take more than two minutes to reach them. Karstil wanted to soften the impact before he reached the 1,200-meter range of their TVLGs.

"Sickle Two-six. On the way. Wait." The fire mission had been accepted by the supporting artillery and the round was on the way. Karstil scanned the DDP, searching for active vehicles in support of the infantry. So far nothing showed. The platoon and its supporting infantry continued to cover ground at 20 meters a second. The formation was holding, though the Viper was dropping behind. Not good.

"Sickle Two-six. Splash. Over."

As the round hit, the DDP flashed a yellow spot near the targeted infantry, the HAFE indicator showing that the artillery had fired flechette.

"Market Two-two-six. Add one hundred. Left two hundred. One round. Fire for effect," Karstil directed.

"Sickle Two-six. One round. Fire for effect. On the way."

The infantry must have known they were about to get pounded. Karstil saw the target circle begin to move as they attempted to avoid the incoming rounds. Moving infantry was dangerous, but at least the cannon on the vehicles had a better chance to hit them. The DDP showed another yellow circle over the vacated infantry position.

"Sickle Two-six. Fire mission complete."

The moving infantry had created a gap in the defensive edge of the TOG forces. They had been positioned at 1,000-meter intervals, allowing their TVLGs to provide overlapping fields of fire. With one squad rooted out of their position, it had opened up a space wide enough to allow the platoon through. All the Liberators needed do was steer closer to one of the flanking positions to avoid the fire from the opposite squad.

"Quent. Open on the moving squad as soon as we're in range. We'll see if we can hurt them before we get close. Spint, bear a little to the right." The 150mm gun fired, the blue halo of light expanding at the muzzle. "Whoop, wheeeeee," sounded the laser warning klaxon. They were still too far from the infantry for the pedes to be painting. Karstil checked the DDP. There to the left was an active vehicle.

"Target identified. Horatius tank. Range two-two-double-zero. Bearing five-eight-double-zero." He felt the turret swing away from the infantry and toward the identified tank. The concentric aiming circles on the ballistic computer tracked across the screen, centering on the red blip that had shown itself. He pressed the laser painting treadle.

"Target identified. Lock achieved." The 150mm cannon opened at once. Blue light swept over the turret, the scream of the heavy laser close behind. Red dots appeared in the circle indicating hits.

The klaxon continued to scream its warning. The ballistic computer remained calm, reporting the identification of the target and lock. To the right and left, Farwell and Mullins opened on the Horatius. The painting laser was doing very well. At that range, it should have had a 10 percent chance of success, taking into account the flicker shields of the Horatius. Karstil's cannon and laser fired again. More hits. That Horatius was going to die hard. He knew he had scored four hits. With Mullins and Farwell also shooting at the same target, it should have vanished in a ball of fire by now. And it hadn't fired back. The crew must have been stunned by the first hit, or else the turret and hull weapons had been destroyed.

"Target identified. Horatius tank. Range one-six-double-zero. Bearing four-four-zero relative." Another Horatius to the right of the first one. "Quent. Switch targets." The turret swung right, the aiming circle crossing the new target.

"Target identified." He hit the painting laser. "Lock achieved." This was great shooting. The cannon and laser fired together. More red dots indicating hits.

"Market Two-two-six, Two-two-two. Targets bogus. I say again, targets bogus. Just transponders." The voice of Mullins remained steady. For some reason, he had determined that the targets were just transmitter units being used to confuse the attackers and make them waste their fire.

All this for a damned decoy.

37

Alsatia, Caralis
The Commonwealth
6 January 6831

Somewhere out there were the real tanks, still concealed and waiting. The platoon was spread out, engaging fake targets. No wonder the shooting had been so good. The tanks were abreast of the infantry positions now, too deeply committed to change the plan.

"Market Two-six, this is Market Two-two-six. Many bogus targets," Karstil said.

"Market Two-six, this is Market Two-one-six. Confirm bogus targets," Broast called in. As did Ventis. "Market Two-six, this is Market two-three-six. Confirm bogus targets."

All three platoons of the Second Century reported the same condition. There was no telling how many TOG defenders were in the area, or even where the front-line actually was. By now, the entire Century was deep into the enemy position, picking up TOG tanks that evaporated when engaged.

"Market Two-six," Freund came on. "Tanks up. Two-three-six, deploy and dig them out. Two-one, break. Two-two, push 400 and hold."

To the rear of the platoon, the Viper grounded in a cloud of digging charges, the infantry pouring out to meet the TOG legionaries face to face. The tanks moved on until they were 400 meters beyond the infantry fight. "Two-two-three, on line with me. Break. Two-two-two, echelon left." Mullins would protect the left rear of the position while Farwell linked with the first platoon on the right. Karstil's Liberator pushed through a clump of trees, the trunks shearing off as they came in contact with the forward hull. Spint was careful not to take a tree between the two arms, which would have made the TVLGs mounted between them unusable.

The DDP continued to show the bogus Horatius tanks, one of them within 50 meters of Karstil's Liberator. He searched the ground under the trees to his right, trying to find the transponder. He saw a small, camouflaged box, about half a meter on each side, covered with bushes. With no targets ahead, he swung the turret to the right and fired the 50mm cannon. The metal box disintegrated under the impact of the APDS round and the red circle vanished from the DDP.

Behind the tanks, Karstil could hear the Vipers pounding away at the bunkers with their SMLMs. That let them stay out of range of the infantry weapons while keeping the enemy pinned down. Their own infantry closed the positions under cover of the attack, rushing the positions as the last of the missiles exploded on the sides. The stunned TOG defenders were faced with immediate combat as the fresh attackers closed to point-blank range and opened fire. With their overlapping fires disrupted by the artillery attack, the defenders found themselves attacked from flank and rear. The TOG infantry fought valiantly, but the odds were against them. Karstil heard the Renegade infantry reporting captured soldiers as position after position fell.

Even the positions not attacked were in trouble. The Vipers called artillery fire onto the remaining bunkers, pinning the infantry inside for elimination by HELL rounds. It was all very methodical, but it was not an advance. The tanks waited for orders from Century while the prisoners were herded to the rear.

Karstil watched his DDP, scanning the distance for targets. The noon sun burned down on his back, sending warmth across his shoulders. He felt his eyes getting heavy, and he wanted to sleep. With the hull of the tank becoming hotter under the hammer of the sun, they'd need thermal nets over the tanks if they were going to stay here. Otherwise, they would start to glow like beacons to anyone watching with a heat sensor. Still no orders came from Century.

Certainly anyone out there knew of their presence. They had done enough shooting to give the alert of their presence on the front. The TOGs must be waiting for some signal. He looked into the fighting compartment to check on his crew. Podandos was slumped forward on his ballistic screen, his breath coming in long gasps. Spint looked alert, though Karstil suspected that he, too, was fighting fatigue. Karstil wished Freund would send the infantry forward to secure the ground at least out to TVLG range. That would keep the TOG infantry away and provide a screen of painters when the attack came in. All infantry squads were equipped with hand-held laser painting devices, and they could paint targets as they came within their 200-meter range. This was the same situation he had faced before; tanks alone were not sufficient to hold a defensive position.

Then the computer called out, "Unidentified target. Range three-zero-zero, double zero. Bearing zero-zero-one-zero mils relative. Speed four-two-zero. Target closing." At last. The TOGs were coming. At that speed, the enemy would be on them in just over three minutes. They had to be at treetop or low altitude to be moving at that rate.

"Market Two-six, this is Two-two-six. Bandits. Extreme range. Closing fast."

"Two-six. Roger bandits. Have acquired. Artillery on the way."

"I have them," said Podandos over the intercom, and Karstil marveled at how fast his gunner could snap to consciousness. The turret swung right to pick up the targets.

"Unidentified target. Range two-two-zero, double zero. Bearing unchanged. Speed three-six-zero. Target closing." Karstil reckoned that there must be many vehicles clumped together, which was why the computer was having difficulty separating them. The enemy had slowed, probably getting ready to drop to normal flight as they came within range. He saw the single circle split into parts.

"Target identified. Two Horatius tanks, one Trajan tank. Range one-six-zero, double zero. Speed two-eight-zero. Target closing." The TOGs were attacking with tanks only. Not a bright thing to do, Karstil thought. Not if Freund would deploy his own infantry.

"Market Two-three-six, this is Market Two-six. Rally on me," Freund ordered. No! thought Karstil. Don't pull the infantry away now! Behind him, he heard the Viper rise on its grav drive and turn. There was no saving the situation now. He would defend the position without the painting and TVLG support of the pedes. On screen, he saw the blue square move toward the right to form on Century Headquarters 8 kilometers away.

"Target identified. Two Horatius tanks, one Trajan tank. Range one-two-zero, double zero. Speed two-four-zero." They'd be on the deck now, skimming over the ground with no chance for the defenders to attack bottom armor. Karstil felt the tension in his stomach, realized that his shoulders were rigid, his arms flexed. The way those TOGs were coming on, it seemed like they wanted the ground.

"Target identified. Two Horatius tanks, one Trajan tank. Range eight-zero-double zero. Speed two-four-zero." It would only be moments now. He could see the rooster tails of the tanks against the skyline. Even at 8 kilometers, the height of the dust cloud was easily spotted.

"Two, break Three. Go for the Trajan first." Karstil then flipped to intercom. "Quent. Go for the Trajan. We'll worry about the medium stuff second." There were two ways to attack a mixed force: lights first or heavies first. Both theories had advantages. Karstil hoped that the combined fire of the stationary Liberators would damage the Trajan enough that the Horatius tanks would be easier targets. By concentrating all paint and fire on the one target, he hoped for a lucky hit. The target circle on the DDP switched to the Trajan indicator. I hope that's a real tank, thought Karstil. I don't want to end up shooting at this guy and have him turn out to be a bogus target.

He examined the approaching tanks with his monocular, trying to separate the heavy Trajan from the two Horatius medium tanks. The range was still too great for positive identification, but he was sure he could see the broader hull of a heavy tank in the center of the TOG formation.

"Target identified. Trajan tank. Range three-nine-double zero. Speed two-four-zero." He hit the laser painting treadle, knowing that Mullins and Farwell were painting as well. "Target identified. Lock achieved. Target painted." Karstil almost thought the ballistic computer sounded surprised. The range was still too great for the 150mm cannon, but the heavy laser whined to life. Someone in the platoon had painted the Trajan, and even though the lasers could not penetrate the front, multiple hits would begin to wear away the armor. He saw a huge blue ball erupt from the center of the TOG formation as the Trajan's 200mm cannon spoke. He heard the round rumble by off to this right. The Trajan was returning fire with the 200, even though Karstil's Liberator was beyond its maximum range. Perhaps the commander had been spooked by the laser hits. The klaxon began to whoop its warning.

"Target identified. Trajan tank. Range three-zero-double zero. Speed two-four-zero. Lock achieved. Target painted." A brilliant flash of light to the right caught Karstil's attention. He saw Farwell's Liberator surrounded by a cloud of molten sparks and shimmering iridescence. The DDP showed that the Sergeant had been painted; every TOG tank had opened simultaneously on his tank. The twin sponsons melted away under the torrent of hits. The 150mm cannon took a direct hit on the muzzle brake, peeling back the gun tube all the way to the mantlet. The tank was enveloped in smoke as Farwell backed down, covering his own retreat with quick-blooming smoke grenades. As the tank turned to bring its undamaged side armor to bear, a 200mm APDS round struck the 50mm laser mount, ripping the weapons from the turret and flinging them into the air.

"This is Privet Sickle," came the voice from artillery command. "Thor strike. Danger close."

The DDP flared with a forest of red circles, posting information as the enemy targets were identified. Two more mixed platoons of Horatius and Trajan tanks appeared on the right flank opposite Broast's platoon. At 1,200 meters, the display came alive with infantry symbols. It was TOG infantry, lying hidden and silent all across the front of the Century.

"Flicket Market. Flicket Market. This is Flicket Market Two-six. All Flicket Market units withdraw to rendezvous Toga Regal four-three-five-zero. From right to left. On my command." Centurion Freund must have seen enough, had enough. Now he was going to pull the Century back before it was destroyed.

While withdrawing during contact with the enemy, the least heavily engaged units went first, falling back to covering positions. Thus, the Century withdrew the least-involved platoon first, then the next, and finally, the most heavily engaged. Optio Broast, with first tank platoon, had not yet made contact with the TOG advance, except for the infantry. He would be able to get away to establish a blocking position to the rear. With him would go the Century headquarters, engineers, and artillery commands. Following would be the infantry platoon, and last of all, the second tank platoon, Karstil's, would break contact and flee.

"Flicket Market Two-one-six, this is Flicket Market Two-six. Break contact." First tank platoon was away, safe.

For Karstil, the theory of least heavily engaged first would hold. Mullins, to the left rear, would break first, taking up a position 600 to 800 meters to the rear. Then Karstil would leap-frog that position to one 600 to 800 meters beyond that. Farwell, assuming he could get away at all, would be the last out. That made Farwell the sacrifice allowing the platoon to escape. There was no use trying to save his tank. Better to lose a little of what was already gone than try to salvage the situation and his tank by expending another. You bury and decorate tankers in groups of three.

Karstil directed his tanks. "Two, this is Six. Paint Horatius tanks. Incoming Thor. Quent, switch to the Horatius tanks. Take the one on the right." The turret swung slightly and Karstil treadled the painting laser. Thor attacks did not need painted targets, but Karstil, like most ground commanders, distrusted indirect artillery fire that had a mind of its own. He wanted the targets painted, just in case.

"Target identified. Horatius tank. Range one-six-double zero. Speed two-four-zero. Lock achieved. Target painted." A grim smile spread across Karstil's face. It had been his laser that had painted the target at extreme range. Whoever had this painter before he got it had been one lucky man. Or else the combination of parts used to make up this boneyard Liberator had meshed in such a way that it was now better than average. The klaxon continued to whoop.

"Flicket Market Two-three-six, Flicket Market Two-six. Break contact." On Freund's order, the infantry were on their way to safety. Time to start withdrawing his tanks.

"Two-six. Break contact."

"Two. Negative. I'll cover from here."

"Two-six. Break contact. That's an order. Now go!"

"Two. Roger. I"ll meet you in the rear." Mullins was gone.

"Privet Sickle. Splash. Wait."

One of the Horatius tanks had broken away from the tight wedge pounding on Farwell and was headed toward the left of the platoon position. Karstil was still targeted on the other Horatius. Mullins had taken the free one.

The Thor satellite had been 700 kilometers above the battle. When the artillery mission warning order came in, the satellite rotated to bring its bundle of depleted-uranium javelins into the correct firing configuration. Then it waited for the ground station to download the fire mission into the ballistic system. The onboard computer analyzed the request for fire, comparing it to its own mission requirements, calls from other locations, threat assessment, and current ammunition load. That process took only micro-seconds. Analysis complete, the Thor selected the target areas and number of javelins to be launched.

Each of the javelins, 25mm in diameter and 1.5 meters long, was launched with an initial velocity of 3,200 meters/second. Not that the initial velocity had much to do with the final velocity—the acceleration of gravity having more effect than the initial speed. Nevertheless, by the time the javelin reached the surface, it would be incandescent from the speed of its transit through the atmosphere. When a long-rod penetrator of that size and mass struck an armored target, the results were spectacular. The tip of the molten rod spreads out over the surface of the armor, forming a pool of metal so hot that it instantaneously brings the armor to a molten state as well. As the rest of the rod continues on its course, this liquified globule drives through the armor until the rod exits the underside of the armor or strikes the ground.

The Thor satellite above Century Secundus processed the request for fire relayed from Privet Sickle Two-six. It selected two clusters, each containing three uranium javelins, from the racks on board, and fired them at the battlefield. The rods exploded from the launch tubes. To control the wobble from the launch, the satellite fired engine stabilizers to maintain the correct station for the launch platform. The rods on the way, the Thor turned its attention to other matters, allowing the javelins to hurtle toward the surface of Caralis.

The descent from 700 kilometers took three minutes. The javelins took most of it without additional control, for the vector established at time of launch was enough to direct them toward the fighting. By 100 kilometers, they were cherry red, with onboard sensors scanning the surface below, searching for vehicle signatures identifying TOG vehicles. Five of the javelins acquired lucrative targets. The sixth vanished in a spectacular burst of light and heat, no doubt having malfunctioned. The other five continued to drop toward the surface.

The Horatius tank continued to traverse the platoon position, trying to reach the location of Mullins' retreating Liberator. Karstil tracked it with the Liberator's hull TVLG system, swinging the tank to the left to bring the missile arc of fire onto the Horatius. The turret continued to track the other Horatius as it approached Farwell's dead tank. The flanking Horatius was moving fast, and Karstil was having trouble bringing the hull-mounted missiles into line. It was possible to swing the tank around fast enough, but he didn't want Podandos, controlling the turret, to be thrown off the acquired target.

The first Thor javelin struck the Horatius turret just behind the 3/6 laser mount, smashing through the painting laser and into the turret-top armor. A millisecond later, the second javelin struck alongside the first. The searing ball of molten uranium and titanium from the first strike burned through the roof of the turret and into the commander's station. The second hit, in almost the same hole, continued the process, driving through the fighting compartment, targeting computer, and weapons controls to exit the vehicle through the bottom. The force of the javelins pinned the Horatius to the ground. The tank, moving at 240 KPH, came to a complete and abrupt halt. Anything not secured to the interior broke loose and hurtled against the front of the fighting compartment, including, of course, the three crewmembers. The trauma of severe deceleration should have been enough to kill all three crewmen, but no one would ever know because the Horatius tank split apart in a spectacular fireball as the javelins sliced it in half as neatly as a knife.

The second Horatius tank had grounded to the right of the position, its grav coils spread across the Alsatian landscape, the 150mm cannon burrowed into the ground. The undamaged turret swung toward Karstil and launched a SMLM missile, followed by fire from the 3/6 laser and 50mm cannon. Just beyond it lay Farwell's tank, smoke spewing from the hatches and the gaping wounds on the hull and turret. Bringing its main gun to bear, the Trajan poked through the smoke, swinging its hull toward Karstil.

"Driver! Back down! Back down!" shouted Karstil into the intercom, and he felt the Liberator slide. Spint had seen the approaching Trajan, and knew that the tank, with its damaged rear, could not afford to turn away. The Liberator continued to move backward, gaining speed.

The wooded knoll where Karstil had placed his tank was a finger of high ground extending into the battlefield. To the right and left, the finger sloped away sharply. Though a tank could back up, the speed at which it was possible to control one moving in reverse was limited to approximately 36 KPH. A Liberator's thrusters could reach that in thirty seconds, going even faster if required. But at speeds above 36, control of the vehicle was difficult. Spint, in his haste to escape the Trajan, exceeded the safe reverse speed. The Liberator slid over the side of the knoll, crashing through the trees to the bottom of the gully.

From his position, Karstil could see the wreck of Farwell's tank, now aflame. He could also see at least one crewmember huddled in a crater to the rear of the tank. Evidently, Farwell had managed to fire his digging cannon before evacuating the tank, giving the survivor a place to hide. The rise of the knoll blocked the second Horatius tank, but it was still within SMLM range. The Trajan, unseen but recorded on the DDP, continued to prowl the area.

Beyond Farwell's tank, Karstil saw movement in the brush. As he watched, a Viper poked its nose from the screening vegetation and crept forward. He recognized it as one of their own APCs, supposedly withdrawn long ago on Freund's orders. The Viper TC was fully exposed in the right hatch, searching the area with his monocular vision device. The Viper continued to creep forward at less than 6 kilometers an hour, moving so slowly that it emitted almost no thermal signature.

Karstil's DDP showed that the Trajan was coming up the opposite side of the knoll. The TOG crew obviously knew where Karstil was, and may have guessed that he was in difficulty. Now the huge tank was creeping forward to bring its heavy lasers and cannon to bear on the Liberator. When it came over the edge of the ridge, all its weapons would be at point-blank range. In a stand-up, nose-to-nose fight with a Trajan, the Liberator was a dead duck. Even a hit from its 150mm cannon followed by a heavy laser would not be able to knock out the Trajan. Neither would the pair of TVLGs assure destruction.

The Trajan, on the other hand, had three weapons that could slice through the Liberator's armor with ease. The pair of turret-mounted 7.5/6 lasers would penetrate the ceramic armor no matter where they hit, and the 200mm cannon would enter cleanly anywhere but the turret face. Added to this was the tank's SMLM and TVLG load.

Even faced with the immediate threat of the Trajan, Karstil could not take his eyes off the drama to his right. The Viper commander had spotted the survivor hiding behind Farwell's tank. He was bringing the Viper closer and closer to the flaming Liberator, using the tank's thermal emissions as a shield against the sensors of the grounded Horatius. Neither the Viper nor the Horatius could see each other, but there would come a moment when the flames no longer protected the Viper. On came the APC, its hull just centimeters above the ground. It was being very, very quiet.

The Horatius, on the other hand, had traversed its turret to the right, ready to fire its SMLM at Karstil as soon as the Trajan had cleared the edge of the ridge and painted. He held his breath, watching the DDP screen and the approaching Viper, trying to calculate which tank would reach its objective first. If only he could see the Horatius, he could keep it occupied while the Viper stalked. The infantry vehicle had its turret rotated toward the Horatius, ready to paint the grounded tank as soon as its weapons would bear. With its TVLGs mounted in the hull, it would take but a moment to bring them onto the Horatius. The turret-mounted SMLM launcher would get off its shot just behind the paint attempt.

Karstil glanced at the DDP. The Trajan was almost to the edge of the knoll, moving slowly through the trees. The low main gun and twin sponson design was not meant for forest movement, and so the driver was taking the trees outside the protruding arms rather than in between them on the center hull. The Viper was almost clear of the flaming tank, with just 30 meters between it and the survivor.

The Viper accelerated, crossing the distance in a single bound, swerving to the right to face the grounded Horatius. Karstil could see the portside infantry doors snap open, men leaping to the ground to cover the retreat of the survivor. The TVLG racks on both sides of the forward hull flashed fire, their missiles screaming toward the hidden enemy tank. The starboard SMLM rack fired a moment later, and Karstil could see the 25mm cannon pouring out shells at a fantastic rate. The missiles were the deadly weapons, the 25mm Gauss cannon only a mild annoyance.

Above him, a tree crashed across the lip of the gully, and the DDP showed the Trajan almost on them. The infantry were dragging a figure from the crater, firing weapons to cover their retreat. Another tree thudded to the ground as the bow sponsons of the Trajan appeared.

The infantry were pushing a figure, perhaps two, into the armored compartment. Karstil could see their legs pumping under the covering shroud. The other TVLG rack fired along with the last SMLM. The Viper was empty now except for its 25mm cannon. The great barrel of the 200mm Trajan cannon cleared the lip, followed by the bow plane.

"Get ready, Quent."

"I'm on him, sir."

The bulk of the Trajan blotted out the sky above the Liberator, and in a moment, would reach its center of gravity and tip down into the gully.

"Target identified. Trajan tank. Range two-zero." Podandos hit the painting treadle. "Lock achieved. Target painted."

"Tank!"

"Identified!"

"Fire!"

The command was reflexive and superfluous. Karstel knew Quentain would not wait to fire on a painted, locked target 20 meters away. The battlefield belonged to the quick and the dead, and everyone knew it. All three turret weapons fired together, the blast of the 150mm cannon deafening in the confines of the gully. The blue ball of ionized gas leaped from the muzzle, reaching and enveloping the underside of the Trajan.

The titanium armor, thicker on the bottom than the Liberator carried on its sides, absorbed the damage. A surge of molten metal swept down the gully, engulfing the bow of the stranded Liberator. The Trajan, wounded but not killed, sank onto the edge of the gully, tottering. In a moment, all its drives and helm shot away, it would tilt far enough forward to depress its weapons to engage its tormentor.

"Again! Again! Shoot! Shoot!" It took time for Gauss cannon and heavy lasers to recharge. A seemingly infinite amount of time. The Trajan tipped forward. Green lights sparkled across the DDP, indicating that weapons were charged again. Karstil hit the painting treadle. "Lock achieved. Target painted."

Podandos didn't even wait for the cue. He saw the green lights flash and thumbed the master firing switch. Again the turret weapons spoke as one. Again the blue glow of the 150mm cannon enveloped the Trajan. Again Karstil fired the TVLGs.

This time there was no hope for the damaged heavy tank, whose forward bottom armor had been ripped away by the previous attack. Grounded at the edge of the gully, the Trajan could present nothing new to its lighter adversary. The laser, cannon, and missile fire burrowed deep into the hull, ripping through the already damaged helm and drive controls. When the heavy laser and one TVLG struck the 200mm ammunition stored in the bottom, the hull ripped apart at the joint where the sponsons attached to the main hull. One arm melted away in the fire, the other was propelled downward over the Liberator's turret.

The concussion of the blast caught Karstil square in the chest, pounding the breath out of him and throwing him against the rear of the hatch coaming. He felt a sharp pain across his back, felt something snap high in his left shoulder. Then he was driven into the fighting compartment to crumple on the grated floor at Spint's feet.

"Get us out of here," was all he could say before blackness swallowed him whole.

Alsatia, Caralis
The Commonwealth
6 January 6831

It was disaster all along the line for the Commonwealth/Renegade Legion. Cohort Harras had been repulsed at the right shoulder of the bulge, the others along the front. TOG Centuries, attacking in waves of Horatius and Trajan tanks supported by Romulus APCs, turned back the 2567th Renegade Infantry Legion (Provisional). Massive fire support from both Pompey grav artillery units and Thor satellites covered the attacks. Waves of fighters overwhelmed the 2567th's air defenses, smothering out the Air Defense Century.

Century Secundus broke contact with the TOG units, falling back 40 kilometers to a high ridge. There they reorganized the shattered force that remained. All three platoons had taken casualties, although the only vehicle lost was one of Karstil's. Freund did not have time to heckle Karstil about the loss, however, being too busy coordinating the next move with Harras.

Besides that, Karstil was temporarily unavailable for harassment. The medical orderly had diagnosed a cracked rib or ribs in the upper back as well as a possible fracture of the scapula. Karstil was one banged-up soldier. Immediate evacuation and rest were prescribed.

Prescribed, perhaps, but not applied. No one who could walk, crawl, or fight a vehicle was leaving the Century or Cohort. There were men hurt worse than Karstil who stayed in the ranks. Instead of evacuation, they swathed the side of his body in tape and gave him a massive dose of local pain killers. Anything general would have made him groggy and unfit to command, and he would definitely be needed.

Even Farwell, wounded and without a vehicle, was sent as a replacement to a damaged Liberator in another platoon that had lost most of its crew. Karstil was sorry to see him sent away, but he was also happy that the man had survived. He made a mental note to find the Viper commander if he made it back alive. The sergeant should get some kind of a commendation for his act.

Over the commlinks, the men of Cohort Harras could hear the reserve units committed to battle. Cohort Primus went in with a rush to stem the TOG attacks, and the excited chatter of the Cohort was distinguishable above the general din of combat. They knew full well that they were the last hope of the Legion. Commanders did not like to commit the reserve to save themselves from disaster; reserves were for exploiting victory. At the moment, there was no other alternative. Prefect Kenderson was trying to save the shattered remnants of his force, but it was too little, too late. There were just too many TOG tanks, too few Deliverers.

One by one, the command stations of the Cohort Primus, or First Cohort, signed off in the heat of battle. Century after Century reported itself destroyed, the commanders noting overwhelming odds. Even the dashing riders of the heavy tanks were not enough to plug the gaping holes that developed in the front. It was time to trade space for time.

Cohort Harras was assigned as the covering force for the right-hand Manus as it tried to withdraw to better positions. Its mission was to defend the front in small packets, covering the withdrawal of the Manus elements, fighting at long range, forcing the enemy to deploy. Once the TOG units were ready to attack in force, the elements of the Cohort would fall back to other positions in the rear. The watchwords of the operation were to stay out of close range, and to avoid commiting the units to a stand-up fight unless absolutely necessary.

Karstil watched the narrow valley that stretched out in front of his position. The area that had been thick with retreating units just hours before now stood deserted. He had watched the support vehicles of the Legion flow past him as they sought safety in the rear, using the floor of the valley to mask their own movement. The first to go by were the supply types, long lines of Asinus, Equus, and Chuckwagon carriers. Some were crammed with equipment and support troops, their loadbeds packed so full that men and equipment hung from the sides in disarray. Others were neatly packed, the drivers and assistant drivers sitting in their seats, the support troops quiet in the cargo bays. Others were nearly empty, the drivers swerving in and out of the mass to pass the slower vehicles.

Next were the artillery and engineer vehicles. The units showed the frightening scars of combat, the armor on the Peddens and Constructors gouged and torn, and the wounded laid out on the flat spaces of the hulls. The closer to combat the vehicles had been, the more sullen and grim were the crews. Grimy faces, red-rimmed eyes, and set jaws marked the combat support elements. Last of all had come the fighting men of the Legion. The units were small, and Karstil read the hull numbers of the vehicles to determine how they had done.

Most of the Centuries were down to three or four combat vehicles out of the nine or ten they should have had. Most were damaged. A Liberator crawled past, grav coils hanging loosely from its under-carriage and bouncing off the ground in showers of sparks. Another's turret was completely destroyed but for the turret ring, exposing the entire fighting compartment. The only visible crewmember was the driver, who wore his face-mask down to protect himself from the dust of the road. There were few Vipers or Wolverines. Either they had taken a different route, or they would not be coming back at all.

Behind Karstil, supporting him from a secondary blocking position, was Mullins. He had seen it all before in that other retreat on Caralis, the 2567th's previous disaster. Once more, the Legion had been crushed by superior forces, forced to retreat. Once more, there had been disaster in the Air Defense Century. "Every day we die a little" was the unit's unofficial motto, and today they were dying a great deal. Somewhere, hundreds of kilometers to the rear, were the lines of the Commonwealth 2031st Strike Legion. If the 2567th could get back to those lines, they could be evacuated to some distant continent or planet to re-fit and re-arm. All they had to do was survive until the passage of lines.

Karstil's DDP flashed its warning. Fifty kilometers in the distance were the first of the TOG units. Closing fast, they skimmed across the terrain at 600 kph, using Low-Altitude Flight in their efforts to close with and crush the last elements of the retreating Legion. He felt himself tense. The numbers of red squares and triangles was impressive even if they were not yet identified by type. At that speed, the enemy would be on him in five minutes. His one assigned Pedden artillery support vehicle would have to do some fancy shooting.

"Gable Fungus Two-two-three, this is Teacher Haddock Two-two-six. Fire mission," Karstil clicked in.

"Gable Fungus Two-two-three. Fire mission. I'm right behind you. Have them on my screen."

"Haddock. Prepare to fire HELL to the right of the road. I want to force them to the left to get good shots on bottom armor at long range. I don't want to let them get much closer than two klicks before I break away."

"Fungus. Negative on HELL. I have HAFE, ADM, smoke, and GLAD."

Karstil paused. Without the powerful HELL rounds, there would be no hope of stopping the TOG vehicles. His only chance was to make the enemy believe he faced a much stronger force to the front. At an approach speed of 600 kph, that would have to happen very quickly.

"Haddock. Open with GLAD at once. Fire one smoke into the area to the right of the road. I want them to know the area is targeted."

"Fungus. Negative GLAD. That requires a painted target for a good chance of a hit."

"Haddock. I understand that. I want fire at long-range to break up their formation. I don't care if I hit anything."

"Fungus. That is not the correct use of the GLAD round."

"Haddock. This is not the time or place to debate the theory of artillery deployment. You are attached to me. You will follow my orders. Shoot GLAD."

"Fungus. I will record in my log that I do so under protest."

"Haddock. Noted. Shoot GLAD."

"Fungus. On the way."

Karstil heard the low-pitched thud of the artillery piece firing. With any luck, the TOG commander would know that GLAD was being fired, know that this was an inappropriate use of artillery, and begin to suspect a trap. There was no reason why the Renegades would fire GLAD at extreme range unless they had so much artillery that they didn't care or else had infantry with painters close by to mark targets. Or both.

Karstil knew there are old commanders, and there are bold commanders, but no old, bold commanders. The TOG commander had obviously been around, for he was playing his hand by the book. Karstil knew that TOG regulations did not allow commanders to rush headlong into a suspected trap. As the first of the GLAD rounds dropped into the enemy's oncoming forces, his opponent made an instant decision.

Karstil could see the red squares and triangles, now no more than 40 kilometers away, apply negative thrust and begin to swerve. At that range, there was little chance to hit anything even when the target's vector was known. Once the targets slowed and turned, the possible target zones multiplied rapidly. There was no ballistic computer in existence that could solve that firing equation.

"Fungus. Target turning. Fire mission complete."

"Haddock. Negative. Continue to shoot."

"Fungus. I have no firing solution," the Pedden commander protested.

"Haddock. Make it up. Use your imagination."

"Fungus. Against regulations."

"Haddock. Shoot. Two more rounds."

"Fungus. Under protest."

"Haddock. I am about to send a very irate platoon sergeant to your location. This man will sit on your shoulders and make you do what I tell you. Now shoot."

Hidden in his vehicle to the rear of his commander, Mullins heard the exchange between Karstil and the artillery sergeant. A grim smile spread over his face. Through the intercom, to no one in particular, he said, "I guess we'll stay with our young hero. He seems to have a decent grasp of the situation."

Manus Headquarters was in chaos. Men were running everywhere, trying to sort out where was the front, what units were still operational, who was still fighting. The Optio grounded his Equus light grav sled just within the perimeter and watched the situation. The exact location of the command vehicle was not immediately discernible in the confusion.

There, under a stand of trees, he saw the radar and commlink antennas that marked an important vehicle. A modified Spartius had had its turret removed, replaced by a phased array communications system. The rear loading doors on both sides had been lowered, and tent extensions erected over them. Knots of men, probably officers, stood around the vehicle. Here was a lucrative target.

The Optio dismounted from the Equus, indicating to the driver to move the vehicle away from the area. As the sled drew away, the officer opened a small pouch attached to his belt. Inside were several rank and branch insignia. He studied the assortment, looking for a rank high enough that his presence at a Manus command would not be questioned, but not so exalted that he would be questioned. He also wanted an appropriate branch. He selected the rank of Centurion Maximus and Medical Support Service as the branch. The insignia and rank on his uniform, he picked up his small bag and moved toward the Spartius.

The confusion around the vehicle allowed him to approach within 10 meters before he was challenged, but it was perfunctory at best. The Triarii on sentry duty was obviously new and scared, and the grim-faced Centurion Maximus did not look like someone to be trifled with. The guard allowed the officer to pass without forcing him to give the countersign.

The Centurion Maximus walked up one ramp, through the operations center, and out the other side of the vehicle. He set the bag down beside the vehicle, opened it, and extracted a 50-centimeter lance-point antenna. Glancing around quickly to see if he were being observed, the Centurion Maximus placed the antenna on top of the vehicle amid dozens of other similar antennas. The antenna, its base a magnet, snapped onto the top of the Spartius.

The Centurion Maximus closed the bag, passed through the operations center, and left the vehicle. He glared at the Triarii as he passed through the security cordon, then walked briskly toward the grounded grav sled.

On the top of the Spartius, the antenna began to send out a coded signal, whose frequency would manifest as only a fuzz on the normal frequency of a standard commlink. Hundreds of kilometers away, the DDP of a TOG receiving station marked the transmission with a single red dot. From now on, that Manus Headquarters vehicle would be a "painted" target for any artillery or air attacks. It would not last long. The Legatus Maximus standing behind the systems operator smiled. He would deal with the Renegade Manus in due time.

40

Alsatia, Caralis
The Commonwealth
6 January 6831

The gorge was the last defensible position for the next 45 kilometers. There, well to the rear, were the lines of the Commonwealth 2031st Strike Legion, and safety. The 2031st had had enough time to prepare its lines with minefields and other obstacles, a defense in depth that would at least hold the TOG forces while the 2567th evacuated off the Alsatian continent.

For thirty-six hours, the men of the 2567th had been trading space for time, making the TOG attackers deploy and probe while the defenders slipped away. The strategy had not always been successful. In one Manus, three Centuries had been overrun, destroyed when the Manus headquarters had come under heavy air attack. The headquarters had been well hidden in the terrain, its thermal nets in place, but the TOG *Pilum* and *Martiobarbulus* fighters had discovered it and spent an hour turning the target into so much rubble. Bereft of their control headquarters, the Centuries had been shattered by the onrushing TOG forces.

Karstil stretched his legs as best he could in the cluttered fighting compartment of his Liberator. He couldn't remember when he had last eaten, yet the floor of the fighting compartment was littered with numerous emergency combat ration wrappers. Food was not really the problem; lack of sleep was. His eyes were inflamed and his ribs and shoulder throbbed with pain. Having long since used up the local painkillers, he dared not use the general sedatives that remained. At his current level of fatigue, they'd put him asleep in an instant, and Karstil didn't want that. There was no telling if he would be able to rouse himself in an emergency. Anyway, the pain kept him awake.

The early evening light cast deep shadows in the 60-meter crevice through which the road wound toward the TOG forces. The sharp ridges on either side made movement dangerous except on the road itself, as it would force the vehicles out of the cover provided by the valley. It was along that route that the remnants of the 2567th had passed just moments ago. To operate above the ridge lines would force vehicles to present their undersides to defending forces, and he was sure the TOGs would not be coming on at Tree-Top Flight Mode or Low-Altitude Flight Mode. They had done that already, moving high and fast to get behind the defenders. It had worked, and several times the retreating Renegade forces had been forced to deploy to brush TOG defenders off the route of retreat. But they had paid a high price.

More than once, Karstil had kept his Liberators hidden in the valleys, attacking bottom armor on the Aeneas and Lupis vehicles as they went by. There were enough wrecks strewn across the distant battlefields to prove the value of bottom attacks. When he picked up the infantry squad, the attacks became even more deadly. The infantry painted well, and they had plenty of TVLGs, which they were using to better and better effect.

He had lost the Pedden artillery support, its sergeant happy to leave the tanker's control and rejoin his battery. The cannon were now deployed well to the rear, behind the covering lines of the 2031st. They were still his on-call artillery, but they would operate as a battery now rather than as single units spread across the front. Not that he really trusted them.

The last time Karstil had called for support from the artillery, there had been a mix-up in the mission. He had called for an artillery-delivered minefield across his position just in front of the TOG forces. The mines had arrived on schedule, but they had fallen 800 meters behind his own position rather than that distance in front of it. Luckily, the TOGs had seen the mines deploy. Suspecting a trap, they had halted until they could bring up their own Remus engineering vehicles. Karstil had used that time to make his way through the minefield. But it had been close, and Karstil had never again called for artillery support.

Now the infantry and one tanker from each tank were out in front, planting a hidden minefield between two clusters of trees. The men didn't like it. Placing mines was stoop labor that required much digging for no immediately apparent reward. It was even more discouraging when the troops knew artillery could do the same job in a tenth of the time and at no cost in energy. But they did it because they were told to. Told by a young Optio who was playing it by the book.

The troops placed the mines in staggered lines between the trees, and on down the steep slopes of the gully, a task made even more difficult because the sides of the gorge were so sharp. It required a fine sense of balance to carry one of the 15-kilo mines up the hill, place it in the finished hole, and then arm it. The real challenge was replacing the soil around the mine. The fuse was a proximity type that detonated only when a vehicle passed over it, but the troops still didn't like the idea of pushing dirt on top of an armed bomb. Karstil had to emplace the first few mines himself, just to show that it could be done. He had tried to do it in a semi-jaunty manner, despite the pain in his shoulder, but he had sweated through the whole operation.

With the mines deployed at last, he stationed his tank where he could see well down the road. Mullins was behind, his cannon aimed to the rear edge of the mined area. The infantry were deployed along the crests of the gorge.

The plan was simple. All the vehicles would shut down, covering themselves with their thermal nets to remain invisible to TOG sensors. No active emissions would be allowed. With passive-only sensors, Karstil would be able to detect the TOG approach at 4 kilometers. In the darkness, he hoped that the enemy would stay below the crests, using the deep valley as concealment from the distant Renegade forces. Karstil had listened over the commlink as all the other outposts were withdrawn.

The 2031st should have called him in by now, too. It made no sense to leave a lone strong point this far ahead of the main line, when all the others had left. The Centurion in charge of this sector must be very slow, thought Karstil, for his unit should have been up and gone by now, too. He didn't dare attempt to contact him, though, for the TOGs would surely pick up the signal. And complaining would do no good. When the Century was ready, they'd let him know. He settled down to wait for the next fight.

It was more than an hour after full darkness that the DDP flashed its first warning. A column of red squares appeared on the screen, moving slowly down the valley. They were advancing with such stealth that even the passive sensors did not pick them up until the lead vehicle was three kilometers away. Not bad, thought Karstil. The 2031st probably doesn't even have them on their screens. A shiver coursed through his body, activating the pain in his shoulder. It stabbed through him, making his head swim. Careful, fella, he told himself. Don't black out now. Just hold on for one more hour.

"Quent," he whispered over the intercom, "you know the plan. Wait until the head of the column reaches the near edge of the minefield, then take out the last vehicle you can target. Mullins will get the lead."

"Got it."

Karstil watched as the column of red squares on the screen came ever closer. He could no longer tell if they were moving slower or not. Perhaps it was his imagination. He wanted to talk to Mullins, to make sure the Platoon Sergeant was alert and tracking the column. What if Mullins couldn't see them yet? What if Mullins were asleep? What about the infantry? They were so quiet that Karstil didn't have them on his screen at all. Were they still there? Were they awake? Would they follow the plan?

"Getting closer, Quent. Get ready."

"Yes, sir."

There had been no real reason to talk to Podandos. He knew the plan and would execute it to the best of his ability. But Karstil had to share his concern with someone, even if it were just unnecessary chatter. Podandos didn't seem to mind. Perhaps he shared Karstil's feeling.

The leading red square was almost at the near end of the mined area. There were no more targets appearing at the tail of the column, though Karstil couldn't tell if that were because the column had ended or because the sensors were not picking up any more vehicles. He took a deep breath, holding it for a moment. He flipped the commlink to open traffic; Mullins and Podandos would get the commands simultaneously. Wait. Wait. Wait.

"Tank!"

"Identified."

"Fire!"

The Liberator jumped, slamming Karstil against the front coaming of the hatch, stunning him for an instant. A brilliant blue ball of ionized gas expanded from the muzzle of the 150mm cannon, and the 50mm began to chatter. He saw the tracer element of the main gun round streak into the inky darkness, saw a second round flash before his eyes. There was a deafening explosion 75 meters away as Mullins' HEAP struck the side of an Horatius tank.

With the sensors on passive-only, they had not distinguished the target types, only that they were there. Karstil saw the flank of the Horatius glow as Mullins' heavy laser struck home. The ballistic computer showed that the leading vehicle had been painted, and he thumbed the missile switch. The one TVLG missile left in the rack flared across the distance. It would never penetrate the tough front armor of the Horatius, but the combined hits of missiles and shells might panic the TOG crewmen.

Outlined in the glare of battle, the Horatius swung to the right to engage Mullins. Far to the rear was another Horatius, its turret belching smoke. Podandos had been dead-on, the laser following the 150mm HEAP round into the crater left by the shell. Karstil could see the sparkle of 50mm hits rake across the wounded turret. Between the two tanks were half a dozen Lupis carriers, their line-of-sight and access blocked by the two medium tanks. The SMLM racks on the leading vehicles were elevating to bring their missiles to bear on the Liberators that had sprung the trap even as they tried to climb the walls of the gorge.

The leading Horatius was turning broadside to Karstil to bring the hull-mounted 150mm cannon to bear on Mullins, but the commander must have hesitated when Karstil's TVLG struck home. The TOG tank began to swing back. The turret had been fully traversed to engage Mullins, and it continued to pound away at him. Mullins, all his weapons able to bear, was giving better than he got. Deep in the gully, Karstil saw three SMLM missiles spring from their racks, arcing over the edge of the ridges to search for Mullins. He could see the fire trails of the missiles streak through the intermittent darkness, hesitate in their course, and plunge toward the Platoon Sergeant's tank.

"Watch out!" shouted Karstil, forgetting that all the circuits were still open.

He need not have used the energy. The Vulcan III system on Mullins' Liberator was tracking the incoming missiles as they left the tubes. With the missiles all approaching from the same vector, the anti-missile system hardly had to raise a sweat. All three SMLMs disintegrated long before they closed. It was the first time Karstil had seen the Vulcan in action from the role of pure spectator, and he was impressed.

The hatches on the near Horatius popped open, smoke exploding from the vents. With the crew bailing out, Karstil disregarded them. Tankers without tanks are not much of a threat to anyone but themselves. Behind the tank, the Lupis APCs were climbing the sides of the gorge, blocking the line-of-sight to the rear Horatius. Podandos changed target and began to hammer at the flank of the nearest APC. At that range, the heavy laser was accurate enough that painting was almost unnecessary.

The Viper burst into flames, the infantry blowing out from the side hatches in an attempt to escape. Behind it, another Lupis crested the ridge, its infantry access doors snapping open. It was too late. The Renegade infantry, lying atop the ridge, opened up with their TVLGs. The Lupis took a TVLG square in the bottom. It turned to the right, lost helm and drives at the same time, and grounded on the edge of the ridge. Then it slid over the crest and crashed to the bottom of the gorge, rolling over and over as it fell. It burst into fountains of flame.

The burning vehicles supplied plenty of illumination for the grim scene that was unfolding. The lead Horatius was fully involved. Behind it, the Lupis lay on its back, spouting fire. The APCs to the rear were trying to climb the walls of the gorge, only to receive point-blank fire from the hidden infantry atop the crests.

The rear Horatius, Karstil's original target, was pushing forward through the debris of the column. It began to climb in an attempt to get by a crippled Lupis, turning straight into the minefield laid hours before. The underside of the tank flared in a series of explosions as it crossed the thickly strewn mines. The 150mm gun drooped, digging into the ground. The tank stopped.

"One, this is Six," Karstil shouted. "Get out!" He would give the infantry a thirty-second lead, then he would withdraw his own tank. Mullins would be the last to go, covering the retreat of the others. He had to call the 2031st to tell them he was coming.

"Sealskin Sword Three-six, this is Bicycle Gadfly Two-two-six," Karstil called out.

The infantry squad leader was quick to respond. "Gadfly, Sword Three-six."

"Gadfly Two-two-six. Am withdrawing now."

"Roger, Gadfly. Come to mother."

"Six, One. Mounting now. It's time to get the hell out of Dodge."

"Roger One. I never liked Dodge that much anyway." The Viper APC screamed by overhead, its driver choosing to use LAF at full power, trusting in speed to get him to safety. His trust was well-placed.

"Two, Six. Cover me."

"Two. Roger."

"Spint, back her down. Don't turn until we're well clear of this mess." Karstil's Liberator shuddered as the grav drives came on, the tank rising and backing in one movement. Well clear of the gorge, it slowed and pivoted, then moved forward to pass Mullins' tank. He was already at a hover, turning the hull to follow Karstil. He waved as they passed. Home was going to look very good.

BOOK III
FULL POWER

41

Alsatia, Caralis
The Commonwealth
7 January 6831

The Cohort meeting was smaller than the one that had taken place five days earlier, with many seats in the briefing tent vacant. Everyone looked tired and drawn, even the members of the staff. There was a different feeling in the room, too. The last time, the air had been charged with a mixture of excitement and dread. Excitement because they were going into combat as a full-strength, well-trained unit. Dread because there were so many men who had never faced the ultimate test.

At this meeting, Karstil sensed stoic resignation and relief instead. Resignation because the Cohort had passed the test of combat, but had lost the ultimate battle. Relief because it would soon be all over. They were being evacuated to accept replacements, new equipment, and rest. Rest. That was the key to the operation now.

Centurion Moldine Rinter began the briefing, looking even more tired than the rest of the officers. As Operations Officer for the Cohort, she was supposed to have her finger on the pulse of the unit at all times and be available at the critical moments. But there was no way of knowing when those times would come. The usual result was that an Ops Officer tried to be awake all the time, treating even routine reports as though they were the beginning of something big. Her only relief came in the form of Bonto Lavayal, the Centurion who handled the Intelligence Section of the headquarters. Technically, Lavayal was the Deputy Operations Officer and should have stood half the watches in the Operations Center. But that never happened. Not in Cohort Harras, nor in any other Cohort, Manus, or Legion. Ops was in control most of the time, with the DOO relegated to minor functions.

Rinter began the briefing with a report on the current situation on Caralis. The 2031st Commonwealth Legion had been hastily deployed across the line of retreat of the 2567th to prevent a complete breakthrough to the more populated areas of the continent. It was a veteran Legion whose original mission was that of continuing the attack through the 2567th. When the 2567th collapsed, the 2031st had been thrown in to hold the line. That line was now stabilized, but the 2031st was under increasing pressure and needed help.

The TOG forces now in contact with the 2031st included the 149th Praetorian Guard, the 3241st Strike Legion, and the 13379th Legion, the Harbingers of Death. The 13379th was an old adversary on Caralis, the 3241st was new. New and of a different organization. There were significantly more heavy vehicles reported in the 3241st, the tank platoons being of mixed weight rather than only one type of vehicle. This was why the 2567th had encountered so many Trajan/Horatius platoons in recent combat. The heavy units all had a Trajan configuration, but the Century headquarters was assigned a Remus engineering tank in addition to the standard equipment. The engineering vehicle gave each Century increased capabilities in both attack and defense, especially when attacking prepared defenses.

The officers in the briefing room listened with only slight attention. As far as they were concerned, all this was just history that could as easily wait until they were on their way in transports. What they really wanted to know was whether there would be turn-over for leaving the vehicles, or if they would have to evacuate the vehicles as well as the personnel. Fond as many were of their tanks, they wanted to get away as quickly as possible. Some of the officers actually dozed, relying on their senses to awaken them when something important came along. More often what they really depended on was a quick poke in the ribs from the man sitting next to them. Assuming, of course, that he wasn't napping as well.

As the reports continued, some of the men began to sit up straighter and listen harder. Suddenly this was beginning to sound more like an attack briefing than the prelude to an evacuation. Shocked faces stared back at Rinter as she spoke. This *was* an attack briefing! The officers began to take notes.

Seeing that the younger officers were beginning to catch on, Centurion Rinter smiled inwardly. She had never said they were going home, only that this was a briefing for the next operation. But she knew that the rumor mill had been hard at work; now it would be easier for Harras to break the news. There would be no trip to safety, at least not for a while. For many of them, the trip to safety would never come. The background report finished, she turned the floor over to Harras.

"The mission, gentlemen," he began, "is to make a spoiling attack on the TOG forces to our front." Harras looked over the audience, detecting disappointment in some faces and resignation on others. "The 2031st is holding now, but there are indications, as the Centurion has said, that TOG is building up for the big push. What we'll try to do is give them a bloody nose, make them pause long enough to allow the Commonwealth to get reinforcements here. We need five days."

Karstil absorbed the news of the attack with mixed emotions. He hadn't really felt good about leaving the embattled continent. If it hadn't been for the destruction of the Air Defense Century and the massacre of the Manus headquarters, the Legion would have been fine. To retreat in the face of such overwhelming odds was no disgrace. It would go in the books as a retreat, but a successful retreat was sometimes a victory in itself.

With the Air Defense Century gone, Prefect Kenderson faced a difficult decision. The combat elements of the Legion were capable of withstanding air attacks, but the support units, lacking heavy weapons, were sitting ducks. To defend the supply and support units, he would need to pull combat vehicles from the already-strained front line. That would have made the rear echelons defensible, but weakened the leading edge of the Legion at the same time. It was, as they say, "Damned if you do, and damned if you don't." Kenderson had kept the front line intact. The result had been TOG fighters chewing up support troops all over the field.

For Karstil, the prospect of evacuating Alsatia had left him with a sense of unaccomplished objectives, the feeling that there was more the Legion could do. Now they would have the chance. He wondered at his own attitude. Faced with the choice of safety or possible death, he seemed to accept danger as the preferable condition. It wasn't out of any special loyalty to the 2031st, for it wasn't much more than a unit number to him. As for sheer patriotism, the Commonwealth seemed too big, too distant, to evoke emotional ties. And the Renegades were just a name for an unknown dream. What was it, then, that drew him willingly to face the enemy?

Perhaps, Karstil thought, it was because he liked being a soldier. The world of combat, with its risks of sudden death and horrible wounds, was all too real, but he felt at home in it. It was more than the excitement, more than the adrenaline rush that came from contact with the enemy. It was the sense that he was doing a responsible job and doing it well. Nowhere else could a man so young be given the responsibility for such important decisions. Eight other men, and actually many more, depended on him to make the correct choice at the correct time. He was proud of what he had done, of how much he had grown. He liked being a soldier.

And soldiers fight, that was their reason for being. Now the Legion was being asked to do what they were trained to do. Climbing onto the transports for safety was all well and good, but if there was still fighting to do, he was glad to be going back.

The plan for the spoiling attacks was simple. Elements of the 2567th, including Cohort Harras, had been assigned sectors in which to operate. As they found opportunities, they would stage attack/raids within their sectors. Short, sharp jabs at the TOG forces would keep the enemy guessing about the purpose and weight of the Renegade moves. It also would force the TOGs to reinforce their own front to defend themselves, disrupting their plans for attack. If units could break through the front, they would drive deeply into the TOG area, withdrawing when the enemy massed against the penetration. Then the attackers would flee back to their own lines, leaving the riposte to fall on empty air. It was exactly the sort of thing a mixed force of tanks and infantry could do well. It would also be a chance to be daring without endangering the rest of the Legion.

Harras concluded the briefing by turning the meeting over to Centurion Jantus Golliatus, the Supply Officer. Supply was going to be a touchy part of the operation. In some cases, the attacking units would be outside the normal supply radius, making conservation of ammunition important. The evacuation of casualties was another subject of interest. As there would be no battle ambulances with the attacking units, men wounded in action would have to remain in the combat vehicles of the forces involved. Anyone who required immediate medical treatment would have to be left to the TOGs. That sounded harsh, but the more seriously wounded would have a better chance as prisoners than of being carried to the rear by their own men. Commanders would have to make such difficult decisions on the spot.

That was a responsibility Karstil did not want. He was a fighter, a tanker, not a medical officer. He had had the same medical training all officers receive at Officers Training School, but that did not prepare him to make medical decisions. How was he, with his limited knowledge, going to know if a man could live long enough to make it back? He thought of the surviving members of the platoon. There was no way he would abandon any of them to the tender mercies of the TOGs. The Toggies didn't mistreat prisoners, but they weren't kind to them, either. He hoped never to face the necessity of leaving one of his men behind.

He remembered the actions of the infantry squad leader when it came time to pull out of the defensive position during the first withdrawal. That Sergeant had chosen to risk his vehicle and his squad to save the survivors of Farwell's tank. That squad had been lost in the first retreat, possibly because it stopped to save a friend. That was not an acceptable risk, but Karstil knew that he would have done the same.

When he returned to his platoon with the news of the attack, most of the men griped, which was exactly the response Karstil had expected. Yennan, the new gunner in Mullins' tank, was the most vocal. As the youngest member of the platoon, he felt he had done his part and didn't see why they needed to do more. "Let the 2031st do some of the dirty work for a while," he moaned. The others had kept quiet, not wanting to threaten Karstil's position as commander. It was Mullins who settled it.

"You can't live forever," he said. "Anyway, it's 'Dulce et decorum est pro patria mori.'"

With that, the men of the second platoon returned to their tanks to prepare.

42

Alsatia, Caralis
The Commonwealth
7 January 6831

The plan for the morning fun was simple in the extreme. Both the first tank platoon, Broast's, and the second, Karstil's, would be reinforced with one of the two remaining infantry squads. Both platoons would attack on broad axes of advance, able to maneuver as long as they didn't interfere with the adjacent platoon. Each was to advance as far as possible, refusing to become deeply committed to any assault. As soon as the TOGs reacted, the platoons, operating independently, would be recalled. The plan did not call for the capture or retention of any specific ground.

Five thousand years earlier, commanders had used their horse cavalry in much the same way on Terra. It had made and broken the reputations of those officers. Now grav tanks would perform the same functions, generally raising havoc behind enemy lines, destroying what they could, and escaping when the counterblow was delivered.

Platoon Sergeant Lucifer Mullins watched his young Optio, who was excited by the prospect of combat. He had seen the symptoms in young commanders before, but it usually happened before they had seen any action. Karstil was becoming a veteran, or close to it, by now. He should be facing the prospect of action with a certain sense of resignation, instead of seeming happy as a clam at being able to lead the platoon. Mullins thought maybe they were making young people different these days.

Karstil had chosen a platoon column as the formation for the attack. Mullins was just as happy to play tail-end-Charlie in the formation. It would mean that he covered the rear of the three-vehicle formation, with the Viper APC sandwiched between the two Liberators. He would have liked to have Farwell with him, but who knew where he was. There were no replacement tanks or crews available, and the third vehicle would be the APC, a slender reed when one was contemplating armored combat.

Mullins was disappointed that the Legion was not being pulled off Alsatia. After some sixteen years as a tanker, he could feel the Legion disintegrating under the constant tension. It had not been so bad early on. The Legion had not committed any major errors after reaching the surface, and things had been quiet since he found the demo charge in Karstil's Liberator.

Then had come the abortive attack on the TOG positions. Nothing had gone right after that. He knew from rumors flying through the sergeants' network that the Air Defense Century had been caught napping again. They had not been able to acquire or lock onto any of the attacking TOG fighters. After the Century was destroyed, the TOG fighters were all over the field. It was loss of the air defense that resulted in the destruction of the Manus headquarters. How the Legatus could have allowed that to happen was beyond him. Men in that position were supposed to be qualified to run their commands. And if they couldn't, there was no excuse for getting caught with their pants down. There should have been enough senior sergeants around the headquarters to camouflage their superior's blunders. Well, he thought, that was just the way things went in the good old 2567th.

Mullins didn't think much of the present plan, either. Charging into TOG positions, only to run away when attacked, sounded more like desperation than a good plan. He was sure that, one by one, platoons all down the line would be destroyed for no gain. It was almost as if the High Command had decided to sacrifice the 2567th because the Legion had proved to be of no real value. This would allow the higher-ups to disband the Legion after commending its brave fallen soldiers. The good thing about the plan, if there was one, was that no disaster would destroy more than one platoon at a time.

Mullins was a survivor. He had been a survivor in his other Legions, and he would be one now. There was a thin line between being loyal and being stupid. As the last tank in the column, his would be the one to cover the retreat if any other vehicles were able to escape. He liked Karstil, thought he would make a good Centurion if he lived.

"Placid Gargoyle, Placid Gargoyle, this is Placid Gargoyle Two-six. Prepare to execute Spider." Karstil heard Centurion Freund pass the word over the commlink that they were about to attack. He waited for Broast to acknowledge and then did the same. The 2031st would open with tanks, infantry, and artillery, covering the front with area fire. After a five-minute barrage, the platoons of Cohort Harras would roll forward through the friendly lines. The 2031st would provide support and covering fire for the first three kilometers. After that, the platoons would be on their own. He heard the first of the HAFE rounds rumble overhead.

All across the front, the air rocked with the blast of many weapons firing at once. Even at a one-meter hover, he could feel the shaking as the gravitic waves were bombarded by concussion. If the blast effects were impressive kilometers behind the lines, they would be even more so for those on the receiving end. He watched the seconds scroll by on the chronometer. Time to move.

He stood in the turret, craning over the bulk of the armored house to see the smaller Viper hidden in the trees to the rear. He waved to the TC and pointed forward. "Go," he said over the intercom, and Spint applied maximum thrust to the Liberator. The jolt of movement and the subsequent acceleration threw him against the rear of the hatch coaming, sending a sharp pain through his shoulder and back. Even with plastic armor across his back, it was painful to be thrown against a solid object. I'll pay for that in my old age, Mullins thought. Probably be so crippled I won't be able to move.

The Optio had heard the plan for the attacks, had even been responsible for drafting some of the orders. He had been so busy at Legion headquarters that he had been unable to slip away. And he felt he was being watched. He couldn't put his finger on the watcher, but a sixth sense told him that there was someone out there. He had scanned the faces at Legion headquarters, but could see no change in personnel. Now he had an important job to do.

It was all well and good to be given the mission of sabotaging the equipment of the 2567th. He and his contacts had done a good job, but their other mission was to keep their own headquarters aware of what the Legion was doing.

Though the report was based only on rumors, he had sent off word that the Legion was to be withdrawn from Caralis. Now he wished he hadn't presented it as hard fact. His superiors were not going to be pleased when they found the 2567th attacking. They would be doubly displeased if the 2567th disrupted their own plans for an attack. Displeased superiors were not nice people to deal with, especially when they were TOG Generals.

The Optio was amazed at how soft and stupid the Renegades were. NaBesta Kenderson was unfit to command a TOG force above a platoon. He had allowed things to happen within the Legion that would never have been tolerated in a TOG formation. The men of the headquarters treated the Prefect with so much familiarity that many were on a first-name basis with him. The man actually seemed to care whether the troops liked him. A TOG Prefect told his underlings what to do, and the underlings did it. The idea of asking after his men's health or offering to relieve them at some task was enough to make a true officer vomit.

But the Optio had to put these thoughts aside and find a way to let his superiors know that the 2567th was attacking and what the attacks meant. With the TOG defenders so informed, they could lay a trap for the unwary Legion. With any luck, the entire Legion could be destroyed. That would make him an important agent in the eyes of his superiors, perhaps even lead to his immediate promotion. This was an opportunity on a silver platter.

The report of the Legion status and the complete plan of attack was to be sent to Commonwealth Planetary Defense Headquarters on Rolandrin. Each of the Cohorts and Centuries had submitted a detailed description of where and how they would attack so that other Legions operating in the area would know that the 2567th was out in front and that they should provide fire as needed by them. Planet had to be informed so that they could provide air and satellite support, if available. Because of the length of the report, a special channel on the commlink had been opened with Planet. But that commlink had been established in one of the communications vehicles and had not been slaved through to the Legion command post. The link was for a one-time message and reply. After that, the link would be broken. The Optio had been given the responsibility of establishing the link and transmitting the message.

The communications vehicle was well away from the main headquarters. Security was only part of the problem. Because the message would be sent on a very narrow band, it was important that the sending unit be able to trace an unimpeded vector from its dish to that of the orbiting satellite. From the satellite, the message would be bounced planetside to another receiver. The satellite would take the scrambled message, decode it, then re-scramble it, and send it planetside. There would be a double encoding process, making the message from the satellite virtually unreadable to any but the authorized recipient.

The Optio, however, had another plan. As he sat at the commlink console attempting to link with the satellite, he would arrange for the transmission to be sent on a second frequency as well. The second frequency was far enough away from the authorized one that there would be no bleed-over into the satellite send. The second frequency was his private link with his superiors. He was to send to them only at special times, and this would not be one of them. But the receiver at TOG headquarters was on listening silence all the time. It would receive the message and store it in its files. When the operator came on duty, all he would have to do was check his messages and play back the transmission. It might be a little late, but there was so much in the message that even a little late was good enough.

The communications sergeant recognized him as he entered the vehicle, another of the Spartius APCs that had been converted to another use. The headquarters was full of them. This was a new sergeant in the headquarters, but the man had obviously been told that the Optio was coming and was ready for him. The man had been lounging in the seat, his feet propped up on the desk in front of the commlinks. The Optio suppressed his normal response, which would have been to chew the man from one end to the other, but that was not the way things were done at the 2567th.

"You ready to send?"

"Sir."

"What?"

"Sir. You are supposed to say 'Sir' when you address an officer."

"Right. Sir, you ready to send, SIR?"

The Optio could feel his neck beginning to get hot. This was typical of the attitude that infected the entire Legion. Here was an unknown communications sergeant addressing an officer in that tone of voice. He gritted his teeth, counting silently, slowly, to ten.

"I'll take the commlink now."

"I'll stay here and help you."

The Optio gritted his teeth again. This sergeant was going to be a problem. "No, sergeant. I can do it myself. This is highly classified material."

"No problem. I got clearance for it."

"I'm sure you do," said the Optio, slowly and firmly. "But you do not have a need-to-know. I do. Please exit the vehicle."

The Sergeant dropped his feet to the floor and stood. His left arm was in a sling, and he moved as though in great pain. The Optio could see the bandages under the combat coveralls. He seemed hurt at being ejected from his comfortable location by something as unimportant as a Top Secret message to Planet, upon which might hang the fate of the galaxy. The Optio didn't even watch him go.

The set-up for the transmission took no time at all. It was merely a process of opening the secret channel as well as the one to the satellite. The entire plan ran to seventeen typescript pages, all of which had been encoded into four-number groups for transmission. The decoders were using one-time tear sheets to decode the message after it was scrambled by the satellite. The message could be broken, as could any transmission, but it would be useless by that time. The four-number groups were transmitted to a disk that would send the signal in a single, two-second screech.

Perhaps screech wasn't an accurate description. The message would go by laser to the satellite, which was one of the reasons why the vehicle's position was so important. From there, it would go via another laser to the ground station at Planet. Unless someone managed to intercept the beam of light, there was no way another receiver could read it. The laborious process of encrypting and scrambling was to ensure that, if this did happen, the interceptor would not be able to read the message.

The Optio heard the satellite signal. It was transmitting its standard call sign, informing ground stations of its presence. There would be no answer from the TOG station; there never was. He held his breath and keyed the transmission switch. Three seconds later, he heard the satellite acknowledge the transmission as received. He closed both channels, twisting the frequency read-out dials so that no one would know the previous positions. After closing the commlink, the Optio left the van.

43

Alsatia, Caralis
The Commonwealth
7 January 6831

The ground was covered in a thick pall of smoke and dust. Indeed, the air was so clouded that Karstil was not even aware of the friendly lines when he passed through them. His sensors showed the positions of the 2031st as a series of blue squares, but he didn't see any actual vehicles. Not that he would or should. The fighting positions of the defending Legion were 800 meters apart, and each of them was protected by overhead cover as well as thermal nets. It was only the firing signatures of the weapons, identified by the sensors as friendly, that allowed the positions to appear on the screen at all. There were no red TOG indicators.

The platoon passed over the minefields laid in front of the 2031st positions. Tiny send-only pylons were placed in the gaps so that they beamed their messages only toward the friendly lines. The sensors in the vehicles picked up the coded pulses, displaying the information as single blue dots on the DDP. All the tanks had to do was follow the dotted line, marking each pylon as it was crossed. The pylons had anti-tampering tremblers built into their bases. If someone tried to move one, the home station would detect the tampering and explode the pylon. That usually discouraged further tampering.

It was perfectly possible for the vehicles to cross the minefield at any location. The mines had an Identification Friend or Foe (IFF) system built into them, but there was no use taking chances with a faulty send unit. An exploding mine did as much damage to a friendly vehicle as it did to an enemy, and the 2567th did not have any extra vehicles to spare.

"Placid Gargoyle Two-six, this is Placid Gargoyle Two-two-six."

"Gargoyle Two-six."

"Two-two-six. Passed Ratchet. Spider now operative."

"Roger, Two-two-six. Passed Ratchet. Spider operative. Control loose. Weapons loose."

"Two-two-six. Wilco." They were on their own now. Ratchet, the designation for the front-line members of the 2031st, were to the rear. The plan, codenamed Spider, was operative in this area. Karstil leaned back against the coaming, twitching forward as pain reminded him of his damaged scapula and cracked ribs. Better to lean forward than back, he thought. Not as relaxing, but more comfortable under the circumstances. He checked the DDP. Behind him the other two vehicles were following in a ragged column. They might look new and ready in the late morning sun, but they weren't.

Karstil's Liberator still had that gaping hole in the left sponson. He had tried to have it repaired, but there was not enough time. The crew had stuffed their duffles and other personal gear into the opening, but Karstil knew that it was only to make themselves feel good. A 150mm round in the same hole would hardly be deterred by the presence of the kits. The Viper had lost one of its SMLM launchers, a serious problem because it reduced the tank's limited long-range fire by 50 percent. There were plenty of TVLGs on board the APC, the crew having stored an additional fifteen missiles inside the infantry compartment. They knew the risk they were taking, but assumed that if it came to the point of the extra ammunition exploding, they were already dead.

Mullins' Liberator was in the best offensive shape of all the vehicles in the column. It had taken a near-miss with a heavy shell that jolted the tank, resulting in the TS&R systems becoming misaligned. The systems had come from different tanks in the boneyard, and perhaps they never did get along well together. Most of the time they functioned normally, but the occasional tendency to lose control created some interesting maneuvers by the tank. Sedgwick Abul was a good driver, and so he did not augur in when the TS&R went bonkers, but it had been close. Karstil distrusted the TS&R. It was a clever system, but like all such things, when it decided to do something strange, it was really strange.

The first objective was a rocky knoll to the left front of the operational area. The slopes were gentle on the near side, dropping sharply on the back. From its elevation, he would be able to observe the wide valley that lay beyond. The knoll was not large enough to hold a strong TOG force, and so anything there should be a reasonable match for the platoon.

The sensors showed no enemy located on the knoll, but Karstil felt that the TOG would not leave it undefended. His sixth sense told him to expect an outpost, and he was mentally prepared for a squad supported by their Lupis and perhaps an Aeneas. The only danger from a Lupis was its SMLMs. The Aeneas carried a light laser and a 100mm cannon. As long as the battle stayed at 2 to 3 kilometers, they should have no trouble.

As they approached the knoll, Karstil put the platoon into a wide vee, with Mullins on the right, the infantry well to the rear and centered. The arms of the vee were a thousand meters apart. No matter when or where the enemy showed himself, the unengaged tank would be able to flank the position. Simple and effective.

"Quent."

"Sir."

"Take a look at the top of that knoll. There's some kind of big lump just to the right of the top. As we cross three kays, see if you can hit it with an APDS round."

"Got it, sir. Firing at three." The platoon cruised on over the open ground, closing on the objective at 120 KPH. In a minute, they would be within range of the main guns, and the lasers could already hit any target. Karstil felt the turret move as Podandos brought the main gun to bear on the distant knoll. Major shifts were accomplished by moving the turret, and the gun itself made all the fine adjustments. "Laid on. Firing at three."

Karstil watched the targeting information on the DDP. The lump had been acquired, but the ballistic computer refused to recognize it as a real target. It would not scroll any information on a target that was not stored in its capacious memory banks—and rocks were definitely not in memory. The numbers flashed as the range decreased. At 3,000 meters, the 150mm cannon thumped, the blue ball of ionized gas expanding around the muzzle. Just for the fun of it, Podandos followed the round with a blast from the 5/6 laser.

Rock does not really burn, but rock dust will explode. The 150mm APDS round struck the lumpish outcropping directly in the center, pounding the rock into a cloud of microscopic particles. The laser bolt struck the cloud of dust, bringing the particles to incandescence in an instant. The entire cloud flashed in a brilliant explosion. Very impressive.

As the detonation spread across the knoll, the DDP came alive with red circles. The infantry, hidden around the outcropping, were sprinting away from what was obviously the target for the main gun. "Tallyho!" shouted Karstil over the commlink. "Get 'em, Quent! Get 'em! Rake 'em over! Hey, Spint. Straight at 'em." The Liberator changed course slightly and began to accelerate. The main gun fired again, and another cloud of dust appeared on the knoll. Shooting infantry with a 150 was like trying to kill mosquitoes with a hammer: not efficient but spectacular when it worked. All Karstil really wanted to do was to keep them running so that they could not regroup and return fire.

Two red circles appeared on the DDP behind the knoll. Grav drives on some vehicles had fired up. The sensors did not have line-of-sight, so the targets couldn't be identified. Mullins, however, was off to the flank. He'd be able to see them soon enough.

"Unidentified targets. Range one-seven-double zero. Bearing zero-one-zero relative. Targets stationary." The ballistic computer had seen the targets but had not yet determined what they were. It would search its memory and give him their best guess, based on the output of the engine. "Engine power indicates probable light tanks and carrier." He had been right. Unless the TOGs were playing games with their drives, Mullins would find a Lupis and Aeneas behind the knoll. The painting laser warning whooped and began to scream.

So much for keeping the infantry busy. The squad, or least a portion of it, had gotten itself together to paint his tank.

"Swing left, Spint. We'll try to attract their attention." The Liberator swerved, and Karstil brought his arm up just in time to keep from being thrown against the side of the coaming. The turret slewed to the right. In the infantry position, there were a pair of explosions followed by streams of fire indicating TVLGs. The peds were getting organized. From behind the knoll, a single fire trail indicated that another missile had joined the barrage.

Behind his left shoulder, the Vulcan III rotated on its mount, tracking the incoming missiles. Its own ballistic computer analyzed the threat posed by the missiles, determining which, if any, would strike the tank. It rejected as inappropriate targets those that were sure to miss, engaging only ones with a chance of striking the tank. The multiple light laser sprang to life, and two of the missiles vanished in spectacular bursts of fuel and warhead.

The red dots were crawling away over the crest of the knoll, trying to reach their supporting tank and carrier parked in the rear. They were a beat too late. Mullins and the Viper APC had swept around the right of the knoll and were now positioned on the flank of the evacuating force. The Aeneas was faced with the choice of abandoning the Lupis to save itself or staying to trade shots with the heavier Liberator. The Lupis was faced with the choice of abandoning the infantry to save itself or remaining to pick up the pedes before running. The Lupis chose to stay. The Aeneas chose to flee.

Mullins took a quick shot at the fleeing Aeneas with both the heavy laser and the 150mm cannon. Both shots hit the stern, and the light tank disappeared in a cloud of smoke. It emerged an instant later, slower and still trailing smoke, but it would live to fight another day. The Lupis paid for its loyalty to the bounce infantry. With the Aeneas a difficult target, Mullins switched to the APC.

The infantry had just closed the access doors when the first 150mm round struck the flank. One of the doors spiraled away, and another slumped on its hinges. The Lupis staggered, its 25mm gun spraying Mullins with tiny slugs. The gunner had fired one of the SMLMs, with the other rack awaiting lock-on by the painting laser. It should have fired earlier. At 1,000 meters, there was no advantage in waiting for the painting laser to decipher the flicker shields. Had he fired the SMLM, he would not have died with the missile in the rack, though the exploding round had not added much to the detonation of the vehicle itself.

Karstil brought his Liberator over the crest just as the Lupis took its first hit from Mullins. The range was less than 200 meters, and he didn't wait for the targeting laser to paint the target. The heavy laser, 150mm and 50mm cannon, and one TVLG struck together. The 150 fired HEAP, the 50 joined in with APDS. The two rounds struck within a meter of each other, ripping open most of the rear armor. The TVLG smashed through the remaining titanium armor and ceramic protection to burst in the engine compartment. Grav coils and circuitry vaporized. The force of the explosion threw the Lupis forward, driving the nose shield into the ground. The heavy laser struck in the shattered stern, boring through the wreckage and drives.

The explosion began just behind the last infantry access door and spread forward over the vehicle. One moment, there had been a Lupis carrier, the next, there was nothing but a ball of fire and boiling smoke. Parts of the carrier rained down on Karstil's tank. The patter of falling pieces continued for many seconds.

"Placid Gargoyle Two-six, this is Placid Gargoyle Two-two-six."

"Gargoyle Two-six."

"Two-two-six. Objective Zephyr secured. No casualties."

"Roger Two-two-six. Interrogative. Enemy?"

"Two-two-six. Negative. One fleeing Aeneas. No other TOG vehicles in sensor range or sight. Aeneas fleeing three-two-zero-zero actual. Damaged."

"This is Two-six. Wait."

The plan, Karstil knew, was to hit and run. The plan did not call for waiting. Freund was not going with the plan. Now he and his platoon, successful in their first attack, were being asked, told, to wait until some decision was made at Century.

"Placid Gargoyle Two-two-six, this is Placid Gargoyle Six."

Karstil stared at the commlink speaker. Placid Gargoyle Six? Placid Gargoyle Six was Centurion Maximus Milton Harras. The Cohort commander wanted to talk to him.

"This is Placid Gargoyle Two-two-six." Best not to keep the Centurion Maximus waiting while a mere Optio pondered the honor of talking directly with the Cohort commander.

"This is Six. Can you continue the advance?"

"This is Two-two-six. Yes, sir."

"This is Six. No need to use 'sir' on the commlink. Have you taken any damage?"

"This is Two-two-six. No, sir…I mean no…Negative. No damage."

"O.K., son. We're going to send you deeper. The other attacks were not as successful. Get out there and kick some butt. Use your own initiative. Come back when it starts to get busy. We'll keep you informed."

"Two-two-six. Wilco." Karstil felt his heart expand in his chest. Harras had as much told him that he was the best platoon leader in the Cohort.

"This is Placid Gargoyle Six. Good hunting, Karstil."

Alsatia, Caralis
The Commomwealth
7 January 6831

The platoon skimmed forward, still in the wide vee they had used to begin the attack. Any other formation was no use, for there was no telling where they would encounter the enemy. As the kilometers rolled past and the unit moved deeper and deeper into TOG territory, Karstil felt elated at penetrating so far into enemy territory. By noon, however, with no contact and no enemy on the DDP, they were at extreme friendly artillery range. If they advanced any more, they would really be on their own.

When Karstil reported that they were leaving their own support range, he was told to keep going. Perhaps because of the range or perhaps because of TOG interference, the commlink with headquarters was faint and garbled. He didn't like either, but on they went.

By mid-afternoon, the platoon had crossed into an area littered with wrecked tanks and parts of tanks, obviously the scene of recent violent combat. A Liberator turret perched on a low ridge, staring sightless over the debris. Beyond it, a Trajan had buried its bow in the ground, its 200mm cannon crumpled and twisted. Grav coils lay like miniature straw piles across the ground. There was no telling what they had come from, but there were several from Class 2500 engines. Heavy tanks had either died in the area or limped away to be succored by their maintenance people.

"Unidentified multiple targets. Range two-zero-zero-double zero. Bearing eight-double zero relative. Target velocity three-six. Tracking." Karstil glanced at his DDP. A string of faint red squares had appeared 20 kilometers away to his right front. They were moving as slowly as bounce infantry, but the size of the marks indicated vehicles of some kind. The computer was searching its files. Based on the limited information available, it could not come up with a solution.

"All Gargoyle. Bandits at eight-double zero relative. Close on targets. Maintain current formation. Guide on me." The platoon turned to the right and began to accelerate. Karstil checked the red squares on the DDP. They were fainter than anything he had seen before, and moving slowly. The platoon skimmed over the terrain at 180 KPH. He indexed the targeting computer for additional information, and numbers scrolled across the screen. The information that appeared showed the time until the computer felt the target could be identified.

In less than five minutes, the ballistic computer would have the target identified. In six minutes, he would be able to paint and fire his heavy laser. He could change any of the numbers by increasing or decreasing speed, but 180 was well within safe speed for the terrain. Decreasing speed would only give the target more time to react to his presence. If they were unsure of what he was doing so deep in TOG territory, they might not react to his first attack.

"Unidentified multiple targets. Range one-seven-zero-double zero. Bearing zero relative. Target velocity three-six. Tracking." The ballistic computer was still unsure of the target, waiting for at least a 70 percent solution before it made its best guess. The targets were moving down a road in heavy woods. Unless they made it to an open area, they were at a distinct advantage over the grav tanks.

If the platoon came to normal flight, he would have to attack the unidentified column head-on in the narrow confines of the trees, sacrificing heavy firepower to stay at normal flight, or attack from Tree-Top Flight so that all the platoon's weapons could fire. The disadvantage of Tree-Top Flight was that it gave TOG adversaries a chance to hit the relatively soft underside armor.

"Unidentified multiple targets. Range one-four-zero-double zero. Bearing zero relative. Target velocity three-six. Tracking." They were still there, still in column, still in the woods. Decision time was coming up fast.

"Two, this is Six. I'll go down the road to meet them. Take three with you and circle to the right. Try to flank them if you can."

"Two. Wilco."

Karstil watched as Mullins and the infantry carrier bore away to the right, sweeping in on the target. "Unidentified multiple targets. Range one-one-zero-double zero. Bearing zero relative. Target velocity three-six. Tracking." They were still moving through the woods. He glanced at the DDP; it showed the road snaking through the timber. Another minute or so and he'd be in the trees.

"Spint. We're going down that road ahead. Be careful. We'll probably want to slow down as we enter. Something around 70, I think."

"Roger, sir. I'll brake to 70 as we enter." The Liberator turned to bring the opening in the treeline centered on the bow. Karstil could see the break in the heavy woods, the forest verge thick with brush.

"Unidentified multiple targets. Range seven-eight-double zero. Bearing zero relative. Target velocity six-zero, accelerating. Target breaking up. Tracking." The faint red squares had changed from their column into a pair of wedges, the flanking vehicles in the woods. "Unidentified multiple targets. Range seven-five-double zero. Target velocity six-zero. Tracking." Still no information on the nature of the target. The Liberator slowed as it neared the trees.

Spint did not apply maximum deceleration, instead letting the tank coast down toward 70 KPH. He was aware of Karstil's injury, and saw no need to slam the Liberator around unless absolutely necessary. Soon enough, they'd be thrashing about plenty. The gap in the trees came toward the tank with disconcerting rapidity, but still with no line-of-sight to the enemy vehicles. "Targets stopped. Targets firing," purred the ballistic computer.

What could they be firing at? There was no line-of-sight, no way they could be shooting at him.

"Incoming artillery," continued the computer. "Area targeted." A series of red circles centered on the DDP over his location, separating as the computer tracked the incoming rounds. The outer circles carried "ADM" notations, the center one was notated as "HELL." The platoon had stumbled onto an artillery battery, which had now opened fire.

"Break right. Accelerate!" They'd have to chance the Artillery Delivered Mines rather than face the HELL round. The Liberator turned sharply as Spint responded to his command, the right sponson scraping the ground in a panic turn. The Liberator skidded momentarily, then righted itself as the vanes controlled the turn. Karstil bounced back and forth in the hatch, pain searing through his back and shoulder. He felt his vision going gray.

The Liberator was clear of the incoming shells before they landed, the HELL round producing a white ball of fire to the rear. The ADM bursts scattered hundreds of mines which struck in the field. The DDP noted their fall, recording their location for the future.

It was standard military philosophy that one does not chase tanks with artillery. The tubes could not be tracked fast enough to catch the tank, and the tank's speed and maneuverability would always let it dodge the incoming rounds. But that meant the tank was dodging shells instead of serving its primary function as an offensive weapon. If a tank did nothing but dodge, it couldn't be attacking the artillery—or anything else. Even with an almost infinitesimally low chance that artillery would hit the tank, the law of probability guaranteed that, if enough rounds were fired, sooner or later, one of them would hit.

Karstil understood in his gut that it was just a matter of time before one of the HELL rounds got him. All he could do was to bob and weave, reducing that chance to as near zero as possible. If he could do that, the other vehicles of the command might be able to close and destroy the target. There was no use trying to run. The artillery pieces could fire out to a range well beyond 100 kilometers, and even at maximum speed, he would be a target for too long. Besides that, the tank would have to travel in a straight line, making it an easy target.

The DDP told the story. Three of the artillery vehicles continued to track his Liberator while the others turned on the flanking units. Other red circles began to chase Mullins and the infantry vehicle. His own tank continued to dodge rounds, the circles appearing on Spint's screen in time for him to maneuver away. But they weren't any closer to the artillery pieces.

Time was on the side of the enemy's guns. Aside from the law of probability, the TOGs must surely have notified their headquarters of the presence of the Renegade tanks. Somewhere, even if from a great distance, support vehicles had to be on their way. When they arrived, the scales would definitely turn against Karstil. He had to do something.

"Spint, turn toward them rather than away," he said tersely. "Let's see if we can get close enough for a shot." In response, Spint swerved the Liberator back toward the woods. Accelerating, he brought the tank to treetop level.

"Target identified. Six Kershaw Special Artillery Platforms. Range four-zero-double zero. No lock achieved." Karstil didn't recognize the name. He hit the "Interrogative" switch on the DDP to gain more information, and a display of data appeared. It told him that the Kershaw Special Artillery Platform was a tracked vehicle, modified from a Kershaw ground tank into a tracked artillery carrier. It was slow and weakly armed and armored. The display also informed him that the GPE-5B artillery tube gave the vehicle a 75-kilometer range, and that it was most often found in second-line TOG Legions.

At least Karstil knew what he was fighting, and a second-line Legion at that. From the statistics on the vehicle, he saw that an attack from the rear would be best, but the enemy battery had circled the vehicles, with all of them facing out. The front armor was not that thick, there were no flicker shields to deflect the heavy laser, and the only weapon they had was the main gun. If he could close the range, they would be easy pickings for the heavier, faster tanks.

"Spint. Close fast. We'll make a pass over the battery. Try to evade their shots as we go in. Quent, fire everything at the first target you can acquire. They have no shields."

The Liberator swerved violently as Spint tried to throw off the tracking of the artillery pieces. Sooner or later, they would realize that the tank was going to make a firing run over the position and adjust their own fire accordingly.

"Two, Six. I'm making a pass over the target. Follow me in."

"Two. Roger." Mullins' Liberator was several kilometers away from the battery position, still dodging the rounds that chased him. The Viper was even further away, unharried by fire but unwilling to make a nuisance of itself for fear of retaliation.

"Three, Six. Close to within two klicks. I'll try to paint one as I pass. Launch the SMLM as I close. I'll try to guide it in." The infantry carrier acknowledged and turned toward the battery. Karstil's Liberator roared over the trees, closing on the battery. Red circles appeared on the DDP ahead of the charging tank. Each one bore a notation of the ammunition being fired, but Karstil was too busy coordinating the other vehicles of the force to worry about what they were. Let Spint worry about them, he thought. He'll pick the lesser of the evils.

The treetops passed in a green blur, the taller ones whipping against the outstretched arms of the forward hull. Artillery rounds burst in the trees to the right and left, and to the rear, another blaze of white light indicated a HELL round. The tank juked right and left, avoiding the mine-scattering ADM rounds.

The red squares on the DDP were almost under the location indicator. Karstil saw a small clearing in the woods, tracked vehicles parked on the perimeter under the trees. He had a momentary impression of huge cannon pointing skyward, the muzzles as big as trash cans. Then the Liberator rocked as Podandos fired the three turret weapons together.

A series of explosions raked the artillery position, the glow of molten armor followed by clouds of dense, gray smoke. Then Karstil's Liberator was gone, across the trees. The artillery tubes would not have time to track 3200 mils that quickly. They had been laid on him as a primary target, the real threat to their existence, and now they would have to acquire a different target and traverse to it. For the moment, he was safe.

The Liberator shuddered in a sharp left turn, throwing Karstil against the coaming, his right shoulder coming up hard against the rim of the hatch. The only good thing was that Spint had turned to the left, bruising the strong right shoulder rather than the other, injured one. Karstil's eyes grew gray from shock, then gradually cleared. He could see Mullins' Liberator bracketed by exploding shells while still a kilometer from the TOG firing position. A series of explosions in the treetops blotted out the tank, and then it appeared again, streaking away from the target. Mullins hadn't made it across the battery.

The Liberator circled to the left as the artillery shells began to chase it again. In the distance, Karstil could see Mullins and the Viper turn back toward the battery position. If they rushed the guns all at once, they just might have a chance. The DDP had shown that there were only five targets now, the Liberator's guns having destroyed one of the vehicles. There was no way the KSAP could take that kind of pounding and survive.

"Two, Six. We'll rush them together this time. On my command," Karstil ordered.

"Two. Wilco. I'll bring the infantry with me."

"Three. I'll blow my pedes just as we cross the target."

"Three, Six. Drop them 600 meters short. No use having them caught in the blast."

"Three. Wilco."

With three vehicles crossing the target's 200-meter-wide area at high speed, there was no use risking the mounted infantry in the area. Karstil leaned against the front of the hatch, waiting for the other vehicles to get into position.

"Check the DDP, sir." It was Podandos. "Friendlies in the area."

Karstil leaned back and looked at his DDP. There, scattered around the KSAPs were a series of blue dots, friendly infantry. And a blue square appeared nearby, an infantry carrier.

"Now! Charge now!" he shouted into the commlink. "Maximum thrust."

Spint hadn't waited for the command. The Liberator surged forward, its hull skimming the tops of the trees. In the distance, Karstil saw Mullins turn and charge as well, the Viper close behind. An explosion rocked the clearing ahead, a second column of smoke blending with the one caused by Karstil's attack. Shells stopped exploding in the trees.

As he crossed the battery position, Karstil saw two of the TOG vehicles blazing fiercely. Another one had the tube depressed, the muzzle pointing into the deeper woods. The Liberator banked slightly, the turret swinging to the left as the three weapons fired at one of the KSAPs the DDP indicated as still functioning. The HEAP round struck the rear of the turret, followed by the heavy laser. The tinkering Mullins had done with the sights paid off; the laser followed the same hole as the 150mm round. There was a flash as the turret disintegrated, then the hull began to blaze.

Karstil was aware of a blur to his rear. It was Mullins crossing the target just seconds after he had cleared. His own tank banked left again, and he could see the bounce infantry blasting out the sides of the Viper. Infantry liked to deploy under the protective outer shield of the Viper if they could. Being expelled with explosive violence was not the safest way to exit a vehicle. He could see the bodies of the infantrymen crash through the trees as their grav belts began to impede the fall. That, he thought, was a hell of a way to go to work.

Mullins must have scored a hit, because there was another flash and ball of fire in the clearing. The DDP was down to three red squares, and then another one winked out. The Liberator continued to turn back toward the area of combat.

"Unknown Renegade tanks, this is Empire Hearty Three-one-three. We have surrendering TOG troops in the area. Do not fire." The transmission was accompanied by multiple shells bursting over the clearing.

"Empire Hearty Three-one-three, this is Placid Gargoyle Two-two-six. Will circle the area. Break. Two, Six. Friendlies in the area. Will circle. Cover me."

"Two. Wilco."

The Liberator circled slowly over the clearing. Below, inside the ring of trees, Karstil could see four tracked vehicles burning brightly in the late afternoon sunlight. The long shadows cast by the trees intensified the glare. Among the vehicles were numerous men, many of them in combat armor and power packs he recognized as Renegade bounce infantry kits. There was another smaller knot, hands folded behind their heads, forming to one side. In the center of the clearing was a Viper APC, its 25mm "pop-gun" aimed at the rear of the turret of a tracked vehicle.

"Ground it," he said.

Spint brought the Liberator to a 1-meter hover beside the Viper and then let the tank sink nicely to the ground.

Alsatia, Caralis
The Commonwealth
7 January 6831

The infantry squad leader was sitting on the turret of the Viper, watching the Renegade infantry round up the last of the TOG artillerymen. Karstil crawled painfully from the turret of his own tank and lowered himself to the ground between the forward booms. Each movement was an effort that sent stabbing pain through his back and shoulder. He leaned against the right sponson, supporting himself with his good arm while his vision cleared.

Glancing over at the Viper, he could see that the vehicle had been through some desperate combat. The doors had been blown from the left side and the protective outer shroud had been hit so many times that almost nothing remained. The driver's cupola had been crushed, now little more than a gaping hole where the vision blocks and hatch should have been. The smoke grenade packs on the front of the turret were gone, as were the twin SMLM racks that should have been on the sides. Karstil couldn't tell if the accessories had been blown away in combat or ripped from the turret by the vehicle's passage through the woods.

The Sergeant jumped down from the turret and came to where Karstil stood. Karstil straightened slowly, trying not to reveal that he was in excruciating pain. The low sun glared off the visor of the Sergeant's helmet, making Karstil wince. He returned the salute.

"Thanks for the help, Sergeant."

"Thank you, sir." The voice was soft and musical. "We never expected to find a friendly unit this far in the rear." When the helmet came off, it revealed a wealth of auburn hair that glowed in the sun. "We didn't know what to do until your tank came across the opening in the trees."

Karstil's jaw dropped. The girl was twelve centimeters shorter than he was, her dark brown eyes set in a rosy face. Not what he had been expecting. "Uh," he stammered. "Uh. Who are you?"

"Sergeant Honor Ross, sir. Third Squad, First Platoon, Third Century of the 2031st Legion," she said. "Or what's left of the squad. We're down to five men and me. And the Viper's in pretty bad shape." She met his eyes. "We'll be glad to get out of here."

"Well, Sergeant Ross. It is Ross?"

She nodded.

"Well, Sergeant Ross. I'm not here to get out. We're on a raid as deep as we can go, and I haven't received orders to pull out."

The Optio and the Sergeant stared at one another in silence, neither wanting to be the first to suggest a course of action. It was obvious that Ross wanted to be gone, but he had received no word to pull back. He'd have to check with headquarters before he did anything else. The stalemate broke when Mullins grounded his Liberator and joined the group.

"Sir. Sergeant. Excuse me, sir," he broke in, "Big Six is on the horn. Wants to talk to you." He gestured toward his own tank. "I've got him five by five, and Quentain says he can't raise him. You'd better use my commlink." He reached out to take Karstil's arm.

Harras did, indeed, want to talk to him. Mullins had reported the action and its results, and the Centurion Maximus was ecstatic. He ordered the platoon to press on, while the 2567th attacked in its wake to apply more pressure to the TOG forces. There had been a major foul-up in the TOG's plans, and everything was in a state of flux. Pressure, especially pressure in the rear, was just what was needed. Karstil signed off with mixed emotions.

He really wanted to pull back. The pain in his shoulder and back was becoming so bad that he had trouble breathing. He had to take short gasps, holding his breath until the pain subsided. He knew that the pain would be forgotten when things heated up again, but he wasn't sure how much longer he would be able to concentrate on what needed to be done. Luckily, Mullins came up with a plan for the immediate situation.

With evening coming on, it was decided to turn the damaged left side of Ross's Viper into a prisoner holding cell. After they had crammed the artillerymen in, the perforated shroud was bent down to secure the opening. They had to use Mullins' tank to crush the side of the Viper, for the titanium armor was too tough to be moved by hand. That done, they used the Viper's 25mm cannon to destroy the other Kershaws. It took longer, but it saved the Liberators more valuable 150mm ammunition for later.

By the time they had cleaned up the area, destroyed the artillery pieces, and secured the prisoners, it was fully dark. Now the problems of crew fatigue and vehicle repair became paramount. Ross's Viper had been damaged more than it showed, for she had taken engine hits that slowed the vehicle to half-speed. Again, the veteran Mullins came up with the solution. The command would drop back from the scene of action to the debris-littered battle they had seen earlier. They would rest there for the night, and might possibly salvage enough parts from damaged vehicles left in the area to repair Ross's Viper.

As the vehicles approached the area, drifting along at 2 KPH to keep from alerting any sensors, a pair of blue squares flashed on the DDP. Karstil wondered who it was out in the darkness, friend or enemy. He set the Liberator down, letting the other vehicles in the command ground nearby. In a quick council of war that included Mullins, Honor Ross, and infantry Sergeant Dunstan Crown, they came up with a plan.

Crown would lead a foot patrol across the 10 kilometers to observe the intruders. There was something about the vehicle signatures that made Karstil uneasy. One showed steadily as a Wolverine, the other showed intermittently on his screen as an Eradicator antiaircraft unit. All the Eradicators were supposed to have been destroyed, and the TOGs would certainly have gone after any survivors. Now here was one deep behind their lines.

The patrol departed on foot, not using their bounce packs for fear of alerting any sensors in the unknown vehicle. The rest of the command settled down to await developments. A 10-kilometer hike through the darkness, even with thermal sights and helmet heads-up-displays, would take some time. A man could march 5 kilometers in an hour, but that did not allow for the need to be sneaky. It was a good three hours before Crown called in.

The command spent the time hunkered down in a slight depression in the open field. They were formed in a wide triangle, with Ross's wounded Viper in the center and Karstil's point of the triangle closest to the unknown station. It was not a time for rest. Besides the major damage that had been inflicted on all the vehicles, there was minor damage that they could repair now. Mullins' training had become reflexive for the tankers, and they were out checking equipment as soon as the vehicles had grounded and shut down. Seeing the tankers at work, the infantry followed suit. Even in the darkness, there was plenty to be done. Karstil tried to help, but the throbbing in his shoulder wouldn't let him. He sagged against the side of the tank.

"Can I help you, sir?" It was Honor Ross, come over from her own vehicle. She had planned to talk to him about pulling back, calling the mission accomplished and running for home. The walk to the command Liberator had given her time to organize her argument. The condition of the command, the depth into TOG territory, the prisoners, the dwindling supply of ammunition, and the fatigue of the troops were all part of her logic. Now she found the commander near collapse.

"I'm all right, Sergeant," snapped Karstil, "What's the problem?" He was sorry that the words had come out in that tone of voice, but it seemed to be happening quite a lot lately. He would have to begin to think before he opened his mouth. No use dumping on the troops.

"That shoulder looks bad, sir. It probably needs to be rebandaged. Your crew's busy. I could do it."

He knew she was right. He could feel that the bandage had slipped, losing support for the damaged shoulder. He tried to think of a reason why she shouldn't do it and gave up. He was just too tired. "What makes you think you're a doctor?" Again, he regretted the words and the tone. Her presence was as unsettling as had been Julianna Pope's two months before on the transport ship.

He had been trained by his family and by the military to view women as equals. He had accepted it in his instructors, had accepted it in Julianna. The Operations Officer of the Cohort was a woman, and he had taken her orders as though from a man. It had been drilled into him: Women were equal. Treat them as you would anyone else.

But now, with a woman in his command who was a subordinate, he didn't know how to treat her. She stood there, the dim light from the interior battle lanterns reflecting from her eyes. I give up, he thought. I surrender. "Sorry, Sergeant. Do what you can."

With only one good arm, it was almost impossible to break open the combat coveralls. Ross had to help him open the battle suit and peel it away from his shoulders. He was aware of his own odor. He had been in these coveralls for a week without a chance to clean himself. That might be acceptable around the men of the platoon, but it felt humiliating in the presence of Ross. If he hadn't been so tired, in so much pain, he would have been embarrassed.

She removed the plastic shield and then cut away the soiled bandage with her combat knife to reveal the cracked shoulder blade and bruised ribs. She was no doctor, but she had certainly seen bruises and broken bones before. What she hadn't ever seen was what an injury looked like after several days and with no doctor around to do his magic.

The left shoulder slumped as though it had lost its support, and she could see the angle of the broken scapula pressing against the skin. The swelling extended from the center of his chest, over the shoulder and around the back, all the way to the spine. Most of the area was a deep purple-black, but the area around the shoulder itself had turned a dark green. And it smelled as though there were something dead under the skin.

Karstil stood braced against the sponson between the extended forward arms of the tank while Ross retrieved the aid bag from the Liberator's fighting compartment. Podandos and Spint eyed her warily.

"This is going to hurt," she said, then pressed the bulge of the scapula down until the two parts were almost aligned. Next she taped it in place. There wasn't much she could do for the ribs except pad the area. She knew that taping ribs was not the best way to deal with them, for it would only drive any broken part into the chest cavity, perhaps puncturing a lung. She replaced the plastic shielding.

Karstil let her poke and prod, gritting his teeth to fight back the pain. Standing half-naked in the darkness while an unfamiliar woman worked on his back was not so terrible, though. Her hands were soft and gentle, and she certainly smelled better than anyone else in the platoon. He wondered if she used perfume.

With the bandage applied and his uniform closed, Karstil felt better than he had in days.

"You wanted to see me, Sergeant?"

"Yes, sir. It's about the plans for the command." She got ready to present her argument for making a break for home.

Just then, the commlink in the Liberator came to life with a suddenness that made both of them jump. "Six, this is Three." Karstil reached for his combat helmet, swung the boom mike away so that he could use it without having to put it on.

"Three, this is Six."

"Three. They're friendlies, sir. But you won't believe what we've got. Better join us."

"Six. On the way." Karstil began to climb the front glacis of the Liberator. "Thanks for your help, Sergeant," he said in a business-like way. "I'll call your Viper to pick you up here." He turned back to his tank. "Spint! Podandos! Fire her up. Let's move."

46

Alsatia, Caralis
The Commonwealth
7 January 6831

The targets were indeed a Wolverine and an Eradicator, or what was left of them. Crown had obviously spent some time interrogating the crew, and he felt they were legitimate.

As the command moved up to the grounded vehicles, Karstil could tell even over the DDP that the Eradicator was damaged. The blue indicator light kept blinking on and off as though the power plant were malfunctioning. The Wolverine showed a steady blue square, which meant the light tank was functional. The Sergeant in the Wolverine was the first to greet him, obviously glad to have another friendly in the area.

As for the Eradicator, it was a mess. The turret had been blown off by an internal ammunition explosion. The driver had been thrown clear. The other survivor was a Legatus from the 2567th Legion's headquarters. Karstil could have hugged him. At last, he thought, someone to take command of this circus. He saluted the Legatus, reporting the mission and status of the command.

"Have you taken a good look at me, Optio?" They were standing in the darkness, and Karstil could just make out the man's shape.

"Sir?"

"Have you taken a good look at me and my rank?"

"No, sir."

"Well, do it now."

In the dark, Karstil could just make out the crown and sword on the collar of the battle dress uniform. "I don't understand, sir."

"Look a little harder, Optio, and you will see that suspended from the hilt of the sword is a small 'C'. The 'C' means that I may be wearing the badge of a Legatus and the branch designator of air defense artillery, but that I am actually a correspondent. The Legatus rank is purely honorary. I get to eat in the officers' mess. That sort of thing."

Karstil felt his heart sink. Just what he needed: a Legatus with no real rank.

"I'm sure the others have noticed the 'C,' Optio. This is your command. I will just ride in the Eradicator. What do you think?"

What do I think? thought Karstil. What do I think? I think that I don't need this. My platoon is down by a third, I have an infantry squad from another Century, another squad from a different Legion crammed with prisoners, a Wolverine from I don't know where, and a useless Eradicator carrying a pastiche of non-combat types. What do I think? I think I'd rather not deal with it.

"Sounds like a good idea, sir," replied the Optio. "We'll go with it."

"Great! By the way, my name is Lurron Johnston. I'm with holovid station GHTY."

The name rang like a warning bell. Something about GHTY was familiar, and Karstil searched his memory. Ah, yes, now he remembered where he had seen the GHTY logo before. Judith Westover had been wearing it on her jacket the night at the reflecting pool. If it hadn't been dark, Lurron Johnston would have seen the young Optio go pale.

The two officers made their way back to the assemblage. Mullins and the Wolverine Sergeant had begun to swap lies, commonly called war stories, about the recent action, and the Platoon Sergeant joined Karstil at once.

"Sir, Sergeant Glover says that there aren't any TOG units within kilometers of here," began Mullins. "He says there's lots of activity toward our lines, but nothing further back." Mullins waved the Wolverine commander toward them. "This is Sergeant Jason Glover from the light Cohort of the Second Manus. He's been behind TOG lines for five days."

"Glad to meet you, Glover. What's up?"

The Wolverine Sergeant saluted. "Not much, sir. Been back here so long I don't really know what's happening. I picked up those two in the Eradicator last night. They seem as lost as we are. The driver's fine, but that correspondent is a bit goofy." He noticed the Legatus standing behind Karstil in the darkness. "Sorry, sir. I didn't see you there."

"That's all right, Sergeant," said the Legatus. "I don't mind being lost. I've talked with the Optio here, and he will remain in command of this force. I will act on his orders."

The four Sergeants exchanged glances. A Legatus turning command over to an Optio was not a normal, everyday occurrence, even if his rank were only honorary. Something was brewing, and they didn't know if they liked it.

Karstil called for a status report on the new equipment. The Wolverine was fully loaded, not having fired a shot since landing on the planet. The Eradicator was badly damaged, but the driver's station was functional and the right hull missile rack was operational, along with its datalink antenna. Unfortunately, with no DDP at the fire-control station, it was impossible to expend the ammunition. The most immediate problem for the stragglers, including Ross's squad, was the lack of food. The platoon shared what they had.

The force bedded down for the night in a tight formation. Karstil wasn't worried about becoming an artillery target. Even if a satellite spotted them, he hoped that the number of vehicles would appear as a single presence rather than a sizable force. He wanted to attract as little attention as possible. The crews needed rest, and he reasoned that a tight formation would require fewer men on watch. He, too, needed sleep. With his shoulder feeling better than it had in some time, he was getting drowsy.

The red battle lanterns in TOG Planetary Headquarters turned the syntho-leather tunics almost black. Six men stood around the tactical display, pondering its meaning. The air, even though it was cleaned and circulated, was heavy with smoke that rose from the cigars of the officers. There was no talking, only anticipation.

The center of the tactical display flared into life, a beam of light descending from the overhead projector. The light sparkled for a moment, then the diminutive figure of an officer appeared. The laser hologram of Grand General Oliodinus Severus Septimus turned to face the General. "Caesar hails you, General Arcadius."

"Hail, Caesar," replied the General, stiffening to attention and saluting.

"We are concerned," continued the hologram. "Concerned about your reports of activity on Caralis. Your Legions were supposed to be on the offensive as of two days ago. We have received no confirmation of victories."

Brigadier-General Arcadius remained at attention, but his toes tapped nervously inside his armored boots. He had known this interview would be coming, known that it would not be felicitous. The Grand General had used "we" in his opening remarks, and Arcadius didn't know if the pronoun indicated concern at headquarters or was the Imperial "we" to indicate interest at the highest governmental levels. He hoped not the latter.

"According to our information," the Grand General continued, without allowing Arcadius to speak, "you were supposed to attack all along the front forty-eight hours ago. We are also informed that you are now on the defensive." Even in the 25-centimeter tall hologram, the tight smile was clear.

"There has been," broke in the Brigadier-General, "a small change of plans." Arcadius knew that little lie might not qualify as one of the great understatements of the millennia, but it certainly was up there. "The Renegade and Commonwealth forces on the planet seem determined to destroy themselves on our swords. They have launched a desperate assault all along the lines." He spoke faster now, trying to get the speech in before he was interrupted again. "We have information that has allowed us to blunt their attacks and to make them pay a high price." He finished and waited for a reply.

"For your sake and the sake of your family, I certainly hope that is true. The government has given you the resources you asked for, with the intention of seeing you crush the Commonwealth units on Caralis. Your actions must now justify that faith." The hologram never took its eyes off the General.

Arcadius stared back at the column of light. He hated holographic confrontations. There, in front of him, was the disembodied image of his commander, so fragile and yet so real. If only he could reach out and break up the patterns of light, crushing the life out of the shimmering shadow. He much preferred commlink or face-to-face. In commlink, the interrogator couldn't see one's eyes, and in face-to-face conversation, there was so much to be learned from the feelings in the air. This holographic stuff gave neither opportunity. The interviewee couldn't hide, but there was no feeling in the air to guide the answers. He opened his mouth to utter assurances, but the hologram cut him off. "Hail, Caesar," it said, and then vanished as Grand General Oliodinus Severus Septimus broke the connection. The "Hail, Caesar" from the officers fell on empty air.

Brigadier-General Arcadius faced his officers. One of them, he knew, was assuredly a spy, was sending reports to Grand General Septimus. That was not surprising. He had done it himself just a few short years before. Every commander in TOG had someone reporting his activities to his superiors. It was a system that kept all commanders on their toes, but it didn't give a man much leeway when things got out of hand. Which they definitely were right now.

"Legatus Maximus Philippicus," he said to one of the officers, who braced to attention in response. "Have we anything more from your source?" He had been careful to use the words "your source."

"No, sir. We are still digesting the original information. Unfortunately, our analysts did not get it as promptly as we would have hoped. Some things in it are a puzzle." Philippicus paused, weighing his next words.

"Go on."

"Well, sir. It seems so genuine, so detailed. We have everything, down to attack times and even locations for platoons. It's almost too detailed."

"Are you telling me you think it's false? That you have been fooled? That you have given me an incorrect estimate?"

"I don't know, sir. Everything in the report is wrong. Either we've missed a coding cue or the entire report is an incredible lie."

General Drusus Arcadius bent closer to his unfortunate Intelligence Officer. He spoke slowly, biting off each word. "Legatus Maximus Antipolous Philippicus, you are my chief of intelligence. You are supposed to know whether or not the reports you receive are real or if they are nothing but smoke and mirrors. Now you are telling me that the information you paraded in front of me and my staff may be so much hokum. Your great intelligence coup is nothing but dust."

Philippicus leaned backward as his commander confronted him, his feet rooted to the floor of the headquarters. "I will know the truth within the next twelve hours, General."

Legatus Maximus Philippicus fled from the headquarters to his own staff. Nothing would keep him from finding out the truth. The report had been so complete, so detailed. He could recite its main points almost by heart: the 2567th to be evacuated from Caralis; the 2031st to defend in a wide cordon; the remnants of the 354th to initiate spoiling attacks; no new Renegade forces to land. Even the location of the attacks and their time had been given. Now the report was contradicted by action. The 2567th had attacked, often successfully. At least one new Legion had landed. The 354th had not attacked at all. The report had everything backward. Someone had to know what was going on.

Earlier that day, he had sent Legatus Targus Vortrun to the headquarters of the Manus opposite the center of the 2567th attacks. Vortrun was to evaluate the situation and report. With secure, land-line communications to the Manus headquarters, Philippicus would be able to talk to Vortrun in complete security. He placed the call.

The communicator was answered, but the line was so filled with interference that Vortrun sounded as though he were screaming into the comm. Philippicus could barely make out what the Legatus was saying, though it sounded like, "Attack! Attack! Attack!" Then the line went dead. Philippicus stared at the communicator for some moments, then softly replaced the handset in its cradle.

Alsatia, Caralis
The Commonwealth
8 January 6831

The day was well along before Karstil got the platoon on the move. Mullins had found enough parts to jury-rig the grav-drive engines on Ross's Viper to bring it up to full speed. He was not sure how long the repairs would last, but at least she would be able to keep up. There was nothing to be done for the Eradicator, whose damage was too extensive. He had, however, been able to rig a modification. By slaving his DDP through the Eradicator, Mullins was sure the vehicle could fire at least one of its anti-aircraft missiles.

The repairs, most of which had to be carried out in daylight, made the platoon late in leaving its night bivouac. Not that Karstil minded much. Though he had slept well for the first time in days, he had awakened stiff and sore. Honor Ross volunteered to reset the bandages, but Karstil turned her down. Quentain did the job instead, and afterward Karstil wished he had taken her offer. Podandos tried hard, but he just didn't have Ross's touch.

With the Wolverine in the lead, the platoon moved out. The tanks followed on line, with the three other vehicles strung out behind. Ross came first, followed by the Legatus in the damaged Eradicator, and finally Crown in his Viper. That way, reasoned Karstil, he had strength at both ends, with the lame ducks in the center. Ross would probably not be able to maneuver well, and it was best to have her close at hand. There may have been some other reason to keep her close at hand, but Karstil didn't dwell on it.

The terrain was rougher than the day before, the rises becoming sharper, the woods larger and more dense. Karstil kept the speed low, not wanting to stumble without warning onto anything strange. All active sensors were closed down because the sensor signature could be detected well beyond the range the active sensors could identify a target. A vehicle could sense a sending unit at, say, 50 kilometers, while it could identify a target through active sensing at 25 kilometers. Targets at 50 kilometers would not be identified by type, only by nationality. All vehicles went to listening silence for the same reason.

With the Wolverine 25 kilometers in front, there was little chance that the platoon would contact the enemy by surprise. At 1100 hours, the Wolverine turned back toward the tanks, skimming the ground at 120 KPH to close on Karstil's Liberator. Glover waved for Karstil to stop, signaling Mullins, 400 meters away, to do the same. Both Liberators came to a 1-meter hover, the vehicles behind following suit.

Jason Glover scampered onto Karstil's Liberator to deliver his information. "I've got a flock of red indicators on the far side of that ridge, sir," he said. "I got out of there as quick as I could. Don't think I was spotted."

"What exactly is a 'flock,' Sergeant?" The one thing Karstil didn't need was an exaggerated report. "Try to tell me exactly what you saw."

"Yes, sir." Glover's enthusiasm was undiminished by Karstil's rebuke. "There were at least twelve, sir." He was making it up as he went along. He had not counted the red squares, just knew that there were many of them. "Most of them were in a tight formation in the valley, with a couple posted around an extended perimeter. Looks like a command post."

"Was it a command post?"

"I don't know, sir."

There were woods some 1,500 meters to the rear of the last Viper, and Karstil signaled all the vehicles to join him there. He used a hand-held laser torch to signal, not trusting the commlink if a TOG formation were that close. When the last vehicle grounded, he called the command ers together to hear the news.

Glover poured out his report, as Karstil silently noted that the "flock" of a dozen had now grown to "fifteen or more." He didn't correct or rebuke his recon Sergeant. Glover was so obviously excited that it was probably his first chance at combat.

Mullins pondered the news. "Perhaps we should avoid them, sir. Looks like a lot."

Glover's face fell. He no doubt wanted to charge the whole mess, cannons blazing. He stood back and pouted. Even Crown looked disappointed, but it was Ross who broke the silence. "We're not here to avoid contact," she said, glaring at Karstil. "If I remember our discussion of last night, you said we were the point of an attack. If that's a headquarters unit, maybe we should attack it."

"We hardly have the strength to take on a headquarters, even if it's only for a Cohort."

"But they don't know that, my boy," interjected Johnston. "Perhaps we could convince them that there are more of us." He disregarded the stares from the other members of the council, and cleared his throat. "I used to be in the business of make-believe," he said. "All you have to do is convince the eye, not the mind, that something is true. A couple of palm trees and a reflecting pool, and you have an oasis in the desert. It's all very simple, really."

The council of war looked at Johnston, their faces reflecting their moods. Glover, Crown, and Ross were excited, Karstil interested, Mullins skeptical. "I believe," he continued, "that each of the vehicles has a gizmo that sends out an identification code. Sergeant Glover said he could tell what people were before they actually made contact." He looked to see if his lack of technical expertise had made an impression. Their faces hadn't changed.

"What we must do is give the TOGs more than they can handle. With our four different vehicle types, we should be able to represent a large force by spreading ourselves out. Who knows what they'll do if they think they're being attacked by a lot of us?"

"And when they do find out," interjected Mullins, "they'll blow our asses into the next county."

Johnston look chagrined. "It was only an idea, Sergeant. Better than running away."

Karstil was pondering Johnston's idea. "They can tell what we are, even without the transponders. Remember how we were fooled by those bogus Horatius tanks in the attack. We could pull all the sending units from the vehicles and give them to the infantry. That would make us seem to double in size."

As enthusiasm swept the group, even Mullins had difficulty suppressing a smile. The thought of giving the TOGs some of their own medicine had a definite appeal.

While the crews pulled the transponders from the vehicles, the Sergeants and Optio Karstil set the plan. Johnston and the Eradicator would carry the infantry forward to a blocking position. Glover and his Wolverine would accompany them to provide commlink and DDP information as well as the fire support of his 100mm cannon. The other vehicles would be divided into two groups: Mullins and Crown in one, Karstil and Ross in the other. Karstil would lead his force in a sweep to the right, with Mullins and Crown making a wider sweep beyond. When both tanks were opposite the TOG formation, they would turn to attack. Deployment of the tanks would depend on the terrain and the situation. Navigation would be by guess and by God, for the attackers would not activate their sensors until they had closed to 20 kilometers or less. By 1330 hours, they were ready.

Karstil made some quick calculations and plugged them into the onboard computer. What he really wanted to know was how long it would take to close from various ranges after detection. Their outside limit was 20 kilometers. He hoped to be able to get closer before the TOG defenders took any action. The answer scrolled across the screen.

A chart appeared indicating the time it would take to cover the ground to the target, based on the speed of the attacker. According to the computer, that was five minutes to close from 20 kilometers, at a maximum speed of 240 KPH. If the unit were not detected at that range, the reaction time for the defending TOG units would be reduced even more.

He studied the numbers. The TOGs could probably pick him up at 20 kilometers, would assuredly have him at 15. Assuming that he was sensed, it would take some time for the TOGs to react. Say, two minutes. At the end of that time, they would be going into their defensive positions, and that could take another minute. A three-minute grace period for the attackers. If the TOGs were slower or sensed him at closer range, all the better. The 240 KPH speed looked the best. It would keep them at a safe speed for ground-level flight, and even if the TOGs sensed them at 20 kilometers, they would have only a minute and forty-eight seconds before Karstil and his unit appeared over their positions. Given that, he could begin to shoot lasers at four kilometers, with the enemy still confused when the first shots arrived. It was the best he could hope for.

The infantry, with Glover and Johnston, moved first, closing on the target at a speed of 25 KPH. At that speed, it would take them nearly two hours to reach their blocking positions. It was a long time, but a greater speed would make them easier to detect. The tanks moved a half-hour later, Mullins and Crown leading, Karstil and Ross following fifteen minutes behind. All vehicles were on listening silence until contact.

Legatus Targus Vortrun studied the tactical display supplied by the Manus operations officer. A series of blue circles, squares, and triangles spread across the screen that covered a 500-kilometer circle showing where the TOG units were located. Because of reports from Planet Headquarters that some of the units in the display were no longer in existence, Vortrun wondered if the display were being produced for his benefit. Legatus Maximus Philippicus had given him an intelligence update before he had left Planet, and Vortrun knew there had been Renegade incursions into the Manus's area. None of them showed on the map.

Legatus Affilios Kendiliapos had been Vortrun's classmate at the Academy, and now he stood in the rear of his headquarters, awaiting the decision. Targus let him sweat. Typical of the offworlders, Affilios was anxious to please the TOG overlords. They may have been classmates, but Targus had always disliked the other man. Now the Manus commander was trying to put on his best face after a disaster in his area of operations, while trying to fool his Legion at the same time. Well, thought Vortrun, we're going to hang you out to dry as an example to the others. He turned to Kendiliapos and smiled.

"So this is the most accurate information you have?"

"Yes, Targ," Affilios said, approaching the display. "As you can see, we are doing quite well."

The use of the familiar "Targ" made Vortrun smile even more. When he dropped the hammer, this man was really going to squirm. It was fun to have the goods on his victim and then watch him twist and turn as the screws tightened. He searched the display, finally locating the symbol for Artillery Century Tertius. There it was, a blue square near the front line. The Century had been reported destroyed, overrun by three Centuries of Renegade tanks, late yesterday. Now Affilios had it in position, ready to support his front. Either he was trying to fool someone, or he was incredibly stupid. Either way, he would have to go.

"This unit"—Vortrun reached forward with his light scepter to touch the artillery symbol—"seems to be out of place." The symbol vanished, and Vortrun looked up to see Kendiliapos's discomfort. He touched another symbol, and another. Beads of perspiration began to appear on the Manus commander's forehead. "You seem to have a number of misplaced units, commander."

"Surely you know that there may be some slight errors in the display," Affilios said. "These things are not always completely accurate. There is always a lag between the report and the actual situation."

"I'm sure that's true, commander, but this is more than information lag. This is outright falsification. You have been submitting fictional status reports to Legion headquarters. There are Renegade units in your area that do not appear on your display. Please post them now."

Kendiliapos touched the controls of the tactical display. There was a slight wavering in the screen, as blue symbols moved or vanished and red symbols appeared. "This can't be right," said the Manus commander. "Notice that there are Renegade symbols around the Manus headquarters. The display must be incorrect."

Targus Vortrun examined the tactical display. There, around the Manus headquarters, were a series of red dots that indicated Renegade activity. He had expected to see indications of enemy penetration into the Manus's area, but not this. Perhaps Affilios was correct and the tactical display was malfunctioning. He fixed the unfortunate commander with a withering gaze. "You had better check all your sensors, Legatus. And do it now."

Legatus Affilios Kendiliapos backed away from the display, turned, and entered the intelligence section of the Manus headquarters. The Centurion and his staff were standing at attention, awaiting his arrival. Kendiliapos decided that if he were to go down, he was going to take someone with him, and the intelligence officer was the best choice. The Renegade units near Manus headquarters would be the cause of the Centurion's downfall.

Kendiliapos kept his voice soft and pleasant as he "explained" the "correct" situation to the Centurion. By the time he was done, the Centurion had issued orders to the perimeter security to withdraw to the maintenance area to have their sensors checked and calibrated. The red dots disappeared from the intelligence display. Kendiliapos returned to his visitor.

"There," said the Manus commander as he entered. "I think that is more accurate. It certainly conforms with the information we have from our prisoner."

"You have a prisoner? You had not mentioned that before."

Kendiliapos smiled. At least there was something the rear-echelon people didn't know. "Yes. A Renegade Centurion, a military-police type, whom we picked up yesterday morning. He has become quite cooperative." Affilios felt the mood in the room change. Now he was in charge. Perhaps the situation could be salvaged after all. With his old classmate on the defensive, he might be able to convince him that all was not completely lost. There were only those little red dots to deal with.

"He has confirmed that the units we face are incapable of anything but retreat. They may have had one last spasm in them, but that is all. That spasm is what we have been witnessing. Nothing to be alarmed about at all." He watched the face of his inquisitor become more tranquil. There would be, could be, no adverse report to Planet Headquarters. "Would you care for some refreshment?"

The situation had certainly changed, and Vortrun felt it as much as had Affilios. Slight falsification of status reports was something that occurred at all levels; it was part of the system. Perhaps Kendiliapos had been wrong, but he was glad he had not dropped the axe just yet. Let the situation clarify itself a little before he made his report. "Yes, Legatus," he said amiably, "I think I will."

The Manus commander touched a button on the console. Almost immediately, a curtain parted to reveal a Mastati carrying a silver tray and goblets.

Alsatia, Caralis
The Commonwealth
8 January 6831

The DDP in Karstil's tank flashed with red triangles, and the ballistic computer told him that unidentified enemy units were sensing at 45 kilometers. The computer almost sounded a bit annoyed that its own sensors were all passive. But perhaps it was because Karstil was upset to be discovered well beyond the range he had calculated as optimum.

He had not known the exact location of the target, had plugged the approximate coordinates into the computer, based on what Glover had told him. Both he and Mullins, 12 kilometers ahead, had maneuvered based on the information. The red triangle had appeared slightly farther away than expected, but it was within the mean probable error. What he had not counted on was having the enemy sensors acquire him as a target at 45 kilometers. He wondered if Mullins had seen the triangle, if the same outpost had sensed him. Karstil also had to worry about the Wolverine and the wrecked Eradicator. If he had been sensed, surely they had, too. He contemplated breaking commlink silence. No one was to talk until they had made contact with the TOG units. Did being sensed at 45 kilometers constitute "contact"? He made the decision to make no decision. He hadn't gone over what to do if they were discovered at extended range. If the others said nothing, neither would he.

The Liberator and the damaged Viper continued on course, skimming the ground at 180 KPH. Karstil kept a close eye on Ross's APC, worrying that it would not be able to keep up if he called for full speed. The carrier was staying with the tank, cutting around the small hills and copses in a dainty dance that made the heavier Liberator seem clumsy by comparison. Karstil approved. Ross was obviously driving, and she certainly was good. Either she was showing off, or she was an excellent driver.

Karstil felt his stomach tighten into a knot. He wished he hadn't listened to Johnston, wished he had kept his command together, wished he had listened to Mullins, wished...wished he had done something, anything, that would have prevented the current situation. Here he was, his command spread over 50 kilometers, with no idea of the enemy's actual location, no commlink with anyone, and with the enemy very probably aware of where he and his men were. Added to that disaster was the throbbing pain of his shoulder and back.

The two vehicles continued on their course, skirting trees and small hills, ducking into ravines as they appeared. Karstil watched the red triangles, kept listening to the whining voice of the computer tell him that there were unidentified targets at 43 kilometers, 39 kilometers,

35 kilometers. He hoped one day to meet the people who had programmed the nagging voice.

Then the screen went blank. One instant, the display of red triangles had been there. The next instant, they were gone. He stared. The ballistic computer noted, smugly, that the targets had vanished. It was too good to be true. He tapped the screen, a reflex action that could not possibly affect the situation. No matter that it was an exercise in futility. Karstil tapped the screen again.

He pressed the "recall" control, and the red triangles reappeared. They were broken outlines this time, indicating the last known position of the targets that were no longer identified. They were the best he had to indicate the location of the TOG unit, and so they would have to do.

The minutes ticked by as the Liberator and Viper continued to sweep toward the flank. Karstil could see the blue indicator of Mullins 12 kilometers ahead. Both forces maintained course and speed, the broken triangles edging down the screen until the blue forces bracketed the red. Karstil gave the order to turn to the left and increase speed. Mullins' indicator followed a moment later. Either the Platoon Sergeant had been waiting for Karstil or he had made the decision independently.

Karstil watched the ground speed indicator rise to the maximum 240 KPH. The ground flashed by in an ochre blur dotted momentarily by clumps of green vegetation. The terrain rose gently toward a distant ridge, behind which the TOG unit should be. It had been on that ridge that the red triangle had appeared. Somewhere off to the right, Mullins and Crown were closing on the same target. Ross was still behind, her APC following in the Liberator's wake. She had dropped back far enough so that if Karstil were targeted by artillery or hit a minefield, she would be able to react.

The crest of the ridge came closer and closer. The sensors, still set on passive mode, were being blocked by the terrain. Somewhere on the other side was a TOG unit, its readiness a riddle. They did not have active sensors or they would have appeared on the DDP, just as the first ones had. By now, an outpost guard could have made visual contact, could have used commlink or land-line to notify the target. The enemy could be lying in wait, weapons trained on the crest, ready to ambush him as he appeared. Or they could be gone, having slipped away to some other location, with artillery on call to blanket the valley. Karstil took a deep breath, as deep as he dared against the pain in his back and shoulder, trying to force the growing lump in his stomach to dissolve. He could feel the moisture on his palms and the beads of perspiration forming around the band of the combat helmet.

Four kilometers from the crest, he energized the active sensors. The DDP screen splashed red. Triangles, squares, circles, and dots appeared. Karstil's mouth dropped open in disbelief. These were the "dozen" targets Glover had mentioned?

"Targets identified," said the computer. "Six Romulus B-2 command vehicles, three Nisus B-7 commlink vans, four Lupis B-9 repair vans, five Remus engineering vehicles, seven..." Karstil didn't need to listen any longer. He had no idea what a Nisus was, in any configuration, but he recognized the Remus as a worthy combatant. "Range three-two-double zero. Targets stationary. Range closing." The Liberator shot over the crest of the hill.

Karstil's mouth gaped open. In the valley below lay more than a score of TOG vehicles clustered in groups of a half dozen or so. There were more vehicles than he could count. A forest of communications antennas stretched into the air. Most of the vehicles sported huge dish laser receivers and rotating radar grids.

If Karstil were surprised, struck dumb by the sight, Quentain Podandos and Duncan Spint were not. The 150mm Gauss cannon fired as the Liberator started down the slope into the valley, the high-velocity HEAP round striking the door of one of the Lupis grav vans. Its armor no match for the HEAP round, the door blew off, scything across the ground into a clump of men. The turret controlling the rotating antenna was lifted from its mount to topple backward onto the ground. Smoke and flame spewed from the van.

More from reflex than anything else, Karstil treadled the painting laser.

"Target identified, Nisus B-7 commlink van. Range three-three-double zero. Lock achieved." He heard the heavy laser whine as the turret traversed the area, throwing him against the coaming. He wasn't aware of a hit with the laser, and the main gun fired again before he could see any additional damage. Once again, he hit the painting treadle.

"Target identified. Lupis B-9 repair van. Range eight-double zero. Lock achieved." By reflex alone, he triggered two TVLG missiles and felt them whoosh off the front rack, their fire trails curving to the left in search of the painted target. He could feel the Liberator rising from its normal 1-meter cruise height as the enemy vehicles seemed to leap at him.

Spint took the Liberator over the top of one group, the twin sponsons of the tank smashing through the antennas as though they were a field of wheat. Karstil ducked as pieces of duralloy tubing bounced off the top and sides of the turret. The 150mm cannon pierced the center of a bed-spring configuration, ripping it from its mount. The spring slid the length of the barrel and came to rest against the turret.

The Liberator banked hard left as it finished its run over the area. Karstil looked past the 50mm cannon mount as the tank turned. He could see the whole field now, an ant hill stirred by a giant's stick. Dozens of vehicles were scattered across the valley in clumps of four or five, their thermal covers protecting them from sensor observation. Against the edges of the surrounding trees were more vehicles parked under the outstretched branches. A conservative estimate would have been at least a hundred pieces of equipment, ranging from grav transports to command posts, to generators of various sizes and shapes. It was a "target-rich environment" if he ever saw one.

It was too rich. No one of the TOG groupings was a match for his tank, but together they posed an almost insurmountable problem. Even if each man in the enemy camp were armed with only a pistol, their combined fire could be devastating to his vehicle. Many of the enemy would die, but if their attack was organized, the Liberator would eventually be swamped. That was the solution. He had to keep moving and shooting so they never had the chance.

The ballistic computer was spouting information as fast as it could, the voice overlapping itself as it tried to identify targets. The 150mm cannon fired again and again, the blue ball of incandescent gases boiling away as the turret swiveled back and forth to engage new targets. Podandos could not control the main and secondary armament, so control of the lighter weapons passed to Karstil. He didn't even try to engage with the TVLGs, but just kept firing the 50mm and laser as targets swept past. He caught sight of another Liberator churning its way across the valley, its own weapons flashing as it skimmed the ground.

Because the ground was so littered with enemy equipment, movement at normal flight altitude was virtually impossible. Spint brought the Liberator to treetop flight so that he could maneuver the craft without having to dodge clumps of vehicles. All over the valley, smoke was rising in thick, oily columns. As the Liberator burst through a pillar of smoke, a large cluster of vehicles appeared 500 meters ahead. Six of the Romulus vehicles were grouped together under a double layer of thermal nets. Thick snakes of cable spread from the vehicles toward outlying communications and sensor vans. The tank had slowed to ten kilometers an hour, because a greater speed made target identification and acquisition almost impossible in the obscuring haze and smoke.

Karstil pressed the firing switch of the 5/6 laser and saw a huge rip appear in the thermal net, the smoldering edges peeling back to reveal the interior of the cluster. The 50mm cannon fired through the hole, striking the port fender of a Romulus. The Hammerhead round penetrated the mudguard and exploded through the central pair of support stanchions. The vehicle lurched under the impact of the light round, then sagged to its side as the outer supports collapsed as well, unable to bear the weight of the vehicle. The hatch on top of the Romulus slid open, revealing the interior. An officer, clearly distinguishable in his red battle suit, was standing in the entryway. He held a commlink handset and was screaming something into the microphone. Karstil could clearly see his mouth, the lips pulled back, teeth exposed. The officer raised his left hand to point at Karstil as he yelled into the commlink.

Their eyes met in pure hate. Then the 150mm cannon fired, and the man vanished in a ball of brilliant white light.

The covey of vehicles trembled as though alive, a living organism attacked by an unknown virus. Parts of vehicles rose through the air, gouts of flame exploded from behind and through the cluster. A turret spiraled away to vanish in a tower of smoke that rose from the stricken vehicles. Men, some of them with their uniforms on fire, raced away from the doomed carriers. Nosing through the smoke came the bow of a tank. Karstil swung the turret to the side to engage and then recognized the blunt nose of a Wolverine. It was Glover. He was high in the command hatch, his uniform stained with smoke and lubricants. He held his helmet in his right hand, waving it excitedly as he plowed through the debris of the command post. The Wolverine was at normal flight, its bow pushing the flaming wrecks out of the way as it churned through the debris.

As Karstil's Liberator swept over the Wolverine, he waved at Glover. The commlink was no use. With the man's helmet off, there was no way to make contact. Karstil smiled. At last, the recon Sergeant had something to shoot at. It would probably rank as the high point of his military career. More TOG vehicles appeared ahead, and Karstil turned from the happy Sergeant to the more mundane task of making small pieces out of big pieces.

Less than 800 meters away were a pair of Aeneas tanks, grounded and with turrets pointed away. The ballistic computer noted their presence and announced acquisition and lock. The scattering of red target indicators vanished from the DDP, to be replaced by the pair of triangles indicating "real" targets. Karstil treadled the painting laser, and the DDP flashed "no shields detected" across the screen. Grounded, unshielded targets—a gunner's dream.

"I've got it, sir," said Podandos, indicating that he had regained control of all the weapons. Karstil felt the turret tremble as the gunner carefully lined onto the rear of one of the Aeneas tanks. The main gun fired first, the 150mm HEAP round striking between the rear lights. The 50mm fired next, its own HEAP gouging more armor and ceramic shielding from the battered stern. Then the 5/6 laser hummed and the wreckage of the ceramic glowed again as the light bored into the bowels of the grounded tank. A huge jet of flame roared from the stern of the Aeneas, and the hull sagged in on itself. The turret sank into the glowing mass, its 100mm cannon pointing skyward as the bulk of the turret slumped into the molten pool.

The finger of the main gun continued to track on the disintegrating Aeneas as though contemplating its handiwork. It contemplated too long. The crew of the other Aeneas had seen their sister tank erupt in fire and death, and they had no intention of meeting the same fate. The light tank sprang from the ground, accelerating at full throttle as the turret swung to engage the slow-moving Liberator. The crack of the 100mm cannon brought Karstil out of his trance as the APDS round struck the front left sponson of the Liberator. He laid the painting laser on the rear of the fleeing Aeneas and treadled the activator.

"Target identified. Aeneas tank. Range one six-double zero. Target locked," said the ballistic computer, as though this was another assured kill. With all turret weapons under gunner's control, Karstil triggered a pair of TVLGs, which roared from the bow launch tubes. Simultaneously, the warning klaxon began to scream in his ear. The Aeneas launched its own TVLGs in return. This assured kill was going to fight back.

The Vulcan III flicked the incoming TVLGs aside as a second 100mm APDS round struck the front slope in a shower of fragmented armor. A huge chunk of unsupported titanium wilted away. The 150mm Gauss cannon bucked, both TVLGs found their target, and the Aeneas was wreathed in smoke and flying fragments. A cloud of impenetrable white blossomed from the turret as the light tank attempted to hide within its own smoke. The 50mm round penetrated, but the smoke was enough to dissipate the 5/6 laser shot.

By the time the Liberator had dodged around the tendrils of haze blotting the Aeneas from view, the light tank was skittering toward a clump of trees. The turret had been shattered by TVLG and cannon hits, but the hull was still intact. Before Podandos could train the turret on the dwindling target, Karstil saw a Viper appear from the trees. The 25mm cannon was hardly a danger to the armored hull of the Aeneas, but the Viper gunner was taking carefully aimed shots at the damaged turret. Karstil could see the slugs burrowing into the crumpled armor as the Aeneas passed the Renegade APC and it almost made the safety of the trees. The last shot from the Viper's cannon finally reached a critical portion of the turret, and the structure split just behind the gun mantlet. The Aeneas plunged into the forest as a huge flare of super-heated titanium rose from the back of the mortally wounded tank. Careening off the tree trunks, the hull erupted in a fountain of flame. A final, violent explosion marked another warrior's demise.

Alsatia, Caralis
The Commonwealth
8 January 6831

Karstil's Liberator glided through the valley, where the debris of battle lay scattered about in smoldering mounds. Mullins' Liberator, the Wolverine, and the two Vipers were on similar missions, checking the destroyed and abandoned TOG vehicles for signs of life and fight. There were occasional explosions as damaged vehicles cooked off or when the prowling Renegade tanks found and destroyed functioning TOG equipment. Guarded by the infantry from the two Vipers, a group of prisoners was forming in the center of the valley. Spint grounded the Liberator beside the sullen group of TOG legionaries.

The prisoners were sitting in a large mass, the Renegades so busy just rounding them up that they hadn't yet separated the officers and enlisted men into two groups. There were, Karstil estimated, more than two hundred TOG soldiers gathered in the valley. He assumed that his infantry had disarmed them, but he couldn't be sure. Now that he had them, what was he to do with them?

Well beyond the growing prisoner group, Karstil saw Johnston's Eradicator grounded beside a glowing hulk. The man was probably gathering background for some story, or getting his picture taken next to a TOG vehicle so he could have it on file. Then again, maybe he shouldn't be too hard on Johnston. It was he who had come up with a decent idea for dealing with the TOG installation. He looked back at the conglomeration of prisoners and sighed.

Disarmed TOG soldiers were approaching the cluster, passing through the widening ring of Renegade guards, who gave them a perfunctory check for weapons. Something would have to be done and done soon. Karstil wished that the rest of his force would finish the mopping up so that he could assemble what resources he had. It was getting late in the day and he didn't want to have to deal with a great wad of TOG soldiers at night.

"Spider Dolphin Two-two-six, this is Spider Dolphin Six." The commlink, quiet for almost a full day, crackled to life. Karstil was surprised at the strength of the signal. Either Harras was quite close or the atmospherics were very good.

"Dolphin Six, this is Dolphin Two-two-six."

"Six. How are you doing, young man?" Harras sounded chatty, but Karstil wondered what the Cohort commander really wanted.

"Two-two-six. Have overrun a bad guy unit at…" He paused to get the location from the inertial guidance system attached to the DDP. The satellite navigational system was more accurate, but not having had a check from it for more than two days, Karstil wasn't sure he could get a good fix without some work. "Kilo Magnus three-three-four, five-one-three. Many prisoners. Current force augmented by two APC, one recon, and one Flyswatter type."

"Six. Nice going, son. Situation still quite fluid. Our friends on the other side seem quite confused, not that we, and you, didn't have something to do with that. Press on another five-double zero or so and give me another call. As to your unwanted guests, why not just 'lash the rascals naked through the world,' as one ancient bard put it. Or at least, just into the woods without their shoes or shorts."

Karstil smiled into the mouthpiece of the commlink. The thought of two or three hundred TOG soldiers wandering about the woods at night without boots or trousers was pleasant to contemplate. "This is Two-two-six. Wilco on both the press on and the naked rascals."

"Six. Good job, Two-two-six."

Karstil switched off the commlink as Mullins' Liberator grounded gently to his right. The Platoon Sergeant was begrimed with smoke and dust from the fires through which he had obviously driven. The Liberator itself was covered with pockmarks, probably from small particle hits made by close-range explosions. Mullins looked quite pleased with himself as he dismounted and approached. He threw Karstil a crisp and exaggerated salute. "Goooood afternoon, sir. Nice boneyard you seem to have created." Mullins looked over the growing bag of prisoners. "And quite a lot of meat on the hoof as well."

"You have a marvelous grasp of the obvious," replied Karstil as he returned the salute with equal exaggeration. "Now we have the problem of what to do with them."

"I know how they deal with Renegade prisoners," answered Mullins, with a grimness in his voice that startled the Optio. "But I don't suppose we really should do that. An example or two might…" He left the suggestion hanging.

"No." The response was sharp and definite. "Another suggestion is that we order them to remove their boots and trousers and then we turn them loose."

A smile of satisfaction passed over Mullins' face. "Nice solution, sir."

"Not mine," said Karstil. "It came from our big Six. He gets the credit for that one. And he wants us to press on another five hundred or so klicks. I'm not crazy about a night move, and we don't have that much daylight left."

Mullins glanced at the setting sun and then at his perscomp. "By the time we get these clowns out of their gear and gone, it'll be full dark. We ought to get some distance between us and here, just in case some of these guests make it to a commlink. That'll mean we have to go one direction and then turn for the run." He was holding his combat helmet in his hand while he tugged at his ear. Unable to come to a recommendation, Mullins broke open the front of his coveralls and extracted a cigar.

Karstil watched his Platoon Sergeant perform the ritual, knowing that he would speak not another word until the cigar was well-lit. He also knew that the cigar would not light until the man made a decision. There was no use hurrying the process. Glover's Wolverine coasted to a halt behind the Liberator. Even without a plan from Mullins, things needed to be done.

While Mullins contemplated the movements of the force as well as its resupply, Karstil set Glover, Crown, and Ross to the disrobing of the TOG prisoners. Some of the enemy were against the process, but the blunt ends of the assault rifles persuaded them to comply. While this was going on, a commotion occurred along the fringe of the group. When Karstil looked up, he saw a Renegade Centurion stalking toward the command group. The officer was walking stiff-legged, an angry man with a mission. He reached the bow of Karstil's tank and stood at rigid attention.

Karstil eyed the Centurion from atop his Liberator. He had no idea why the man was just standing there, because he should be reporting his presence and his status. It slowly dawned on Karstil that the Centurion was waiting for him to report. He shrugged and dismounted over the bow of the tank. The Centurion was quite clean, certainly cleaner than Karstil. Even in the falling light, his rank insignia and Military Police branch designator glowed on the collar tabs of his blue uniform. The Centurion stood rigid, eyes straight ahead. Karstil approached and threw a less than snappy salute. The Centurion returned it crisply.

"Optio Roglund Karstil, sir."

"You should have reported as soon as you were aware of my presence. Who is in command of the unit and where is he?"

"This is Task Force Karstil, sir, and I am the commander."

"Nonsense," snapped the Centurion. "They do not put Optios in command of attacks on a TOG Manus headquarters. You must be a surviving officer."

"No sir," said Karstil slowly, as though explaining to a child. "This is, in fact, my task force. The attack on the Manus headquarters was, uh, accidental."

"Accidental!" snorted the Centurion. "A typical response by an 'accidental' officer. A professional would never have that experience."

Karstil was beginning to grow tired of the interview. He was deep in enemy territory, with some 300 prisoners on his hands and an order to push on another 500 kilometers. He did not need a Military Police Centurion heckling him. "Is there anything I can do for you, sir?"

"It is not what you *can* do for me. It is *what* you will do for me. I will assume command of this unit. Summon your Sergeants to me now."

"Excuse me, sir. My Sergeants and I are on a mission to penetrate the TOG rear areas. We are currently dealing with 300 TOG prisoners. We have battle damage to make good and ammunition to distribute."

The Centurion glared at Karstil. He spoke again, very slowly and through clenched jaws. "Perhaps, Optio, it is common for tankers to dispute the orders of their superiors. In the Military Police, and I stress the 'Police' aspect of the branch, this does not happen. I could place you under arrest. And I'm sure you know that. Now where is your Sergeant?"

Several possible actions coursed through Karstil's mind. He could disregard the Centurion and continue on his mission. This would leave an unhappy Centurion, who was, as he had pointed out, a member of the police. He could turn over command and let Harras deal with the problem when and if they reached friendly lines. That could have disastrous consequences for the mission of the Cohort and the Legion. He could attempt to reason with the Centurion, but that was probably out of the question. He could shoot the Centurion and forget the whole thing. Inclined to the last solution, he fingered the flap on the pistol holster. Unfortunately, his holster was on his left hip and it was impossible to draw the weapon with his left hand. It would require a cross-draw, and the butt of the pistol was facing the rear.

"I think I've got the problem worked out, sir." Mullins had approached the officers, unaware of the situation. He recognized the Centurion. "Evening, sir," he said and saluted.

"Are you the Platoon Sergeant of this unit?" asked the Centurion. "I am Centurion Abalard Bronsus. I am taking command of this unit. Prepare to move at once. We are returning to friendly lines." Mullins let his mouth drop open, apparently in shock. He looked at Karstil. "You do not seem to understand, Sergeant," continued the Centurion. "I have relieved this officer of his duties. I have taken command here."

"Excuse me, sir," said Mullins. "We have a mission to penetrate another 500 kilometers into the area. Surely you are not going to abandon that? And what about the prisoners?"

"Who told you that you were to penetrate 500 kilometers into the area, Sergeant?"

"Optio Karstil, sir. He got those orders from Cohort."

"Did you hear the orders, Sergeant?"

"No, sir. Optio Karstil heard them, sir."

"Then you have new orders from me. I am the ranking officer, and you will obey me."

Mullins knew that there was something wrong, but years of training, years of response to orders, did not allow him to question the situation. Centurions outranked Optios as surely as Optios outranked Sergeants. The man with the highest rank was in charge. That was the way the military worked. If the Centurion had been a Commonwealth officer, there might have been some recourse. But the Centurion was a Renegade, and that settled that. The darkness was almost complete, and they needed to get going. Going anywhere was better than standing around. He could see the last of the prisoners, including the ones previously entombed in Ross's Viper, being herded unshod and untrousered into the far woods. "Yes sir," said Mullins.

"As soon as you have the command assembled, I will speak to them," said Bronsus. "Until then, you will place this Optio under arrest. Put him in one of the light vehicles. I will command from his tank."

Both Karstil and Mullins recoiled. In this darkness, thought Karstil, no one will see who fired the shot. He began to fumble with the holster flap. I don't care how bad this hurts. I'm going to blow this man into the next klick. He felt a hand close gently but firmly over his left wrist. From behind him came the voice of Mullins. "Easy, sir. Easy. It'll work out." Karstil could feel tears beginning to well up in his eyes, partly from pain, partly from frustration.

"Is there some new development?" This time, Karstil recognized the disembodied voice of Lurron Johnston rising out of the darkness. Just what he needed, a television reporter to make his relief public. He saw the shape of the reporter loom closer.

Centurion Abalard Bronsus whirled to face the intruder. "I am Renegade Centurion Bronsus, Military Police. I have relieved this officer of his command and have assumed that role myself. We are returning to friendly lines. Who are you?"

Johnston came close enough to be seen by the others. "I am Renegade Legatus Lurron Johnston, Air Defense Artillery. I don't understand why we are returning. I think the Optio has indicated that we were to continue."

"I'm sorry, sir. The Optio didn't tell me that you were in command."

"The Optio didn't tell you that I was in command, Centurion, because I am not in command," said Lurron softly. "I have relinquished that position to him."

"Then, as the ranking officer capable of taking command," continued the Centurion, "it is my right to be the commander. Sergeant," he said, turning to Mullins, "carry on."

"Perhaps," broke in Johnston, "I have not made myself clear." Karstil closed his eyes and lowered his head. The honorary rank of Legatus had obviously gone to the reporter's head. He was going to do something stupid, and at the distance he was from the Centurion, the "C" on his rank would be clearly visible. Karstil glanced imploringly at the make-believe Legatus.

The "C" was gone. Karstil stared through the gloom at the reporter's rank insignia. He was not mistaken. The tiny "C" suspended from the sword and crown had been broken off, either by accident or on purpose. He suspected which it was.

Johnston drew himself up to his full height and looked the Centurion in the eye. "I did not say I was not in command, Centurion. I said that I had relinquished that command to the Optio. Technically, that makes me still in command of the unit." Karstil marveled at the timbre of the reporter's voice.

"As a fully capable combat officer, and I believe that Air Defense Artillery is a combat branch, while Military Police is a combat support branch. I have determined that Optio Karstil is in command of this unit." His next words were very slow and very even. "It is my intention that he will remain in command of this unit until I deem him no longer capable of that function. At that time, I will determine who is in command. Do I make myself clear, Centurion?"

Mullins watched the reporter with mixed emotions. Certainly he was acting for the good of the command, but that did not change the situation. Mullins knew that the reporter had no command responsibility, knew that the MP Centurion was the ranking officer. Stuff the Centurion, he thought. I'd rather be under Karstil's command than this doofus from another outfit. Mullins decided to say nothing.

"I'm sorry, sir," stammered the Centurion. "I didn't understand fully." The Centurion began to recover. The bit about Air Defense Artillery being a combat branch while Military Police was a combat support branch sounded wrong. "But I don't see how the two of us can remain in the same unit."

"In that case, Centurion," Johnston said, "you may leave the area the same way you arrived. On foot." Here came the part that would make or break the situation. "You will either leave this area and this unit, or I will have the Sergeant strap your ass to the front of the Optio's tank as additional armor. Sergeant Mullins, escort the Centurion to the woods and return." He nodded to Mullins and then turned to Karstil. "Optio. Take command of the force and prepare to move."

With that, Johnston, the imitation Legatus, turned on his heel in the most military manner he could muster and vanished into the darkness.

50

Alsatia, Caralis
The Commonwealth
9 January 6831

It took several hours for Task Force Karstil to prepare to move, as "ordered" by the Legatus. The force had been scattered over the valley, and the infantry had still to render the last of the TOG prisoners deshabillés. The transponders, removed earlier from the vehicles, were replaced. In addition, other Renegades, held prisoner at the TOG headquarters, appeared. They were a mixed bag that included an Engineer and a Maintenance Sergeant, a Mastati trained as a topographical intelligence specialist, a Principes communications specialist, and three Triarii who were a second cook trainee, a cornua player (no horn found in the rubble) from the Legion band, and a ground transport supply specialist.

The new men were about to be scattered through the operational vehicles, when Honor Ross reported that she had discovered a damaged Spartius APC. The twin 5/6 lasers were fully functional, but the power plant was damaged and possibly leaking radiation. The Maintenance Sergeant offered to make a check to determine if the Spartius could be moved safely. The Engineer Sergeant volunteered to help. An hour and a half later, the Maintenance Sergeant reported the vehicle safe but producing only half the thrust usually available. Karstil decided to drag it along. All the new men were armed with captured TOG infantry weapons and placed in its infantry compartment. In the darkness of a new day, the unit moved.

When Karstil reported the movement to Cohort Headquarters, he referred to his unit as "Vexillary Karstil," a title suggested by Johnston. "Vexillary" was the ancient term for a special unit on detached service. As they were now larger than a platoon and not yet a Century, Johnston thought they had to have a name. Karstil acquiesced, too tired and too much in pain to argue. He even allowed Ross to reset the bandage on his left shoulder.

Food and ammunition were becoming a problem for the Vexillary. The original rations had been for a force of fifteen, which had grown to thirty-two. Some food had been salvaged from the wreck of the TOG Manus headquarters, but Karstil had sent much of that with the "escaped" prisoners. The Renegades were on emergency rations only, and even those were beginning to run low. It didn't bother Karstil that much. By now, he was totally constipated, and the pain in his shoulder seemed to drive away all thoughts of food.

The TVLGs, so plentiful when the mission began, had been reduced to the ammunition in the racks and four for each of the infantry squads. Main gun rounds were a little low, with only a couple dozen remaining in each Liberator. The 50mm cannon were in better shape.

Glover's Wolverine had forty-seven 100mm rounds available. The lasers were going to be the primary defense.

Legatus Maximus Antipolous Philippicus glanced at the intelligence report he had been studying for the past three days. It had seemed so valuable, but now he decided the report had to be false. With that, he flung the useless thing across the room. From now on, he thought, he would believe only reports from the front. And there were plenty of those.

He stood beside the tactical display, staring down at the blue triangles and squares that marked the locations of the principal units on the surface. With a control wand, he reached over the display and erased the Manus Headquarters that had so recently been occupied by his Legatus. Declare it gone, he thought. Then let the other information be posted. The Renegade force that had destroyed the headquarters was of unknown size, but it had to be at least Cohort-strength. Fine. Place a Renegade Cohort there. Done, and done, and done.

Philippicus stared at the display. With that same Cohort, he touched the other locations of reported, and disregarded, contact with the Renegades. A pattern began to appear. This was no random movement. The Renegade Cohort had followed a steady course through the TOG rear area. Where were they going?

Philippicus extended the line of the Renegade advance. There, 800 kilometers beyond the Manus, was the forward planetary headquarters. That was it! Somehow the Renegades had discovered the location of the planetary headquarters. This must be a Cohort-sized raid designed to destroy or capture the headquarters and Brigadier-General Arcadius. He must notify the General!

Or must he? What would happen, Philippicus wondered, if the General were not informed? He would make other mistakes. He would be criticized, perhaps even removed, by Grand General Septimus. There would be an opening at General rank that needed to be filled. A hero, a man who had saved the day, would be promoted. It would be even better if Septimus was in on the whole scheme, or at least enough to see that Arcadius was doing the wrong thing. Philippicus recalled the original tactical plot, the one showing the location of the Manus headquarters, and posted it to the commander's display. He then replotted his estimate and sent it directly to Area Command. From there, it would be uploaded to Septimus.

That accomplished, Philippicus opened a secure commlink with the Cohort of Trajan tanks that formed the headquarters guard, the "palace guard," so to speak. The commander of the Cohort knew Philippicus, knew that there was tension at the headquarters. He made an instant decision. Philippicus, he decided, was the path to the future. Drusus Arcadius was on his way out. He agreed to follow Philippicus's orders.

The plan was a simple one. A Renegade unit was deep in TOG territory. They would have to climb the escarpment that broke the plain between the lower areas and the high mountains. There was only one pass where the Renegades would be able to attack the Legion headquarters He would station his Trajans, supported by their own infantry, around the mouth of the defile. When the Renegades emerged, it would be a turkey-shoot. Ten minutes later, the TOG Cohort moved quietly away from the Legion headquarters.

Vexillary Karstil formed into its narrow vee as before. Sergeant Glover and the Wolverine became the point, operating two kilometers ahead of the main body. Karstil and Mullins moved abreast on a 1,200-meter front, each followed 600 meters to the rear by a Viper carrier. Centered in the force and even with the carriers came the damaged Eradicator carrying the imitation Legatus. Behind it was the Spartius. Karstil had put his slowest vehicle in the rear on the theory that it would give the Spartius a head st. t if they had to break contact and escape. The force moved at 120 KPH, well within the safe speed limit for the terrain. At that speed, dawn would be breaking just at the 500 kilometers that Harras had ordered. They would then be able to start their withdrawal in full light.

The wide formation did not last long. An hour into the march, they encountered the scarp of the mountains that crossed the area like a huge spine. The peaks reached 4,000 meters above the surrounding plain, and the foothills were a series of jagged ridges rising 2,000 meters in abrupt inclines. The passes through the mountain wall were high and narrow, approachable along narrow routes that switch-backed their way along the faces of the precipices. This was mining country, or had been before the TOG invasion. The walls of the mountains were dotted with huge, open-pit mines that carved gigantic craters into the walls of rock. Some of the holes were several kilometers broad and as many deep. Other mines were deep caverns that bored horizontally into the wall to become a maze of passages and galleries.

The open-pit mines appeared on the DDP as great voids. Even with active sensors on high power, there was no way to discern what was in the depths until the bow of the tank cleared the edge. The caverns were the same. The mouths of the caves appeared on the DDP, but the sensors could penetrate only two or three hundred meters, and not even that far if the gallery made a sharp turn. It was not a situation to make rapid movement desirable or comfortable. The Vexillary slowed and compressed.

Glover remained in the lead, with Mullins and Crown following. The 2-kilometer gap between the forces shrunk until Mullins moved just fast enough to keep the Wolverine in easy sensor range. The tight turns and steep mountains meant that there were times when he was less than 600 meters behind the scout. Karstil led the main body, with Honor Ross and her Viper close behind. The Eradicator and the Spartius brought up the rear.

The narrow gorge broke the mountain wall like an axe cleft. The base of the notch was 100 meters wide, with the road filling 10 meters of that. The rest of the opening was taken up by a roiling mountain stream that crashed and roared down the canyon over huge boulders and into deep pools. Tank-sized rubble was strewn on the banks, mute evidence of spring freshets that filled the valley in time of flood. The road hugged the left side of the cut, the wall of the mountain rising sheer for 500 meters before it gave way to craggy pinnacles and outcroppings. Karstil wanted very much to send one of the vehicles up to take a look over the edge, but he was worried about what he might find, or what might find him. The power required to make that climb would have made the vehicle stand out like a beacon to any waiting TOG forces. He sagged in the hatch, trying to decide whether or not to take a look himself. He was too tired to make a decision.

A large, four-legged creature with mottled, long hair, sprinted across the road in front of him. "Watch out!" he screamed into the headset as the thing vanished.

"What?" came the response from Spint.

Karstil blinked into the darkness and realized that he had been hallucinating, so tired that his mind was playing tricks on him. "Nothing. Never mind." Either he would have to be more alert or he would have to sleep. He wondered if the others were having the same trouble. He closed his eyes and let his head sink down on the DDP screen. The tank swerved slightly, throwing him against the coaming. There was no use trying to sleep.

With his face still pressed against the DDP, he opened his eyes. The screen glowed with crawling, blue squares, the assault column working its way through the valley. The Liberator lurched again, bumping the top of his combat helmet against the coaming. The tank had come to a stop. He waited for it to begin moving again. There had been many stops as the column waited for the vehicles ahead to clear an unseen obstacle or work themselves around a tight corner. The maneuver space in the gorge was becoming more and more narrow. The width of the floor had decreased to 50 meters, and the stream was no longer level with the roadway. Off to the right of the road, the banks dropped sharply to the roaring water, unseen below in the darkness. Still the tank did not move. Karstil raised himself and looked at the DDP. One of the blue squares, Glover's Wolverine, was creeping back toward the head of his column, its blue indicator growing brighter as he maneuvered over the void away from the road. The power requirement for movement away from the road bed was such that the vehicle gave off a significant signature when it was no longer able to "hover" over the road.

All the vehicles were on communications silence, and Karstil had given orders that the silence be broken only when the shooting started. He would wait for Glover's report rather than contact him by commlink. The faint hum of the 1250 engine reverberated from the valley walls as the light tank came to a 1-meter hover in front of the command Liberator. Karstil could see the blurred figure of the Sergeant as he dismounted over the front of the recon vehicle and made his way to the tank, climbing over the front glacis to the turret.

"We've got a problem," Glover said, without the usual formalities. He braced himself on the Vulcan III system as he sank down onto the turret. In the subdued glow of the battle lanterns and electronic screens, he looked pale and drawn. Gone was the earlier excitement he had shown when charging into the TOG headquarters. He looked much older now.

"I've got red indicators on my DDP at the top of the gorge. I counted five before I pulled back. The DDP couldn't identify them, but I think, from the size, that they were heavy tanks."

Karstil noted that Glover no longer talked in terms of "a bunch" or "a flock." Now he gave accurate information based on what he had seen. The Sergeant was learning the recon business. Someone else was crawling up the side of the Liberator, and Karstil recognized him as the Engineer Sergeant from the damaged Spartius. He tried to remember the man's name, but couldn't. He nodded to the engineer. "Evening, Sergeant. I can't remember your name."

"Zubin, sir. Dorlan Zubin. Sergeant Known sent me to make a report."

"Go ahead, Sergeant." This could only be more bad news. Probably the Spartius had given up the ghost and Karstil would have to deal with its stranded crew.

"I didn't see it, sir," apologized Zubin, "but Known said he got some red lights on his DDP. They're above us to the left and right, and he said there were lots of them."

51

Alsatia, Caralis
The Commonwealth
9 January 6831

Karstil felt the weight on his shoulders. It had all been easy up until now, nothing to do but charge forward and shoot. Now he was surrounded, or close to it. The only salvation was the fact that the TOGs didn't know where he was or didn't know that he knew of their presence. He would have some time to make a plan and perhaps be able to slip quietly away.

"Pass the word, quietly. Shut down. Turn everything off. All vehicle commanders to report to me here. And do it qui-et-ly." Glover and the Engineer Sergeant dismounted and disappeared into the darkness. Alone in his tank, Karstil tried to think. Going forward was not an option. The TOGs at the mouth of the gorge would be expecting him. Going back was the only hope. It would be difficult to turn the column around in the road, but it was possible. Getting the tanks to the new front of the column would be a problem on the narrow way, but could be accomplished. It would require significant thrust on the part of the maneuvering vehicles, and that thrust would, or could, produce a signature that the TOG DDPs would see. If he didn't reverse the order, he would have to lead with the Spartius and Eradicator, not a great solution.

As he wrestled with the problem, the vehicle commanders began to appear out of the darkness and to climb onto the top of Karstil's Liberator. Karstil waited for all of them to appear before he began his briefing. He was making it up as he went along and he didn't want to repeat the plan more than once.

"As I'm sure you all know by now," he began, "we're surrounded. The TOGs have a group of heavy tanks at the head of this valley, and they probably have more along the flanks." He watched the faces of the Sergeants. They showed no surprise. "We're going to have to slip away to the rear. The best thing would be to reverse the whole column, getting Glover into the lead. But we can't do that. The thrust required to get the Liberators past the other vehicles could alert the TOGs. We'll have to turn around where we are and move that way. When the terrain widens out, we'll get the heavy stuff up front. I'll ride on the Spartius."

The Sergeants exchanged glances, but none offered a suggestion. Each one reflected on his own skill, preparing himself for the coming operation. It was Mullins who finally spoke. "Sir, I think it would be best if I rode the Spartius." The tone of his voice was almost fatherly, as though he were talking to a favorite son. He locked eyes with Karstil. "It would be better if you led the tanks, just in case we make contact. Someone has to control this mess, and you're it." The eyes of the two leaders continued to lock. It was Karstil who broke first.

"O.K., Sergeant." Mullins was right. He was the commander of the column, and he couldn't risk losing control by being out of communication with the others if trouble came. "We'll be moving slowly. Take part of Crown's squad with you. They can sweep ahead and support you if you run into trouble. Glover will stay with me until the valley widens, then I'll send him forward to you. Place him where you want." He turned to the others. "All commlinks off, not even listening silence. Don't turn them on until the shooting starts or until you get word from me personally. Sensors on passive. We'll follow Mullins' moves. Back to the vehicles." He turned to his Platoon Sergeant. "Mullins, move when you're ready."

"Right, sir. I'll have Yennan in the command chair. Abul's the best driver I've seen. He'll stay at the controls." He turned to Dunstan Crown. "Dunny, give me some of your walking wounded for the point. See ya, sir." The vehicle commanders slipped off the sides of the Liberator and disappeared into the darkness.

It was five minutes before Karstil saw the Spartius begin to move. Spint had let the Liberator slide backward, twisting slowly to the right as he brought it around to face down the road. Honor Ross's Viper glowed blue on the DDP, and Spint brought the medium Liberator up as close behind it as possible. He would take it around the Viper as soon as he had the space to do so. Ross had been visibly upset when Karstil had sent Crown's squad to act as point. She was closer to the front of the column, and it would have been just as easy—easier, in fact—to use her squad. Karstil had used Crown because he knew the men of that squad were part of the family that had started the operation. They were used to Mullins, and both groups would trust the other. He hoped she understood and would do nothing foolish.

The column crept down the road at a walking pace. Karstil made a mental estimate of the TOG deployment. He assumed that the last TOG vehicle was two kilometers to the rear. The infantry could cover 100 meters in a minute when marching, and half that when moving cautiously. That would give the column a speed of 50 meters a minute. It would take twenty minutes to cover a kilometer, forty minutes to reach the last TOG vehicle. With each column made up of seven vehicles and each one taking up 25 meters of space plus the distance between them, the column would be almost 200 meters long. The last vehicle would be past the last TOG four minutes behind the first one. In an hour, they should be clear.

In the darkness, Karstil was aware of a figure walking beside his Liberator. The man tapped the side of the tank, waving when Karstil acknowledged him. It was the gunner of Glover's Wolverine, walking the flank to tell him when the pass was wide enough to get the tank past. Three minutes later, the man tapped again. It was wide enough to slip the Wolverine past, and Spint brought the Liberator to a stop and hover, nudging the right sponson into the cliff face. The Wolverine drifted silently past, squeezing in between Karstil and Ross. There was no additional glow from the Wolverine, and Karstil was glad that he had decided not to reverse the organization of the column. If the TOGs were above and waiting, they might have missed the move.

The column continued to creep down the road. Glancing at his perscomp, Karstil saw that 20 minutes had elapsed since they'd started the retreat, a kilometer covered with no problem. He felt the Liberator stop as Spint tailored his movement to that of the Wolverine ahead. Karstil waited for movement to begin again, for these momentary halts were common. But nothing happened. The blue indicators of the other vehicles showed no movement except that the trailing tanks were closing on the center. Karstil didn't like that. Even with 25 meters distance for each vehicle, they were terribly close together. If the TOGs opened on the column, there would be almost no maneuver room. He would have to warn the trailing drivers about keeping their distance. The sound of footsteps in the darkness brought him back to his other problem. An infantryman from Crown's squad clambered up the Liberator to report.

"Infantry crater in the road, sir," he panted. "And Mullins says there's a tank beyond. Probably a heavy. He can't get a good read on it because it's behind a sharp turn in the road. He thinks there's infantry with it." Before he had finished his tale, Mullins appeared on the

Liberator to confirm the report.

The two leaders discussed the situation. The time for subtlety had passed. There was nothing to do but blast their way through the road block. "The problem," said Karstil, "is that we can't get to him until we're around the corner. He'll eat us alive as we make the turn. At that range, he can't miss with his main gun, and we've all had so much damage that we can't stand any pounding. We've got to make him come out where that Spartius can get a shot." Karstil rubbed his eyes, and saw yellow and green spots swarm across his vision. "Get the other commanders here. I have a plan."

With the other Sergeants clustered on the Liberator, Karstil explained what was going to happen. The infantry on the point would make their way toward the infantry craters, while Mullins grounded in the Spartius to target the curve where the Trajan would have to appear. At the same time, Karstil would take his Liberator wide of the road. The thrust required would certainly alert the TOG heavy that he was coming. Just short of the turn, Karstil would open fire with his 150mm cannon, shooting high into the rocks above the enemy tank. There was no chance of a hit, but he hoped to antagonize the Trajan into creeping forward to bring its main gun to bear on the Liberator. With any luck, it would disregard the shutdown Spartius until it was too late. The infantry would do what they could. When the Trajan died—he used "when" rather than "if" in the briefing—the column would go past at maximum speed until it had covered at least a kilometer. Commlinks would go on with the first shot. As the Sergeants departed, Ross was the last to go. "Take care of that shoulder, sir."

Karstil smiled at her for the first time.

Left alone in the darkness, Karstil waited three minutes to make time for orders to the others. The only ones who really had something to do were the infantry out front. With the minutes passed, he ordered Spint to fire up the Liberator, and he switched on the active sensors as the Class 2000 engine roared to life. Almost at once, the ballistic computer acknowledged the Trajan's presence. The Liberator swerved out of line and over the deeper gorge to the left of the road, the thrusters powering to Tree-Top Flight mode to maintain the tank level with the others. The Liberator edged past the others. Watching the DDP, Karstil calculated the fluorescent line that showed the intervening terrain.

"Good, Spint. Stop her here. Quent, hit the rocks above him." The words were hardly out of his mouth when the 150mm cannon fired its APDS round high into the rocks. The blue flare of the muzzle wiped out whatever night vision Karstil had. The round crashed into the hill and exploded, sending a shower of pebbles down the slope. The next time, the 150 and the 50 fired together. More rock scaled away as larger pieces crashed down. Karstil watched the DDP for signs of activity on the part of the Trajan. On the third volley, he saw the Trajan rise to a hover and begin to move forward.

"Back a little, back a little. Quent, keep shooting high." The Liberator edged backward as the hull of the Trajan cleared the corner of the obscuring terrain. The Trajan commander was, obviously, playing it cautious. This is not for the faint of heart, thought Karstil. The Toggie would be better off if he charged forward. The Liberator continued to back away. The bow of the Trajan was clear of the hill.

"Shoot at the rock," said Karstil. "I don't want to spring the trap too soon." The cannon fired again, and Karstil saw a large chunk of stone bounce off the left sponson of the Trajan. To his right front, he saw Mullins bent over his sights in the Spartius. "Come on, you sucker. Just a little more," he mumbled. He could see the 200mm tube of the hull weapon of the Trajan as it probed the darkness. It was traversed far left, but it still couldn't reach the Liberator.

The Trajan commander had had enough of the rain of stone. The tank surged forward, turning left as it cleared the edge of the cliff. He treadled the painting laser. "Target identified. Trajan tank. Range two-double zero. Target locked."

"Tank. Two hundred. At the hull. Fire HEAP!" shouted Karstil.

The turret wavered. "Identified," came the word from Podandos.

"Fire!"

"On the waaaay!" shouted Podandos as all three turret weapons triggered together.

The hull had been the only clear target, and Karstil had not wanted to wait for the turret to come into view. The quantity and rapidity of hits were more important than quality. He launched his last two TVLGs as the turret weapons fired. To his right, he saw the lasers on the Spartius glow red at the muzzles as they added their fire to that of the Liberator. Two TVLGs and an SMLM rose from the infantry carrier as well.

The cannon and laser shots slammed into the left front hull of the Trajan, a shower of titanium and ballistic armor spewing from the side. The missiles, arcing high over the combatants were engaged by the Vulcan IV system on the turret of the heavy tank, and three of the incoming missiles were pulverized. The other two, a TVLG and the SMLM, got through. The glowing crater produced by the cannon shots absorbed both the missiles, and Karstil could see a great chunk of the armor slide from the left sponson just in front of the 200mm mount.

The gaping maw of the Trajan's cannon continued to swing toward the Liberator. A blue ball of ionized gas expanded from the muzzle, and Karstil felt his heart stop. The 200mm round was wide, but not wide enough. The HEAP round struck flush on the muzzle of the 50mm cannon mounted on the left side of the Liberator turret. The cannon, laser, and elevating mechanism vanished in an instant. Karstil was slammed against the hatch coaming, the force of the blast driving him into the fighting compartment. He felt his combat helmet strike the side of the opening, and his eyes filled with stars.

His arms were still outside the hatch, and he struggled to pull himself level with his tactical display. The DDP was blinking wildly from the shock of the hit. He stood on the commander's chair. His eyes cleared as his head rose above the turret edge. The Trajan was still there, fully illuminated in the fire of Karstil's 150mm cannon. To the right, he could see Mullins standing on the top of the Spartius and waving his arms. The lasers from the APC continued to bore into the front of the Trajan, firing through the gaping craters caused by the cannon and missile hits.

Deep in the hull of the Trajan, one of the laser hits bored through the shattered armor and ballistic protection. The driver, his hands clasped around the control mechanisms, never felt the impact of the aligned light. The combat helmet vaporized first, followed in a microsecond by his face and head. The nerves and muscles, tensed to control the 377-ton tank, reacted one last time. His left foot came down hard on the thrust pedal as both hands jerked backward. The tank responded at once.

The acceleration thrust of the Trajan was among the best of the TOG heavy tanks. Karstil was aware of the tank as it surged past him, climbing into the darkness. Multiple TVLG hits sparkled across the bottom armor, the missiles fired by the Renegade infantry huddled in their craters. In the glow of the explosions, Karstil could see the TOG tank commander high in the turret of the Trajan. He pointed at Karstil, shouting something into his microphone as the turret swung to follow his arm. The heavy lasers on the turret of the Trajan were swinging to engage the damaged turret of the Liberator.

To the rear of the column, the Wolverine and second Liberator, now with clear shots at the Trajan, opened simultaneously. As the Trajan rose past the column, it exposed its already savaged bottom armor. A great cloud of molten titanium spewed from the underhull, one of the grav coils blasted into atoms by the rain of shells. The Trajan couldn't recover. The turret continued its traverse even as the hull nosed over. With the driver's foot still locked down on the thrusters, the tank continued to accelerate as it plunged into the darkness beside the road. Karstil's last impression of the Trajan as it went over the side was of the turret still turning toward him. Then it was gone in the darkness to explode deep in the crevasse. The noise of the explosion reverberated through the gorge, amplifying from the surrounding peaks.

Karstil felt the Liberator surge forward as Spint hit the thrusters. There was no time to gloat over the kill. The column had to get as far away as fast as possible. The Liberator roared down the gorge, well clear of the road. Maximum safe speed in the gorge was only 50 KPH, but that was fast enough to get them clear of the scene in only a few minutes.

52

Alsatia, Caralis
The Commonwealth
9 January 6831

"Pull it up, Spint. Pull it up!" Karstil felt the Liberator slow as the driver responded to his command. "Ground it near that outcropping ahead." The tank slowed more as Spint searched for the designated location in his driver's DDP. The tank slowed even more, finally coming to a halt behind a boulder that jutted from the right side of the cliff.

The column was badly strung out in the gorge, and Karstil wanted to get them under control before he decided what to do. The first tank to arrive was Glover and his Wolverine. Karstil signaled him to continue down the valley for another kilometer to see what was ahead. As the others arrived, he placed them in position. The last ones to arrive were Crown and Mullins. Crown had stopped to pick up his squad, and the Spartius was slow because of the damaged grav drive. At last, all the vehicles were in place. Reports from the commanders showed only one infantryman wounded, hit by fragments from one of his own TVLGs.

"Six. This is Four." Jason Glover, a kilometer down the valley, had something to say. Radio silence had been lifted when the shooting started and Karstil hadn't imposed it again.

"This is Six."

"Four. Bad news, boss. I've got a red screen at forty kays. The bad guys don't like us."

Forty kilometers, thought Karstil. That would put them at the mouth of the gorge. Both ends of the tunnel were closed. It looked as though Vexillary Karstil were about to be destroyed. "All units," he said into the commlink, "this is Six. Passive sensors. Break. Four, stay where you are. Break. All commanders rally on me." The decisions about the future would have to be discussed with the rest of the command; this was not one he was going to make alone.

"Six, this is Five." Even with the distortion of the commlink, Karstil recognized the soft voice of Honor Ross. "Intruder at four-eight hundred relative. On foot. Range six hundred. Sending a patrol to investigate."

"Six. Roger. Take prisoners if possible."

"Five. Wilco."

As the tank commanders began to appear, Karstil was surprised by how quickly he could discern them in the darkness. It was only then that he realized that the gorge was becoming lighter. He looked at the sky. What had been inky black with a covering of stars had given way to pale light. There was a slight mist of ground fog rising from the cleft where the stream tumbled beside the road. Morning was coming on. In the gorge, the deeper black was shattered by a short burst from a 5mm Gauss rifle, the high-velocity projectiles ricocheting in a shower of sparks against the rocks. The Sergeants froze, turning to face the fire.

"Six. This is Five. We've got a prisoner. Bringing him in."

The others waited in silence for Ross and her prisoner to appear. It was not that they were so interested in the prisoner, or that he would be able to change the situation, but rather that it represented something that they could handle, unlike the TOG units closing on the mouth of the gorge. Ross, a squad member, and a man wearing civilian clothes, appeared out of the morning mist. Ross and her soldier showed signal deference to the man. They stopped beside Karstil's Liberator.

"Doctor Ambrose Rondthaler, at your service, sir." The man was fully two meters tall, his gaunt face outlined in salt-and-pepper hair and beard. The voice was soft and comforting, and though his clothes showed some rough wear, they were of fine material and cut.

"He didn't try to run away," broke in Ross. "He just waited until we took a shot, then put up his hands and waited to be captured."

Rondthaler glanced at Ross with a look that said that he would have gotten away if he'd wanted to. "I don't really think of myself as being captured, Miss. I prefer to think that I approached you voluntarily."

"Right." Karstil didn't need to split hairs with Ross or this doctor. "What were you doing in the gorge?"

The doctor gave Karstil a tight smile. "I was surprised to see a Renegade unit here. The TOGs have held the area for the past three months, and I and my companions have been in hiding since then. The TOGs, as I'm sure you know, are not easy on civilians. At any rate, a sentry of ours heard you go by last night, and I came to the road to make contact with the rest of your force. Now that the road is clear to the Commonwealth area, we will move to the valley, where the rest of your units are currently located. We heard your tanks in the valley earlier today."

Karstil rubbed his eyes. "I'm sorry to disappoint you, doctor. But what you see is what you get." He watched the doctor, waiting for the reaction of dismay. There was none, almost as though he had not spoken. "We're a raid, doctor. Those tanks in the valley are TOG, not Renegade. We're actually surrounded. About to be destroyed."

"Oh my." Karstil had finally gotten a reaction from the doctor, who pulled at his beard. "Then we must make plans to be away."

"I'd love to 'be away,' Doctor. But unless you have a hidden door to this valley, there is not much likelihood of that."

"There is another valley, over there," said Rondthaler, pointing into the gloom on the other side of the gorge. "That's where the rest of my people are hiding."

"It doesn't show on my DDP," sneered Karstil. "What I mean is, I have no way of knowing where it is or where it leads."

Rondthaler either didn't hear or chose to disregard the tone of Karstil's statement. "There's a valley that leads off at right angles to this one. It's the one we came up when we escaped. All you have to do is climb that ridge and you're there. That's how I got here."

Karstil stared at the precipice that formed the opposite wall of the gorge. A lone man might be able to scale it, but taking a column of tanks over the terrain would be a bit more difficult. The thrust required to climb the wall would make them visible to any TOG units in the area. And the TOGs would know that they had gone down another route. It wouldn't work.

"The transponders again." It was Johnston who spoke. "If we leave the transponders behind, wouldn't they see them? Would that cover our climb?"

Karstil thought for a moment. "It would mean leaving a power source with them. That would mean a vehicle, and we don't have one to spare."

"Why not the Eradicator?" asked Mullins. "It's only carrying two people now."

"Excuse me for butting in, sir," said the Sergeant, whom Karstil remembered as commanding the damaged Spartius. He couldn't remember his name. "The Spartius will never make a full-thrust climb. We should leave it. There are five of us in the vehicle, but we could ride the outside of the Eradicator."

Karstil looked at the men around him. He could see the obvious excitement in their faces. Before they had been depressed, ready to accept defeat and destruction. Now they were looking forward to escape. They had a plan. He turned to the Maintenance Sergeant. "Can you slave the transponders through the Spartius power pack?"

"It'll take some time, sir, but I can do it."

"Get on it. The rest of you, dump everything you don't need. Load the missile racks and dump the rest. Make room for the men in the Spartius. If there isn't enough room, Mullins and I can probably squeeze one into each of the Liberators." He turned to the Maintenance Sergeant. "I can't remember your name, Sergeant."

"Known, sir. Herman Known."

"Right. Can you rig a time fuse in the Spartius? No need for it to fall into enemy hands."

"I'm afraid that's out of my line, sir, but Engineer Sergeant Zubin may be able to. He's into demolitions, you know."

Karstil, of course, had no idea what the men in the Spartius could do, but he was willing to take Known's word as bona fides for the other Sergeant. "Have him talk to me. The rest of you get going."

While the Sergeants scattered to prepare their commands for departure, Karstil called Glover and told him the rudiments of the plan. There was no use going into detail, just in case the TOGs were listening. Essentially, Glover was to remain on passive until the last moment. When he pulled back, he would dump his transponder at the Spartius, pick up the Sergeant there, and escape over the mountains. Half an hour later, all was ready.

Mullins and Crown led the column, with Ambrose as their guide. The doctor would remain on the crest as the others pulled out, riding the final leg on the Wolverine, along with Sergeant Known. Mullins and Crown departed up the valley before applying full thrust to make the 1,000-meter climb to the ridge. The noise of the grav drives filled the gorge, the whine reverberating from the rocks. As the tanks crossed the ridge, the valley was filled with a sudden silence. Johnston and Ross took their damaged vehicles out next, their whine cut off as they cleared the ridge as well. The departing vehicles cut their commlinks as liftoff began so there was no way for Karstil to know if they were safe. He just hoped.

"Four. Six. Move." He switched to the intercom. "Spint, up the valley and begin the climb." The Liberator swung around until it was facing back up the gorge and began to move. As they rounded a corner, the tank drifted over the mist-shrouded stream bed and began a steep climb. Halfway up, it slowed as Spint turned the vehicle in the narrow confines of the valley and then applied full power as he aimed for the crest.

Below him, Karstil could see the gorge, the road twisting down the side and the bowl of the valley still filled with the rapidly disappearing mist. Far below, he could see the Wolverine begin to make its way from the assembly area, a diminutive figure riding the outside of the turret. Many kilometers away, he could see the open plain that was safety. An instant later, the towering peaks blocked his vision as Spint turned the Liberator down the notch. The tank swept between spires of stone no more than 10 meters apart. Down below, the figure of the doctor waved as they went past.

Then they were in another cleft that twisted and turned past jagged minarets and razor edges. Now the stone dropped away to reveal a small valley, no more than a kilometer square, that sparkled with water amid patches of verdant growth. Seeing the Viper and Eradicator grounding near some trees, Karstil directed Spint to do the same.

53

Alsatia, Caralis
The Commonwealth
9 January 6831

Karstil had underestimated the "companions" to whom Rondthaler had referred during their first conversation. Instead of finding maybe a dozen civilians, he encountered more than a hundred scattered through the valley. Whole families had assembled there, along with all their worldly goods and vehicles. There were at least twenty wheeled vehicles of all shapes and sizes, and in various conditions of repair.

For an officer, used to the military hierarchy, dealing with a mass of civilians was a lesson in frustration. An officer is used to turning to his Sergeant and telling him to do it. The Sergeant goes away and returns when the job is done. Not so in civilian life. Every decision must be discussed in full, with everyone having his say. Then the motion is put to a vote, and the majority rules. Unless, of course, there is someone who still disagrees, in which case, all the arguments are trotted out again. New motions are called for, a new vote is made, and perhaps the decision is acceptable by all. All this takes time and leads to compromises that may or may not support the original concept.

Upon being informed of the extent of the refugee problem, Karstil made the instant decision to "mount up and move out." This was greeted by wails of protest. It would take hours to load everything. Some of the vehicles were out of fuel. The people were about to have breakfast. Someone was staying with another family last night, and she hadn't come home. Wouldn't it be better to wait until dark? Why not stay here? Did the TOGs really know where they were? Shouldn't we vote on this? Let's call a council. Let's talk this out.

Rondthaler nudged and cajoled, prodded and pushed, but it was like trying to move the sea with a fork. A council of the leaders was scheduled. Karstil presented his plan. It was essentially the same: pack and move. Not acceptable. It was coming on lunch time and the people needed to be fed. There was the decision as to who would lead the column. Would the Renegades guarantee the safety of the column? No. Why? Because, with six vehicles, that was impossible. Why?

The only good thing about dealing with the council, made up of both men and women, was that they talked one at a time. When Karstil met with the heads of households, those with primary responsibility for the children, they all talked at once. Worse, they brought their children with them. No sooner did a conversation start than it would end or be transferred to another. He stalked away from the group, followed by a trail of people who wanted answers he did not have. Then they broke away from him to reform under the trees. Karstil was astonished. First they were after him and then they were gone. At least he wouldn't have to deal with them for a while. The council was ready for its decision, and he had been summoned to hear what they had to say. As he moved to where the council was seated under another clump of trees, he saw the second group clustered around Sergeant Honor Ross. Good, he thought. Let her deal with them. Let her earn her money for a change.

The TOG *Gladius* fighter drifted along through the thin atmosphere. The controls were on automatic, allowing Carlin Fulmin, the pilot, to lounge in his seat with almost nothing to do. The vector thrusters fired occasionally to maintain course and speed. Behind the pilot, the weapons officer scanned his ground sensors. The left-wing hardpoint had been equipped with a ground sensor pack, and this provided information on what was far below. He could see the contours of the cleft that broke the escarpment. Deep in that cleft should be a column of Renegade vehicles, reported at Cohort strength. He had seen nothing to indicate that.

The display flashed. Far below, in a tiny coulee, the sensor pack had discovered something. The Weapons Officer increased power and magnification. The information appeared: civilian vehicles hidden along the edges of the trees. "Carlin," said the WO, gaining the attention of the pilot. "No Renegades, but I've found some civvies hidden in the woods."

"No sign of the Renegades?" asked Carlin.

"Nope."

"Well, we've got weapons on board, and we could do with some excitement. What say we kick some butt?"

"Sounds good to me."

Fulmin grasped the control yoke, flipping the master switch to regain command of the fighter. The right wing dropped sharply and the *Gladius* rolled into a dive.

The eleven men and women of the council were seated on stumps and rocks under the overhanging branches. The air was cool and still, unlike the blazing heat in the center of the valley. The soft sound of falling water came from somewhere under the trees. If it hadn't been for Karstil's sense of urgency, which the others obviously did not share, this might have been a quiet meeting of town leaders on some distant planet far from strife. A thin, hatchet-faced woman rose to speak as Karstil entered the circle.

"We have been discussing, young man, the proposed withdrawal from our valley." The voice was as sharp as the face. Karstil glanced at the others. From their expressions, he could tell that most of them were in this one's camp. To one side stood Doctor Rondthaler, looking like a defeated man. "You have created a number of problems for us," continued the speaker. "By coming here, you may have given away our whereabouts to TOG. That is very bad. You should have considered our safety when you made your move."

She paused to look at the other members of the council. Karstil could feel the heat rising under his collar, even in the coolness of the shade.

"Now you come to us with a proposal to move out into the valley, to take our chances on the unknown. Added to that, you will not guarantee the safety of the populace. This council has established itself as the governing body of the local population. As a member of the armed forces, you come under our control. As you have already admitted not having contact with your headquarters, you will function and conduct yourself as *our* armed force.

"With that in mind, we charge you with the task of evaluating the present situation to determine if evacuation is necessary. Next, assuming it is, you will present a plan for the safe withdrawal of all civilians and their goods. You will present your evaluation tomorrow after breakfast, and your evacuation plan after dinner. I think that should cover it."

Karstil was dumbfounded. If the civilians wanted to stay, that was fine with him. All he really had to do was order his tanks to move, and they would be gone. The civilians could fend for themselves. But some of what the woman had said was true. His escape into the hidden valley could have alerted TOG to the presence of at least another way out. They would be closing in soon, and the civilians were sure to take the brunt of the casualties. He had some responsibility for the current situation.

"I'm sure, ma'am," Karstil said, "that the TOG forces at least suspect the presence of the valley. My suggestion is that we load up what we can on the vehicles that will run, dump the rest, and get out. We should do it at once."

"That was your earlier proposal, Optio," said the hatchet-faced woman, "It was as unacceptable then as it is now. Please do as the council has ordered or we will be forced to relieve you."

Karstil was saved having to respond by the violent explosion that shook the valley. The shock wave flattened the council, tumbling Karstil over a stump to land in a heap under the trees. As a cloud of smoke and dust blotted out the center of the clearing, he leaped to his feet and began to run toward the opening. His left side hurt terribly and his arm hung useless at his side. Something seemed to be wrong with his right foot as well. He reached the site of the crater in time for the smoke to clear. High above, he could see a fork-like craft still climbing into the sky. The ship did a hammerhead stall high in the air, turning around to make a second pass at its target. Karstil started to run.

He was still in the clearing when the *Gladius* fighter released its bomb. The shock wave would have sent him straight into the trees had not a hand grasped his ankle, bringing him down with a crash in a small crater. Another body landed on top of him as he fell, and the shock wave passed over them. Even with the wind knocked out of him, Karstil could smell the odor of stale cigars.

"Sorry, sir," said Mullins, still lying atop his commander. "Not a good idea to be running about when the bombs are landing." With that, he was on his feet, pulling the still-gasping Karstil after him. That done, the Sergeant took off at a sprint toward his grounded Liberator. Karstil sagged to the ground, too tired and too hurt to run after him. As Mullins ran, he signaled wildly toward Lurron Johnston, who was standing in the Eradicator's turret.

By the time Mullins reached the Liberator, the Eradicator was powered up and at a 1-meter hover nearby. The Platoon Sergeant scrambled over the glacis and into the turret just as his own tank began to move. Sedgwick Abul, the driver, had seen Mullins as he sprinted across the field. The two vehicles cleared the edge of the trees and grounded.

High in the sky, the *Gladius* made another hammerhead stall, swooping down on the valley. The pilot must have been surprised to see the two Renegade tanks at the edge of the trees. There was no way he could know that the Eradicator's turret was virtually destroyed, thus altering the recognition signature of the vehicle. In addition, with its transponder removed, the anti-aircraft vehicle had no recognizable electronic signature. It would have been too late to change the trajectory of the run anyway.

Mullins worked frantically, trying to disregard the approach of the TOG *Gladius*. The Eradicator was unable to fire its remaining missile because of the damaged DDP, but as he had told Karstil, the weapon could be slaved through the Liberator's DDP. Now he was going to have a chance to prove it. The external electrical ports of the two vehicles were close enough that all he had to do was run the slave cable from one vehicle to the other. His own DDP had acquired the incoming target.

On the other side of the clearing, Mullins could hear the whack of Karstil's 150mm cannon open on the diving fighter. An instant later, Mullins' own 150 fired, followed almost immediately by the sharper sound of the 50. Yennen was attempting to drive the fighter away with ground fire.

As the TOG pilot dropped another of his 500-kilogram bombs, Mullins' two 150mm shells hit the fighter in quick succession, the first on the bow, the second on the right side. Neither shot penetrated, but the fighter shook under the impact. Almost immediately, the fighter spiraled away from the hidden valley, streaking toward the void of space. He must have decided to leave ground combat to the ground-pounders. But that wouldn't stop him from reporting Renegade tanks in the valley.

Sitting at the firing board of the Eradicator, Lurron Johnston kept his finger on the firing switch even as he watched the *Gladius* scream down at him. The procedure was for Mullins to attach the slave cable, count two, and then fire. The count of two was to give the missile a chance to load the information from the Liberator into its warhead. It was also intended to give Mullins a chance to clear the cable. The *Gladius* pulled out of its dive and began to climb away. Damn, thought Johnston, he's going to get away. He triggered the firing circuit.

eside the Eradicator, Mullins had almost seated the slave cable when the firing circuit called for power. Mullins had his left hand on the cable, his right on the side of the Eradicator. The spark of electrical energy arced across the space between the cable and the access port, and Mullins felt the jolt to his toes. White light flashed across his eyes as he was thrown to the ground. The cable hit beside him, the electrical sparks continuing to snap across the ground. He was dimly aware of a fireball on the Eradicator as the missile left its compartment to rise into the air.

The *Gladius* pilot was momentarily aware of an explosion in his bomb sight as he climbed from the target. He was confused. There should have been no secondary explosion unless a previous hit had finally triggered a reaction. He took his eyes from the sight to scan his panel, but got a green board. By the time he looked back into the sight, he could see the anti-aircraft missile centered in the dissipating fire ball, a tiny dot riding a circle of fire. He wrenched the stick to the left and back, all thought of reporting the target driven from his mind by the sight of the oncoming missile.

He was a fraction of a second too late. The titanium armor of the *Gladius*'s stern absorbed most of the damage, but the HELL missile was stronger than any armor any fighter could carry. There was penetration to the interior. In the instant that remained, the pilot and weapons officer saw warning lights flash on: life support leak, decompression, strut fracture, bulkhead collapse. The next moment, the *Gladius* exploded in a brilliant fireball that scattered its parts all across the tiny valley.

240

54

Alsatia, Caralis
The Commonwealth
9 January 6831

The council was sullen, the hatchet-faced woman furious. They had summoned Karstil even before the last of the fighter's parts struck the ground.

"Now you've done it! It's not enough that you showed the TOGs where we were. Now you've shown that we are a military force. They'll bomb us! Have you no regard for civilians?"

Karstil almost answered with a resounding "no," but thought better of it. He had already made up his mind. He was here to tell the council he was leaving.

"The council will have to decide what to do with you," continued the speaker. "You are under my command—our command—report here in four hours to hear our decision."

"In a pig's eye." Karstil could stand it no longer. "You can take your council and your decision, and stuff them. As of now, my only responsibility is to the men and women of my command. We're pulling out, and if you want to come along, that's up to you. We leave as soon as our column is ready to move."

The hatchet-faced woman stared at him. "You can't do that. I forbid it. I will have you placed under arrest. I am Muriel Walker, the president of the council, chief officer of this valley. My word is law. You will do as I say. If you do not, you will be reported to the Commonwealth." The grove of trees was suddenly still, except for the soft rustling of leaves. The two stood face to face, each one having stated a final position.

A woman's voice broke the silence. "Nolan, we're leaving." Every head snapped toward the speaker. She was a small woman, neatly attired in trousers and leather jacket, her white hair pulled back in a bun. She stood with her hands on her hips, staring at the gathered leaders. "Didn't you hear me, Nolan. We're leaving with the soldiers." She glanced at one of the women within the circle. "Vincenta. Your husband is leaving, too. You'd both better come." Two rose to their feet and left the circle. "The other families are packed, too. You people had better shake a leg. With that fighter down, they're sure to come back with more." She turned and left the grove.

As Karstil turned to limp after her, he saw the other members of the council rising to leave. Walker was still standing in the center. "Wait," she snarled. "You can't all leave. We have things to do." The others paid her no heed. "Come back," she called. "I'm in charge here."

The woman who had broken the silence was well into the clearing when Karstil reached her. She didn't break stride as he came alongside, still dragging his right leg. "I think it's time we left, young man. Your Sergeant Ross explained it all to us, and we've decided to go with you. I'm only sorry that we didn't move sooner. Perhaps we could have saved that man of yours." She stopped to face him. "I'm Regina Nabalus. My husband Nolan is one of the councilmen. They spend too much time talking when a decision needs to be made. And now it's time to go. Oh, here comes that nice young lady of yours."

Sergeant Ross joined the pair. "Excuse me, Mrs. Nabalus. Sir, the column's about ready. Glover has already left to scout the way, and the first civilian vehicles are beginning to move. The troops are all loaded." She took Karstil by the elbow and began to lead him away. "Excuse us, Mrs. Nabalus. We have to go." As they moved on, Ross spoke again, her voice lower. "Sergeant Mullins is unconscious, but I think he'll be all right. The same with Johnston. The Eradicator is finished. That last missile burned out most of the interior when it fired."

Karstil stared at Ross, not knowing what to say. Either she should be criticized for doing too much or praised for doing the right thing. He hurt too much to decide. He'd put that off until another time. "We're ready to move?"

"Yes, sir. Locked and loaded." In the distance, he could see a group of civilian vehicles moving out of the valley.

"Then let's do it."

"Right, sir. Moving now. I put Johnston in my vehicle. Crown has his driver. Mullins is in his own tank. When he wakes up, I'm sure he'll be all right." She trotted away toward her Viper. Karstil watched her go. The combat uniform didn't do a thing for her, but even from behind, there was something delicious in the way she moved and the way the sun sparkled off her auburn hair. He shook his head. Then his Liberator grounded next to him, and he caught Quentain's eyes. The gunner was watching Ross as well, obviously enjoying the sight.

A column moves at the speed of the slowest vehicle, which meant the column often came to a dead stop. The sedans and vans of the civilians were not in good shape when the trek began, and it wasn't long before they began to break down. After a flurry of attempted repairs, it usually turned out that nothing could be done. The family would then plead that their goods be loaded onto one of the still functioning carriers. At first, Karstil waited for the load to be transferred, but by the third breakdown in an hour, he was reaching wit's end. The transfer of cargo was slowing movement to a dead crawl, and each passing minute gave the TOGs a better chance of finding them. It was Honor Ross and Regina Nabalus who made the decision.

Regina was standing beside a van with a broken front suspension, when Karstil walked up. "Dump it all," she said. "We can't wait any more." Three men were frantically pulling parcels and boxes from the rear of the van, stacking them neatly beside the road. "We can't waste any more time with this." She turned to Karstil. "Young man, I suggest we dump the lot over the side. From now on, we just leave broken cars behind."

Tough lady, thought Karstil. I'm glad she said it and not me. Easier, though, when it's someone else's gear that's being left behind. He looked at her. She was grim, the lines around her mouth and nose deeper than ever.

"You're right, ma'am. We'll leave it."

"Will you tell them? Or shall I?" she said softly.

"I'll do it." Karstil turned to the men who were unloading even faster than before. "No use, gentlemen. We'll have to leave it. Get back on your trucks and keep moving." He turned to remount his Liberator. "Thanks, Mrs. Nabalus."

She nodded and turned away. Karstil saw her tremble slightly as she turned. When he looked back from the turret of his tank, he saw her leaning on the van, her head buried in her arm. She was sobbing. Then her husband led her away to mount an already dangerously over-crowded sedan that had stopped alongside.

It was full dark by the time the column broke clear of the massif. The journey from the hidden refuge to the plain had been no more than 30 kilometers in a straight line, but the vehicles had had to cover at least five times that distance because of the broken ground. The entire trip had taken nine hours, slightly faster than the pace of a walking man.

Karstil was frustrated. One of the great assets of grav vehicles was their mobility. With the civilians attached to the column, and wheeled vehicles at that, this advantage was lost. He felt himself leaning into the hatch of the tank, willing the column along. It was no use.

There had been little TOG opposition to the trek. Glover, well out in front, had twice reported contact with enemy units. Once he had moved forward to investigate, but the contact had vanished like a will-o'-the-wisp as he approached. The second time, he discovered a damaged Lupis infantry carrier. When he called for reinforcements, Karstil sent Ross and her depleted squad in support. The Lupis had been destroyed and the squad scattered among the crags and outcroppings.

Late in the afternoon, Mullins reported in. He said he was awake and ready to take charge, but Karstil thought he sounded a bit woozy. He decided to use Mullins carefully until he had the chance to talk to him, eyeball to eyeball.

The little column circled at the mouth of the valley beside a small lake formed by a stream that tumbled down the gorge. Karstil put the combat vehicles in position on the plain, keeping the civilian vans and sedans against the mountain wall. He was down to two Liberators and two Vipers, along with Glover's Wolverine; seven vehicles reduced to five. Behind him, twenty civilian wheeled transports were left from the thirty-one that had left the grove of trees.

The Wolverine grounded beside Karstil's Liberator, and the Recon Sergeant made his report. He had made a wide sweep beyond the valley mouth, a 30-kilometer radius out into the darkened plain that had taken him most of an hour.

"I got some indication of TOG units on both flanks, sir," he reported. "They seemed to be moving very slowly, but they are approaching. I also got some chatter on the commlink. I couldn't tell if they were our guys or theirs, so I didn't try to make contact."

"Do you think you were spotted?" asked Karstil.

"Don't see how they could help seeing me, sir. They didn't react, but I have to assume that if I could see them, they could see me. I kept my sensors on low power so I was only picking up their readings."

The command group was silent. "O.K.," said Karstil. "We've been spotted, but the TOGs may not know our strength. Most likely, they'll probe the perimeter before very long. Let's say two hours. I don't want to be here when they arrive."

"It'll take a bomb to move those civilians," muttered Mullins, tugging on his ear. Karstil was glad to see his Platoon Sergeant returning to his old ways. He even had the dead end of a cigar clamped in his teeth.

"Then we'd better get a bomb. Mrs. Nabalus should be able to do it."

"Yeah," said Crown. "That's one tough broad."

"Lady," said Ross. "That's one tough lady."

"Lady," said Crown, chastised by the diminutive Sergeant. He looked at Karstil.

"Lady," said the Optio. "Now, let's go." Karstil broke up the meeting. "Glover, take the point. Mullins and Crown on the left flank, Ross and me on the right. We'll put the civilians in the center with Dr. Rondthaler, Mrs. Nabalus in the rear to 'encourage' the stragglers."

"With a whip, I assume," said Mullins.

"With a whip if necessary," replied Karstil.

55

Alsatia, Caralis
The Commonwealth
9 January 6831

They were ready to move in forty-five minutes, a good quarter of an hour faster than Karstil had planned. Most of the civilians were too tired to argue with the decision, and Rondthaler and Nabalus managed to silence Walker when she started to protest. It was obvious that the command structure of the party had changed, and it was not the council who was in control. Karstil wanted to take advantage of the situation, knowing it wouldn't be long before the council reasserted itself. He just hoped it would be Ambrose Rondthaler and not Muriel Walker who emerged as the new champion of civilian rights.

The doctor had been more and more in evidence as the party made its way out of the mountains. He seemed to have recovered from the council's decisions, which he had obviously resisted. As a member of the "do it" faction rather than the "talk it to death" group, Rondthaler had been the loser in the first argument. Now that they were on the way, the doctor became one of the leaders again. Karstil was glad to see it. He wanted the doctor in control when the shooting started.

The move over the plain was easier on the vehicles than the trek from the mountains. The rolling hills were passable, even traveling across country. Karstil had the drivers break out the front parking lamps on the vehicles, leaving only the rear lights operational. Even these were shrouded by pieces of "thousand-kilometer-an-hour tape," a ubiquitous substance with the reputation of being able to seal anything while withstanding tremendous speeds. There was a story, probably apocryphal, of a *Guardian* fighter that had flown a mission with its cockpit sealed with the tape. It was only on recovery to his carrier that the pilot realized that a 25mm hole in the fuselage had been sealed with the tape and been inadvertently painted over in the rush to ready the fighter. Such were the legends surrounding "thousand-kilometer-an-hour tape."

With the tail lights reduced to mere dots of light, one vehicle could follow the other across the plain. All the light switches in the vehicles were taped closed so that the driving lamps could not be turned on involuntarily.

Glover and the Wolverine led the group, with the Liberator/Viper teams on the flanks. Speed in the darkness was kept low, a steady 20 kilometers per hour for the wheels, though even that would make the sedans pitch and roll. On the flanks, Karstil and Mullins cruised at 60, keeping their speed up just in case faster movement were suddenly necessary. At 60, they would be able to ground without damage or accelerate to battle speed in an instant. Karstil had no idea where friendly lines might be, but he estimated that they should be able to make some kind of contact in six to eight hours. If they hadn't found friendlies by then, the dawn would reveal just how weak his force really was.

He was passing back down the flank of the column, five kilometers to the right of the civilian vehicles, when his DDP flashed red. He switched from passive to full-power active scan, and the red squares solidified into targets that the ballistic computer identified at once.

"Targets identified. Three Aeneas light tanks, one Lupis infantry carrier. Range two-zero-zero-double zero. Bearing four-eight double zero relative. Targets closing at six-zero. Lock not achieved."

He thumbed the commlink control from listening silence to full power active. "Three, Six. Turn left. Accelerate to one-twenty. We're going in. Break. All stations. Intruders to the left of the column. Am engaging." The Liberator made a sweeping turn to the left and began to pick up speed. Karstil saw Ross's Viper make the same turn to fall in on his left flank. The amber triangles that marked the civilian column dropped behind. The DDP did not identify the vans as friendly because it had no program that recognized civilians as anything but unidentified targets. The Viper, 500 meters away, showed blue, but the other combat vehicles, their transponders lost the day before, became amber triangles like the vans.

"Targets identified. Three Aeneas light tanks, one Lupis infantry carrier. Range one-eight-zero-double zero. Bearing six-four double zero relative. Targets closing at one-eight-zero. Lock not achieved." The computer paused. "Targets separating."

A glance at the DDP proved the computer correct. Two of the Aeneas tanks continued to come straight in, the third one and the Lupis carrier moving to the left as though to flank the Liberator and Viper.

"Three, Six. Accelerate to two hundred. We'll blow right through them. Concentrate fire on the left-hand one. Once by, we'll make a turn to the left and chase the other two. We can't let them get to the column." Karstil's voice sounded steady. "Break. Four, get your butt down here. We need help."

"Six, Four." Glover responded instantly. He must have been listening intently for Karstil's command. "I thought you'd never ask, boss. I'm already on the way."

A little less levity on the commlink, thought Karstil. The others had already taken Glover's lead and were also calling him "boss" on the air.

"Targets identified. Two Aeneas light tanks. Range one-three-zero-double zero. Targets closing at four-double zero. Lock not achieved."

Life was going to get interesting. With only the TVLGs and the 150mm cannon on the Liberator, and with the Viper short its SMLM launchers, Karstil's flank was terribly weak to face the two Aeneas tanks. Luckily, his own Vulcan III system was still functional, while the Aeneas had nothing with which to defend itself against missile attack.

"Targets identified. Two Aeneas light tanks. Range nine-zero-double zero. Targets closing at four-double zero. Lock not achieved."

He glanced at the DDP. Ross's Viper had moved slightly ahead, her speed some 10 kays faster than his own. The red indicators of the two Aeneas tanks held steady in the center of the display. Far to the left, he could see the other indicators of the flanking TOG units. They were just beginning their turn toward the column. Further to the left was the amber triangle that would be Glover's Wolverine. A single Wolverine would be no match for the Lupis and the Aeneas. The best they could hope for was a running battle until the Liberator was able to join up.

"Targets identified. Two Aeneas light tanks. Range five-zero-double zero. Targets closing at four-double zero. Lock not achieved."

He treadled the painting laser. There was no need for the TOGs to suspect that his own long-range laser had been destroyed. They would expect to be painted at long range, and wouldn't disappoint them. His own warning klaxon began to howl; they were painting back.

"Targets identified. Two Aeneas light tanks. Range four-zero-double zero. Targets closing at four-double zero. Lock achieved."

That should make them wince, thought Karstil. His painting laser had to be the luckiest one in existence; he painted every time he tried. Too bad there was no heavy laser to take advantage of the lock.

"Targets identified. Two Aeneas light tanks. Range three-zero-double zero. Targets closing at four-double zero. Lock achieved."

The 150mm cannon responded at once, the blue flame at the muzzle smothering Quentain's call of, "On the way." The blaze of light blinded Karstil. He looked down to confirm the hit. The DDP circled the Aeneas on the left, a "T" appearing to show a turret hit. The warning klaxon continued to whoop in his ear. It was a comfort to know the TOGs hadn't been successful in painting him.

To his left, he saw the Viper bathed in a shower of molten titanium as a pair of lasers struck the front glacis. They hadn't been trying to paint him at all. They had chosen to pick on the lighter of the two targets first. The 150mm cannon fired again, and Karstil saw the HEAP round burst on the targeted Aeneas. The DDP showed another "T" on the hit indicator. It wouldn't be able to stand much more of that.

"Targets identified. Two Aeneas light tanks. Range two-zero-double zero. Targets closing at four-double zero. Lock achieved."

Still too far for the TVLGs. The 100mm cannon on the Aeneas tanks fired together, the rounds screaming into the night ahead. They were still shooting at the Viper, still trying to destroy the lighter target first. One round splashed on the turret, while the other lost in the darkness. A missile lifted from the rack, riding a cone of fire into the black sky. Stupid, thought Karstil. Don't fire a TVLG at 2,000 meters when the missile only has a range of 1,200. Then he laughed. "They" didn't know that. They would expect an SMLM at that range.

"Targets identified. Two Aeneas light tanks. Range one-five-double zero. Targets breaking right. Bearing eight-double zero. Lock achieved."

Sure enough, the Aeneas tanks were turning away. The launch of the TVLG, fired against the painted Aeneas on the left, had been enough for it. With its turret shattered by hits from the 150mm cannon, the Aeneas knew it could not stand a missile hit.

"Three, Six. Break left. Spint. Emergency turn to the left." The Liberator canted hard as Spint pulled emergency power to make the turn. The left sponson shuddered across the ground, clods of dirt and sparks spraying into the darkness. Karstil braced himself in the hatch and watched his DDP bring the other TOG vehicles into the center. He was aware of Ross's Viper flashing by as she tried to make the turn herself. Her higher speed and slower reactions meant that she had to turn wider and then accelerate to catch up.

The DDP showed Glover locked in with the other Aeneas and the Lupis. The swirl of combat was drifting toward the civilian vehicles as Glover sought to interpose himself between the enemy and the column. He was doing all right. Then Karstil saw a flash in the screen, mirrored by a distant explosion. The Wolverine swerved away in a sharp right turn; the TOG tanks broke for the column.

"Targets identified. One Aeneas light tank; one Lupis carrier. Range two-five-double zero. Range steady. Lock achieved."

He swung the turret to aim at the Aeneas.

"Aeneas."

"Identified."

"Fire!"

"On the way." The 150mm cannon bloomed blue flame. Two and a half kilometers away, the HEAP round found the rear of the Aeneas. The light tank must have had some damage already because it slowed perceptibly. The stern of the tank continued to glow.

In the distance, the sky lit with missiles as the Lupis tried to slug it out with the Wolverine. The Wolverine had the advantage in that exchange. While the Lupis could fire its SMLMs one at a time, the Wolverine was launching two-missile salvos in return—and the TVLGs had better penetration.

"Target identified. One Aeneas light tank. Range two-zero-double zero. Target closing at one-zero-double zero. Lock achieved."

The 150mm cannon fired again.

The Liberator rocked from the concussion of a hit on the rear armor, a cloud of titanium droplets fanning away. Karstil glanced at the DDP. He had been so busy chasing the flanking tanks that he had lost sight of the original adversaries. There they were now, two kilometers behind and gaining.

"Three, Six. Take out the Aeneas. Spint. Hard left." The Liberator executed another emergency turn to face the oncoming Aeneas tanks.

"Targets identified. Two Aeneas light tanks. Range two-zero-double zero. Targets closing at four-double zero. Lock achieved."

There was no way of telling which one was the damaged vehicle. He would just have to shoot and hope. He swung the turret to the nearer of the two.

"Identified."

"Fire." Through the blue muzzle blast of the heavy cannon, he could see both light tanks return fire. One of the shells struck flush on the turret face, the other was lost. You're good, he thought, but not good enough. Both of those shots should have hit. Then an explosion far to the right told the story. The second tank had fired at the column.

Armored fighting vehicles were designed to give and take punishment, and a medium tank could usually take significant damage before becoming non-combat worthy. Lucky hits could kill a tank in seconds, but usually the commander saw the armor melting away in time to make a run for it. This was not true of civilian vans. The 100mm HEAP round struck flush on the high side of the van, expending most of its energy inside the passenger compartment. The van exploded in a ball of flame, the blast silhouetting what had been in the compartment's interior. One full figure was starkly etched against the flame before it dissolved.

"Switch targets!"

"Identified."

"Fire! Turn right!"

The Liberator swerved parallel with the column, racing down the exposed flank to engage the attacking Aeneas. The TOG light tank fired again, and another van exploded in a ball of flame.

A 100mm APDS round struck the left side of the Liberator's turret, knocking the tank sideways. A ball of fire and molten armor swept over the top of the tank, and Karstil could smell something burning. Spint fought the controls to bring the 273-ton monster back on course. The main gun fired again.

Karstil reached up to adjust the combat helmet. It was gone. He ran his fingers through his hair and felt it crumble under his touch. It was his own burning hair that he smelled. He searched around the top of the turret for his helmet. It had been blown against the 150mm mount. He extracted it just as the gun tube depressed. The helmet would have been crushed had it remained there a moment longer. The plastic was still hot enough to scorch his hands.

Another 100mm round swept overhead. His main gun fired again. To the right, another van burst into flames. The Aeneas was huge in the ballistic sights. Smoke poured out of the Liberator's fighting compartment as ceramic ballistic armor melted under the hammering of the 100mm rounds.

He glanced at the DDP. Far to the rear, he saw the Aeneas and Lupis grounded near each other, the Viper and Wolverine circling like a pair of hungry wolves. That thrust had at least been blunted.

The Aeneas Karstil had been attacking turned away, its turret rotating to engage the charging Liberator. The other Aeneas, left behind when the Liberator turned, stopped firing at the tank and began to take on the column. To his right, another vehicle flared.

"Left. Turn left." The Liberator failed to respond. "Left, I said. Turn left!"

"Left vane out, sir. Turning right."

The damage to the tank was beginning to take out its systems. With the left steering vane out of action, the tank could turn only to the right. Away from the Aeneas.

The wreckage of the column swept across the bow of the Liberator. There were enough burning vehicles to illuminate the area, and many of the civilians had managed to turn on their headlights despite Karstil's earlier precautions. It looked like a convention of crazed fireflies as the vehicles dodged away from the tanks. Through the flame and drifting smoke came a broad, double-prowed shape, a rooftop adrift in a sea of grass. Karstil stared at the sight. The house erupted in a brilliant blue ball, and it was only then that Karstil recognized the shape as that of Mullins's Liberator. He had abandoned his left flank guard to come to the aid of the right. Who, thought Karstil, is minding the store?

The Aeneas tanks, already damaged by Karstil, could not stand against the reinforcements. Light tanks did not slug it out with mediums. Not for very long, that is. Mullins's heavy laser took out the first with a single shot. The night sky glowed with a fireball as the ammunition and missiles cooked off from the heat. The second Aeneas made a dash for home, but it was too close, its drives too badly damaged to make it away before Mullins had him locked. The Aeneas died in a shower of sparks. At the head of the column, the other TOG vehicles met the same fate.

It took half an hour to round up the twelve surviving vehicles. Five had been destroyed by the fire from the TOG tanks, two had broken their suspension during flight, one was unaccounted for. The latter was Muriel Walker's sedan, and Karstil was torn between making a detailed search of the area or just getting on with it. In the end, they swept the area once and kept moving.

The civilian vehicles had turned on their lights during the fight, and Karstil decided not to extinguish them. He was sure the TOGs had reported the column, sure that they would soon attract more enemy interest. There was no use being sneaky about the movement now. With lights on, they could pick up speed to 30 KPH, not a terrific rate but still faster than before.

Casualties among the Renegade vehicles were not too bad. Ross had lost two of her remaining men to the TOG missiles, and Glover's driver was dead. He took Johnston's old driver as a replacement, and was soon at the head of the menagerie, snooping his way across the ground. Spint had been burned when one of the 100mm rounds penetrated the side of the Liberator, but he had begged to be allowed to continue to drive. Karstil decided that his tank was in no shape for combat anyway, so he let Spint stay. There was no use putting a healthy man in a sick tank.

There had been some talk of burying the civilian dead, but Karstil didn't want to spend the time. They loaded the easily located bodies onto the good vehicles, where people were as quick to offer space to the living who lacked transport as to those who would never need it again. Boxes and bags, so carefully packed the day before, were unceremoniously dumped to make room. There was even some light-hearted banter about what they were dumping. An air of camaraderie had taken over the party. They would all make it together, or...

The vehicles, now more a horde than any sensible formation, moved across the plain. Glover continued out front, but Mullins and Karstil no longer acted as flank guards. Instead, they followed along behind, sweeping up stragglers and keeping the strays from wandering too far from the center. Karstil had Ambrose Rondthaler, with a compass and a heading, in the center. The doctor followed his course, and all the other vehicles were to guide on him. Which they did, more or less. That was the reason why Ross and Crown made their occasional sweeps to the flanks, turning back those who had straggled too far away.

The convoy continued without serious incident. Once an Aeneas approached the rear, but Mullins fired a shot or two with his heavy laser, and the TOG light tank evidently thought better of trailing that close. He dropped back and continued to shadow at 45 kilometers. Glover and Ross both reported the presence of an Asinus light grav sled well off to the right. It was traveling at high speed toward the TOG positions, and Ross had swept out to make contact but had failed. The light sled had continued on, eventually lost as it went out of range.

As dawn came up, Glover reported that he had picked up blue indicators at 50 kilometers. Friendlies at last. He closed with the column to 40 kilometers and sent the Sergeant forward to make contact. He was back in half an hour, his turret and hull scoured by HAFE rounds.

"They won't let us in," he reported.

"What?"

"I tried to contact them on commlink, and they told me to buzz off. Or words to that effect." Glover was livid with frustration and rage. Karstil saw that the Reconnaissance Sergeant had been wounded by one of the flechettes. His right shoulder and neck were covered with blood, and a thick pad of bandaging bulged under his coveralls. "They said they didn't recognize us. Said we could be TOGs trying to slip into their area." He put his hands over his face. "Then they started shooting at me."

"You stay here. I'll do it."

Karstil had a quick conversation with Mullins. He wanted him ready to move as soon as he made contact. That solved, he moved forward until certain he was in commlink range of the unknown friendlies. He didn't want to approach too near until they told him to come in. When he had closed, slowly, to 10 kilometers, he opened his commlink.

"Spider Dolphin, Spider Dolphin. This is Spider Dolphin Two-two-six." He waited for a response. When none came, he tried again, this time on a broad frequency band. "Spider Dolphin, Spider Dolphin. This is Spider Dolphin Two-two-six."

"Unknown Station, Unknown Station. This is Net Control. Get off this frequency."

"Net Control, this is Spider Dolphin Two-two-six. Request permission to approach."

"This is Net Control. Get off this frequency and stay off."

"This is Spider Dolphin Two-two-six. Have civilian and Renegade forces with me. Request permission to enter your lines."

"Net Control. Permission denied. You TOG pond scum can stay where you are."

"This is Spider Dolphin Two-two-six." Karstil could hear the frustration in his own voice, and wondered if it translated across the commlink. "This is Optio Karstil of the Two-five-six-seventh Renegade Legion. I am returning from a patrol. I have civilians with me. Request permission to enter your lines."

"Nice try, Unknown Station."

"This is Spider Dolphin Two-two-six. Nice try, like hell. Can't you bozos recognize one of your own vehicles?"

"Yes, we can recognize our own vehicles, Unknown Station, and you are not one of them. Karstil has been reported lost in action. Now get off this frequency."

The transponders, thought Karstil, the damned transponders. Without them, he had no IFF signature. The ballistic computers must certainly see him, but without the transponders, he could be anyone. And if he was officially dead or captured, there was no way they were going to let him in.

The Liberator made a wide turn to the right, leaving the area just as the first HAFE rounds crashed into the ground. So much for the direct approach.

Karstil returned to a very subdued group of troops and civilians. The troops had been able to hear the conversation on the radio and knew the problem. The civilians, without access to a commlink, were just tired and letdown after a night of tension.

"We could make a run for it," suggested Crown. "Sooner or later, they'd have to realize we're friendlies."

The suggestion was greeted with stony silence. It was the "later" that had them worried.

The command group, all the Sergeants and Karstil, stood or crouched between the sponsons of the command Liberator. Even the Engineer and Maintenance Sergeants were there. The only missing commander was Lurron Johnston. As no one considered him a real commander, no one asked for or about him.

"Night infiltration seems to be the only hope," said Mullins. "We'd have to ditch the vehicles and go in on foot."

"Forty kilometers is a long way for the civilians to go on foot," said Ross. "Some of them are pretty well spent."

Karstil knew she was right. Most of them had been without sleep for twenty-four hours, and added to that was the tension and excitement of the last day. Even now, they were awake and puttering around instead of taking the opportunity to rest. "We might be able to make 40 klicks in a night, but we're not really up to it, either. And there's also the wounded to carry."

"Look this way and smile." The words were so incongruous that the whole group turned toward the voice. It was Johnston, now dressed in civilian clothes, standing atop one of the vans. He had rigged a tripod on the roof of the vehicle, and had mounted a holovid camera there. How he had found the time or space to salvage the rig was a mystery, but there he was, big as life, and looking like a holovid reporter.

"What the hell are you doing?" It was a virtual a cappella chorus from the group.

"I'm going to transmit the glorious return of Vexillary Karstil to the bosom of its friends. Let's see if we can do it while I still have enough light."

It didn't take the Sergeants and Karstil long to disabuse Johnston of the idea of a return, glorious or otherwise. Sneaking in at night meant that he would have to ditch the camera, and that he might very well get shot by one of the Renegades they were trying to reach.

"By the way," said Karstil, "not that I am interested in how you managed to save the rig when I told everyone to dump the nonessential, but how did you plan to transmit your story? You have no one to transmit to."

"Not true, my lad. Not true at all. It's obvious I have no ability to tape my broadcast, but I do have the ability to send. GHTY, the leading edge of news reporting, has subsidiary stations on this large chunk of rock. They may not compare with the magnificent edifice that is the home of GHTY News, but they are capable of receiving and sending broadcasts on certain wavelengths. I was planning to beam the broadcast to one of them. There has to be a station somewhere in Commonwealth space able to pick it up and either play it or save it. I'd take the part of the second hero. You, Optio, would play the lead. Pretty nifty, eh?"

"Would the broadcast be seen here on Caralis?"

"Of course. They, the lucky devils, would have less interest in it, as they are actually taking part in the show. But yes, they'd see it."

"The broadcast from here. Hmm. Maybe one of those stupid doinks who won't let us come home might see it. It can't hurt."

"A capital idea, lad. You guys smile. No, go ahead. Look angry. That's it. Lights, action, camera. Good afternoon, my friends, this is Lurron Johnston, broadcasting live from Vexillary Karstil."

Prefect of the Legion NaBesta Kenderson sifted through the reports that littered his desk. There was such a thing as having too much information. Why didn't the Manus commanders handle some of these reports? There was no need to deluge the Legion commander with the details of Century operations. He even had some reports about various Platoons. Not my job, man. Not my job. "Lartur. Get in here," Kenderson barked into the inter-office commlink. His Operations Officer appeared almost immediately.

"Sir?"

"What is all this? Do I need to know about platoons?"

"Let me see, sir." Legatus Mantelli Lartur took the report from the Prefect of the Legion and studied it for a moment. "Sir, this is a report of the destruction of a successful long-range patrol. This Optio Karstil and his platoon penetrated 1,500 kilometers behind TOG lines. He was destroyed some time yesterday. He was from Centurion Alanton Freund's command."

"And I need to know this?"

"Well, sir. I thought we could make a hero of the boy. You know, for the home front. Glorious death and all that. No survivors. It would be good for troop morale. What the Legion has become."

"You sure he's dead? I mean, really sure?"

"Certainly, sir. Thinking of that, maybe it would be better to make a live one a hero. Maybe the Centurion. Oh, and this just in. Some TOG forces are probing our lines. They're getting ready to attack, probably tonight, and they're trying to infiltrate storm troops dressed as civilians into the lines."

Kenderson stared off into space. The Renegades certainly needed heroes, alive or dead. And the 2567th probably needed them more than most Legions. "All right. Put one of them in for a commendation. Might as well go for the Gold Palm. It will probably be disallowed, but it's worth trying."

Lartur nodded and left. Kenderson stretched in his chair, feeling his knees and shoulders pop. He decided to walk through the operation area. It would be good for the others to see him taking an interest in their work.

The rows of desks faced each other, allowing conversation over them. Each station had a read-out station connected to the central computer for the headquarters. Above the room, as Kenderson knew, were the thousands of antennae that connected various portions of the Legion with the headquarters. Each of the antennae was designed to accept calls from a limited number of sending stations. The multiple antennae made the headquarters conspicuous, but it also meant that TOG jamming would not affect all the stations simultaneously.

As he entered the room, he saw a group of people surrounding one of the desks. "I thought you said that this was foolproof. We're supposed to be receiving from satellite only. How can it be jammed?"

"Sir, we're picking up this signal on a civilian frequency." One of the observers reached for the screen and twisted a dial. Kenderson stopped to observe. Like magic, the screen cleared to reveal the face of a man, warped slightly, but definitely the face of a man.

"...broadcasting live from Vexillary Karstil. We have tried to approach what are purported to be friendly lines, but they keep shooting at us." The camera swung away from the speaker to pan across a horribly damaged tank. Kenderson, a tanker for fifteen years, had momentary trouble recognizing it as a Liberator. The problem was that the left side of the turret had been blown away, and much of the armor on the bow and sides had been crushed. He doubted that anyone could have survived all that.

"The tank you're seeing now," continued the commentator, "belongs to Optio Roglund Karstil, the commander of the Vexillary. After many narrow escapes, he has brought us to within 40 kilometers of friendly lines. From here, we will attempt to infiltrate tonight. . . "

"Lartur!" Kenderson exploded. "According to the report you gave me, that man is dead. You'd better get him in here and get him fast. I want an operation mounted at once to bring him in. Find out where that transmission is coming from. Call the unit opposite it, and tell them to get the lead out."

"Yes, sir!"

"And find out what the hell a Vexillary is."

"Yes, sir!"

57

Alsatia, Caralis
The Commonwealth
10 January 6831

Karstil stood in the commander's hatch of his Liberator and watched Johnston continue his program. The hesitant Legatus had become the consummate reporter. His deep, well-modulated voice swept over the listeners. His pacing, too, was excellent. Even though he was directing the camera by remote control, he never seemed to fumble on his lines and he knew when to step in front of the camera and when to let the picture do the talking. The transmission signal was strong enough that Karstil was able to pick it up on his own DDP.

"...And so, ladies and gentlemen, this broadcast comes to an end. Late tonight, I will be crossing into friendly lines. The next time I talk to you, I will be with the victorious Renegade and Commonwealth forces on Caralis. This is Lurron Johnston, bidding you a fond good evening." The screen fluttered, went blank, and then filled with the amber and blue indicators of the current positions. Across the top of the screen, 40 kilometers away, were the faint blue indicators of the Renegade front lines.

The blazing sun of noon hammered down into the slight depression where the vehicles had gathered. The civilian vans were clustered near the center, around and under a small grove of trees. The tanks were hull-down around the edge. Glover and Mullins' tanks faced toward the TOG forces, Karstil toward the Renegade lines. The flanks were watched by the two Vipers. It was Mullins who reported them first.

"Six, this is Two."

"Six."

"Two. I have a red screen. Many hostile vehicles at 50 klicks and closing."

"Six. Roger. Break. All units, rally on Two," Karstil ordered.

As Spint moved the damaged Liberator across the depression, Karstil could see the two Vipers heading in the same direction. The civilians watched the movement with interest. As Karstil passed the trees, Ambrose Rondthaler jogged up to the tank. "Trouble?" he asked as the tank slowed.

"Trouble," Karstil said. "TOGs are headed our way. We don't know if they're after us or after the Renegade lines, but it's trouble in either case."

"What do you want us to do?"

"For now, just sit tight. Get everybody loaded and ready to move. I have a flare pistol, and if I fire a red star cluster, you get out. Make a run for the lines and hope for the best."

"And what about you?"

"We're tankers." As if that were the answer to any question.

"That's not much of an answer."

"It's the best answer I've got, Doctor."

"Good luck, son."

The Liberator accelerated toward the rim of the hills. Glover and Mullins had already begun to place position stakes in proposed firing positions, and the slope was dotted with red markers below the crest. All a driver had to do was bring the bow of his tank up to a post. He would know that he was in hull defilade without having to guess. Each tank would fire once from that position and then back down, pulling forward into a different position for the next shots. That would keep the TOG units from concentrating too much fire on one vehicle. They would be able to "see" the tanks on their DDPs, but they wouldn't know which tank was going to move to a firing position. It wasn't much of an advantage, but it was all they had.

Karstil put the Wolverine in the center of the line, with Mullins and Crown on the left. He put Ross to the right, 600 meters from the recon tank, with his own tank another 600 meters beyond. All the tanks would have ample maneuver space and yet be close enough to support one another if necessary. The infantry dismounted and occupied prepared craters blasted by the infantry carriers in a shallow depression 400 meters ahead of the ridge line. From here, they would be able to paint targets for the tanks as well as engage enemy armor with their dwindling supply of TVLGs. The tanks didn't expend their digging charges. Being in hull-down positions, they didn't need the additional protection of a crater. They would use the charges later if the battle moved into more open ground.

By the time all the preparations were made, the TOG formations were 30 kilometers away and closing. Sensors went to high scan and radio silence lifted. "Targets identified. Many Horatius medium tanks, Aeneas light tanks, Lupis infantry carriers. Range two-eight-zero-double zero. Bearing six-four-hundred relative. Targets closing at one-eight-zero. Lock not achieved."

The same reports were coming in over the commlink from the other vehicles. The DDP showed more armored targets than Karstil had ever seen before. He was seeing a TOG Manus in attack formation.

The two Cohorts of the Manus were attacking abreast. Each Cohort was deployed in two lines, the three light Centuries leading, followed by the three mediums. The Centuries were on line, each with three Platoons up, and one back around the Century Headquarters. All Platoons were supported by infantry carriers. It looked, thought Karstil, like an antique cavalry charge from some holovid. He and his companions were the infantry that would try to break the charge. Or be broken by it.

"Targets identified. Many Horatius medium tanks, Aeneas light tanks, Lupis infantry carriers. Range two-five-zero-double zero. Bearing six-four-hundred relative. Targets closing at one-eight-zero. Lock not achieved."

All the vehicles were in turret defilade, the entire vehicle protected by the hill. The only parts of the vehicles that rose above the surrounding terrain were the tops of the turrets and the sighting systems. From that position, the tanks could sense and paint targets while remaining completely protected. All tank commanders were up, Karstil having moved from the normal command hatch to the central, driver's hatch at the rear of the turret. It had a DDP repeater so that he could control the battle from the more elevated position. Though it was less safe because he was fully exposed, it was easier to see the rolling plain ahead. Karstil knew the lower commander's hatch was just as good, but he wanted to actually see the oncoming TOGs rather than merely sense them through electronic means.

"Targets identified. Many Horatius medium tanks, Aeneas light tanks, Lupis infantry carriers. Range two-two-zero-double zero. Bearing six-four-hundred relative. Targets closing at one-eight-zero. Lock not achieved." He tapped the display, calling up the estimated attack time from the computer. There was a slight pause while it calculated the information.

"At current speed, enemy targets will be within four-kilometer painting range in six minutes. Targets will be in the three-kilometer main gun range two-zero seconds later. Targets will be in the one-two-hundred missile range three-six seconds later."

Six minutes and twenty seconds to make any changes in the deployment. Six minutes and twenty seconds to think about all the things that could go wrong. He looked back at the grove of trees a kilometer to his rear. He could barely see the civilian vehicles huddled under the protecting branches. No figures were moving outside the vehicles, for the civilians were ready to pull out when he gave the signal. And ready to pull out even if he wasn't.

"Targets identified. Many Horatius medium tanks, Aeneas light tanks, Lupis infantry carriers. Range one-nine-zero-double zero. Bearing unchanged. Targets closing at one-eight-zero. Lock not achieved." Five minutes to contact. Karstil felt his stomach tighten. Far away, he could see the faint plumes of dust, rooster tails churned up by the speeding tanks. Grav drive meant that there was no contact with the ground, but a 273-ton vehicle travelling at 180 KPH stirred up the air around it. That air sucked up clouds of dust, which rose behind the tank in a telltale plume.

"Targets identified. Many Horatius medium tanks, Aeneas light tanks, Lupis infantry carriers. Range one-six-zero-double zero. Bearing unchanged. Targets closing at one-eight-zero. Lock not achieved." Four minutes. Through his monocular, Karstil could see the shimmering shapes of the tanks. The rising heat from the plain blocked vision, making objects appear distorted and taller than they really were. Being able to see was not the advantage he had thought. He swept the horizon. It was dotted with shimmering tanks.

"Targets identified. Many Horatius medium tanks, Aeneas light tanks, Lupis infantry carriers. Range one-three-zero-double zero. Bearing unchanged. Targets closing at one-eight-zero. Lock not achieved." Three minutes to laser contact. It was time to gain the commander's hatch. He dropped down past Spint, huddled over his control, watching his own DDP as the red shapes came closer. He had opened the vision periscope so he could see the marking post. Karstil eased past his driver, who looked up and returned his Optio's grin. Why either one of them should be grinning right now Karstil didn't question.

Podandos was completely engrossed in his ballistic display, moving the sight circle over the approaching targets. With only the 150mm cannon left in his arsenal, his job was going to be easy. Karstil plugged the intercom jack into the commander's outlet.

"Targets identified. Many Horatius medium tanks, Aeneas light tanks, Lupis infantry carriers. Range seven-zero-double zero. Bearing unchanged. Targets closing at one-eight-zero. Lock not achieved." One minute. It shocked Karstil to think that the trip from the turret top to his battle station had taken two minutes.

"Tank. Aeneas. Bearing six-three hundred," he said into the intercom.

Podandos responded at once. "Tank. Aeneas. Bearing six-three hundred. Not identified. Blocking terrain."

"Driver, prepare to move."

"Up."

"Target identified. Aeneas light tank. Range-four-zero-double zero. Bearing on. Target closing at one-eight-zero. Lock not achieved." No time left. Karstil treadled the painting laser, heard it whine to life even as the warning klaxon sounded in his headset.

"Target identified. Aeneas light tank. Range three-five-double zero. Bearing on. Target closing at one-eight-zero. Lock achieved. Target painted." Good. Let the TOG commander worry.

"Driver, move!"

"Moving." The Liberator surged forward, the turret rising from the ground.

"Tank. Aeneas. Range three thousand. HEAP, fire shot!"

"Identified."

"Fire!"

"On the way." The Liberator vibrated as the 150mm HEAP round screamed toward the rushing Aeneas. An instant later, the shell blossomed on the turret.

"Shot loaded. Identified," came the report from Podandos.

"Fire!"

"On the way." The tank shook again as the APDS round followed the HEAP shot into the target. Karstil hoped that the second shot would hit the same area as had the blast of HEAP. With any luck, the HEAP would have torn a chunk of armor off the turret, allowing the APDS round to penetrate and explode in the vitals. The DDP indicated a strike on the turret.

"Target. Driver, back up." The warning klaxon screamed.

Spint, the rear thrusters already engaged, popped the control. The Liberator leaped down the slope as three shells screamed over the position. Behind the slope, the Liberator moved to the right. With the left steering vane gone, there was no way to turn left. That kind of turn would require Spint to spin the tank to the right until it was facing to the original left.

Karstil watched the DDP. A Lupis carrier was breaking toward the flank of the position. He snapped the ballistic sight over the APC and treadled the painting laser. "Target identified. Lupis carrier. Range two-seven-double zero. Bearing on. Target closing at one-eight-zero. Lock achieved. Target painted." There was no need to paint targets, he was doing it by reflex and because there might be someone else who could use the advantage.

"Tank. Lupis. Range two-seven hundred. HEAP. Fire HEAP."

"Tank. Lupis. On. Not identified. Blocking terrain."

"Driver, move."

"Moving," Spint acknowledged.

"Tank. Lupis. Identified."

"Fire."

"On the way."

"Load HEAP."

"Up. Identified."

"Fire."

"On the way."

In the distance, Karstil saw the second round explode on the side of the infantry carrier close to the impact point of the first. Smoke poured from the side of the TOG vehicle. "Target. Driver, back up."

The plain was dotted by plumes of smoke. Karstil glanced at the DDP. The weight of the TOG attack had shifted toward the left, away from his position, either by design or accident. From the display, it looked like the TOGs were trying to sweep that flank, trying to get to the rear of the depression and cut off retreat. Karstil fired at one last target, then told Spint to take the Liberator across the rear of the position to aid Mullins. Ross would have to guard the right flank alone.

As the Liberator blasted its way across the depression, it passed close to the trees. Karstil saw Rondthaler wave as he went by, then raise both arms in a questioning attitude. Karstil shook his head and pointed to the trees. The doctor nodded and returned to his vehicle.

Along the rear of the slope Karstil could see smoke pouring from Glover's Wolverine. The cannon was still firing, and a blackened and scorched figure remained in the commander's hatch. The air around the tank was crisscrossed with TVLG smoke trails interlaced in a fantastic fabric. The ground in front of the Wolverine exploded in a shower of dust.

To the left of the position was the glowing ruin of Crown's Viper. Unexpended 25mm ammunition popped in the wreckage. At least the infantry squad had been dismounted before contact. They would be holding that section of the line a little longer, until the tanks came forward and dug them out of their holes.

Further on was Mullins' Liberator, also showing the scars of combat. The right-front sponson extender had been torn from its arm and now hung limply from tendons of armor. The right access panel on the rear side had been blown off, exposing some control cables. There was probably internal damage that he couldn't see. The command was being worn down to nothing. Karstil reached into the turret, extracted the flare pistol, and fired. It wasn't a coherent thought pattern, just a reflex action.

The DDP was red with tanks. As the Liberator crested the ridge, an Horatius appeared 600 meters away. It had been sneaking around the flank, trying to get past the defended positions. Karstil was almost as surprised as the TOG commander. With no transponder in the vehicle, the enemy had not gotten a good read on the approaching Liberator.

"Fire!" shouted Karstil. "Driver, move up." There was no use being in hull defilade at this range, and he wanted to be able to fire the TVLGs while he had the chance. He treadled the painting laser.

"Target identified. Horatius medium tank. Range six-double zero. Bearing on. Lock achieved. Target painted." The first round had struck flush on the Vulcan mount.

"Fire!" The main gun bloomed again as the turret of the Horatius began to traverse. The driver had grounded the vehicle and was swinging left to bring the main, hull-mounted gun to bear. Karstil triggered a pair of TVLGs. The face of the enemy turret glowed as all three shots struck the canted armor between the 3/6 laser and Vulcan mounts. Titanium slag dripped down over the turret ring. Then the laser and 50mm cannon fired back.

Karstil didn't see the hits on his turret, but he felt the ceramic armor go instantly too hot to touch. The acrid fumes of melting ballistic protection stung his nose and eyes. He triggered the last TVLGs as the main gun of the Horatius swung into position and fired.

The 150mm HEAP round found the already shattered face armor of the Liberator's turret. The DDP screen shattered, fragments raking across Karstil's face. The sensing and targeting computers came apart in a shower of sparks, cables, and computer chips. Blinding, choking smoke filled the fighting compartment. Deep inside the tank, an expanding orange glow, instantly doused by the fire retardant system, showed momentarily. The glow returned, was doused again, returned again and began to expand.

"Out!" he shouted into the intercom, even as he realized that there were no more communications with the crew. He kicked at Podandos, saw the gunner struggling to rise from his chair. He reached into the turret and dragged the Triarii from his position. There was no way both of them were going to get through the same hatch together. He dropped into the smoke-filled interior and boosted Podandos through the opening first. The gunner hit the top of the turret and rolled off to the left. Karstil followed him out.

This tank had finally fought its last battle.

Alsatia, Caralis
The Commonwealth
10 January 6831

Karstil crawled away from the burning Liberator, his body wracked with violent spasms as he coughed out the smoke. His cracked ribs sent stabs of pain with each breath. He rolled further down the hill, then tried to rise. The ground kept shaking his feet from under him. The horizon swam crazily across his eyes.

He was aware of a Liberator roaring by, smoke pouring from the hull. The right sponson extender had been shot away, but still hung from the tortured hull by a strip of armor. Mullins' tank was totally out of control. The boneyard beauty's TS&R systems, grafted from two different tanks, had finally decided that they couldn't work together any longer. The tank spiraled into the sky, rotating around and around on its long axis. In Karstil's last view of the tank, it was engulfed in flames, plunging straight into the ground.

As he staggered to his feet, the bow of an Horatius rose over the crest of the hill and started down the slope. The turret was firing at some target to the left, the main gun moving back and forth in its mount like the nose of some giant beast sniffing for prey. The gun found what it was looking for and fired. The blast knocked Karstil to the ground.

He was on all fours, crawling away from the Horatius, then looked back. The side of the tank bloomed with an explosion that rocked the whole vehicle. He gaped as the tank began to swing toward its unseen adversary. The driver wasn't fast enough and a second heavy round struck behind the cleft of the jaw-like right projection. The tank shook again, driving the left edge into the ground. Smoke poured from the holes blasted in the side. The tank commander vaulted from his position as a jet of white-hot vapor exploded from the hatch. The tank settled quietly to the ground. The jet of vapor continued to scream from the turret.

The sun was blotted out, and Karstil looked up to see the gigantic hull of a Deliverer rumble past, the red Renegade "R" scrawled on its side. Behind it came a Spartius APC, the grav-pack infantry moving along beside. Then there were hands pushing him to the ground. "Easy, fella. It's all right now," came a voice from a great distance.

The sky kept spinning, filled with disembodied heads looking down at him. One of them seemed much closer than the rest, and he tried to concentrate on it. If only they'd stop moving, he thought. Karstil concentrated on the face. Slowly it became stationary, suspended upside down in front of him. He could see the lips moving, but couldn't hear what was being said. "I think he's conscious," said the head. "Don't try to move. You're strapped to a litter."

The upside-down head grew shoulders as it came closer. "Can you hear me, Optio?" Karstil blinked. Yes, he thought, I can hear you. Why do you ask? He tried to lift his arms, but he was unable to make them move. They felt very heavy. He wiggled his fingers and felt them against his leg.

"Don't try to move," said the head and shoulders. "You're strapped to a litter."

He raised his head and looked down. There was a blanket over the rest of him. That's probably my body, he thought. He moved first one foot, then the other. The blanket responded. Good, he thought. Most of the major parts were in place.

The people standing around reached down and picked him up. The gaping maw of a Pilus ambulance appeared, and he was gently placed inside, feet first. The other seven racks were already occupied, intravenous tubes inserted into the soldier's arms. Then the door closed and it was too dim, too much effort, to look around.

The regional hospital was a sprawling complex of semi-permanent buildings. They were labeled semi-permanent because they had been built as temporary, "for-the-present-emergency," structures designed to last five years. That had been twenty years ago, and they were still in use. The architect had left the buildings ugly, on the assumption that the life span of the structures would be brief.

Karstil sat beside a bed that held a patient so completely swathed in bandages that only the eyes and mouth were visible. Numerous tubes entered the gauze coverings bringing in, and draining off, the fluids keeping the patient alive. Only the shallow, steady rise and fall of the chest showed that the occupant was alive. The eyes were closed, as they had been for the two weeks since he had been brought in. Karstil looked up from his book as Doctor Ambrose Rondthaler approached the bed. "I'm afraid we're losing him," he said.

Karstil nodded. "I just wish he knew what happened."

"Have you seen the others?" asked the doctor.

"Yes," replied Karstil. "They've taken Sergeant Crown's body home for burial. Spint, too. They promoted him posthumously to Sergeant. That may be some consolation to his family."

Rondthaler leaned on the footboard of the bed and stared at the electronic read-out above the bed. Respiration and heartbeat were lower than they had been the day before. The massive damage and extensive burns were taking their toll. Emergency surgery had repaired the bones, but the Human body, even with the extraordinary measures available to modern medicine, could withstand just so much trauma. "And the others?"

"Quentain was released last week, along with Sergeant Glover. They should be back with their units after convalescence leave. Abul and Yennan were unaccounted for."

"By the way," said the doctor, "I was checking hospital records the other day and found a Sergeant Hampert Farwell of the 2567th listed as an outpatient. He was listed as having been with your Cohort."

Karstil's face brightened. "Well, that's good news. I'd been hoping that he made it. That leaves only one tank commander still in doubt."

Rondthaler cleared his throat. "I asked the computer to check on the other infantry squad leader. Sergeant Ross, I believe." Karstil's head turned ever so slightly. "She has reported back to her command. Evidently, she's all right."

Karstil felt his face begin to flush. He had not mentioned Ross, nor asked the doctor to check on her. He had intended to do it himself upon discharge from the hospital. He looked back at the figure lying in the hospital bed. "I guess the unofficial motto of the Legion is still apt: 'Every day we die a little.' Maybe it's his turn."

"It's not my turn, and I ain't dead yet," croaked the bandage-encased figure of Sergeant Lucifer K. Mullins. "Maybe every day we do die a little, but the TOGs die more. Let's keep it that way." The head turned toward Karstil. "Sir? You wouldn't happen to have a cigar?"

Optio Roglund Karstil reached inside his bathrobe and extracted an evil-looking black object.

"As a matter of fact, Sergeant," he said, "I do."

Epilogue

Alsatia, Caralis
The Commonwealth
25 January 6831

SPECIAL ORDER 6825-417
  Centurion Alanton H. Freund, 715-332-9638, awarded the Commonwealth Legion of Merit.
  Centurion Alanton H. Freund, 715-332-9638, awarded the Renegade Distinguished Service Order.
  While commanding his Century, the above-named officer planned and executed a series of spoiling attacks against a superior Terran Overlord Government force. Through his control of the operation, elements of his command were able to break through and disrupt a series of prepared positions and to destroy an enemy Manus Headquarters.
  Under his direct supervision and orders, civilians, trapped behind enemy lines were rescued. This final operation was carried out successfully, despite heavy casualties for his own force.
  In the planning and execution of this mission, Centurion Alanton H. Freund has shown himself an officer of exceptional ability. He reflects the highest traditions of the Commonwealth and the Renegade Forces in Shannedam County.
  By order of Gregory Gitimus, General, Commanding.

  Prefect NaBesta Kenderson looked at the never-diminishing pile of paper that covered his desk. No matter how hard he tried to move all the reports from the "In" basket to the "Out," he never seemed to make any headway. Why, he thought, are there never enough subordinates? The answer came to him immediately: more subordinates made more paper work. Each one of them "knew" that the commander just had to have his report.
  From deep in the desk, a buzzer sounded, so softly that only a man sitting there could have heard it. Kenderson reached under the central desk drawer and pressed an unseen button. Behind his chair, a wide panel opened silently in the wall. Without turning his head, he offered his greeting. "Come in, Stone."
  Centurion Lawrence ("Just call me Larry") Stone shuffled through the opening and seated himself in a leather chair that stood before the desk. His bulk dwarfed the desk.

"I have your final report here," said Kenderson. "It makes interesting reading." He looked up at the intelligence officer. "It's too bad one of them got away in that grav sled the night before Karstil got back, but we have the others dead to rights. Your recommendation to terminate seems reasonable."

Larry Stone looked carefully at the Prefect. He usually distrusted officers outside his own branch, but this was a Renegade officer, and much worthier than a Commonwealth officer of the same rank. He rose from his chair. "I'll get started on it tonight. The rest of my people are in place. It won't take long." He turned toward the opening in the wall as the communicator on the desk buzzed.

Kenderson picked up the receiver, holding up his hand to keep Stone in place. The Centurion stopped beside the desk as Kenderson spoke into the instrument.

"Yes, sir," said Kenderson. "The report is accurate." There was a pause. "I'd rather go with the proposed solution," he said, waving Stone back to the chair. There was another long pause as Kenderson listened to his invisible interlocutor. "Yes, sir," he said softly, replacing the instrument in its cradle and staring up at Stone.

"There will be no termination of the infiltrators," Kenderson said.

"What?"

"No termination."

"But why?"

"It seems," said the Prefect, "that you reported too well. Your report was so devastating, so detailed, that Planet Headquarters has taken charge of it. I don't know how they got their hands on it, but they did. Now some twit has decided that the problem is too widespread to be dealt with on a unit-by-unit basis. Commonwealth Intelligence has taken over."

"But that shouldn't mean we can't handle our problem, should it?"

"What it means," said Kenderson, rubbing his face with his hands, "is that we are forbidden, and I stress the word forbidden, to take any action that might indicate our knowledge of the TOG plants. And that includes your termination plans."

"I could make it look like an accident."

"No, Larry. Not even an accident."

Stone slumped in the chair. "We can't just let them get away with it. They'll go on to other units, and we'll lose track of them. We've got to do something!"

"No 'we' don't. Try anything, and the Commonwealth types will be down on us like a kiloton of lead."

"So we sit here and do nothing." Stone shook his head. "I guess it's true what they say...Damned if we do..."

Kenderson laughed humorlessly. "...and damned if we don't."

GLOSSARY

GROUND FORCE TECHNOLOGY

GRAV DRIVE

The most important advance in ground propulsion was the development of the Grav Drive in 2210. Named after its inventor, the Marshman Drive allows an object to fall parallel to the ground rather than toward it. Specialized anti-grav steering vanes allow the device to change direction. The military immediately saw the possibilities for the development of the modern-day Grav Tank.

The Grav Tank has significantly changed the nature of ground warfare. Depending on its altitude, a Grav Tank can travel from 100 KPH up to 900 KPH. At such speeds, a grav-mounted Legion can cover the distance between the old Terran cities of New York and Chicago in an hour and a half. With its terrain-following radar, a Grav-mounted tank can maneuver in the densest terrain at unprecedented speeds. The firepower available to a Grav Strike Legion could defeat a 20th-century army. Because of its great speed and ability to concentrate rapidly, a Grav Legion can attack or defend an area hundreds of kilometers across. Grav Armor has become the decisive arm of ground combat.

One of the disadvantages of the Marshman Drive is that it cannot operate farther than 15 kilometers above the mean surface of a Terra-like planet. Thus, most spacecraft use anti-grav generators for atmospheric flight. Even with its disadvantages, the Grav Tank has significantly changed the nature of ground warfare.

ARMOR AND PASSIVE PROTECTION

A Grav Tank's standard armor is crystalline titanium alloy that is molecularly wedded to a ceramic matrix. It is proof against old-style shaped charges and low kinetic energy weapons, very resistant to hyper-kinetic energy weapons, and offers good protection against most other energy weapons.

A Grav Tank's interior is also well-protected. All major components have redundant circuitry built into them, along with self-repair capabilities. A totally separate secondary system is provided for such critical components as shields and terrain sensors. Additionally, energy-absorbing foams and fire protection equipment are standard passive ballistic protection on all combat vehicles.

SHIELDING

Grav Tanks are protected by flicker shields. The flicker shield is a thin wave of pressure-gravity that would normally be impervious to all forms of energy. Because power demands are so high, it was necessary to design a shield that flickered on and off instead of remaining permanently on. A flicker shield is effective against lasers, thermonuclear explosions, energy weapons, and low-mass projectiles. As the flicker rate increases, the power usage increases geometrically. No matter how fast the flicker rate, at least 10 percent of all shots get through.

PAINTING LASER

The Painting Laser marks a target with a laser, then the sensors in a missile or artillery munitions home in on the reflected laser light. As long as the laser is held on its target, the accuracy of the guided munition approaches 100 percent. When a Painting Laser hits a shield, the targeting vehicle can use the reflected laser light to analyze the defending shield's flicker rate. It car .nen target its combat lasers to slip in a shot during the flicker shield's off-cycle. The flicker rate can also be downloaded into other friendly fire-control systems and to the electronic circuitry of any guided missile.

As a countermeasure, the shield can be distanced from the hull of the vehicle so that attacking laser light bounces off the hull and then strikes the reverse side of a shield in an "on" cycle. This reduces the amount of reflected laser energy and makes it difficult to lock onto shields with high flicker rates.

MASS DRIVER CANNON

The most modern form of projectile weapon, the MDC usually consists of a long tube made from superconductive material, to which twin rails of magnetic material are attached. A strong current passes through the tube, accelerating slivers of hardened steel, down the barrel on the crest of a magnetic wave generated by the tube and the rails. Because of its weight and ineffectiveness against shields, MDCs are most often mounted on spacecraft or space-defense vehicles and installations.

GAUSS CANNON

A popular ground vehicle weapon, the Gauss cannon is a direct-fire ballistic weapon that functions similarly to a Mass Driver Cannon. The shells cannot be turned by shields and they use hyper-kinetic energy to penetrate a target's armor.

APDS Round

Armor-Piercing Discarding Sabot (APDS) Rounds use kinetic energy to penetrate their target. The round consists of a long, thin depleted uranium penetrator surrounded by a container, or sabot. Once the round has left the cannon, the sabot slips off to reduce drag caused by air resistance.

HEAP Round

The High-Explosive Armor-Piercing Round is similar to an APDS Round except that it has a directional explosive charge directly behind the penetrator that detonates when the penetrator enters the armor. This drives the penetrator deeper into the armor and causes some lateral damage.

Hammerhead Round

The Hammerhead round consists of a nose and a lateral-shaped charge. The nose has a self-destructive X-ray laser. When the round hits the side of a vehicle, the kinetic energy released is converted to X-ray energy. This energy is focused back toward the vehicle through a special crystal, causing it to laze. The laser bolt drills a hole through the armor, while the lateral-shaped part of the round passes down into the vehicle. When it strikes the bottom of the laser hold, the charge explodes perpendicularly to the sides.

MISSILES

Anti-vehicular missiles are fairly large, bulky, and have limited ranges. All missiles can be guided to their targets by an active Painting Lasers, allowing for both direct or indirect firing. If the target is not painted, the gunner locks onto the target, fires, and then the missiles internal guidance and control systems home in on the target.

SMLM

The Sub-Munitions Laser-Guided Missile (SMLM) is a standard, heavy anti-vehicular missile. When the missile approaches its target, it explodes and showers the target with high-velocity sub-munitions that can scour off large blocks of armor. If the missile is able to penetrate to the vehicle's interior, the explosion is directed laterally, causing extensive internal damage.

TVLG

The Tube or Vertically Launched Laser-Guided Missile (TVLG) is lighter and shorter-ranged than the SMLM, but has greater penetration. Its warhead is a modified 100mm Hammerhead Round. Infantry squads normally use it as their primary anti-vehicular missile, with the indirect fire capabilities removed.

ARTILLERY

All field pieces are now mobile, armored, and capable of firing on the move. The guns utilize electromagnetic accelerators and rocket-assisted projectiles to respond with unheard of speed and accuracy to fire missions from the forward combat elements. Artillery's ability to totally destroy any target that has stopped moving for more than one minute has ensured the Grav Tank's supremacy over cheaper and more easily constructed ground vehicles.

HAFE ROUND

The Hypervelocity Airburst Flechette Explosive (HAFE) Round explodes into a cloud of thousands of explosive flechettes, which are too large to be stopped by shields. Moderately effective against vehicles, HAFE rounds are most useful against infantry targets and to clear wooded areas for easier passage by grav vehicles.

ADM ROUND

Each Artillery-Dispensed Mine (ADM) Round contains hundreds of mine sub-munitions. When the round arrives over its target, it scatters these mines over a diameter of 600 meters. Each mine is keyed to explode if a grav field passes over it or if it is touched. The mine is equipped with a transponder receiver that identifies friendly passing vehicles or infantrymen. Enemy units can clear ADM minefields by using Engineering Vehicles or Anti-Mine Artillery (AMA) Rounds.

GLAD ROUND

The GLAD Round is a laser-guided anti-vehicle round. When the round arrives over the general location of its target, a parachute is deployed. Sensors in the round then search the immediate area for a target being designated by a friendly laser. If there is no laser designation, the round chooses its own target and launches itself.

SMOKE ROUND

A Smoke Round sets up a dense barrier of smoke that is opaque in the visual electromagnetic and infrared spectra. Smoke can be used defensively to cover the withdrawal or shifting of troops. Offensively, a barrage of Smoke can be laid down in front of an enemy making a high-speed advance into built-up area. The smoke blinds the enemy's terrain-following radar and will cause the vehicle to crash.

CRATER ROUND

The Crater Round is an artillery version of the Digging Charges that all vehicles carry. They are used mainly to hastily create a defensive zone for a retreating force. They can also be used to quickly create dug-in positions for an attacking force.

HELL ROUND

When a HELL Round detonates, it releases enough gravitic energy to cause a small, uncontrolled fusion reaction. This type of round is very clean, leaving little tactically significant radiation, but it does totally destroy any buildings, vegetation, or unshielded units in the blast radius. Shielding does reduce the blast effects of a HELL Round, making it less effective against stationary vehicles than GLAD Rounds.